PJ Grondin

b/ 20/ 2019

Drug Wars

PD House Books

PD House Holdings, LLC
4704 Venice Road
Sandusky, Ohio   44870

www.pjgrondin.com

pjgron@pjgrondin.com

ISBN: 978-0-9984644-0-4

Dedication

This story is dedicated to the men and women who work in law enforcement at all levels in the United States of America. Their job has recently become more dangerous due to the actions of a minority of officers in their ranks, and a firestorm of media attention to a relative few incidents. I pray that the bad apples are identified and removed, and trust is restored between the general public and those brave men and women in the law enforcement profession.

Acknowledgements

As usual, my dear wife, Debbie, deserves a medal for her patience as this story developed. She provided invaluable feedback as I described the plot to her over numerous evening meals. I must give a shout out to Tom Pascoe. He read an early version of the manuscript and provided frank comments on the storyline. Finally, my editor, Elizabeth 'Bee' Love for her detailed review and markup of the manuscript. Without her input, the manuscript would not be ready for publishing.

Drug
Wars

PROLOGUE

Saturday, August 10, 2013, 1:45 AM

Two agents from the Savannah satellite office of the Drug Enforcement Administration moved through the front door of the house one-quarter mile east of Downtown Savannah, Georgia. Stale, acrid odor from burnt marijuana filled the small living room in the rundown, cinderblock house. Two other team members handled the back entrances. All wore black tactical uniforms with "DEA" in large gold letters on their front and back.

"Living room clear," team leader, Vincent Mercado, uttered into his headset microphone.

As Mercado made his way deeper into the house, he saw the green laser-dot from Agent Alex Smith's LAR-15. He was coming through the patio door in the back of the house.

He heard Smith in his earpiece, "Dining room, kitchen clear."

* * *

Crouched in a bedroom closet with a cordless phone and a twelve-gauge shotgun, twenty-one year old Weston Ross cowered with his hands covering his face. Seized by fear, he was certain that the intruders could hear his body shaking. Time crawled, the seconds dragged. Every sound from outside the closet echoed in his ears. The windows were buffeted by the light breeze. To him, it seemed as though they would shatter with every slight gust. Even the sound of the crickets belting out their chorus tweaked his anxiety. Sweat poured down his brow into his eyes. His tee shirt stuck to his drenched body.

But the sound he feared most was one he hadn't yet heard: the sound of the bedroom door followed by footsteps. He knew they would be coming for him and he knew why.

From his early teens, trouble followed Weston. He started using and selling drugs when he was in junior high school and never stopped. His parents threatened to throw him out. At sixteen, his father followed through on their promise. He was on the street with nothing but the clothes on his back.

But Weston had cash and dope. His friends were happy to give him shelter. They just gave their own parents a sob story about how their good friend's parents threw him out into the street. It didn't take long for his friends' parents to see that Weston Ross was trouble.

Three months after being kicked out on the street, his father was killed in an automobile accident, leaving his poor mother a widow in an empty home. Weston seized upon the opportunity and moved back home.

She tried to lay down the rules, to reel him in and steer him away from his business partners. It was too late.

He countered her attempts with lots of cash. It saved her from bankruptcy. She wouldn't have to sell the house and the car and it put food on the table. She could buy new cloths. And she could party with her son's "friends." The pain and sorrow of a lost husband washed away in a river of booze and the haze of pills. Before long, she was nothing more than a party favor for her son's business partners.

* * *

The night of the DEA raid, Weston's mother, Paula Deming Ross, had had enough. She'd sobered up enough to know that she was no more than a drunk and an addict. In the bathroom off the hallway, she wiped the thick film of grime off the mirror. She was forty-three, but the old hag in the mirror looked to be at least sixty with pronounced facial wrinkles, hair turning gray at the roots, puffy bags under her eyes, and thick mascara now running down her face from the sweat, mixing with tears.

She thought of her dead husband and how he stood by their family, listening to her defend their son. *He's just confused, influenced by his stupid friends. He'll grow up and get on the right path*, she had said.

Her husband was patient, but did not understand why she was soft on their only son. He wanted the best for his son. He expected his own flesh and blood, the child that they raised to follow the rules, to be a productive member of society, to find a perfect girl and marry, and produce grandchildren. He didn't expect them to turn into a gangster, a thug, and a criminal. Her husband compared their son to his cousin, Jarrod Deming, her brother's son. *Jarrod's going to be a cop. Why can't he be more like Jarrod?* But her husband knew it was time to force their son to make hard choices, to either sink or swim. They had to think about their own futures, their own sanity.

She looked into the mirror again. She'd become worse than her son. It was time.

She had found one of Weston's many handguns in the bathroom vanity, a Smith and Wesson 9mm. She picked it up and looked at it for a long moment. The feel of the plastic handle was rough and cold. The magazine was full and the safety was off. Her vision clouded as tears welled up in her eyes.

She locked the door to the bathroom. She knew that the flimsy door wouldn't hold back anyone intent on entering. She believed it to be her last defiant move, separating her from her son and all the pain he'd brought down on this house and their family. She took a deep breath before sitting down on the edge of the tub, still holding the gun.

Even though the temperature in the house was nearly eighty-five degrees, she felt cold. She lifted her face to the ceiling, intending to ask her husband for forgiveness before she took the final step. But she stopped, noticing the dust clinging to the cob webs hanging from the ceiling. This made her laugh and shake her head. A moment later, she started crying in earnest.

She took a final deep breath. In a voice broken by deep sobs, she whispered to her husband and to God and any other spirits that were listening, "I'm sorry."

* * *

Mercado and his team continued their slow, methodical sweep of the house. All was proceeding as planned until they heard a loud, but muffled bang. They immediately knew the sound of a gunshot originated from somewhere inside the house. Mercado, in a hoarse whisper filled with tension, ordered, "Reports, Smith."

"Clear."

"Deming."

There was silence. Mercado paused, then repeated with more emphasis, "Deming!"

"Clear."

"Deming, you hit?"

"Negative." A pause. "Let's go."

* * *

Weston Ross heard the loud *bang* from the bathroom. It sounded like a gunshot, but his mom was the only other person in the house. *She wouldn't do anything that crazy, would she?*

The scent of gunpowder reached his nostrils. He jumped up from the closet floor, grabbing the shotgun and ran into the hallway to the bathroom door. "Mom?" Silence. "Mom, you okay?"

The scent of cordite was strong. He was growing tense. He tried the door, finding it locked.

Louder and in a near panic, he yelled, "Mom! Mom, are you in there?"

Finally, he backed up, then charged. The flimsy, hollow-core door with the cheap lock popped open.

A night light shed a dim glow throughout the bathroom. When his right shoe hit the floor, it slid nearly causing him to lose his balance. He looked down at the dark liquid, confused until he saw his mother's body sprawled in the bathtub. The bullet had entered at the right side of her head. The left side of her skull was blown away, with bits of brain and skull mixed in the pattern of blood on the mildewed tile wall.

The big macho kid who stood up to his father, who had a swagger in his walk, who talked like a thug, dropped the shotgun against the wall, turned, and vomited into the sink. His body convulsed twice more. He ripped off several sheets of toilet paper from the roll that sat on the vanity and wiped his lips and chin dry. He picked up the shotgun and backed out of the bathroom into the hallway, his brain on overload. He leaned the shotgun against the wall in the hallway and wiped his face with both hands.

The image of his dead mother flooded his mind, like a scene from a horror film. *What have I done?* In an instant, like his mother, he realized what he'd become, and he hated himself for it. He grabbed the shotgun and turned towards the living room.

A moving green dot appeared on the wall. He quietly took two more steps, then stopped to listen. He shifted the gun to his other hand. When he did, a man dressed in a robotic looking outfit came around the corner of the hallway. A bright green light was at the tip of whatever robot man was holding.

Weston started to raise the shotgun to his shoulder. In a flash, Jarrod Deming unleashed three rounds into Weston Ross' chest killing him instantly.

He didn't hear his cousin say, "Sorry, Wes."

* * *

As soon as the remaining rooms were cleared, Vincent Mercado yelled orders. The DEA van backed into the driveway up to the garage. A flurry of activity followed as several trash bags laden with marijuana and cocaine were hauled into the house. Crime scene photos were taken of the drugs and cash. Mercado called District Attorney Andrew Newsome and sent him pictures of the bust via cell phone. The raid was a profitable one for members of the Savannah Drug Enforcement Administration.

Chapter 1

Twenty-Two Months Later
Tuesday, June 16, 2015, 10:20 AM

Peden Savage, owner of Savage Investigative Consultants, sat at his nineteenth-century mahogany desk, waiting for a call from the manufacturer of a tiny spy camera. The device was disguised as a tie-clasp. Testing had not gone well with the gadget. Savage and his only full-time employee couldn't get the video and audio to transfer to the host server. In his line of work – private investigations, law enforcement consultation, and surveillance equipment supply and support – flawless device performance was expected. Worse, they planned to use the device in the field in less than twenty-four hours. If the manufacturer couldn't resolve their problem, they had to go to plan "B," and there was no plan "B."

Savage Investigative Consultants provided support services to law enforcement agencies from the Federal Bureau of Investigation, the Drug Enforcement Administration, all the way down to local law enforcement agencies like the Savannah-Chatham Metro Police Department. They all had a high degree of confidence in Savage's work, even the FBI. Four years earlier, Savage was forced out of the Bureau amid an internal scandal and no small amount of distrust between Savage and his coworkers. He had planned to blow the whistle on agents who were illegally planting evidence to assure convictions in high profile cases. He resigned from the Bureau, but only after receiving assurances from management that they would fire the dirty agents.

Savage and Sparks had been on the phone numerous times with the manufacturer's technical expert trying to find the bug with the camera. *We'll call as soon as we have a solution for you*, he had said. That was hours ago.

Savage was surprised when he answered the phone on the first ring and the husky, female voice of Special Agent Megan Moore asked, "So, who do you think the killer is?"

He replied, "Miss Scarlet in the Billiard Room with the lead pipe."

He knew she was smiling on her end of the receiver, as much as she ever smiled. She said, "Peden, have you seen the news this morning? It's on every channel except Disney."

"Sorry, Megan. I've been busy, you know, making a living."

Moore didn't reply, though he could hear her breathing through the receiver. Megan had been his partner at the FBI during his short tenure there. Her face was model thin with eyebrows perpetually sculpted into an angry look, and framed by light blonde hair that hung just below her cheek bones. Savage wasn't sure if her eyebrows were naturally that way or if she purposely penciled in the scowl.

She and Savage had a history, but not a sexual one, though he couldn't convince his wife that was the case. In fact, Megan Moore was one of the reasons that his wife was now his "former" wife.

Finally, she said, "Tune in to any TV station. I'm sure you're going to want to see it for yourself. No doubt the boss will be calling you."

He frowned. 'The boss' was Roland Fosco, Special Agent in Charge of the FBIs Savannah office. Fosco was Megan's boss, and had been Savage's boss. Since Savage was in business for himself, and since his wife left him nearly five years ago, he really didn't have a boss. That is, unless you count the hundreds of clients of Savage Consultants. Fosco was one of those clients.

Before he could ask about Fosco, a dial tone buzzed in his ear. He hung up and grabbed the remote for the flat panel TV, clicked the power button and watched as the screen came to life. Another beautiful, serious-looking blonde, this one a news anchorwoman with shoulder-length hair, was introducing the reporter on location.

The picture on the screen shifted to the front steps of the Drug Enforcement Administration's Savannah office where a crowd of about fifty people had gathered. Most of the crowd appeared to be employees of one news organization or another with microphones in hand or cameras hoisted up on their shoulders. A news conference was about to start.

Savage hit the button to increase the volume. He noticed the caption in the lower right corner that stated the clip was previously recorded. The anchorwoman had just warned the audience that the clip contained graphic images. A man in an expensive-looking suit stepped up to the bank of microphones. There was no podium, just a few chrome and black stands. Several of the microphones were held to each other with duct tape or Velcro.

The man faced the crowd flanked by another man and a woman who were a few feet to his backside. The reason for Special Agent Moore's call became crystal clear. Peden recognized the man stepping up to the microphones. It was Jarrod Deming.

Savage first met Deming when his company established business ties with the Drug Enforcement Administration. His appearance on camera didn't do him justice. The combination of the light gray suit and the natural tendency of television cameras to distort a person's true stature made him look less impressive than he was in person. In reality, he was built like an athlete at the height of training for a championship game. There was not an ounce of fat on him. He was well over six feet tall, muscular, handsome, with a narrow face. His wide neck appeared to go straight to his ears. He could have been a model for a military action figure. Savage believed that he could have been a middle linebacker for the Atlanta Falcons. Deming had played college football at the University of Georgia in his freshman year, but wasn't committed to the game.

Savage had heard that Deming was a rising star, but not

on the football field. Many felt that he'd eventually be among the leadership at the DEA, at least at the Georgia field office in Atlanta. But there he was on TV, his title still listed as Special Agent Jarrod Deming. Savage thought that something must have happened to stop his upward movement in the agency. Or he simply could have decided that he wanted to stay in the field.

On screen, Deming looked to either side. The man and the woman both nodded. The camera slowly zoomed in on his face so that the people on either side of him were barely visible. His features were now vivid. Reaching into his suit coat he pulled out several pages and unfolded them. He cleared his throat, took a deep breath, looked up, his eyes seeming to fix on a point in the distance, then he moved slightly to his right and opened his mouth to speak.

From that moment, it was total chaos. Three cracks could be heard, like firecrackers exploding in quick succession, followed by a fourth crack. Deming fell backwards. As he did, the camera angle changed. The images on the screen were in continuous motion, just streaks and swirls of color. Savage tried to make out any of the images to no avail as the cameraman scampered for cover.

The audio was only slightly better. Between the screams and shouts from the crowd, Savage could hear panicked voices yelling, "He's been shot! Call 911!" and "Oh my God!" and "He's bleeding!"

After a few seconds, the cameraman got himself together and started panning the crowd. He turned to Deming as the agent lay on the steps, bleeding from the chest. The film clip was immediately cut off. Savage waited while the stunned anchorwoman regained her composure, then she continued.

Special Agent Jarrod Deming was shot and killed less than twenty minutes ago in a hail of gunfire as he was preparing to deliver what a source close to the agent described as a scathing report about tactics used by the Drug Enforcement Administration. The details of Agent Deming's disclosure of alleged wrongdoing by members of the DEA are not known. Speculation was mounting that high-ranking officials of the federal agency were concerned that this announcement would hurt the DEA and cripple its mission.

The shots appeared to have come from the parking lot just beyond the DEA's office, though information about the exact location, if known, has not been disclosed.

The Savannah-Chatham Metropolitan Police Department has cordoned off the entire parking area in hopes of keeping the crime scene undisturbed. A crime scene investigations team has been called...

Savage was listening to her account of the shooting when his phone rang again.

It was Megan. "So, what do you think?"

In a relaxed tone, Savage said, "I think the anchorwoman is hot. The field reporter isn't bad either."

Moore didn't respond and let the silence get her message across that she wasn't in the mood for his sexist humor.

He replied honestly, "I'd say that it's far too early to speculate on anything. It doesn't look good for the agency, though. If I was Cliff Metzger, I'd be watching my six."

Cliff Metzger was the current head of the Drug Enforcement Administration in Georgia. No doubt he would soon be on the hot seat, if he wasn't there already.

"What are you going to tell Roland?"

"That my fees just went up. Maybe he'll get a different consultant."

Megan replied, "Fat chance, Pedee. Later."

Savage hung up. He hated when she called him Pedee.

Savage started thinking about the murder...assassination really. He thought it would be insane for anyone at the DEA to order the hit.

Savage was deep in thought, replaying the newscast over in his mind when the phone rang again, jolting him out of his thoughts. It was the manufacturers' representative calling about the micro-camera. The software update was sent via file attachment to Lee Sparks' e-mail with instructions on how to copy the code into the program. Savage should have been elated, but his priorities had changed in the last ten minutes. Besides, Sparks could take care of the software issue. He now had bigger irons in the fire.

Chapter 2

Assistant District Attorney Elizabeth Sanchez was at her desk at the Chatham County Courthouse when one of her peers ran into her office, waving her arms, and yelling something about a shooting. Sanchez had a difficult time understanding a single word. She raised her hands and told the woman to calm down when a second co-worker yelled, "Hey, ya'll, a DEA agent's been shot. It's all over the news."

Sanchez leapt up and ran down the hall with the other two women to a conference room. On the screen of a seventy-inch flat panel TV, a pretty, young field reporter stood in front of the Drug Enforcement Agency office building southwest of downtown. The sun was bright. A breeze pushed the reporter's hair into her face as she tried to maintain her composure. Obviously, she hadn't had time to primp for the cameras before the live broadcast. Behind her, several uniformed men and women were in a semicircle, their attention focused on what appeared to be a man in a suit, though all Sanchez could see were his shoes and the cuffs of his pants.

The reporter did her best to ad lib.

...just as Deming stepped to the bank of microphones, shots rang out. At least one of those shots struck the agent in the chest. Officers, who were on duty here, rushed to his aid.

A vehicle with a loud siren approached the scene, drowning out the reporter for the moment. Once the siren shut off, she continued describing the chaos behind her.

Uh...paramedics are now on the scene...and, uh...have taken over the lifesaving efforts. It is unknown at this time where the shots came from.

The reporter looked around the grounds in front of the DEA office, then took a deep breath before refocusing on the camera, continuing her report. *The shots echoed off buildings in the area, making it difficult to pinpoint their origin.* The anchorwoman from Channel 8 asked the field reporter, *Did Agent Deming pass out copies of his remarks before the shooting? Do we know any specifics about the content of his accusations?*

The reporter nodded her head as she received the question in her earpiece, then shook her head and said, *No to both of your questions, Stephanie. None of the reporters on the scene here received an advance copy from the victim and none of his accusations were made public.*

There was a flurry of activity behind the reporter. Her cameraman was zooming in on the paramedics. *It appears that the paramedics are attempting to move Agent Jarrod Deming, quickly putting him on a stretcher. Police are moving people out of the way to make a path for the rescue...*

When the reporter said the name *Jarrod Deming,* Sanchez's jaw dropped. She covered her mouth with both hands and tears welled up in her eyes. She hadn't seen Jarrod Deming since he and her best friend, Sylvia Mason Deming graduated from the University of Georgia ten years ago. Sanchez didn't realize that her old friend and her husband were back in Savannah. She wasn't even sure that they were still married.

Sanchez continued to watch the TV, but no new information was forthcoming. Jarrod Deming was shot and the shooter was still at large.

In the courthouse, a loud buzzing sound pierced the air. A booming voice filled the halls and offices of the Chatham County Courthouse. *"Your attention please. Your attention please. The Chatham County Courthouse is now on lockdown. All doorways into and out of the building are closed and locked until further notice."*

After a ten-second pause, the entire announcement repeated. A number of groans could be heard throughout the building, but most folks were resigned that they weren't going anywhere for the time being.

Back in her office, Sanchez decided to use the lockdown time to track down her friend, Sylvia Deming. She started with the small address book that she kept in her purse. She had Sylvia's parents' home number, the number for their old college dorm room, which she was certain was disconnected, and a cell phone number. *Could she still have her old cell number? It's worth a try. But what would I say. Hey, I saw that your husband was shot this morning. Other than that, how've you been? Stupid, stupid, stupid. Get it together Sanchez.* She thought, *What would I want people to say to me if my husband had just been shot?*

It clicked.

She Googled the white pages using "Sylvia Deming Savannah Georgia." The search returned four possibilities, one of which was Sylvia's cell phone number from her ancient address book. *Now if I can just get out of here.*

She pulled her compact mirror out and inspected the makeup around her eyes. As she did, District Attorney Andrew Newsome poked his head in her office and put on his best smile. He said, "No sense freshening up. We're going to be here awhile." He paused a moment. "Besides, you look beautiful just the way you are." His smile forced his nose to rise. His narrow face, combined with small ears and beady eyes, made Elizabeth think of a rat.

She forced a smile back at Newsome. It sickened her that she had to tolerate his comments which were somewhere between barely appropriate and sexual harassment. Somehow, he knew how to stay on the right side of the line. It still made her skin crawl.

With the exception of the judges in the Chatham County Court System, Andrew Newsome was the top dog in the district. How he got elected with his complete lack of personality, she didn't know. But she did know that he had close ties with at least one judge: Whalen Stillwell.

Judge Stillwell, a Democrat, was the Chief Judge of the Superior Court. He was a powerful, imposing figure, well over six feet tall, perfectly sculpted white hair, and a booming, baritone voice. When he spoke, everyone listened. He ran his courtroom with an iron fist. You didn't argue with Judge Stillwell.

He was also a political machine. When up for election, he rarely faced an opponent because the Republican Party knew defeating him was next to impossible. Putting a candidate up against Stillwell was like throwing money away.

District Attorney Andrew Newsome dressed in expensive suits and still managed to make them look like they'd been purchased at a yard sale. He had a nasally voice and curly, close-cropped hair.

Sanchez knew that he spent a lot of time in Judge Stillwell's chambers. Maybe it was a close working relationship or there was political strategizing going on behind closed doors. Whatever the situation, Sanchez wasn't the only one who noticed. There were plenty of whispers among the Assistant District Attorneys and office staff that maybe there was more to their relationship than judicial machinations. Some thought that the relationship was sexual. Others believed that they plotted to railroad certain cases just to get undesirables off the street, regardless of their innocence or guilt.

Even Stillwell's fellow judges noticed the coziness of the relationship. None were so unprofessional as to reveal their beliefs to mere office staff, but people could tell much by the looks and attitudes of Stillwell's peers.

Just before noon, the lockdown ended, restoring traffic flow in and out of the courthouse. It was business as usual.

Elizabeth Sanchez pulled out her old address book and located Sylvia Deming's cell number. She took a moment, leaned back in her office chair, and looked at the drop ceiling above her desk. She noticed a small chunk of ceiling missing from one of the bright white panels. Shaking her head, reciting the words that she had planned for her call to her old friend, she picked up her desk phone and dialed.

After six rings and no answer, she hung up, and took a deep breath. *I am such a dunce. She's probably at the hospital and can't answer her phone. I'll wait until later this afternoon. Maybe she'll know more about Jarrod's condition by then.*

* * *

DEA Special Agents Vincent Mercado and Alex Smith followed Deming's ambulance to the Memorial University Medical Center emergency room. Within minutes of the shooting, Clifford Metzger, head of Georgia's DEA, called Mercado on his cell phone and ordered the agent to follow the ambulance and guard Deming.

He barked, "Make sure no one gets near him except his doctors and medical staff. Are we clear on that?"

There was only one correct answer. "Yes, sir."

When the doors opened to the ambulance at the emergency room, the two agents were waiting. They knew by the look on the paramedic's faces that there was no need to stand guard, but they had their orders.

With a hint of an Indian accent, Dr. Ari Gupta, the duty emergency room physician, asked the agents to step aside while paramedics pulled the gurney from the ambulance. They already knew Deming's condition, but couldn't make the official pronouncement. That was Dr. Gupta's call. He took one look at Deming, shook his head slightly, then performed a few cursory checks of Deming's pulse and breathing. He also looked at Deming's eyes, which were already glazed over. He looked at his watch and shook his head again.

Mercado saw the gunshots in Deming's chest, his pale, gray skin, and blue lips. A large amount of blood had pooled on the sheets of the gurney near his torso.

Dr. Gupta ordered the paramedics, "Take him inside. Room D."

With that, they rolled the gurney through the open doors of the emergency room. The agents began to follow when the doctor asked, "Are you related to the deceased?"

Smith looked at Mercado with a raised eyebrow, the word 'deceased' not lost on him. Mercado spoke to the doctor. "No, we're his co-workers...from the DEA. Well, I mean, we were."

Dr. Gupta pointed to their left. "There's a waiting room through those doors."

Mercado replied, "Our boss told us to guard this man's room."

The doctor shook his head. "No need unless your boss wants you to guard a dead man." With that, Dr. Gupta headed into the emergency room leaving the agents outside.

Mercado pulled a handkerchief from his pocket and ran it over his brow. Even in the shade of the emergency room marquee, the heat was taxing. He started towards the waiting room door to get out of the heat and to find a quiet place to call his boss. Smith followed without a word.

Once inside the hospital building, the two agents ducked into an empty, small conference room. Smith closed the door while Mercado hit speed dial number three. Metzger picked up on the first ring.

"Deming was DOA."

Metzger asked, "Are you sure?"

"Yeah. He was dead before he hit the pavement. The shots hit his chest dead center. The Doc declared a few minutes ago. There's no doubt."

There was silence on the line. Apparently, Cliff Metzger had a lot on his mind, then he said, "Okay. Spend a few hours at the hospital. If anyone other than family visits, I want to know about it. Is that clear?"

Mercado didn't miss a beat. "Yes, sir."

He flipped his phone shut. He was happy that Jarrod Deming was dead, but so were a lot of others in the DEA and elsewhere. There was a term used for times like these: CYA, or *Cover Your Ass*. Before this was over, CYA was going to be an art form.

Chapter 3

Peden Savage leaned back in his office chair, swiveling from side to side, deep in thought about the scant information that he had on Jarrod Deming's murder. The air around him felt stagnant and humid as sweat formed on his temples. The central air conditioning had been serviced less than a month ago, but something was definitely wrong and it impacted his ability to focus.

The phone rang, jolting him from his thoughts. The caller ID said *Cook*. It was his close friend, Special Agent Marcus Cook of the Drug Enforcement Administration.

He grabbed the receiver. "Marcus, my man, wassup?"

"Peden, I'm black, not you. Can't you just say, *Hey, Marcus...?* Never mind. Did you hear about Deming?"

"Yeah. I got a call from Megan right after it happened. I've been thinking about it ever since. What can you tell me?"

Cook was quiet for a moment, collecting his thoughts. "Whoever did it was really pissed off. Four pops to the chest, any one of the shots fatal. Had to be a pro. No rookie's going to make that pattern on a guy's chest. They worked on him at the scene, but he was dead before he hit the ground."

Savage thought about this first piece of real information about Deming's murder. He couldn't get anything from watching the news accounts. Savage asked, "Any news on the type of gun?"

"Yeah. The rounds were .308s. The direction of the shots was from Deming's front left; more front than left. I got that much from one of my crime scene pals. He couldn't give an exact direction, but it had to be at about eleven, maybe ten o'clock from Deming's stance at the podium." From Cook's description, Savage knew the shooter was to Deming's front-left.

Cook continued, "Rounds penetrated his chest, at least one went clear through. Our boss, Nila West, was behind him. Caught a round on her left arm. Nothing serious. Some antibiotics and a good tape job and she'll be fine."

Savage tried to picture the area in front of the DEA building. As Cook spoke, he pulled up Google Maps on his tablet, zooming in on the crime scene and surrounding area. The property was bounded by Interstate 16 to the north, a large car dealership on the east and a couple small businesses to the west. The main road to the business park where the DEA office building was located was directly to the south. Deming was facing roughly due south when the shots were fired. There was a lot of open area and direct line of sight to where Deming stood. A number of trees and shrubs dotted the grounds, but not enough to block a shooter from getting a clear shot from several angles.

Savage hit a couple keys on his tablet's keyboard. The satellite image of the grounds was now on his fifty-five-inch TV. He could see at least a dozen good locations for the shooter to set up, shoot, and escape. Since no witnesses had come forward, odds were that no one saw the shooter, or had no idea what they were seeing. He thought briefly about the DC Sniper who shot over twenty-five people, all of whom were randomly selected, killing seventeen from the trunk of a car through a hole in the car's body. Nearly all of the shootings were in very public settings.

The roads in and out of the area were plentiful. Within a couple minutes, they could have driven over the Savannah River into South Carolina heading up Highway 17, or headed west on Interstate 16 towards Interstate 95. From there, the possibilities grew exponentially.

"Peden, you still with me, my man?"

Savage shook his head at the futility of catching a gunman in flight. "Yeah. I was just looking at a map. Lots of escape routes. Shooter would have had to screw up big time to get caught."

Cook said, "You know, I've been with this gang for about two and a half years. I got to know Deming some. When I first got here, he was all gung-ho, kick-ass, kill-the-bad-guys kind of guy. Pretty cocky. About two years ago, he cooled off. His mind was always somewhere else. He got called on it, too. Brass told him to get his head out of his ass and back in the game or he was on his way out. Thing is, he didn't seem to care."

Savage asked, "Did he ever let on what was bugging him?"

"Nah, not to me anyway. I was still out of the clique, you know, a newbie. He wasn't gonna confide in me. The only thing he ever said to me was that I should watch my six. I asked him what he meant, but he never said. I just figured he meant in general, like during raids and stuff. But I never played any major roles during raids back then. Still don't, really."

Savage thought for a moment. "You mean, even with all the big busts that the Savannah office has had, you haven't been in on any of them?"

"Not yet. Maybe this will shake things up. We've got an unexpected opening."

Peden frowned. He then asked, "You think this was...?" He left the thought hanging.

Marcus knew what Peden was asking. Could this have been an inside job? Speculation was that Deming was going to blow the whistle on DEA agents' illegal activities. He hadn't leaked any specifics. There was a possibility that no one but Deming knew the details of his planned announcement. If true, the information would die with him.

"Sorry, man. I'm not hearing anything. But I'm not part of the inner circle...yet. I'll be listening. You'll be the first to know."

"Thanks, Marcus. This smells worse than a paper mill on the Savannah River."

"You got that right."

When the two men disconnected, Peden's brain kicked into overdrive. Killing Deming was a mighty risky move, if it was an inside job. *But if they could pin the job on someone else and keep their hands clean...hmm.* Savage was acquainted with many agents at the DEA. Some were still friends. Others, especially those in higher level positions, despised him. He wondered if they might pick a fall guy for the murder. No one on the inside came to mind. But on the outside there were lots of folks who wouldn't mind taking out a DEA agent, especially some of the major dealers.

Then he looked back at his TV and said aloud, "I wonder what happened to the notes he pulled from his coat?"

* * *

After her event-filled day, Elizabeth Sanchez closed and locked her condominium door behind her. She did a quick scan of the wide-open living room, dining room, and kitchen while she pulled off her heels, rubbing each foot in the process. Making her way across the forest green carpet, she tossed her purse on the kitchen counter. She was physically and mentally exhausted from a day filled with bad news and worse news. Even the bright colors and southwestern décor of the walls in her condo, along with the sunlight that streamed through the south facing windows could not lift her spirits. She grabbed a tall glass of ice water, started to take a drink, then dumped it into the sink. Instead, she grabbed a wine glass and hunted in the refrigerator for the open bottle of chardonnay. Having poured a healthy glass of liquid relaxation, she made her way to the living room and plopped down on the couch, nearly spilling her wine. She punched the power button on the TV remote.

The 6:00 PM edition of *Channel 8 News* was on. A field reporter, a young man in a suit coat with neatly prepped hair, was standing in front of the emergency room entrance to Memorial University Medical Center. He was motioning to the Marquee with note papers in his right hand while speaking into the microphone that he held in his left.

Shortly after 10:30 this morning, Dr. Ari Gupta declared Drug Enforcement Administration Special Agent Jarrod Deming dead from multiple gunshot wounds to the chest. In a brief news conference held at 3:00 PM this afternoon, Dr. Gupta said that there was no possibility that Deming could have survived the fatal wounds regardless of the expediency of medical care.

At 4:30 PM today, the Chief of the Savannah-Chatham Metropolitan Police held a separate news conference and had this to say.

The screen shifted to a film clip of the news conference in which the police chief announced that the killer was still at large. He asked that anyone with any information, however insignificant, call the *Savannah-Chatham Metropolitan Police* crime hot line. An 800 number displayed across the bottom of the screen. The screen switched back to the field reporter.

Deming was a ten-year veteran of the Drug Enforcement Administration. He leaves behind a grieving wife. Back to you, Jenn.

Elizabeth sat motionless, stricken with remorse. This news only darkened her already sullen mood.

She stood and went to her purse, pulling out her cell phone with the intention of calling her old friend, Sylvia. Three times she started to punch in the cell number and all three times she stopped. *This shouldn't be this hard. You're just comforting an old friend.* Elizabeth walked back to her bedroom, then back towards the living room with no purpose in mind. She stopped at a mirror in the hallway, faced her image and said out loud, "Stop acting like a baby. She's your friend. Call her."

Now sitting on the couch, she took an extra-long sip of wine, punched in the number again and hit send. Barely one ring had completed when a familiar voice came on the line. The voice was filled with sadness, but it was definitely the voice of her longtime friend, Sylvia Mason Deming.

"Liz…Oh my God!"

"Hey, Sissy." Elizabeth always called Sylvia *Sissy* back in their college days. "I heard about Jarrod. It's all over the news. I'm so sorry."

Through tearful whimpers she said, "Thanks, Liz."

There was a moment of silence, then Sanchez heard the muffled sound of her friend blowing her nose. She continued in a voice with a nasally sound. "Where are you calling from?"

"Savannah, Sis. I work for the DA's office."

This news seemed to lighten Sylvia's mood just a bit. She said, "Oh my God! I can't believe you live here and we didn't know it. How long have you been here?"

"About six years. When I finished law school, I did an internship in Atlanta. But, listen, let's talk about you. What can I do for you?"

There was a moment of silence before Sylvia spoke again. When she did, she was more subdued. "I could really use some company besides all Jarrod's friends. It's been like a parade around here."

Sanchez said, "You tell me when and where, and I'll be there."

Sylvia gave her directions to an address on The Isle of Hope, a nice community southeast of the city.

Elizabeth thought, *Hang on, Sis. I'm here for you.*

Chapter 4

Judge Whalen Stillwell's chambers consisted of two rooms on the fourth floor of the Chatham County Courthouse. The first room was an office area about one hundred forty-four feet square. A large window on the east-facing wall looked out onto Montgomery Street and the Robert E. Robinson parking garage. Not the best view in the city, especially for a high-ranking judge. The second room consisted of a restroom with a vanity and closet where the judge could freshen up. The entire chambers had an abundance of dark, hardwood trim with matching filing cabinets and a massive desk. Incoming sunlight combined with bright fluorescent lights counteracted the dark trim. The office had a sterile, hospital-like aroma with a hint of wood wax.

Three walls were adorned with photographs of Stillwell and various dignitaries, including several senators and house members, Presidents Carter and Clinton, and a host of movie stars. There were a few shots of men in boats with their fishing gear or in the woods with rifles, posing with their trophy kills. In one, Judge Stillwell held the antlers of a large elk, a high-powered Remington rifle with a scope rested across his shoulder.

None of the three men in chambers was admiring the photos. District Attorney Andrew Newsome watched with delight as Judge Stillwell destroyed Public Defender Jonas Cottier. This was Cottier's first job, having passed the bar just nine months ago. He was young and idealistic, believing that defendants would get a fair trial in the United States of America. The three were discussing a recent drug bust in which his client claimed that he had been framed.

The defendant, a twenty-four-year-old white male

named Richard 'Ricky' Armstrong, was caught with thirty-seven pounds of marijuana, four ounces of cocaine, $6754.00 in cash, and several handguns.

Armstrong admitted to his attorney that, at the time of the bust, he was in possession of just under two pounds of pot, but claims he never had any cocaine or guns. He told his lawyer that he never handled coke, that he considered it poison. He only sold grass to a few friends to make enough money to pay for his college classes at Savannah College of Art and Design. He promised his client that he would do what he could to convince the judge that something fishy was going on at the DEA.

"Your honor, my client is a good student at SCAD. He's got a 3.85 GPA and he's never been late for a single class. He's never had so much as a traffic ticket before now. He claims, and I believe him, that he only had a relatively small amount..."

"Stop, Mr. Cottier. Tell me again why this court shouldn't hold ya'll in contempt? And, counselor, ya'll better make it good."

Judge Stillwell's booming southern accent was more than a little intimidating. It was downright commanding and he wasn't about to let a rookie Public Defender control the flow of this, or any, discussion.

He resumed his tongue lashing. "Don't continue to claim that your client had no knowledge of this substantial stockpile of drugs. I read the claim in your motion to suppress. I've heard it too many times already. You can try to prove it in open court during his trial, but your motion is denied. I will not even dignify your client's ramblings with further response. The prosecution has photo and video evidence of the contraband in his home. It doesn't matter if he has a record cleaner than Mother Teresa's. The amount of drugs on hand, and the cash and weapons, all indicate to me that he's a potential danger to his neighborhood, this city, and anyone he meets. Now he has to face the consequences." He looked from Cottier to the District Attorney, then back again. "This part of the discussion is over. Now, before ya'll say another word, counselor, I'm warning you, do not raise this topic in my chambers again."

Andrew Newsome knew that Stillwell didn't want or need the spotlight on his court for holding an attorney in contempt. He just wanted to put Cottier in his place and move on. The bust and trial would generate more than enough publicity for the court and the District Attorney's office.

* * *

District Attorney Andrew Newsome and Judge Whalen Stillwell were having a cocktail at a private club in an isolated room on Skidaway Island south of Savannah. The club was so exclusive that it didn't have an official name, and no signs adorned the building, which wasn't visible from any public road.

"You know, Whalen, with Deming's murder, this case could take on a life of its own."

In typical fashion, the judge replied in his confident, baritone voice, "Andrew, ya'll worry too much. The media focus will be on the trial and what a great job we're doing keeping drugs off the streets. The Deming thing, well, he had it coming, trying to stab his fellow agents in the back. I'm sure that Bobby's going to find the killer." Stillwell grinned, referring to Savannah Chatham Metropolitan Police Chief Robert Chastine. "I expect there'll be a suspect named in short order. Deming's arrested a lot of big-time dealers over the years. We'll probably find that one of those recently released thugs did this." He winked at Newsome and took a long drink from his scotch on the rocks.

Newsome returned a nervous smile and took a sip from his own martini. He wasn't as confident as the judge, plus he'd have to face the journalists' questions during press conferences, something the judge could easily avoid.

Newsome put his drink down. "That reminds me." He reached into his suit coat pocket and pulled out an envelope full of cash. In one smooth motion, he held it out to the judge. In years past, he would appear nervous and look around to see if anyone was looking. Back then the judge had laughed at him and made mocking gestures, ducking his head, looking around nervously, an exaggerated expression of fear plastered on his face. Stillwell had lectured Newsome about how to not look guilty. "Andrew, we're in an exclusive, private club, in a locked room with no cameras and no one around. The walls are as soundproof as it gets. Ya'll don't have to be all 'cloak and dagger' on me. Hell, if you're this nervous now, what are ya'll going to do when things get a little tense?"

Since that first meeting four years ago, Judge Stillwell, District Attorney Andrew Newsome, and a number of DEA agents had made great financial strides, thanks to the War on Drugs. They had taken a lot of drugs off the streets of Savannah, but not nearly as much as they reported. In return for being such great public servants, they had rewarded themselves handsomely.

They were now on track to have the highest dollar total of drug seizures east of the Mississippi River, including the Miami-Dade DEA district. That distinction was making Andrew Newsome nervous. If the news media did a little too much digging, they might ask questions about how the DEA in Savannah, Georgia, was having such success in finding and busting big-time drug dealers in such a relatively small community. Those questions might be difficult to answer.

Stillwell asked, "So, do you have a replacement for Deming?"

Newsome shook his head. It hadn't even been twelve hours since Jarrod Deming had been gunned down and the judge was already pushing to get the Special Operations Team back up to full strength. In Newsome's opinion, replacing Deming quickly was a mistake. The new recruit had to be a good fit with the team and they had to be willing to play by the team's rules, which weren't in full compliance with the law. Apparently, that was something Deming decided he could no longer swallow.

Stillwell stared at Newsome, waiting for his answer. He knew the judge wanted the current pace of the raids to continue. An extended opening on the team would necessitate a slowdown. That would reduce their cash payouts.

Newsome finally said, "We'll work on it. I have to talk with Vince, see what he thinks."

The judge kept staring at his DA, then broke into a broad smile. He polished his drink off, walked over to the serving table and poured himself another. He motioned for Newsome to do the same.

When both glasses were filled, he raised his glass. "A toast; to continuing the good fight...and getting rich in the process."

The men clinked glasses and took a good, long drink.

* * *

Andrew Newsome had a five-minute drive from the club to his forty-five-hundred square foot house on the eastern edge of Skidaway Island. The two-story structure on one acre was eight years old. His wife of eighteen years was elated when they acquired the property during the housing market collapse after the previous owner was forced into bankruptcy. They purchased the home for a song, but the pressure of keeping up appearances to fit in with their neighbors was proving to be expensive.

When he arrived at 7:30 PM, his wife, Meredith, asked about his day and said that dinner was ready. He forced a smile, headed towards the stairs, and said that he needed to change clothes.

He went upstairs to his walk-in closet, pushed his dress pants to one side exposing the door to the four-foot high, built-in safe. Out of habit, he punched the keys in the right sequence and hit the release button. The safe mechanism whirred and clicked as the door bars slid back. He grabbed the handle and opened the heavy door.

To the untrained eye, it appeared that the only thing in the safe were papers that were important only to the homeowner. A closer look revealed that the top section of the safe slid out like a drawer. Behind the fake wall was an additional four cubic feet of storage, which housed stacks of cash. Within a year, if their plan continued on schedule, the space would be filled. He'd lost track of the total amount of cash, but it added up to over one million dollars. All cash, all untraceable, all tax free. Even his wife had no idea that he had the stash. *I wonder what Deming did with his money? Did his wife know about the graft? Does she have it now or did he hide it in a bank deposit box, never to be found?*

He shook his head like an Etch A Sketch to clear his thoughts, then put his most recent take on the shortest stack of hundred dollar bills. He covered his mouth with both hands, marveling at the accumulated Franklins, then slid the unit back in place. He reversed the process, closing the safe door, punching in random numbers to secure the locking mechanism, and rearranged the pants to hide the safe from view. He took one more deep breath and headed out into the bedroom to change into casual clothes for dinner.

Something began to gnaw at his brain – something not related to the safe or the money. It had to do with the Deming hit. He knew that members of the DEA were planning to take Deming out if he went ahead with his press conference, but he didn't know any of the details.

What if Deming had details to support his unspoken allegations? Where would he keep that information? Maybe Deming had a safe like mine? I have to talk with Mercado, see what he knows.

One other thing; when Deming stepped up to the microphone, before he was shot, he pulled papers from his coat pocket. Another loose end. Have to find those notes.

Chapter 5

Wayne Cleaver was a free man at last. Looking around the grimy, run-down motel room, he wondered if his former digs, his two-man cell at the Coastal State Prison in Garden City, Georgia, wasn't a better deal. For twenty-five bucks, the sum total of his "gate money" upon release from the medium security facility, he didn't have to share this room with anyone.

The prison housed male felons considered low risk for violence or flight. Since Cleaver's conviction was on trafficking marijuana, he didn't meet the guidelines for a higher level of security, even though the quantity of pot listed on the official arrest report was rather substantial; fifty-seven-plus pounds. A model prisoner, he was released nearly six years early. The parole board found no reason for him to occupy space needed for more deserving felons.

In addition to his "gate money," he'd saved $58.72 in his inmate account which he received in cash upon his release. He had enough money for one more night's stay and a few cheap meals. He sat on the edge of the squeaky bed and contemplated his next move. Should he retrieve some of the cash that he'd left with his mother in Anderson, South Carolina? Should he lay low for now? With limited funds, he couldn't stick around for long, but he had business to take care of in Savannah.

He took a deep breath to clear his thoughts, but all it did was fill his lungs with the stale, foul air from the motel room. It was mid-afternoon on a beautiful, Georgia day so he opened the window to clear out the musky odor. It took some effort, but the window finally slid to the side. The outside air was stagnant, hot, and humid. He closed the window and reached down to crank the air conditioning up. It was already set on maximum cool. It was going to be a long stay, even if for only one night.

Wayne was a relatively small, passive man, standing only five-feet-eight inches tall, one hundred and sixty pounds. He had a pale complexion despite living in the south most of his life. In stark contrast to his skin, his dark eyes were nearly black, making it difficult to tell where his pupils stopped and his irises began. His face sported perpetual stubble even though he shaved every morning. While in college, he had never cut his hair, resulting in a frizzy, steel wool-looking overgrowth. While in prison, he had kept his head shaved close, for sanitary and safety reasons. He didn't want anyone to have anything to grab if a confrontation erupted. As it turned out, most everyone left him alone.

His dream was to become a graphic artist and work in a movie studio or a marketing agency. He knew computers and how to make them produce images and messages that influenced people.

When he had finished high school in Anderson, he shared his dream of becoming a graphic artist with his mother. She was supportive, but made it clear to Wayne that she couldn't afford to help with financing his college and career aspirations. Being a single, working-class parent left her little cash to work with once the bills were paid. What little she'd saved had to go toward her own future. Wayne's father had left his mother before Wayne was born and she had never remarried.

Wayne got a job in the kitchen of the Mellow Mushroom, a pizza joint and local hangout for college students. He applied for a number of scholarships. Between the two sources he took in enough money to get him through his first two years at the Savannah College of Art and Design.

He had lots of friends from school and work. It was an easygoing crowd. They were young and idealistic and artistic with big dreams. Their generation would make things right with the world. The first female president, the first gay president, the shattering of all kinds of social barriers would be accomplishments that they envisioned seeing in their lifetimes.

Wayne wasn't interested in major social issues, but he did share one thing with the group. That was the habit of smoking a little grass. No one at school or work cared as long as he completed the required assignments, got to work on time, and did his job right.

By his junior year, he was running short on funds to finish his degree. The scholarship money was cut and tuition was raised. There was no way to work enough hours to make up the shortfall, and he didn't want to take on any debt. He and a friend decided that selling a little grass was the answer to the problem.

For thirteen months, it worked like a finely oiled machine. At the start of his final year, sales were good. No one really cared that he was dealing. Even professors at the school were the occasional customer. All in all, his future looked bright indeed.

Suddenly, Wayne's world came crashing down. One of his professors was pulled over for a traffic stop. The officer smelled marijuana when the professor lowered his car window. It took less than a minute's worth of threats from the officer before Wayne's professor was handing over his supplier's name and address and the fact that it was one of his students.

Wayne had lived in a nineteenth-century home that was divided up into six apartment units. The entry to his unit was down a narrow alley protected from street view by a wooden fence. There was no other way in or out. He shared his unit with the student who was his partner. They both were making just enough money to cover the shortfall in their living and school expenses. Business was steady, not growing, just the way both men wanted it to stay. Traffic into and out of their apartment was limited.

One Thursday, around 3:30 AM, Wayne awoke to a loud *bam*, like a bomb going off. Before he could get out of bed, three men in full SWAT gear carrying automatic weapons burst into his room and had him face down on the floor in handcuffs. One man grabbed him by the hair so hard that his scalp bled. When they led him out of the apartment, he noticed several black trash bags stacked in the living room. He never saw his roommate until the two were arraigned.

There was an offer of a plea deal, which Wayne opposed. His appointed public defender recommended that he take the deal. His roommate had already taken a deal and placed all the blame on Wayne for turning him into a drug dealer.

During extensive questioning, Wayne was confronted by a number of Drug Enforcement Administration agents who were involved in the raid. Two names stuck in his mind because they were exceptionally arrogant. They asked who his supplier was, but didn't appear interested in his answer. They took sport insulting him, saying his father was a deadbeat and his mother a whore. The remarks about his father didn't bother Wayne, but calling his mother a whore for no apparent reason caused him to burn from the inside out.

During a break in the questioning, he turned to his attorney and asked him, "Why all the ball-busting over half a pound of weed?"

The astonished look on the Public Defender's face signaled trouble. He'd replied, "Half a pound? Try over fifty. This is serious shit, my man."

The black plastic bags flashed before his eyes. Trying to fight was futile. He later learned that his professor had started the ball rolling, being caught in a simple traffic stop. His roommate had turned on him to save his own ass. But what most infuriated Wayne was the two DEA agents taunting him, calling him names, telling him that he was poisoning kids with drugs. The remarks that hurt most were those about his mother. They intentionally ruined his life.

The two names were DEA Special Agents Vincent Mercado and Jarrod Deming.

The thought of these two getting away with ruining his life just burned within his entire being. Plans of revenge fanned the smoldering visions of each man's face within inches of his own, taunting him, telling him how he'd be mistreated in prison, smiling as they described how his mother would have to take on new 'clients' to pay for his legal bills. Though none of those things had happened, he'd lost over three years of his life on a bogus conviction. Before his arrest, he had respect for law enforcement officers. He would never trust another man in uniform again.

A loud knock on the flimsy motel door shocked him out of his trance.

He looked through the peep hole as another knock shook the door. He saw two men in light-weight, tan suits. One of the men looked towards the parking lot, so Wayne couldn't see his face. He didn't recognize the man facing the door. They both looked big, like they worked out. With the safety chain still in place, he opened the door enough to ask, "Yeah?"

The man who had been facing the parking lot turned towards the door. A shiver ran the length of Wayne's body. It was DEA Special Agent Vincent Mercado.

Mercado grinned, his teeth bright white, his nose, up slightly, showing an air of superiority. "Hi, Wayne." A pause, then, "Mind if we come in and chat?"

A thousand thoughts passed through Wayne's mind causing confusion and indecision. He tried to stall.

"Last time you were in my room, I ended up in prison. What do you want?"

"We just want to ask you a couple quick questions and chat a little bit. No harm in that, is there?"

Wayne took a deep breath. He looked past the two men as best he could, then from side to side. It appeared that they were alone, but there was no guarantee of that. Then he thought, *If they're going to bust me again, there's nothing I can do to stop them.*

He closed the door, unhooked the safety chain, reopened the door, and stepped back. The two agents casually walked into the room. When they were inside and the door was shut behind them, they looked around, raised their noses with man-this-stinks expressions. The man that Wayne did not know turned the wobbly desk chair towards the center of the room and sat, leaning forward with his elbows on his knees. The chair creaked loudly in protest. Vincent Mercado remained standing, facing Wayne.

Mercado spoke. "Isn't much of a step up from Coastal."

Wayne didn't respond. He remained silent and waited for Mercado to state his business, which he figured was going to be a warning to get out of town and to not return. He was wrong.

"Where were you this morning around 10:00?"

Wayne raised an eyebrow. "I'm betting that you already know the answer." He paused and kept eye contact with Mercado. "What's this about?" When Mercado didn't respond, he said, "I was just leaving Coastal in a taxi cab. Came right to this dump and checked in. I've been here ever since."

"Were you anywhere in the vicinity of the DEA office?"

Cleaver frowned. Mercado was leading up to something and it smelled worse than his room. He asked again, this time with just a little more force, "What's this about?"

Mercado ignored the question and asked, "Can anyone verify your whereabouts from 10:00 AM until now?"

Wayne knew that any and all answers that he gave to these two agents could be used against him, but it didn't really matter what he said. It was his word, a convict just released from prison, against two federal agents. He had to temper his answers and remain calm. He also didn't want these guys getting worked up.

In a calm, almost apologetic voice, Wayne said, "Look, I just got out around 10:00 AM. A couple guards and the guy who handles the release log saw me get into the cab. The cab driver delivered me to this motel. I asked him where the closest, cheapest motel was and he took me here. The motel clerk gave me the key to this room. The only other place I've been is the sub shop right across the parking lot. Other than that, I've been in this room."

Mercado seemed to consider the whole story line. "Okay, Cleaver, we're going to check your story. If it checks, you're okay. If not, we'll be back."

Wayne again asked, this time in a voice that sounded almost friendly, "So what's this all about?"

Mercado gave him a snarky smile and said, "Just routine."

Mercado made a slight head motion to his partner towards the door and both men left, leaving the door opened behind them.

Wayne closed the door and said quietly, "Assholes."

After thinking about the encounter, he decided that the visit wasn't "just routine." He needed legal advice, but he wasn't sure where to turn. He knew only one attorney, an old friend, but she was with the District Attorney's office. She was one of them. He picked up the phone book from the table and leafed through to the "S" section and found *Sanchez E.*

He picked up the phone, ready to dial, then thought, *If they know where I am, what's to keep them from bugging my phone?* He shook off his paranoia and dialed the number for Elizabeth Sanchez. After four rings and no answer, he hung up. *I'll try later.*

He turned on the TV. The anchorwoman for *Channel 8 News*, a real looker, was talking about a murder from earlier in the day. At Coastal, when she was on, there were always crude comments from the inmates. On the TV screen, a man walked up to a bank of microphones. Wayne quickly grabbed the remote to un-mute the sound. Just as he did, a woman could be heard screaming and the man at the microphone fell over backwards. Wayne Cleaver understood the reason for Agent Mercado's visit.

The man was Special Agent Jarrod Deming.

Chapter 6

Peden Savage took a quick glance at the old clock on the wall. It read 5:55 but he knew that it ran twenty-five minutes fast. It was actually 5:30 PM. Seven and a half hours had passed since Jarrod Deming's murder. Savage had thought of nothing else since Megan Moore's call moments after the shooting.

Speculation about the murder had reached a feverish pitch, with the general public believing he was killed by a big-time drug dealer or cartel hit man. Personnel inside the Savannah's FBI satellite office believed it was an inside job. Other theories involved common criminals or aliens, but none of the latter had much traction. It was still very early in the investigation. The FBI was the lead law enforcement agency. Any forensic evidence gathered was at the nearest FBI lab, but processing had just begun, so any theories were just that: theories.

In most murders where a spouse is killed, the surviving spouse is typically considered a person of interest. With this murder being likened to an assassination, Megan Moore told Peden that no one planned on asking Sylvia Deming any hard questions. She apparently had an alibi for the time her husband was killed, though it had yet to be confirmed.

Peden was typing his thoughts on the Deming murder into his daily journal. He did this for all his cases. By using the journal, he was able to leave one case for another, then come back and read his notes to jog his memory. The process had served him well over the years.

He hit the save icon and thought about dinner. Pizza and sub sandwiches were out of the question. He'd had Mellow Mushroom fare delivered for lunch for the past three days. He needed something more...sophisticated, but within walking distance. With the yellow pages opened to the restaurants section, he walked his fingers down the list, stopping at a handful of options, but settling on *Garibaldi's*. It was within walking distance, as long as you didn't mind the mile-and-a-half round trip. This time of year, the weather was nice for an early evening stroll through a number of the squares on the west side of the city. He decided to invite Megan Moore so they could discuss Deming's murder. Not the greatest topic while eating Italian food, but at least she was good company.

He reached for the phone, but it rang just before his hand touched the receiver.

"Savage Investigative Consultants."

There was a pause before a man with a gravelly, southern accent asked, "Is this Peden Savage?"

"Yes it is. And you are...?"

"Allen Deming."

Peden's mind went into overdrive. He'd just typed the man's name into his notes. "Mr. Deming, are you Jarrod Deming's father?"

"Yes."

"I'm very sorry for your loss, sir."

After a pause, Deming said, "Thank you." Another pause, then, "I want to hire you."

Peden shifted in his seat. He didn't know Allen Deming from the man on the moon. He asked, "Before I commit to anything, Mr. Deming..."

"Call me Al."

"Okay, Al. How did you get my name? We're not really private investigators. I mean, we don't usually do work for the general public."

"Mr. Savage..."

"Call me Peden."

"Peden. I got your name from my son. He was going to blow the whistle on his DEA team. He was going to name names and provide details of their crimes. The list of crimes is extensive...and they're still happening." Deming took a deep breath. "These guys are supposed to be the good guys, Peden."

Peden looked at the clock, then back at his computer screen. He quickly reopened his journal and scrolled to the bottom. He asked, "Al, how do you know that these things happened and are still happening?"

"Because I used to work for the courts in Savannah, for one judge in particular, and I was offered money to keep my mouth shut. Jarrod was involved in what they called 'payday busts.' " He paused. Peden could hear the man wiping his nose, he hoped on a handkerchief. Deming continued, "My son's conscience got the best of him. His wife, Sylvia, learned what was happening and she gave him an ultimatum. He either came clean or she was divorcing him."

It occurred to Peden that this conversation shouldn't be held over the phone. He said, "Al, can we talk about this in person? It seems to me that you have a lot of information that should be recorded. That way we won't lose anything, if you get my drift."

"We can, as long as you don't mind coming to Arizona, 'cause I'm not going to Georgia. Not even for my son's funeral.

"I spoke with Sylvia just a few minutes ago. She's really torn up. I told her I wouldn't be there for the funeral and she said it was best that I didn't. I hate that I can't go." Another pause, then he said, "Peden, these guys would just as soon kill me as look at me. They have a lot to lose. They'll do anything to protect their little scheme."

Savage said, "I'm not sure how much more we should say over the phone. Are you calling from your home?"

"Nope. Payphone, long ways from my place. If you're worried about your end, I suggest we figure that out now. I can use this phone. Do you have another number where I can contact you?"

Savage thought for a moment, then came up with a simple solution. He said, "Al, you call me tomorrow between 1:00 and 5:00 Eastern Time. I'll have an answer on the communications thing." He still didn't understand what Allen Deming wanted to accomplish by hiring him. "Before we go there, what are you hiring me to do?"

"I want you to find my son's killer."

He paused, then asked, "Why me? There are dozens of guys who could handle this for you, with all the ammunition that you have."

Allen Deming took a deep breath. "Because my son expressly said that if anything happened to him, that I should hire *you*. He said you got forced out of the FBI because you wouldn't go along with some crooked agents at the bureau. He said you were a stand-up guy." Deming took another deep breath. "Was he right?"

"He was right that I was forced out. Stand-up guy? Depends on who you ask. My mom thinks so, but she's biased."

"I was still at the courthouse when I first heard a couple DEA guys use your name in the same sentence as 'shithead,' 'motherfucker' and 'son-of-a-bitch.' I dug a bit and learned why they said that stuff. At the time, I agreed with them. Then I found out what my guys were doing. They offered me hush money and taped me accepting it. They had me. Now I know the real price of playing along. I also know why Jarrod insisted that I call you and no one else."

There was silence on the line. When Peden finally spoke, he said, "Call me tomorrow. If I decide to take this on, I'll give you contact information and let you know my rates and terms. Then you can decide if you want to hire me."

"I already know my answer."

The phone went to a dial tone. Peden hung up and rubbed his face with both hands. The phone rang within seconds. Megan Moore.

Megan Moore asked, "Workin' late?"

"You might say that. I may have a new client. Meet me at Girabaldi's at 6:30 and I'll tell you all about it. My treat."

* * *

Girabaldi's Café was one of Savage's favorite restaurants in the historic district of Savannah. Not only was it within walking distance of his office, which was true with everything in the historic district, it was never too crowded. The décor was beautiful polished wood, chandeliers, and large, arched windows with luxurious drapes. The service was always top notch, the food top notch.

When Moore and Savage were seated, she asked, "So, who's the secret client?"

A waiter walked up, poured their water, and took drink orders. Megan asked for a Pinot Noir and Peden ordered a Blue Moon draft.

When the waiter was out of ear shot, he stated, "Jarrod Deming's old man."

Moore looked astonished. "What, he just called out of the blue and said, 'Hey, I want to hire you.'? To do what?"

"Find his son's killer. Shouldn't be too hard, right?"

"No, except that's what the FBI is doing. Specifically, me. Roland told me just before I left my office that my only job right now was to find Deming's killer. I have a decent budget and a team of agents."

"Great. We can work together."

Moore rolled her eyes. "The last thing that he told me was to keep you at arm's length, to use only your products, not you specifically. He doesn't want you directly involved."

"Look, you're already following the rules. Here you are at arm's length and we're talking about what tools you need for the job. Besides, the FBI didn't hire me. Allen Deming did, or he will tomorrow. Relax, you're following orders like a good bureau soldier."

Megan gave him an evil look, followed by the slightest hint of a smile. "You can be such a dick sometimes."

"So, to get this partnership going, what's the latest intel from the FBI's point of view?"

"Gun was a .308."

"Old news."

"Shots from the south, we don't know the exact location."

"Ditto."

"Shooter was extremely good, probably a professional."

"You're real close to having to pay for your own meal. Even the newsies know that much."

"Okay, wise guy, what do you know?"

Peden sat up straight and was getting ready to talk about Allen Deming's call when the waiter came to the table, delivered their drinks, and asked if they were ready to order. They weren't, but Peden ordered an appetizer to buy some time.

When the waiter walked away, he picked up where he left off. "First off, you have got to keep this between you and me for the time being. Agreed?"

Megan placed a hand on the back of her neck, then said, "Let me hear it, then I'll tell you if I can agree."

"If you don't agree, I can't tell you."

"Hey, I thought we were a team. What, we're only a team when you feel like it? You heard the one about finding the 'I' in 'TEAM'? They found it in the 'A' hole." She gave him a stern look.

Peden smiled and put his hand over his heart. "Wow. That really hurts. Okay, here goes. DEA agents are running scam busts. They are somehow making cash money on each one. Allen Deming got caught up in the scam and was taking hush money, of sorts. Jarrod was going to blow the whistle on them but didn't live long enough to do it."

Megan's mind was trying to wrap around what Peden had just said. She knew it was possible that DEA agents were stealing money from the scene at drug busts, but this sounded like an organized plan. This was much larger than a rogue agent skimming money.

She asked, "Was all this in Deming's news conference notes?"

Peden looked at her and said, "I don't know. I was hoping that you could tell me."

"Sorry, but nobody's found his notes. Somebody at the news conference had to have grabbed them."

Savage said, "Well doesn't that suck. Whoever that is, they're either covering their ass or they're in real danger."

Chapter 7

The sun was low in the morning sky. The forecast called for high heat and high humidity. The heavy morning traffic heading northwest off of Skidaway Island towards Savannah's historic district was a steady stream of BMWs, Lexuses, Cadillacs, Lincolns, and the odd Jaguar mixed with Chevys, Fords, Hondas, Toyotas, Hyundais, and Chryslers. Judges, lawyers, doctors, college professors, and upper-level managers for major hotels and manufacturers headed off the island towards their respective offices for another day of keeping the economy and the government functioning.

Andrew Newsome and Vincent Mercado watched the traffic from Newsome's navy blue BMW 428i parked in front of Cutter's Point Coffee shop. The coffee shop was in a small plaza that had less than a dozen retail shops. It was a busy plaza catering to middle class families. Newsome ordered some kind of sweet smelling latte with cream flavoring. Mercado stuck with Columbian Black, no sugar, no cream. He liked Newsome's Beamer, but not as much as his own gray Acura RLX, which was parked next to them. Mercado did like nice things, but didn't like them so much as to risk being seen as living above his means. He didn't want to draw attention to himself or his team, especially now, with the murder of a fellow agent.

Newsome broke the silence. "Stillwell wants to know if you have a replacement for Deming."

Mercado nearly choked on his coffee. When he recovered, he said, "You're shittin' me, right? He really said that? Deming's been dead less than twenty-four hours."

Newsome didn't turn towards Mercado. "Preachin' to the choir, Vince. He wants to keep up the pace of the busts."

"Tell His Honor," – he said *His Honor* with as much sarcastic indignation as he could muster – "that, no, we do not have a replacement for Deming. You don't just tap a guy on the shoulder and say, 'Hey buddy, you're next.' " He shook his head in amazement.

"Look, I'm with you. We're going to be under the microscope until this Deming thing blows over, if it does. The feebs are going to be on you guys like stink on shit any day now. I heard that Moore's been assigned as SAIC. She's good. Her boss, Roland Fosco, doesn't like you guys...I mean the DEA in general. He's gonna try to tear you guys a new asshole."

Vincent Mercado had been in some tough spots before. He was an Army combat veteran from Iraq, and he'd been up against some pretty tough guys when stationed at the DEA's El Paso, Texas, office. Back then, he had control of the situation. No one was calling the shots or second-guessing his decisions. With Stillwell making demands, he wasn't confident that he could stay under the radar.

He said to Newsome, "Look, if they dig deep and hard enough, who knows what'll surface. I don't believe that there's any way they can trace the money. Once it leaves our hands, in theory, it disappears into the hands of suppliers. Even marked bills can be laundered back into circulation, but we have hundreds of pounds of grass that have been 'recycled.' We might have to move some weight to safe locations to keep the books balanced."

Newsome listened to what Mercado had to say, then asked, "Do you think we can get another bust in before shit hits the fan? That might calm Stillwell down."

Mercado was getting agitated. The judge was in a pretty safe position. The same was true for Newsome. If the investigation got too close, they were insulated from the action in the field. There was no money trail to the judge or the district attorney. But Mercado and his partners, Alex Smith and Pete Nichols, signed for all the seed money when setting up buys. It was their names and their asses on the line if an audit looked real deep into the cash transfers. After the money was in their hands, it was difficult to prove where the money went.

Mercado thought for a moment, taking a deep breath. "We could do maybe one more being short-handed. Going in light is dangerous, but, with the right target, it could be done without a whole lot of fanfare." He paused. "We have a guy we're looking at for Deming's slot. He's pretty new but a real serious guy. Not sure he's up for this kind of work."

"What's his name?"

"Marcus Cook. Former Army Ranger. Big, black dude. Smart. Tough. Maybe too straight-laced for this, but I want to take a closer look."

"Anybody else?"

"Nah. Not right now. Maybe, if we could take a break, we could find somebody. Remember how long it took to get this team together? This kind of shit takes time."

Newsome took a sip of his latte. He knew Mercado was right, but Stillwell wanted action, not excuses. He advised, "Push this Cook guy, see what happens."

Mercado was getting more annoyed the longer they talked. He knew where the orders were coming from, but didn't like the pressure. "Look, it's not my fault Deming got all soft on us." He took a sip of his coffee. "I'll see what I can do, but I'm not promising anything. I'll get a copy of his service record, see if there's anything we can use. Like I said, no promises."

He turned and looked out the window, but all he saw was the side of his Acura. He was tense. It was too early in the morning for that.

Then Newsome shifted topics. "Do we have a plan for a fall guy for Deming? Someone outside the ranks?"

Mercado smiled. "Yeah, I think we got some possibilities. There's a guy we busted three or so years back. Just got out of the joint yesterday. It should work."

Newsome cracked a slight smile. "Did he have a beef with Deming?"

"He had a beef with all of us. He was a real light weight

as far as dope dealers went and we loaded him up with about fifty or sixty pounds. We'll have to do a little work to make him look like he was gunning for Deming, but it should be a slam dunk. He's a loser anyway."

Newsome smiled again. "Good. I'll talk with Stillwell. See if he's good with this."

"I can't imagine that he wouldn't be. He's the one that wants to keep going full speed. If we have to move fast, then this guy's our best bet."

Mercado finished his coffee and stuffed the cup in a paper sack. He held the bag open for Newsome who shook his head. "Not done yet."

Mercado nodded. "Okay. I'm heading in. I guess I've got work to do. Call me, especially if *His Honor* wants to issue any more orders." He opened the passenger door and moved to his own car.

Newsome motioned for Mercado to lower his window. "Let me know how it goes with the new guy."

"Marcus Cook. And don't expect any miracles."

* * *

After Mercado pulled out and headed into traffic, Newsome sat in the parking lot finishing his latte. The drink grew cold, but he liked the flavor that concentrated at the bottom of the cup. He was worried. *We're moving too fast. This is going to blow up in our faces.*

As District Attorney for Chatham County, he made enough money to keep up with his expenses, as long as his wife kept her spending under control. She liked expensive evening gowns, matching shoes, and diamonds. And she liked her Cadillac CTS, but she always wanted the most recent model year. He had warned her that they needed to put money away for retirement, but she was certain that retirement wasn't going to be a problem. She kept her credit cards at the ready and spent what she wanted, when she wanted.

With his wife's spending habits, Newsome believed that he needed to supplement his income, so the arrangement with Stillwell and the DEA team was just what he needed.

Things were going splendidly, until Deming decided he wanted out. Everyone from Stillwell on down was shaken when he told Mercado that he was through. Mercado immediately went to Newsome who, in turn, briefed Stillwell.

Newsome sat in his Beamer thinking about the moment he told the judge the bad news. He had expected Stillwell to explode, pound the table, or throw things around the private room at the club. Instead, he took a sip of his scotch, smiled, and asked, "Andrew, did he threaten to go states evidence or blow the whistle on us?"

When Newsome said no, the judge responded, "Good. That gives you a small window of time to do what you need to do to take care of this little problem."

When Newsome's jaw dropped, the judge mocked him. Without saying the words, the judge was ordering him to silence Deming...for good. That night, less than two weeks ago, his perspective on life changed completely.

He felt alone. His wife was only interested in their social status. The judge didn't care about anything besides himself and his future political career. Stillwell rubbed elbows with the wealthy, connected folks in Chatham County. He could care less about a lowly district attorney.

Only after Deming announced the press conference did he tell Mercado, Smith, and Nichols that they had to eliminate Deming. He was amazed when they said they already knew what they had to do.

Newsome heard a horn blare, then tires screech on the pavement. It woke him from his trance. He looked at his watch and realized that he'd been sitting, thinking for the last twenty minutes. He wouldn't be late, but he would have to get moving.

One last thought crossed his mind. He'd been taking notice of one of the assistant district attorneys. Elizabeth Sanchez had a pretty good track record on cases. Maybe he could give her a raise and take her out for a little celebration cocktail after work. He'd tell her about the rigors of being the district attorney. Maybe she'd see what a man in his position could do for her.

He pulled out into traffic and headed for the historic district and the Chatham County Courthouse.

* * *

By the time he reached the Harry S. Truman Parkway at the Marlborough Way entrance ramp, Vincent Mercado was fuming. *The nerve of Stillwell to toss out orders from his high and mighty position. And to use that weasel, Newsome, as his errand boy. The whole arrangement is unraveling, piece by piece. We should back off and regroup, not blindly hit the accelerator.*

He took a deep breath and looked down at the speedometer. He was hitting eighty miles per hour and the exit ramp for East De Rennes Avenue was coming up quickly on his right. He looked in his mirror, then crossed the slow lane barely making the exit. He had to decelerate in a hurry to avoid rear-ending a Lexus stopped in the line of traffic.

It took several more minutes and the rest of the drive across town to the DEA office for Mercado to get his anger under control. As he walked across the parking lot and approached the spot where Jarrod Deming was supposed to hold his news conference, Mercado, with a snarl on his face, spit on the sidewalk. Under his breath, he cursed his former partner. "I wish I'd been the one to take you out, you snitch-rat-bastard."

Chapter 8

The aroma of freshly brewed coffee filled the office of Savage Investigative Consultants. Peden topped off his mug and grabbed a Cheese Danish and a napkin and sat at the small round table in the kitchen.

As he sat enjoying his morning brew and pastry, he read the *Savannah Morning News*' headline story; a firsthand account of the Deming murder. The headline read "DEA AGENT ASSASSINATED." The subtitle was equally dramatic: "Agent Gunned Down in Broad Daylight as Dozens of Witnesses Scramble for Cover." The reporter, Cline Williston, used the word "assassination" at several points in the story. He was at Deming's news conference, so was also an eyewitness, though he wouldn't be much of a witness in court.

He described the chaotic scene immediately after the shots, which he likened to the sound of firecracker pops echoing off the surrounding buildings. He heard the sound of the bullets cutting through the air, making high-pitched buzzing sounds and the thud as they struck Deming's chest. He described the futile efforts of law enforcement officers and the emergency medical technicians to revive Deming.

Williston gave the text of Deming's invitation to the news conference. In short, it stated that Deming would provide details of illegal activities involving DEA agents and other high-level officials. Advance copies of those allegations were not provided, but they were serious, costing the agent his life.

Peden finished the article just as he emptied his coffee mug. A couple things about Deming's murder bothered him. First, the notes that he had pulled from his coat pocket were still missing. There was no mention of them in any news report. If a reporter had grabbed them and not turned them in to the police, they would be in possession of physical evidence. They would be in ethical and legal hot water.

Could they have just blown away in the wind? That was a possibility, though they would end up somewhere near the DEA office. In the immediate aftermath of the shooting, most people wouldn't be thinking about a handful of paper blowing away on the breeze. The focus of everyone at the scene was on the victim or staying out of the gunman's line of fire.

Who would be concerned about the notes? Peden believed that the only people with an interest in getting their hands on the notes were members of the DEA who might be implicated by Deming's claims. The only DEA employee that he saw at the news conference was Nila West, Deming's boss. Since she was with Deming at the news conference, she must have known what he was about to reveal. Hell, she'd been hit with gunfire, if only a flesh wound, but she was still up there, supporting her agent and in the line of fire. That's a dangerous spot to be standing if you knew Deming was about to be killed.

The second thing that was bothering Savage was the whole notion of a news conference. If the allegations were that damning, then he should have known his life might be in danger. Holding the news conference in such a public place, he might as well have committed suicide. *Was that his intent?*

Peden had heard that Deming was on his way up in the ranks, but something had happened that stalled his ascension. According to Marcus, that had occurred a few years ago.

What happened, Jarrod? What are we missing?

Peden shook off his thoughts, walked into the main office, and sat at his desk. He wondered how different the room had looked back in the mid-eighteen hundreds when the building was first erected. He didn't dwell on his thoughts. He picked up the phone and dialed Lee Sparks' number. Lee answered on the fourth ring, sleep still in his voice.

"Yeah?"

In a cheerful, rise-and-shine voice, Peden said, "Hey, Lee, up and at 'em. The day's wastin' away. We got work to do, places to go, people to see."

The dial tone sounded in his ear. He depressed the button on the cradle then hit redial; this time Sparks answered the phone after the first ring.

"Peden, man, what do you want? I was up nearly half the night fine-tuning this damn camera...which, by the way, is almost ready for prime time."

"Unlike yourself, who appears ready for the morgue."

"That ain't funny. I told you, it was a...never mind. What do you want, and it better be good."

Savage thought for a moment, then said, "How would you like to go on a treasure hunt?"

Sparks replied, "I sure as hell hope you're just messin' with me."

"Well, kinda and kinda not. Get in here as soon as you can and I'll explain."

* * *

Sparks was in Peden's office within forty-five minutes. Peden had a mug of Sparks' favorite brew on the kitchen table and he'd refilled his own mug. Sparks was still yawning when he sat at the table across from Peden.

"I want to run a couple things past you."

Lee held up his hand in a gesture that indicated *Hold on just a minute. Let me get a few sips down before you start talking.*

Peden waited until Lee set his mug down, smiled, and sighed, "Ahh. Okay, now what's this all about?"

Peden laid out his concerns about the Deming murder, from the missing notes to Deming's apparent death wish. He also pointed out that, if Deming's killer was a DEA agent, the news conference forced their hand. They either had to listen to the allegations and face them through legal channels, or they had to eliminate the source of the accusations before they were made public. If the shooter was with the DEA, it was a ballsy move. They had to know that the FBI and any local law enforcement agencies would be hot on the case."

Lee Sparks said, "I know it looks obvious that someone in the DEA was the shooter, but what if they weren't. The general topic of Deming's news conference wasn't a big secret, just the details. What if someone saw this as their chance to nail the guy while pointing the finger in the most obvious direction?"

Savage leaned on the table with his right elbow and rubbed his chin. Who else wanted Deming dead? Some big-time dealers? Anyone else?

He asked Lee if he had any ideas on who else might want to take Deming out.

"Has anyone looked at the wife? The spouse is always one of the first on the list."

Savage rolled his eyes. "It was a professional hit. Marcus said the four shots were within a few inches of each other. Hell, most people would have a tough time doing that at close range."

"Hey. You asked. Just covering all the bases." Lee paused. "How about dealers that he's popped in the past who are now out on the streets?"

"We're looking at that possibility. Marcus is getting a list together. Megan is also looking at that."

He remembered the call from Allen Deming and mentioned, "By the way, I got a new client. Allen Deming, Jarrod Deming's dad. He's living out in Arizona. He said he wants me to find Jarrod's killer, so our little discussion here isn't just friendly chitchat."

Sparks beamed. "You mean this is a paying job?"

Savage gave his partner a hurt look. "Of course I'm paying."

"I guess I better start tracking my hours, huh." He took another sip of coffee. "So, we have the wife, though she's real low on the list; dope dealers; and DEA agents. Did his old man give you any ideas?"

Savage shook his head. "He's looking at the DEA agents. Figures they wanted his son dead. The old man knows for certain that there were some shady dealings at the DEA and others he called 'other high-ranking people.' He didn't name names, but I think he might know a few. Said he wasn't even coming back to Savannah for his kid's funeral. Too scared, thinks he'll get popped, too. Which tilts the scale toward the shooter being DEA."

"I'll say. But we still can't put all our eggs in that one basket."

Peden looked at Lee and asked, "What does that even mean? Never mind. We do have Megan on our side. Fosco wants her to use me for supplies, so we're in. We'll provide a little more than the usual toys. We can hang around at meetings and stake outs 'til we're told to get lost. What do you think?"

"I think I need another cup of coffee. You need a refill?"

Savage looked down at his hands. They were already shaking slightly from the two mugs that he downed. "Nah, I'll pass."

* * *

Peden and Lee's plan was for Lee to do some data mining on the DEA's Savannah office and all the characters the DEA had busted over the past few years. Then dig up all of Jarrod and Sylvia Deming's personal and financial records. All the data would be placed into charts, graphs, and statistical models looking for patterns. If irregularities show up, they could search for explanations. Sometimes those explanations are reasonable, but if there are too many blips on the radar, then you can say that there's smoke. And where there's smoke...

While Lee was making a list of the data to extract from the DEA's database, Peden sat looking at a satellite view of the area around the DEA office building where Deming was killed. In his mind, he drew a line from where Deming stood at the microphones to the furthest point directly in front of Deming to where a reasonably good professional could make the kill shots. That was his twelve o'clock line. Then he made another line heading through ten o'clock. This gave him an upside-down V shape heading away from the DEA's building. The shooter had been somewhere in the area between the lines. He was looking for the best possible hiding spot for a sniper when the phone rang.

He took a deep breath and answered, "Savage Investigative Consultants."

Megan Moore asked, "Do you know who I need to arrest yet?"

Peden smiled. "No, but give me ten more minutes."

"I'll give you fifteen." She laughed a little. "I'm going over to interview Sylvia Deming tomorrow. She doesn't know it yet, but I wanted to know if you had any of those mini-cameras that I could use. I'd like to record the interview. She doesn't need to know."

"Yeah, we can do that. Lee's got a new model he just finished testing, so your timing is perfect."

Megan got a bit more serious. "We were also going to start with the DEA guys later in the day, but they have something on their schedule, some training thing. You know those guys, everything's a big secret."

Savage thought for a moment. Maybe they had another bust going down. He would call Marcus later. He might have some inside information.

He asked, "When are you scheduled for Sylvia Deming's place?"

"About 9:00 AM. Can you have the cameras ready by then?"

"No problem, Megan. I'll invoice Roland. I'll give him the special deal."

"Don't jack the price up too much, Peedee. He can be a real pain."

"Megan, I wish…"

"…that I wouldn't call you Peedee? Yeah, I know."

Peden heard the click, then the dial tone. He shook his head as he placed the receiver on the hook.

Chapter 9

The constant whirring noise from two computers, two servers, and two portable coolers in Lee Sparks' spare bedroom-converted-to-computer-room was starting to distract him. Even with the added foam rubber to absorb the sound, the electronic ringing was wearing him down. It was lunchtime on Wednesday, the day after the Deming murder. His stomach was growling. He thought about what he had in his refrigerator: nothing appetizing. Time for a break.

Hacking into the DEA's Savanah, Georgia, database was child's play for Lee. He routed the search probes through multiple servers across the country and into Canada. He then set blocks so that any attempt at tracing the source of the probes was not possible, except by another hacker better than him. There are a lot of guys like that in cyberland, but only a relative few working for the government.

Sparks wanted raw data from drug raids going back ten years. Then the challenge was to manipulate the data into meaningful information. On paper, it sounded simple. In reality, it was nearly impossible, unless you were a database-geek. Sparks had explained the process to Peden. By the time he finished his explanation, Peden's eyes had glazed over. He had told Sparks, "Just give me the pretty pictures."

It took Lee just forty-five minutes to export the data he needed. Now it would take longer to cleanse the data with his function modules. Once that process was completed, he planned to convert the information into graphs. Putting numbers into graphics helped the layman visualize changes and trends.

He was confident that he would have a pretty picture for Peden by the end of the day. While rubbing his hands together above the keyboard, he rolled his head around in a circular motion. Distinct popping sounds came from the back of his neck, relieving the tension that had built up all morning. He set the function modules in motion and made a final check to make sure that they were chugging through the data.

Standing, he stretched, raising his hands high above his slim, six foot, three-inch frame, nearly touching the ceiling of his computer room. It was really supposed to be a bedroom. When his girlfriend stayed over, she shared his room. If she wanted to use her computer, she sat on the couch and watched the television. She mainly hung out in social media sights. At the moment, she was on a week-long vacation with friends in Key West, Florida, so he had his condo to himself. He grabbed his empty coffee cup and headed for the kitchen. He was about to set his cup down when he heard a loud beep from his computer. He frowned. The computer rarely made that sound.

When he got back to his computer, a warning window was in the center of his larger monitor. "External attempt at access was blocked. Do you wish to allow access?"

While his firewall program did its job, it was disconcerting that someone would come that close to finding his IP address. He answered no to the question and disconnected the computer from the network. Manipulating the data files would be completed offline. Rubbing his right hand down across his face, he wondered who was trying to hack him. He stood thinking for several more minutes. With the computer now safe from being compromised, he decided to take a lunch break. *The nerve of those hackers.*

* * *

Wayne Cleaver didn't sleep well, haunted by the visit from Vincent Mercado and his partner. He half-expected that someone from the DEA would visit him upon his release, but he didn't expect them to imply that he had a hand in a murder.

It didn't make sense. If they truly believed what they said, Wayne would have had to get out of prison, obtain a weapon, know that Deming was giving a press conference, and get to a position where he could pull the trigger.

Thinking back, it also amazed him that they could plant over fifty pounds of marijuana in his apartment and make the case that he was a major dealer. The District Attorney believed that he was a menace to society. To set him up for murder would be child's play. They could easily plant enough evidence for a conviction. Who was a jury going to believe: a department with a stellar bust and conviction rate that the community and the state regarded as heroes for ridding the streets of poison, or a recently released, drug-dealing convict?

Wayne now understood that he was in serious jeopardy. He jammed all of his worldly belongings into a backpack and headed down the road to find new accommodations. One night at the Value Motor Inn was more than enough.

He caught the Garden City transit line to downtown Savannah. From there he caught the Silk Hope bus out Ogeechee Road where there was a string of lower cost hotels. He looked his choices over and decided on the *Deluxe Inn*. He figured that it was better than paying hourly rates at the *Stallion Motel*, which was just up the road.

Standing in front of the hotel, he scanned the four-lane road for cheap restaurants. He spotted the bright yellow sign for a *Waffle House*. He was hungry and didn't want to check into the motel too soon, so he hoofed it towards the restaurant. When he turned to look for a break in the traffic, a Savannah-Chatham Metropolitan police car headed in his direction. Wayne tensed as adrenaline shot through his body, but he kept control and didn't react in any visible way. The police car passed, the officers not even looking his way.

He took a deep breath, looked for an opportunity to cross, and made his way to the restaurant. Paranoia had invaded his mind since the visit from Mercado and Smith the previous day. He kept a close watch in all directions, trying to not look nervous. He wasn't sure that he was entirely successful.

Inside the restaurant, the aroma of bacon and breakfast sausage filled the air, along with pancakes, onions, and green peppers. His mouth watered. He was thinking about a western omelet, but remembered his immediate financial situation. On the menu, he looked for the cheapest, most filling option, trying to preserve his funds. That turned out to be coffee and pancakes.

He grabbed a copy of that morning's *Savannah Morning News* left by a previous customer. The headlines jumped off the page. "DEA AGENT ASSASSINATED." He nearly spit his mouthful of coffee across the table, but grabbed his napkin just in time.

He read the entire story through once, then read it again, stopping at key information that he could use in his defense, committing the information to memory. It was abundantly clear that he needed someone who could help him get out of the area before he ran out of money.

He needed to contact his friend at the DA's office, Liz Sanchez. Even if she couldn't help him directly, she would know who could.

He finished his breakfast, packed the newspaper into his backpack, paid his bill with a small tip, and headed back to the *Deluxe Inn*. Another police car passed him as he crossed the road, but again paid him no mind. That was a good sign. Apparently, he wasn't the subject of a *BOLO*, or *be on the lookout*.

By 11:50 AM on Thursday, just over twenty-five hours after the murder of Jarrod Deming, Wayne Cleaver checked into his second motel. He used cash and gave his name as Robert Smith. The clerk didn't bat an eye at the name and didn't ask for any identification. He asked how many nights to which Wayne replied that he'd be staying for just one night.

After checking the room, which appeared to be remarkably clean for the price, Wayne grabbed the phone and dialed Elizabeth Sanchez's cell phone number.

* * *

Sanchez was at her desk reviewing one of her assigned case files. The file involved a woman who stabbed her husband sixteen times with a paring knife. The paring knife had a one-and-a-half-inch long blade. He survived the attack and didn't want to press charges, but the District Attorney decided that her case needed to go before the grand jury. This was the woman's forth attack on her husband in seven years, all with a weapon of some kind. Plus, the woman had been released from jail just three weeks prior to the attack. She had been arrested for public intoxication. During that arrest, she'd screamed that she was going to kill her husband for snitching on her. With a blood alcohol level of .220, they gave her the benefit of doubt and that she didn't really mean what she was saying.

Her cell phone vibrated on her desk. She looked at the local number on the display, didn't recognize it, and let it go to voice mail.

Her attention went back to the file when her phone vibrated again. She thought it was letting her know that she had a voice mail, but the vibration continued. It was the same local number. After three rings, she picked up the phone and ran her finger across the screen.

"Hello?"

"Hi, Liz. Sorry to call you out of the blue. It's..."

In a happy but hesitant voice, she said, "Wayne. Hi. Are you calling from Coastal or are you out?"

Wayne smiled with amusement. No holding Liz back. "I just got out yesterday. I'm still in town, but I hope that changes soon."

"Yeah, that might be a good idea." She hesitated before asking, "What can I do for you?"

"Well, I'm glad you asked. I need to tell you a little story, but I'm not sure it's a story I can tell you over the phone. Can we meet later? I can't buy you dinner 'cause I'm nearly broke, but I need a small favor. What do you think?"

Elizabeth had always liked Wayne. He was so mellow and easygoing, with long, frizzy hair and quick wit. She wondered what he meant by a "small favor." Meeting him in public would be difficult. It might even be disastrous for her career at the Chatham County District Attorney's office. If word got back to Andrew Newsome that she was meeting with a convicted felon, she might never get a promotion and could even be fired.

As if her thoughts summoned the man, Newsome leaned his head in her office, lit up one of his weasel-like smiles, and said, "Hey, when you get off the phone, drop by my office please. And bring that Solanda Jennings file with you." He pointed to the file that she had been reviewing.

To Newsome, she said, "Okay."

When he left, she said to Wayne, "Sorry about that. My boss wants to see me after we're done talking. You were saying something about meeting up later on? Could you call me right at 5:15? I should be in my car and it'll be easier for both of us."

"Sounds good, Liz. And thanks. I know this is risky for you."

"Don't worry about me. Talk with you in a bit."

When she hit the disconnect icon on her phone, she wondered what Wayne had in mind. She had not spoken with him since he accepted the plea deal that put him in Coastal. That had been arranged and executed quickly and he was gone. Now he was free, but he sounded worried.

She put her thoughts aside, picked up the file, and headed for "the Weasel's" office. She hated being alone with Newsome. It made her skin crawl.

Chapter 10

Megan Moore turned the corner onto Colonel Estill Drive, then followed the left curve where the road turned into Flinn Drive. The neighborhood wasn't too impressive on the whole, but roughly every fifth house looked out of place; a little nicer, a little better maintained, a few hundred more square feet of living space. Homeowners kept their yards well groomed, but not immaculate. Megan did make note of the Neighborhood Watch signs placed every few hundred yards.

As she approached the Deming residence at 19 Flinn Drive, she noted the yard was better kept than most. The roof was new, the trim freshly painted. The house was ringed by a planter that was about one foot above ground level and was in full bloom with a wide variety of colorful flowers.

There were three cars in Sylvia Deming's driveway and one parked on the street directly in front of the house. As she parked, a man in a gray suit and a woman in a dark blue dress exited the house and got into one of the cars in the driveway. She stayed in her car until the couple backed out onto the street and passed her car, heading towards Colonel Estill Drive. The driver glared at Megan as he passed. He had close-cropped, light hair. She thought it was DEA Agent Alex Smith.

After a moment, she exited her green 2013 Honda Accord and headed towards the door. She was on duty and should have driven the FBI duty car, but she preferred to be less conspicuous.

As she moved to ring the doorbell, the door opened and Vincent Mercado's baritone voice said, "Agent Moore, please come in. Sylvia said you'd be coming."

Mercado was easy to recognize. He had skin that looked permanently tanned, probably due to his Cuban heritage. He had dark hair, a face too narrow for his neck, and a thin nose. Megan put him at just over six feet tall with a powerful build that wasn't well hidden by his suit coat. At 11:15 AM, she detected the odor of rum on his breath.

"Thank you, Agent…"

"Mercado. Vincent Mercado. Call me Vince."

"Thank you, Vince. Is Mrs. Deming in?"

"Yes. Head straight back through the kitchen to the back porch."

Megan did as instructed. She made her way through the long foyer. As she passed the living room on the left and a library on the right, she paused. Each room was trimmed in dark wood, finished with a high-gloss varnish. The floors were all solid wood, polished to a fine sheen. Everything in the home was in its place. Megan remembered that the Deming's had no children, possibly accounting for the lack of clutter and the home's pristine condition. She continued through the kitchen and made her way out to the screened-in porch.

There were five people sitting on indoor-outdoor furniture. Megan immediately recognized Sylvia. She wore make-up, a bit on the heavy side, hoping to hide her puffy eyes, red nose, and face. Megan walked over to Sylvia Deming and introduced herself, offering her condolences.

Mercado followed Megan onto the porch and took a seat next to Mrs. Deming. Megan looked around at the guests, seeing if she recognized anyone.

Sylvia, holding a handkerchief in her left hand, said in an apologetic tone, "Oh, I'm sorry." She went around the room, introducing each of her four guests. There were two DEA agents. Mark Willis was actually a retired agent with his wife, Rhonda. The fourth person Sylvia introduced as her sister, Jessica Mason, though they looked nothing alike. Sylvia had dark hair, green eyes, and fair features. Megan thought she weighed one hundred fifteen pounds. Jessica had light hair, dark brown eyes set in a plump face, and easily weighed one hundred seventy pounds. She also had a short, squat nose, where Sylvia's was narrow at the bridge.

Megan again turned to Sylvia and repeated her condolences. She then asked if there was someplace that the two of them could speak in private.

Megan thought that she detected a brief moment of surprise in her face, then Sylvia, in a southern voice said, "Yes, yes. Please, follow me." She turned to her other guests and remarked, "This shouldn't take too long. Please make yourselves at home."

Mercado allowed Sylvia to move ahead, then leaned over and lightly grasped Megan's arm and quietly asked, "Should she have her lawyer present?"

Megan turned and looked down at his hand with her perpetually stern look, then back into Mercado's face. "No. She doesn't. But if you ever touch me again, you'll need a doctor."

He let go of her arm and smiled, but his smile was taunting. She kept her gaze on him a moment longer, conveying the message that she wasn't to be toyed with.

Megan caught up with Sylvia, who made her way into the library. As she entered, she noticed that dark wooden bookshelves completely covered the wall on their left. Oversized leather chairs and a matching loveseat appeared to be seldom used. One of the other walls had a south-facing, three-pane window. Despite a number of larger southern oak trees outside the window, the room was still bright with natural light.

The third wall contained a number of certificates, college diplomas, and other plaques of achievements. Megan turned to face the wall with the doorway through which they had just passed. About a dozen family pictures were hanging, some of Jarrod and Sylvia together, some individual shots, and several photos of Jarrod in his DEA drug raid uniform.

Megan made her way over to the wall where various awards and certificates hung. Two were of Sylvia's and Jarrod's Bachelor of Science degrees from University of Georgia. Another was of Jarrod's certification as a DEA Special Agent. Still another was for completing a special training course for small arms. There were two plaques for marksmanship, then a picture of Jarrod with a sniper rifle. Megan cocked her head for a moment. Something was tugging at her senses, but she couldn't put her finger on it.

Sylvia had been watching Megan as she took in the room, then interrupted her thoughts, asking, "Agent Moore, can I get ya'll anything to drink – a glass of ice tea, water, a soft drink of some kind?"

Megan turned to Sylvia and shook her head. "No. Thank you for asking. I do apologize for going off in a trance like that."

Sylvia just shrugged then motioned for her to have a seat. They each sat in one of the leather chairs, getting comfortable in the furniture, but remaining uncomfortable with tension.

Megan took a deep breath. "Mrs. Deming…"

"Please, Agent Moore, no reason to be so formal. Call me Sylvia."

"Alright, Sylvia. Call me Megan."

Sylvia nodded.

"Sylvia, you can stop this interview at any time. You can have your lawyer present if you wish. As always, with the death of a spouse, we have to question the surviving spouse. We need to ask about what they might know and if they were somehow involved in that death. Do you understand?"

Megan noticed that Sylvia shivered when she nodded that she understood.

"This is an informal interview. We're not recording anything unless it becomes apparent that we need to, for whatever reason. I'm not going to ask any trick questions or try to push you into a corner. Answer the questions honestly and I'll finish up as quickly as I can."

Again, Sylvia nodded.

"Did your husband seem more agitated than what was normal for him recently?"

Sylvia thought for a moment. "He didn't say anything specific to me, but he seemed more tired. We used to go out at least once every week without fail, sometimes two or three times, depending on what was happening around town. For a while now, whenever I'd suggest going to a show or a concert, or even just out for a bite to eat, he'd brush me off. He'd say he was too tired. He even suggested that I go out alone with my friends, but I don't have many friends. The ones I do have are all married. I kept trying to get him to go, but I finally stopped asking."

Moore asked, "When did this shift in attitude happen?"

Sylvia looked up at the bookshelves, thinking. "About a year ago. I remember the exact night. I mean, I remember his attitude, not the date. We were supposed to go out to dinner and a show. When he came in the door, the look on his face was like, I don't know, like his dog had been run down or something. I tried getting him to talk about it, but he said he was tired and just wanted to get a shower and go to bed."

Sylvia put her face in her hands, remembering the day when things started to fall apart. Megan moved to the next series of questions. "Rumor has it that your husband was going to reveal some illegal activities within the DEA at the news conference. Do you know what your husband was going to say?"

Immediately, Sylvia replied, "No. From that day, the one I just told you about, he never told me anything about work. He used to almost brag about how they were cleaning up the streets, busting dope dealers. Then he stopped talking about it." She paused. "You know, his whole personality changed. Something had to have happened that day."

Megan asked a few more questions about Jarrod's work with the DEA. It kept coming back to that day. She believed that if they could figure out what had happened on that day, they might learn why Jarrod Deming was killed. Maybe…

As Megan stood, the door to the library opened. Vince Mercado stuck his head around the door. "Sorry to interrupt. I think everyone's leaving. Is there anything I can do for you before I go?"

"No. Thanks, Vince. Ya'll go on. I appreciate everything ya'll've done."

He went over and hugged Sylvia. As he did, he looked over her shoulder at Megan, a smirk on his face.

She thought, *That's okay, prick. You'll get yours.*

* * *

After Megan left Sylvia Deming's house, she dialed Peden Savage's office number. Peden answered on the second ring.

"Hey, Savage. How'd the signal come through?"

"Perfect. Great shots of the house and clear audio on the interview. Nice touch with Mercado and the doctor comment."

She ignored the Mercado reference, but asked, "Did you get everything recorded?"

"Oh yeah. Lee already checked it out, and it looks and sounds great. Are you still headed this way?"

"Yeah. I should be there in about twenty minutes, thirty minutes, tops."

"Great. See you then."

She continued her drive towards Peden's office, trying to process all that was said, and some things that weren't. She wondered about Vincent Mercado. He was on her list of people to question. It was not appropriate to do it at the home of the victim's widow. When she finished with Peden, she would call the DEA satellite office in Savannah and set up interviews with the agents on Deming's team and their management.

Megan devised her plan of attack as she drove north on the Harry S. Truman Parkway. She thought that a little covert recording might be in order, but no one except her and Savage could know about it.

Her mind kept going back to the interview with Sylvia Deming. It wasn't so much the interview, but something wasn't right. She shifted her concentration back to the drive as she approached the Eisenhower Street Exit. As she slowed for the light at the end of the ramp, she noticed a gray Acura in her rearview mirror. Vincent Mercado was at the wheel.

She made a few turns to see if he would follow her. He did. Finally, she pulled to the side of the road on East Broad Street near Saint Benedict the Moor Church. As Mercado pulled in behind her, she exited her car and walked briskly back to Mercado's.

When his window slid down, she barked at him, "If you're trying to intimidate me, you're making a big mistake."

Mercado gave her an exaggerated look of surprise. "Who, me? Megan, I'm just trying to help you track down a killer. Jarrod was my friend. I want the shooter as bad as anybody."

"Right. And my name is Agent Moore to you. Here's what you can do to help. Stay away from me unless I contact you, and stay away from anyone who might be involved."

Mercado let out a sarcastic laugh. "That might be tough. I work at the DEA and rumor has it that the shooter might be one of us. I'll tell you what. If I hear anything, I'll give you a call."

"Don't worry, Agent Mercado, I'll be calling you soon enough."

She turned and headed for her car. She waited until Mercado pulled away, then made her way to Savage's office on West Liberty Street. Less than twenty-six hours had passed since Agent Deming's murder and the gamesmanship between agencies was already heating up.

Chapter 11

Lee Sparks called Peden to let him know that the data graphs were now in his email inbox. Peden had just opened the first graph when Megan Moore walked into his office.

"Megan, take a look."

He motioned towards the flat panel TV as the first page of graphs from the presentation software popped up. She stood behind Peden, peering over his shoulder. The colors from the graph were bright.

"Hi, Megan." Lee Sparks' voice came over the speaker phone, almost as clear as if he was in the room.

"Hey, Lee. Good work here."

"When I adjust the colors the data will jump out at you."

Peden said, "Okay, this is all nice, but what am I looking at? The first slide's up on the screen."

The slide displayed two narrow bar graphs arranged one over the other. The top graph was titled "Marijuana Busts 2007 - 2010." The graph's horizontal axis was broken into forty-eight bars, each representing a one month period, the color of each bar alternating to show contrast between each month. The vertical axis started at zero and ended at one thousand in increments of one hundred. The unit of measure was pounds.

Lee Sparks said, "Okay. The bars represent the total number of pounds seized for each month. You can see that they vary in height from a low of zero, meaning there were no busts for the month, to a high of two hundred sixty pounds. Are you with me?"

Peden and Megan both responded, "Yes."

Sparks continued, "Okay, the two hundred sixty pounds in August of 2010 was actually three separate busts. The largest was nearly two hundred pounds, the second highest was just over fifty pounds, the third was about ten pounds. The next highest monthly total was one hundred fifteen pounds for two busts. One was nearly a hundred pounds, the other just under twenty. That was in May of 2008. Most other totals were between two and twenty pounds. Nothing too spectacular, right?"

They replied, "Right."

Sparks said, "Now, look at the second graph."

The second graph on the first slide was titled "Marijuana Busts 2011 – 2014." The horizontal and vertical axes were set up the same as the first graph.

Sparks continued, "The first two months of this graph look much the same as the graph from the previous four years. Look what happens in March 2011. The bust total jumps to sixty pounds. Then May is one hundred seventy, June two hundred fifty-five, July two hundred sixty. For the remaining years on the chart, the busts stay at or near two hundred to three hundred fifty pounds. But here's the thing; when you look at the total number of raids conducted by this office, the totals per raid almost always fall in the forty to sixty-pound range."

Megan put her hand on Peden's shoulder and squeezed hard. "That sure is awful tidy. They have to be manipulating data or something."

Sparks said, "Close, but not quite. They conducted actual raids and arrested, or killed, real people, but you're right, something is just too neat here. If you look at the previous four years, the monthly totals are all over the map, even with the small amount of weight per bust. But the last four years...?" Sparks paused for a moment, then continued. "I also have data for cocaine, cash, and weapons seized. Those totals also follow a similar pattern. You'll see it in the other slides."

Peden's mind was in overdrive. "Do you have a list of the dealers?"

"Yeah, but I haven't had time to look at their histories. I'll start that as soon as I'm off the phone. If you flip to the next slide, I'll give you a little more information."

The next slide displayed the length of sentence for each person busted in the raids between 2011 and 2014. There were one hundred eighty-eight arrests with all one hundred eighty-eight doing some amount of time. Additionally, there were three perpetrators shot and killed during two of the raids. Of those incarcerated, fifty-seven were on the streets again, with another twenty-eight up for parole within the next six months.

Sparks walked Megan and Peden through the graph. Peden was most interested in the fifty-seven convicts that were free. To Sparks he said, "You probably already know that I want the names, addresses, and current status of the free birds. If any of these guys had a beef with the DEA, then they might just be mad enough to take out Deming."

"I'm with you Peden. I'll start with them and see if any of them stayed local."

Megan said, "I have to get back to the office. I'm setting up the interviews with the DEA agents who were at the Deming scene yesterday. I know I can't use any of this, but it might help me apply some pressure and ask the right questions."

Peden asked, "What special gear do you need?"

"I think the mini-cam's all I need for now. That reminds me, we have to review that footage from Sylvia Deming's place sometime soon. When's a good time for you, Peedee?"

"Damn it, Megan. Can't you just call me Peden or Pete or…anything but Peedee?"

"Well…I can think of a few names…"

"Never mind. Give me a few minutes and I can drop the clips onto a thumb drive. You can watch it whenever you want. Call me after you do. Nothing jumped out for me during the live feed, but you might see something that I missed.

Lee said over the speaker, "Hey, if you don't need me for anything, I have a bunch of work to do."

Peden replied, "I think we're all set, Lee. Thanks. Call me when you have that info."

"Okay. Talk with you later, Megan."

"Bye, Lee."

Peden grabbed a thumb drive from his desk and plugged it into the USB port on the side of his computer. After a few keystrokes, the video files that were captured when Megan wore the mini-camera to Sylvia Deming's house started to load.

Peden sat quietly thinking as the data copied. There was a slight sheen of sweat forming on his brow. A combination of the ailing air conditioning, the tension from the investigation into Deming's murder, and the computer working hard to transfer the data raised the temperature in the room. Peden thought that Megan looked cool, which bugged him a little. How could she remain calm under this kind of pressure? He knew that Fosco was going to be pushing her for results.

He watched as Megan picked up her purse and looked around his office, eyeing the ancient office's interior. She was methodically taking in each wall in his office. There really wasn't much to see, unlike Sylvia Deming's house.

Sylvia Deming's...the walls were arranged like an art gallery. Everything was in its place. All the family pictures, all the certificates were arranged just right. Each one in the proper place, except...

Again, something was tugging at Peden, something just out of reach, something that wasn't logical. He rubbed his hand across his forehead, wiping the small amount of sweat from his brow. He picked up a paper towel and wiped his hands.

The computer beeped. Peden looked at the computer screen. A small window had popped up stating that the file copy was complete and that the thumb drive could be safely removed.

He pulled the drive from his computer's USB port and stood. When he approached Megan with the thumb drive, she pointed to a cell phone on his desk and asked, "What's the throwaway for?"

As if on cue, his desk phone rang. He said to Megan before answering, "Hang on a few minutes and I'll tell you."

He answered, "Savage Investigative Consultants."

Allen Deming asked, "So, Mr. Savage, ya'll gonna find my son's killer?"

* * *

Peden spent the next ten minutes discussing the specifics of hiring Savage Investigative Consultants with Allen Deming. There would be a minimum weekly update, but Peden explained that the updates were typically much more frequent, especially in the first couple weeks. If the investigation went longer, the calls dropped off. There was a standard fee with expenses. The first payment of the standard fee was due immediately. He would be billed weekly for expenses. If a particular expense was large, such as the need for a very expensive piece of surveillance equipment, then that expense was spread out over a negotiated time period.

Peden explained that he didn't expect the job to last long. He flipped up the throwaway cell phone that he purchased that morning at a big box store and recited the number to Deming. He looked at Megan who gave him a look acknowledging that she knew the reason for the throw away. To Deming he said, "When you want to contact me, use this number. Do not call my office number from this point on. I'll use this phone or a pay phone to call you. Also, call me anytime, day or night, if you feel you have information. Let me decide if its pertinent." He stopped and waited to see if Deming had any questions. When Deming didn't respond, he said, "Okay, Allen, I'm on the clock. I will talk with you soon."

With that, Peden ended the call. Within ten seconds, his throwaway phone buzzed and vibrated on his desk. It surprised Peden because Allen Deming was the only person to whom he'd given the throwaway's number. He picked up the phone and flipped it open. "Allen?"

Deming said, "Hell, in all that contract talk I forgot to tell ya'll, in one of the payday busts a couple years back, Jarrod whacked his cousin."

Savage was caught off guard. Allen Deming had said it in such an offhanded way that he didn't know how to respond.

"Peden, are ya'll still there?"

Dumbfounded, he finally stuttered, "Uh...yeah. Maybe you should start at the top. I'm going to put you on speaker so my partner can hear you."

Deming said, "Whoa, what partner?"

"Megan Moore. She's the FBI's Special Agent in Charge of the official investigation. You don't have to worry; I was planning to tell her everything that you're about to say anyway."

"Well, awright."

Peden hit the speaker button and nodded to Megan so that she could introduce herself.

"Mr. Deming, I worked with Peden when he was in the FBI a number of years back. He and I were partners for a time. I've been assigned by my boss, Roland Fosco, to head up your son's murder investigation for the FBI. Any questions for me before you get started?"

There was a moment of silence, during which Peden thought that they'd dropped the call. Finally, Deming's tinny voice could be heard saying he had no questions.

Deming proceeded to tell the story about his sister's family. He described in detail his recollection of the situation at her home, including how his nephew was using and dealing drugs and how Deming's sister, Paula, and her husband, Richard, had once thrown him out. Then came Richard's tragic death. After the funeral, his nephew moved back home, causing Paula's life to spin out of control.

"That kid, Wes," he said 'Wes' with obvious disdain, "he destroyed his family's lives. Paula was always defending him. Rich, wanted to clamp down and put the fear of God into him, but my sister wouldn't let him do it. Me, I'd've given him the 'old heave ho;' straighten up and fly right or find another place to live."

Peden asked, "So, what happened after Wes moved back home?"

There was another moment of silence as Deming collected his thoughts. When he spoke, the tone of his voice alone pulled Peden into a sullen, gloomy mood. "My sister started doing drugs with Wes and his friends. She was depressed about Rich's death, so she was an easy target. Wes turned the place into a party house for his friends. It was like a dope drive-through store. The neighbors were calling the cops all the time.

"Finally, I talked with Jarrod – he was in the DEA by then – I asked him what could be done. He told me that he'd take care of it." He took a deep, audible breath before continuing. "Two weeks later, the DEA busted the house. During the bust, Paula committed suicide. She was a mess by then. Jarrod shot and killed Wes. The DEA took like sixty pounds of grass and a couple ounces of coke from the house."

Megan looked at Peden with her naturally angry expression. She asked Deming, "Was there an inquiry into the bust, particularly the shooting?"

"There was, but it was a joke. Everybody involved in the 'inquiry' went out and had a few beers afterwards. They're all in this together."

"So everything was handled internally at the DEA?"

"Yeah." Deming took another deep breath. "I think that's when Jarrod started taking stock of hisself, what he and his fellow agents were really doing to people's lives. I started to notice the change right after that bust. Hell, he saw his aunt's body all mangled in the tub, then he shot his cousin dead not five feet from her. That has to weigh on even the biggest asshole of human beings. Pardon my language."

Peden wasn't so sure of that. He knew a few people who would off their parents for a few bucks and not give it a second thought. He said to Allen Deming, "We'll find out who shot your son, Allen. You can count on it."

In a choked up voice, Allen Deming said, "That's all…that's all I want."

Chapter 12

Megan Moore made it back to her office just after 3:00 PM. Traffic across the historic district between Savage's office and the local FBI office on East Bryan Street was light. It took her only ten minutes to drive across town, park, and walk half a block to the office building. She nearly broke a sweat in the afternoon heat. She had a host of tasks to complete before heading home to her Tybee Island condo. The sole advantage to her going home this evening was that it was more comfortable than the office. It was going to be a working night.

After dropping her purse in the bottom drawer of her desk and kicking off her shoes, she started her computer, then headed for the coffeemaker. To her surprise, a fresh pot had just finished brewing. She looked around the small office for the receptionist, but no one was at the front desk. While she poured herself a cup, a tall, slender black woman with shoulder-length, straight, black hair exited the women's restroom, smoothing down her tight dress. Her large hoop earrings dangled nearly to her shoulders.

Shanique King, the resident FBI office receptionist said, "Hey, girl, where you been all day?"

Megan made an "ugh" sound. "It started out on Isle of Hope, interviewing Jarrod Deming's widow. Been downhill ever since. After that, I ran into one of Deming's coworkers, then spent some time at Savage's office." Thinking of Peden's office, she remarked, "I thought *this* place was ancient." She waved a hand around the relatively modern office.

"I had to pick up some hardware over there once. You're right, that thing's ancient. And did you notice that not a thing in that office matches? He's got to get himself an interior decorator, know what I mean?"

Megan nodded as she sipped her coffee. It was hot and tasted perfect. "Thanks for the coffee. It's just what I need right now. Unless I could sneak in a shot of bourbon."

"If I could, I'd spike every pot with a shot. Maybe it'd calm the SAC down a bit."

"Speaking of Roland, is he in his office?"

"Nope. He had an emergency dentist appointment. Chipped a tooth on his coffee cup. Left just about ten minutes ago." Megan smiled at Shanique as she waved her hands in an animated gesture that Roland had freaked out about the tooth. "Anything I can do for you?"

"No. Thanks though. I'll be on the phone, so hold my calls."

"You got it, Sista. Buzz me if you need anything."

Megan closed the door to her ten feet by twelve feet office with a south facing window. Most days, the room was bright with natural light blocked only by thin curtains. She had several flowering plants. They gave the office a nice fragrance, blanketing the industrial strength cleaners and floor wax used by the cleaning service.

She settled down at her desk and looked up the number for the Drug Enforcement Administration's Savannah office. She punched in the number. After only a single ring an electronic voice came on, requesting that she listen carefully to the menu options as they had recently changed. Impatiently, she hit zero. Another female electronic voice came on stating that she should wait while her call was transferred. After four rings, she was just about to hit zero again when a real female voice with a southern accent came on the line. "Drug Enforcement Administration, Savannah. How may I direct your call?"

"Agent Nila West."

"Who may I tell her is calling?"

"FBI Special Agent Megan Moore."

"One moment while I connect you to her office, Special Agent Moore."

Another four rings and a fourth female voice said, "Nila

West."

Megan noticed that Nila West's voice had an edge to it, conveying an attitude that taking Megan's call was beneath her. Megan cranked up her own attitude, not wanting to show any weakness. "Agent West, this is Special Agent Megan Moore. I'm with the Savannah office of the FBI. I work for..."

"Roland Fosco, I know Agent Moore. I've been expecting your call. What can I do for you?"

"I'm the SAC for the Jarrod Deming murder. I need to interview you and the other agents who were present at the crime scene yesterday morning. I'd like to start the interviews first thing tomorrow morning. And I'd like to conduct..."

"That's not possible, Agent Moore."

In a terse voice, Megan asked, "Why not?"

"I cannot give you any specifics, but your interviews would be in conflict with ongoing operations."

Megan took a deep breath and plowed ahead. "Agent West, you've had an agent murdered, literally right under your nose. Surely you want the murderer identified and brought to justice. To do that we need to..."

West again cut Megan off. "Agent Moore, of course we want the murderer apprehended, but we have ongoing operations that take precedence over your interviews."

Megan was getting angry at West's refusal to cooperate. She wanted to drive over to the DEA building, barge into her office, and shake the life out of her. But she tried to calm down. She asked, "When would you and your agents be available?"

"This office will be unavailable until Friday afternoon at the earliest. You'll just have to..."

"Agent West, I don't *have* to do anything. What I *will* do, if I run into further roadblocks is..."

Again, West broke in, a touch of anger in her voice, "Agent Moore, this isn't a *roadblock*! We intend to fully cooperate with your investigation. We can't just stop our work because..."

This time, Megan cut in, clearly not in the mood for

further discussion. With a rising tension in her staccato voice, she said, "All of our efforts – including your agency – should be focused on catching Agent Deming's killer. If you cut me off again, I'll raise this up to Fosco. He can raise it as far as he wishes, but your attitude towards this investigation will be noted. Have I made myself clear?"

Nila West paused as long as she dared. She knew that Moore, as the FBI's Special Agent in Charge of the Deming murder investigation, wielded a lot of power…for the moment. From talking with Vincent Mercado, she also knew of Moore's reputation as a hard-nosed, no-nonsense agent with a solid track record. The only less-than-stellar mark on her record was her association with Peden Savage. It wasn't in her best interest to rattle Moore.

"Yes, Agent Moore, quite clear. I can make my team available for interviews starting Friday morning at 8:00. That's the best I can do."

"I'll be at your office tomorrow afternoon at 3:00 PM. Make sure that you, Agents Vincent Mercado, Alex Smith, Peter Nichols, and Marcus Cook are available and have adequate time, potentially over an hour each, to complete interviews. Also, ensure that we have private rooms available. If you or your people want to have a lawyer present, that is up to you. I will fax this request to you in a few minutes. Copies will also be sent to Roland Fosco and Clifford Metzger." Metzger was West's boss. Megan paused for effect and to give Nila West the opportunity to put her foot in her mouth. When she didn't respond, Megan asked, "Agent West, do you have any questions?"

All Moore heard was, "No." Then a click and a dial tone.

She took a deep breath. "That went well."

* * *

Sitting in the kitchen at the back of his office, Savage opened the box with the calzone from the Mellow Mushroom. It was hot and fresh, the onions, banana peppers, green peppers, garlic, and mozzarella cheese mixing with the Italian Sausage and mushrooms filling the building with an amazing aroma. With a Leinenkugal Summer Shandy in his hand, he closed his eyes and took a deep breath, anticipating a filling dinner. Cutting off a two-inch section of calzone, he whispered a prayer of thanks and raised the cheese-oozing treat to his mouth.

The phone rang.

Damn it.

He dropped the fork back into the box and shut the lid. He picked up the phone and said, "Savage Investigative Consultants."

"Peedee, I just finished watching my interview with Sylvia Deming. Just one thing that I noticed that was odd."

Peden was really hoping to get to his calzone but couldn't just tell Megan to call back later. He said, "Hold on Megan." He took a long pull on his Leinenkugal. "Okay, you have my undivided attention."

"Did you notice that the entire house looked like a highly polished museum? I mean, everything was in its place, front to back."

Peden acknowledged that he felt the same when he watched the video.

"Well, there was one thing that stood out. There was a reflection of something on the floor against the wall in the library. I couldn't really tell what it was, but it looked like a piece of glass."

He was quiet for a moment, rubbing the scar above his left eye, running through the recording in his mind. He didn't recall seeing the glass, but was again focusing on the photographs of the people and the certificates hanging on the walls.

Megan said, "Peedee, you still with me?"

Hearing Megan say 'Peedee' broke his concentration. "Let me bring up the file. I'll let you know when it's up. Where in the video do you see the glass?"

Savage could hear Megan's keyboard rattle. "Look around the 10:17 mark. You can clearly see the piece of glass against the baseboard."

Peden had the video up and was forwarding in ten second jumps to the spot that Megan described. He found the flash almost immediately, then backed up and moved the image frame by frame. To Peden, it looked like a flat piece of glass shaped like an irregular triangle.

He said, "I see the glass. What do you think it's from?"

"It looks like it might be from a broken window or a picture frame, maybe a broken glass, you know, like a cocktail glass."

Savage took nearly a minute, first moving forward, then in reverse, eyeing the images frame by frame. His first impression was window glass, but with such a small image it was difficult to determine whether the glass was flat, like a window, or curved, like a drinking glass.

He asked, "Are there any windows close by?"

"Nope. But there are a few framed certificates above it. Take a look at the video again. It's their "I love me" wall. Mostly Jarrod's stuff, but Sylvia has some stuff there, too. College diplomas, some professional certificates, and a couple of Jarrod's marksmanship certificates. There's also a picture of Jarrod with his sniper rifle on that wall."

Peden thought for a moment when Megan mentioned the wall of certificates. He scratched his head, trying to drag up something that was below the surface. It just wasn't registering.

He asked, "Are you planning to ask Mrs. Deming any more questions?"

"I wasn't, but I can." There was a moment of silence. "What are you thinking?"

After a pause, he replied, "I don't know, but let me go with you this time. We'll get some better pictures, too."

"I'll call her in a few minutes. When would you be ready?"

"Anytime after 10:00 AM tomorrow morning would work for me."

They finished the call and Peden opened the box with his calzone. Suddenly, he was ravenously hungry. He took several large bites and washed them down with sips of Summer Shandy. A smile began to form. He loved a challenge.

Chapter 13

At 5:15 PM, Elizabeth Sanchez drove away from the Chatham County Courthouse. Her boss, Andrew Newsome, had just given her a three percent raise, but his comments seemed to indicate that the raise had strings attached, that she might be doing some after-hours work for him "off the books." She was apprehensive about what that meant.

Her phone buzzed when she reached Martin Luther King Jr. Boulevard. When she hit answer, Wayne Cleaver's voice filled her Chevrolet Malibu.

"Hi, Liz."

In a cheerful voice, she said, "Hey, Wayne. Free at last."

"Yeah, and I want to keep it that way. Is there a safe place we can talk?"

"Yep. I'll pick you up in fifteen minutes. Do you like seafood?"

"I love seafood."

Fifteen minutes later, Wayne jumped into Liz's car. "Where are we headed?"

"I want to surprise you. Don't worry. You'll fit right in. I might not, though."

Wayne wore blue jeans, tennis shoes, and a *Doors* tee shirt. She was still dressed in dark blue slacks, a matching coat, with a white blouse and silver jewelry. In their respective getups, they were an odd couple.

She headed westbound on Interstate 16. Once she was safely in the flow of traffic, he said, "I know you're putting your job in jeopardy just being around me and it means a lot to me."

A nervous smile crossed her lips. She knew he was

right. An Assistant District Attorney socializing with a convicted felon was grounds for dismissal. She also knew that Wayne wouldn't have asked for her help if it wasn't important. It was also why she thought it best that they get out of Savannah to a place where it was unlikely they would be seen together.

They were both quiet for a spell. The sky was a light blue with a few wispy cirrus clouds overhead. The temperature outside was a toasty eighty-eight degrees, but the air conditioner in Elizabeth's gray Malibu was set to seventy-two.

When they passed the interchange with Interstate 95, still wearing her nervous smile, she asked, "So, before we get out in public, how did you get busted with like, fifty-five pounds of pot? You never used to be that stupid."

Wayne shook his head, his eyes widened with surprise. Then he scratched his head, still trying to think about how to answer her question.

"It's a long story. Will I have time to finish it before you have to head back to town?"

She nodded. "We have time. Just tell me what I'm getting into here."

"First, every word that I'm going to tell you is the God's-honest truth. We've known each other for a long time, right?" She nodded. He continued, "Have you ever known me to lie to you or anyone else?"

Her face turned serious, shifting from the traffic flow to Wayne's face, then back to traffic. "No."

Taking a deep breath, he started his tale of woe from the very beginning, which was shortly after the last time he'd seen her. She knew that he'd talked about becoming some kind of commercial artist and she knew he had creative skills. She also knew about his home life, that he grew up without a father. That never stopped him from dreaming big, which is why she was inclined to believe the papers when she read about the bust. She had thought maybe his big dreams clouded his judgment.

What Wayne told her was drastically different than

what she'd read and heard.

* * *

Sandra's Seafood Restaurant in Ellabell, Georgia, was apparently thrown together in a hurry. The building was a former Quick Stop convenience store. A few pictures adorned the walls, none of which formed a common theme. Wayne's first thought was that they may have been placed to hide holes in the wood paneling. The floor was the original asphalt tiles. He could see indents where the store's old shelving had been removed. The furnishings were a mishmash of tables and booths. Few matched each other. But the cool air in the restaurant was filled with the aroma of freshly fried, boiled and steamed seafood.

Wayne and Elizabeth were seated in a booth against the far wall to the left of the front door. When they had pulled into the parking lot, Wayne raised an eyebrow at Liz with a crooked smile. The unasked question was, "What the hell is this?"

She said matter-of-factly, "Hold off on that look until we finish eating, buddy."

The waitresses were all dressed in jeans and tank tops with the restaurant logo. Their waitress was at the table with ice water and hushpuppies just as they sat down. Her nametag said, *Sandy*. She asked Wayne in a sweet southern voice, "What can I getcha to drink, Hon?"

He replied, "Lemonade."

She turned to Elizabeth, "How 'bout ya'll, sweetie?"

"Make it two."

Sandy smiled and headed towards the servers' station.

It was close to 6:00 PM. All but one of the eighteen tables was filled. Wayne saw two other waitresses moving between the tables, but they didn't appear rushed or rattled by the crowd. It was a cheerful crowd, talking amongst themselves, a clamor of dinner noises and pleasant chatter filling the air.

Elizabeth dropped five hushpuppies onto the plate and squirted some kind of sauce over the top. Wayne copied her. She handed Wayne a menu and the list of dinner specials. He looked over the specials first, looking at the prices for the least expensive items.

Elizabeth noticed his discomfort. "Get whatever you want." She smiled reassuringly. "My treat. Besides, nothing on that menu is real expensive."

He smiled, relaxed, and picked up the regular menu. She was right about the prices. When Sandy returned, he ordered the fried catfish platter. Again, Elizabeth told the waitress to make it two.

For the next ten minutes, they talked about old times when they were in high school, reminiscing about old friends, sports, and the senior prom. They'd attended the dance with different dates, but wound up finishing the night together. Shortly after that, they'd graduated. Elizabeth went off to University of Georgia College of Law and Wayne headed for Savannah and the College of Art and Design. They had not crossed paths since high school...until now.

After Sandy returned and left their order, Elizabeth's expression turned serious. As quietly as she could manage, she said, "You spent three years in prison because of these guys?"

Wayne nodded his head as he finished swallowing a mouthful of catfish. "Man is that ever good." He paused for a moment, savoring the taste, then he said, "Yep. I'll tell you something else. I met a guy at Coastal who said he was set up the same way. DEA busted him for over fifty pounds of weed. He told me he had less than a pound when they raided him."

"Oh my gawd!"

Wayne looked at her and whispered, "Keep it down." He continued, "He's kind of a hot head and he tried to fight it. He'll be spending more time than I did because he didn't play along."

"The guys that went to your motel room yesterday, do you know their names?"

"Yeah. Well, I know one name. Vincent Mercado. He was one of the two guys who kept hassling me during questioning after they busted me. The other guy I didn't recognize.

"You said 'One of the guys who kept hassling me.' Who else was there?"

"The other guy was Jarrod Deming, the guy who got killed yesterday. I think this Mercado guy wants to pin Deming's murder on me. Hell, I don't think I was even out of the joint yet when the shooting took place."

Elizabeth froze with a fork full of fish mid-way to her open mouth.

Wayne asked, "What?"

"Sylvia Deming, Jarrod Deming's widow, and I were best friends in college. That's where I'm going tonight. I want to see if there's anything I can do for her. We haven't seen each other in years."

For a fraction of a second, Wayne wondered whether it was a good idea meeting with his old friend, Liz. He felt that he was placing her in a precarious position with work and now with her friend, Sylvia Deming. The thought passed as quickly as it came. He hoped that she didn't read his expression and know what he was thinking.

She said, "You can't go back to your hotel tonight. It's too dangerous."

Wayne's mind shifted into high gear. He wondered how soon Mercado might move to set him up to take the fall for Deming's murder. Or maybe they planned to kill him and then plant evidence proving that he did the shooting. *Dead men tell no lies.*

He said, "I've got to get out of here. Can you get me on a bus to Anderson?"

"That's the first place that they'll look, Wayne. We need to be ahead of these guys. You can stay at my place. I have an attached garage, so we can go in and out of the building without anyone seeing us, and I have a spare bedroom. They'll never suspect that you're still around."

"I can't ask you to…"

"You didn't ask. I insist. Look, Wayne, these guys are looking for a fall guy. That guy is going to be you unless we can prove otherwise. You can't do this alone. Besides, I'm close to all sides here, so I'm in the best position to hear what's going on and maybe have some impact on the outcome."

Wayne was skeptical that she could do much, and he was more than a little fearful that she might put more than her job on the line. If Mercado and the other agents were cornered, they might do more than set someone up for a stint in prison. Since Deming was planning to blow the whistle on his fellow agents, though no one knew the details, it was likely that someone from within the group was the shooter.

She was looking at his dark eyes, letting him know she felt concerned for his safety. His eyes locked on hers. There was an intense energy between them. He reached across the table and took her hands in his. The warmth radiated through her hands and up her arms, her nerve endings igniting throughout her body. He said as quietly as he could, "Liz, I can't let you put your life in danger. These guys are the real deal. I think they killed their partner. If they'd kill one of their own, what do you think they'd do to us?"

She gave his hand a squeeze. "I understand all of that, but I can't leave you out there fending for yourself with no money and no place to hide. We have to figure out a way to stop these guys. Remember, your life isn't the only one they've ruined."

Their waitress, Sandy, walked up with a broad smile on her face and joked, "Ya'll two lovebirds want a couple to go boxes?"

Embarrassed, the tension broken, they let go of each other's hands and laughed at Sandy. Liz said, "Yeah, but just one box. We'll split it up at home."

Sandy cast a smile that said *I know what ya'll are doing tonight.*

Still smiling, Wayne just shook his head. He knew he couldn't continue to argue, but he felt ill at ease with the arrangement. What he really needed was to get to his mother's house in Anderson, South Carolina, where he had some money stashed away. Only then would he feel a bit more in control.

Chapter 14

By 8:30 PM, the western sky was a painting of bright orange clouds with varying shades of contrasting gray, backed by fading blue. Directly above, only the brightest few stars were visible.

Elizabeth Sanchez stopped in front of 19 Flinn Drive on the Isle of Hope. No other cars were visible. She hoped Sylvia was alone. Even after their brief phone conversation earlier in the day, Elizabeth was still nervous. Sylvia's husband's murder was on her mind, but something else nagged her.

Years ago, when Sylvia was away from school attending her mother's funeral, Jarrod Deming had made a pass at her. Sylvia had asked Elizabeth to check her apartment a few times while she was gone. Once while there, Jarrod had showed up, a bit intoxicated, and tried to get her into the bedroom. He was being more than a little aggressive and Elizabeth had used some of her self-defense techniques to get away. She never told Sylvia of the advance, but she let Deming know that if he tried it again, she'd make sure the story got out. He had laughed at her, but after that incident, he never gave her a second look.

At the front door, she took a deep breath and was about to ring the doorbell when it opened. A puffy-eyed Sylvia Deming stood in the doorway. Elizabeth was taken aback at how much older her friend looked than what she remembered back at the University of Georgia. The lines on her face were deep and the skin on her arms was somewhat loose, not taut like she remembered her once athletic friend.

Sylvia walked towards Elizabeth with open arms. The two women hugged for a long moment before either said a word.

Finally, still in their embrace, Elizabeth solemnly asked her best friend from college, "How you holdin' up, Sissy?"

They broke their hold on each other. Sylvia stepped back at arm's length and said in a weepy voice, "Okay, I guess." She grabbed Elizabeth's hand. "Let's go sit."

They walked to the library and sat next to each other on the couch. Elizabeth looked around the room. An empty wine glass sat on the coffee table.

Sylvia offered, "Let me fix you a drink. I've got Merlot, Moscato, and a few other wines. If you want something stronger…"

"I'm fine. I can grab something if I change my mind." An awkward moment passed. They looked at each other, not quite knowing what to say. Then Elizabeth broke the spell. She reached out and put her hand over her friend's. "Do they have any suspects?"

Sylvia's expression went from a blank stare to anguish. Her eyes welled up with tears. The two women embraced again, holding each other for several minutes. Elizabeth had never experienced the heartbreak of losing someone closer than her grandparents. While she loved them dearly, she knew Sylvia's loss was far more painful.

As they held each other, Elizabeth noticed a small shard of glass, across the room lying against the baseboard. It looked like the glass from a picture frame. Above the glass on the wall was a picture of Jarrod Deming with his sniper rifle. She looked away, not wanting to see his image.

She refocused on a painting on an adjacent wall, one that she recognized from their dorm room back at the University of Georgia. The painter was a local, well-known artist who specialized in prints with the theme of forever love. She wondered if Sylvia's love was a one-way street, if Jarrod had been unfaithful throughout their marriage. For the moment, she just hugged her friend, studying the picture, hoping that being here somehow helped.

* * *

Peter Vega had dozed off to sleep at 2:40 AM. He, his

girlfriend, and three friends had partied until past 2:00 AM. The friends crashed in his living room while he led his girlfriend back to his bedroom. His morning class at Savannah College of Art and Design started at 9:30. The professor had warned him that there would be a pop quiz and that he needed a solid score if he wanted to keep his barely passing grade above the red line. He'd added, "I really don't want to have to tell your father that you're failing my class."

They're all afraid of my old man. You would think he was a dictator in some third world country. That was his last thought as he drifted off to sleep with the aid of some very potent weed and a post coital haze. The young woman next to him was already snoring by the time Peter rolled over to turn off the light. Now they both were in a deep slumber.

His dreams were interrupted by his girlfriend pulling on his arm. She was shaking him saying, "Peter, wake up. Somebody's at the door."

"What?" He looked at her with a blank stare, then turned towards the clock, the bright red numbers burning his eyes. "It's three in the morning."

He heard a loud *bang*. The building shook as if it had been struck by a car. The sound of heavy footsteps filled the apartment, the floor vibrating with each step. The door to his bedroom burst open. Three large men in futuristic looking military uniforms, armed with automatic weapons, moved into the bedroom and shouted for Peter and the woman to get on the floor. When they didn't move fast enough, one of the men reached out and grabbed Peter by the hair and dragged him off the bed. The woman next to him grabbed the bed sheets, trying to conceal her naked body, and started to move to the floor on the opposite side of the bed.

One of the military team members shouted, "Stop! You, get over here. And give me that sheet."

He ripped the sheet from her hands. She stood momentarily, trying to cover her body with her arms. The men stared at her, briefly losing their concentration. Terrified that she might be accidently killed by one of the assailants, she laid out flat on the floor.

* * *

Vince Mercado shouted at Peter Vega and his friends to remain on the floor until they could inspect the apartment for threats. After fifteen minutes, Mercado ordered that they move into the kitchen. They were allowed to dress, one by one, while being closely monitored by a member of the DEA team. There were no female team members, so the two females in the apartment had to dress under the watchful eyes of a male DEA agent.

Mercado collected their driver's licenses. As he did, he escorted each individual, women first, into a bedroom with a walk-in closet. When the first woman returned to the group, she was pale and shaking. When the others asked her what was wrong, Mercado yelled, "Shut Up! No talking!"

By the time Peter Vega was escorted to the closet, he knew something was amiss. When Mercado stood beside Vega in front of the closet door, he asked, "How's the old man?"

Vega looked up into Mercado's face. "He's fine and he's going to have ya'll's ass for this. It's exactly why he wants the DEA's budget cut. Spending money on nickel and dime users."

When Mercado opened the closet door, Peter Vega quickly realized that he was in big trouble.

* * *

Andrew Newsome was elated that the bust was a success. They had their target in custody. It was time to play the trump card.

The call to Judge Stillwell had gone well. The judge had been asleep, but knowing the bust was going down, he expected the call. His demeanor was quite pleasant for someone who had been awakened just before 5:00 AM. But he had reason to be pleased, as this particular bust would pay immediate dividends and guarantee federal cooperation far into the future. It also fit his plans for the immediate future, a run for the U.S. Senate.

He asked if there were any complications. When Newsome had said that there were none, he told Newsome to congratulate the team, then call the good Senator and give him the sad news of his son's predicament. Dealing drugs was a terrible crime.

Newsome was taken aback when the judge told him to make the call to Peter Vega's father, the Honorable Senator Armand Vega. He had assumed that the judge would call Senator Vega himself. He advised Newsome to ensure that the senator clearly understood the ramifications of his son's actions.

Newsome took a deep breath as he punched out the final number on his phone. When the Senator's answering service picked up, he identified himself and that he was the district attorney for Chatham County, Georgia. He advised the young man that he needed to be patched through to the Senator immediately. When the attendant asked for the nature of the issue, Newsome said he couldn't divulge that information, but that it would be a grave mistake if he wasn't able to reach the senator right away.

The man on the other end of the phone paused for a moment, breathing deeply into the phone. "I'll ring through to the Senator. Please stand by."

After nearly two full minutes, a clear, deep, authoritative voice came on the line. "Mr. Newsome, this better be good. What the hell is this about?"

"Senator, first I do apologize for the early hour." He looked at his desk clock. It read 5:07. "About two hours ago, the local DEA office carried out a raid in midtown Savannah, Georgia. The team confiscated a large quantity of illicit drugs, including marijuana, methamphetamine, cocaine, and heroin. Your son, Peter, was among the five individuals arrested in the raid." He paused to allow his words to register. Complete silence followed. After nearly fifteen seconds, he asked, "Senator, are you still there?"

"Yes."

The single word response lacked the confidence and force of the senator's initial outburst. The wind had been taken out of his sails, which bolstered Newsome's own confidence.

"Your son is being held at the Chatham County

Detention Center in Savannah. I'll be filing the charges against Peter this morning. He will be arraigned tomorrow...let's see...that would be Friday at 9:00 AM in front of Judge Stillwell. Do you have any questions to this point?"

The senator cleared his voice. "Why are you calling me? Peter is an adult."

Newsome wasn't ready for this. He expected the senator to play the part of the concerned parent. It was time to put up or shut up. "Because, Senator, when the press learns that your son was arrested for dealing large quantities of very dangerous drugs while you want to cut funding for the war on drugs, your constituents might think twice about supporting your campaign."

There was a long silence on the line while the senator considered his next response. Newsome heard another deep breath. Senator Vega then said more to himself, "Aah, Christ." More silence. "What do you want from me?"

They had him, hook, line, and sinker.

"We think that you should reconsider...soften...your stance on funding for the DEA. The agency needs funding to continue the fight..."

"Mr. Newsome, spare me the party line. Just tell me what you want and what you'll do for my son in return."

Spoken like a true politician.

* * *

"He agreed to the whole shootin' match. He's releasing a statement to the press on Friday about his change of heart on DEA funding. We'll meet him at the airport Friday afternoon to discuss the terms of his son's release."

Whalen Stillwell sat stone-faced behind his desk as Newsome delivered the news. It was as he suspected: politics – meaning keeping one's position – and family were more important to senators and house members than the will of the people.

"Don't let your guard down. These guys are like snakes; you cut their heads off but the fangs still carry poison. Have they kept the kid separate from his friends?"

"Yes. He was isolated from the general population as soon as he arrived at the center. We told him that both his roommates rolled on him, so he's pretty scared right now."

"Good. Now let's make sure we're on the same page for when the Honorable Senator from Georgia arrives."

The smile on Stillwell's face gave Newsome chills.

Chapter 15

Peden Savage awoke with a start. Jarrod Deming's murder video played over and over in his mind as he slept. In his dream, Deming would say something that was inaudible, then he would reach into his pocket and pull out his notes, step to the microphone, move to the right, and fall backwards. His hand with the notes would move to the right as his body was propelled backwards. The camera spun out of control.

Each replay of the scene would start the same and end the same. When he finally awoke, he said, "The notes. They had to have dropped to his right side."

Rubbing the sleep from his eyes, he thought who might have seen the papers leave Deming's hand. Nila West was on his right side where he'd swung his arm. She may have seen the papers, but she'd been hit by one of the bullets and was in pain. Who else was behind Deming? His lawyer was on his left. If the wind was blowing from Deming's right to his left that may have brought the papers back his way. Why would he keep Deming's notes secret?

Maybe it was worth another look at the video...after some coffee, eggs, grits, and toast.

* * *

The aroma of Columbian coffee and breakfast filled the entire office at Savage Investigative Consultants. A frying pan with cooking oil sat on the stove over a low flame while Peden stirred a medium saucepan containing slow cooking grits, bits of breakfast sausage, butter and pepper. He was still about ten minutes from cracking three eggs into the frying pan and dropping wheat bread into the toaster.

Peden closed his eyes and breathed in the scent of breakfast cooking. He smiled and thought about what his two girls were doing at this moment. He knew that they were both in college; Kaitlin would start her junior year this fall, Kristi her freshman year. He had hoped that they would attend school close to Savannah. He could have visited and started a real relationship with them. As it stood, they never spoke because of the things he'd allegedly done to their mother. None of it was true.

At 7:35 AM, except for his thoughts wandering to his daughters and the murder investigation of Jarrod Deming, the morning was starting off well. Then his cell phone vibrated. A call before 9:00 AM on a Thursday was never good news. Peden answered, "Savage Investigative Consultants."

"You're up early. Meet me for breakfast?"

"Can't. Already got it cooking."

Marcus Cook thought for a minute. "Got enough for two?"

"Sure. Do you like eggs and grits?"

"Is the Pope a Catholic?"

"It'll be ready in ten minutes."

"For some good eggs, sausage and grits, I'll be there in eight," Marcus said.

* * *

It was more like twelve minutes, but Peden had just finished cooking the eggs when Marcus Cook walked into Savage's kitchen. He stopped, smiled, and inhaled.

"Mmm, mmm! If you had bigger boobs I might ask you to marry me."

"Wait 'til you taste this. You might want to anyway."

Marcus lowered his muscular two hundred forty-five pound frame onto a kitchen chair that protested with a creaking noise. Peden served up a plate filled with three eggs over easy, a generous portion of sausage and grits, and two slices of toast. He pointed to a mug of coffee already sitting on the kitchen table near a place-setting of napkins and silverware.

After Peden dished up his own plate, they sat and dug in, enjoying the meal in silence. The only sounds were lips smacking and the slurping of coffee.

"So, why the rush over here?"

Marcus finished off a mouthful of grits before answering. "We went on a bust this morning around 3:00 AM. An apartment on East 33rd Street, just west of Bull. I was just there to guard the perimeter."

"Still not letting you play, huh?"

"Nope. At least not in busts with any quantity." Marcus paused, forked another mouthful of grits and eggs into his mouth, thinking as he chewed. He swallowed and wiped his mouth with a paper napkin. "This bust was different. Most times, the guys that go in are yuckin' it up. Relaxed, only getting serious when we're within a couple blocks of the raid location. This time everybody was...uptight, tense the entire ride. Even the usual chitchat on the portables was missing."

Peden thought for a minute. "Maybe because the Deming thing was on everybody's mind?"

"Nah." Marcus looked up as if in thought. "Maybe a little, but this was way beyond that. I heard Mercado whisper something to Smith about a 'target' just before we got there. We never used any code words like that before. I mean, they're all professional when the team moves, but this was before the order came down to go and it was just between them two. Normally they identify the perps by name in advance. Not this time. You would have thought we were going after Bin Laden or something."

"What would they mean by 'target'?"

"My guess is they were after someone important. They busted five kids this time, three guys and two gals, but when we booked 'em into Chatham, they separated one of them out from the rest."

Peden asked, "What, was he some kind of badass or something?"

"Nah. They all looked like SCAD kids to me. Artsy, fartsy kind. They definitely weren't hardcore. When I saw them, I thought, 'nickel and dimers.' You know the type; college kids trying to score some stash and spending money."

"What was the take on the raid?"

"I didn't see the official tally, but it looked like about fifty to sixty pounds of weed, a half-ounce of coke, some meth, and a bit of smack. Sound familiar?"

Peden stopped eating for a moment to look at Marcus, reading the expression on his face. He knew that this bust followed the pattern that Lee Sparks had identified.

They continued eating eggs and grits while they thought about the bust. Peden stood and reached for the coffee pot, motioning with it towards Marcus' cup. He nodded and Peden freshened up both their brews.

"When did you learn how to cook grits? I thought you were from up in Ohio, some Slavic community," Marcus said.

"Sheffield Village. When my folks left Ukraine, they settled there. We have relatives who'd moved there before World War II. Anyway, when Susan left with Kristi and Kaitlin, I had to learn how to cook. I was going broke eating out all the time, and the restaurant food was packin' on the pounds. I had a date who offered to cook breakfast for me, but when she looked in the fridge, she laughed." Marcus smiled, thinking back on his early bachelor days. Peden continued, "We went out shopping for breakfast food. She taught me about grits, Cajun spices, how to cook fish and shrimp. It was a real education. The education lasted for a couple months, then some guy stole my teacher."

Marcus smiled as he finished off his grits and wiped his plate with a piece of toast. He asked, "Did you learn anything else besides southern cuisine?"

"Yeah. Not all southern ladies are prim and proper behind closed doors."

Marcus started thinking about the bust again. "When I got back to the office after helping transport the perps to Chatham, one of our guys – Alex Smith – was shredding a small stack of papers. That was weird. We just got finished with a late night bust, we're all dead tired, and he's at the shredder. About that time, our SAIC, Nila West, yells out into the office that we have a mandatory meeting at 7:00 AM. No excuse to miss the meeting. There were some moans and groans, but she says to knock it off, that it was serious." He paused. "At the meeting, she announces to the team that the FBI is starting with their interviews about the Deming murder. First interview is at 3:00 this afternoon. We've been up all night, man. We knew it was coming, but nobody wanted to hear it. She said to finish the paper on the raid, then go home and get some sleep."

"Megan told me that she's starting this afternoon," Peden confirmed. "I'm providing some gadgets and plan to sit in. Fosco says no but I have to provide some 'technical assistance.' Problem is, if I'm in the room with her, they'll clam up. They've all heard about my history."

During Peden's stint with the FBI, he noticed that some of his fellow agents were regularly making false statements and planting evidence to bolster their cases. The targets of the investigations were not model citizens, but it worked on Peden's conscience like fifty-five grit sandpaper. He joined the FBI to uphold the law and not just those that he chose. He knew that his Marine Corps training wouldn't allow him to look the other way without taking action. He did his best to steer clear of the dirty agents, but it wasn't long before the whole issue came to a head.

Jimmy Vignetti, a senior agent, approached him about planting evidence at a crime scene and providing verification of the agent's false statements. Savage refused. He was immediately ostracized. His fellow agents avoided him like the plague.

Finally, Peden threatened to expose the agents and their illegal practices. His boss, Roland Fosco, asked that he not go public, that the FBI would be weakened by the scandal. In exchange for Peden to quietly resign, Fosco promised a major housecleaning at the agency. The only agent close to Peden to survive the cleansing was Special Agent Megan Moore. Fosco was promoted and placed in charge of the retooling effort, hand-selecting new agents. He'd offered Peden an opportunity to rejoin the agency, but Peden refused, deciding to take his skills into the private sector. That proved to be a prosperous decision.

"Yeah, but that shit didn't have anything to do with the DEA," Marcus said.

Peden shrugged. "I still think I'll be more of a distraction than a help."

Marcus thought for a moment. "You know Megan. Maybe that's what she wants: An excuse to bust somebody's balls if they balk at answering her questions. I'm going to hate being in the same room with her today, even though I know she probably won't bust me up like she will some of the other guys."

"So the entire meeting was about the interviews?"

Marcus took a deep breath and leaned back in his chair, which again creaked loudly in protest. He rubbed his stomach and said, "I think I ate too much. Meeting, yeah. That was it. After she finished, she told Mercado to drop by her office for a few minutes. Then everyone took off."

Cook's cell phone buzzed in his pocket. He pulled it out, looked at it, then alerted Peden, "Mercado." He put his finger to his lips in the universal 'be quiet' sign and answered. "Cook."

Peden could barely hear Vincent Mercado's voice from Marcus' phone. He could only make out a few words, but by his friend's expression, Marcus might not get as much sleep as he'd hoped.

After just over two minutes worth of conversation, he punched off the call. He smiled slightly, his white teeth contrasting with his dark facial features.

"I might be getting closer to filling Deming's slot. Turns out that the kid they separated at Chatham is the son of Armand Vega. United States Senator Armand Vega."

Peden's jaw dropped.

Marcus continued, "Mercado wants me available when the Senator flies in. He's going to meet the Senator and handle the 'negotiations' for his son's release, but he wants me on standby in case something goes south."

Peden rubbed the scar over his left eye while he thought

about Marcus being on the inside of the DEA's dirty ops. He wondered what they would want in exchange for a clean slate for the Vega kid. He had smelled dirty politics before, but this was stinking to high heaven.

Chapter 16

A light sleeper, thanks to his stint at Coastal State Prison, Wayne Cleaver learned quickly that his cellmates could be his friend one minute and his killer the next. During his stay, he had observed retribution attacks, but he never let anyone know that he had seen or heard anything – self-preservation in a hostile environment.

The musical sound of Elizabeth Sanchez's cell phone caused Wayne Cleaver's eyes to pop open and his ears to perk up. He remained still, looking around the bedroom, not recognizing his surroundings. Then he remembered that he was in Elizabeth's spare bedroom and made no attempt to get out of bed.

He heard Sanchez groan in the next room as she figured out the identity of the caller. He couldn't hear either end of the conversation but did hear a distinct *Crap* when she completed the call. Within a few minutes, he heard the shower start, then the toilet flush. Elizabeth's day was starting off on the wrong foot.

Wayne sat up in bed, stretched, and rubbed his eyes. Elizabeth's spare bedroom was cheerful, but not dolled up like the rest of the condominium. The walls were off-white. Only a few pictures hung on the walls. A small treadmill was the only other piece of furniture in the room. It looked as if it was getting some recent use. No clothes or towels hung from the machine.

He hopped out of bed and made his way to the kitchen, planning to help his short-term landlord by starting a pot of coffee. He rummaged around in the kitchen, looking for filters and the coffee pot. When he found the Keurig coffee machine, he just stared at it wondering how the thing worked. After several minutes of study, he thought that he had it figured out. Then he found Elizabeth's stash of K-cups and read the various flavors of coffee. *So much for being helpful. I'll just wait.*

Wayne sat at the kitchen counter looking around at the open-floor living space of Elizabeth's condominium. There was no clutter. Everything was tidy.

The kitchen cabinets were natural wood – oak he thought. Signs, with cute sayings like 'Kiss the Cook' and 'As long as we have wine, dinner will be fine,' adorned the red-pepper colored walls.

Wayne turned to face the combined dining area and living room. The dining area was large enough to hold a modest-sized table and chairs, a small china cabinet, and a butler sporting hanging wine glasses. Two separate collages of family pictures in various stages of her youth hung on either side of an archway that led to a hallway.

Beyond the dining area was an expansive living room. A couch and two matching upholstered chairs sat across the room from a large, flat-panel television. The walls in the living room held a number of frames. Some held pictures of family and friends, others with Georgia Bulldog sports shots. A few had more folksy sayings about family and home and cleanliness. No doubt, Elizabeth was an organized person, neat and clean. *And beautiful. She's way out of my league.*

Wayne heard the door from her bedroom creak. Elizabeth walked into the kitchen, her hair still wet from the shower, dressed in a robe. He wasn't sure if she had anything on underneath, but he made it a point to look no lower than her chin.

She must have sensed his unease and smiled. "I guess I should have dressed before breakfast. I forgot that you've been locked up with a bunch of guys for a while." She smiled, trying to lighten the mood.

He exhaled with a loud *woosh,* then smiled back. "Good one." He paused. "I take it from that phone call that your morning is off to a grand start."

She put on a look of disgust. "Ugh. My boss, the DA.

He is such a jerk… correction, an ass. And he looks like a weasel. He's always giving me the perv eyeball. I hate it."

"Kind of like what I just did?"

She laughed. "No. What you just did was try to be a gentleman, but I think you're out of practice. Anyway, I have to go in early, so you're on your own for a while."

That made Wayne nervous. He was used to sitting around all day with little to do, but that was not by choice. Now that he was free, he felt the urge to explore, to get caught up on what was happening in Savannah, but he knew that would have to wait. He also knew that it might never happen.

"So, is there anything I can do around here, maybe clean up a little?" He smiled as he waved his hands around her pristine condo.

"Haha. I know I'm a little OCD, okay, but there are a couple things you can do to help yourself." She walked over to a small desk, picked up a legal pad and a pen, and handed them to him. "Write down everything you can remember about when you were busted. Don't leave out any detail, no matter how insignificant you think it might be."

Wayne was wary about her instructions. He looked at her with a raised eyebrow. "What are you thinking?"

She put one hand on her hip and gave him a look like a teacher disappointed with a student who had talent but just didn't put in the effort. Wayne found the pose a bit sexy, though he figured it wasn't the look she intended.

"I want to compare what you remember with the official account of your arrest. I'm going to do the same thing with a couple other cases from the past few years. Something isn't right at the office. I think Jarrod Deming's murder is somehow connected."

Wayne's wary look turned to concern. He didn't want Elizabeth putting herself in danger on his account. He had seen first-hand that these guys didn't play fair. If she was caught looking at the wrong files or asking the wrong questions, she would be in danger.

He warned, "These guys are already on edge, probably

taking extra precautions. If they catch you snooping around, who knows what they'll do." He put his arms out and she moved close to him. He embraced her. "If something happened to you, I couldn't live with myself."

Elizabeth tried to think of a comeback to reassure him that she would be safe, but her mind was racing, feeling his embrace. She felt awkward, but warm in his arms, her nerve endings suddenly ultra-sensitive. Finally, she assured, "I'll be careful. I won't look at any files while I'm at the office. I'll pack them up and bring them home. We can look at them together, maybe figure out what's going on."

Wayne held her shoulders and moved her to arms' length. He looked at her eyes, feeling a tingle in his spine. He was planning to say something profound, but seeing her beautiful face, her standing in her robe fresh out of the shower, catching the scent of her body, his mind went blank. He wanted to lean in and kiss her.

She said, "You can't do this. Not right now anyway. I have to get to work."

He let go of her shoulders, feeling a bit foolish, as if he was being rejected. "Yeah, uh, sorry. I, uh, maybe I should..."

"You big dork, you don't have anything to be sorry about. Just hold that thought until later. When I get back, I'll bring dinner. There's some wine in the rack. Pick a bottle and put it in the fridge. And write out that stuff on the legal pad."

She closed the distance between them and kissed him lightly on the lips. She backed away. "I have to get ready to go. If you think of anything that you need, let me know before I leave and I'll pick it up on the way home. And pick your jaw up off the floor."

She smiled as she turned back to her bedroom and closed the door behind her.

Wayne stood still as if he had turned to stone. His mind was trying to process what had just happened. After a moment, he smiled and headed back to the kitchen to figure out the Keurig Coffee Machine.

* * *

When Elizabeth finished dressing for work, she stopped in her kitchen and made herself a quick cup of some kind of flavored coffee and toast. Wayne was sitting on a barstool already busy writing down details of his bust on the legal pad. He filled more than two pages of information. When she finished her breakfast, she smiled, then walked up behind him. She put one hand on his shoulder and used her other hand to turn his face to hers. "Call me if you need anything. I should be at my desk after the meeting with 'The Weasel.' Stay out of sight. Especially from my neighbor." She pointed west. "She's getting a little senile, but she can be a busy-body."

"Okay."

Elizabeth leaned over and kissed him on the lips again. This kiss lingered a bit longer than the first. She turned and headed for the door.

Wayne wasn't sure what was happening, but he was beginning to think that this arrangement wasn't such a bad idea after all.

"See you a bit after five."

He smiled in her direction, but was speechless as she closed and locked the door behind her.

* * *

By late morning, Wayne was bored. He had filled out eight full legal-sized pages with details about his bust. He wrote the specifics about how he was selling small amounts of marijuana to friends to pay for his school tuition, room, and board. He also specified the amounts that he had on hand at the time of the bust as well as the amount that was supposedly confiscated in his apartment.

Wayne wrote that his roommate was given a script to follow unless he wanted to wind up in prison for conspiracy. The kid told him that his father was going to cut off his school funding and make him go to a community college closer to home.

Wayne also included how Deming and Mercado badgered him for hours on end. He believed that they were trying to provoke him into lashing out against them, hoping to get an assault on a federal agent charge, but he'd kept his cool.

After he finished writing, he placed a bottle of Georgia blush wine in the refrigerator. Grabbing a bottle of water from the refrigerator, he stepped out onto Elizabeth's patio. It was 11:45 AM. The sun was bright. The scent of flowers on the patio was pleasant. They grew up a trellis, blocking most of the view from the neighbors on either side of Elizabeth's patio. The fragrance of the blooms mixed with various odors from the city and nearby Route 17. Wayne breathed deeply, enjoying the scent of freedom.

"Hi, Elizabeth. Home from work today?"

The voice came from the patio beyond Elizabeth's flowers. It was the voice of an elderly woman. Panic shot through Wayne's body, remembering Elizabeth's warning. He felt like running back into her condominium, but thought better of it. He took a deep breath and smiled just as the woman's head appeared around the edge of a stand of red and pink vine roses.

The woman was startled to see Wayne standing on her neighbor's patio. She frowned. "And who are you?"

"Good morning. I'm Wayne, a friend of Liz."

The woman gave him a skeptical look. "How do you know Elizabeth?"

"We went to high school together." She was still giving him the doubtful eye. He kept his cool, though he didn't feel all that confident. "If you'd like to call her, please do. She mentioned that I might run into you. You have lovely flowers, by the way."

This seemed to divert her attention. She sheepishly replied, "Thank you." She still didn't appear totally convinced, but added, "Elizabeth is the one with the green thumb. She told me the kind of fertilizer to add to each plant. She's really smart."

"Yes, she is. She helped me with my homework when we were younger." He paused, then asked, "Would you like a bottle of water?"

Finally, she smiled a bit. "No, but thank you." She

paused. "My name's Gertrude Francis."

"Wayne…uh…Wayne Johnson."

They talked for a bit longer, the chitchat becoming friendly by the time they'd finished. Wayne bade her good day and headed back inside. Once the door was closed behind him, he took a deep breath knowing that he'd dodged a bullet. But when Elizabeth found out, she was probably going to shoot him anyway.

Chapter 17

Megan Moore, wearing a powder blue, light weight dress suit with a white blouse, and Peden Savage, in blue jeans and a lime green golf shirt, arrived at the Savannah office of the Drug Enforcement Administration on Thursday at precisely 2:45 PM. Their purpose in arriving early was two-fold: they wanted to have time to set up and test their equipment before the first interview and they wanted to establish control of the process. Moore was outwardly aggressive, Savage was more subtle. She was in charge, so he followed her lead.

Two sets of double doors opened into the reception room for the Savannah Drug Enforcement Administration office. A forty-inch-high oak counter approximately six feet inside the entry extended left to right across the entire length of a twenty-foot-wide room. Several banks of fluorescent lights lit the area.

The duo was greeted from behind the counter by a receptionist who stated that they weren't expected and that it would take a few minutes to prepare the meeting room. When Megan stated that she and Savage could take care of the room preparations, the receptionist tried to stall them. Megan would have none of it.

"Miss…" she looked at the name on the desk, "Williams, show us to the rooms and we'll handle the rest."

"But Ms. West said…"

"Tell Ms. West to meet us at the rooms after you escort us to them." Megan's stare could melt steel. She held out her arm as if to direct Miss Williams to get moving. Uncertain what to do, but compelled by Megan's direct manner, Williams stood and pointed towards the door to Megan and Peden's right. She quickly stepped away from her chair and headed towards a doorway. She led Megan and Peden to a closed door. She opened the door, reached in, and flipped a switch, stood aside, and allowed them to enter.

The room was small, only about eight feet by eight feet, with a small table in the middle. The walls were painted industrial light green. The floors were covered in black asphalt tiles. An ancient drop ceiling held tiles that were broken, stained, and in danger of falling. The single incandescent bulb that glowed from its ceiling fixture barely illuminated the space. It was little more than a storage closet.

Moore turned to Williams. "Show us to the second room, please."

Williams appeared nervous, not wanting to say anything to upset the visiting agent. Finally, she said, "There is no other room. Agent West said…"

Megan swept past the shocked receptionist. Peden followed. When he passed the poor woman, he said, "Don't worry, she just finished lunch. You're safe." He smiled as she gave him a puzzled look.

Peden caught up with Megan and they arrived at Nila West's office door together. Without knocking, Megan opened the door and stepped in. West looked up from her desk, surprised by the unannounced intrusion interrupting her meeting.

Moore and Savage looked at the three agents sitting at a small conference table in one corner of West's office. Vincent Mercado, Alex Smith, and Peter Nichols were sitting back in their chairs, appearing relaxed, or fatigued. They had been up all night on a raid.

"You can't just barge into my office. Who do you think you are? And what the hell is he doing here?"

She looked at Peden as if she had stepped in a pile of dog feces. Peden expected no less, knowing it was going to get worse before it got better.

Ignoring Nila West's questions, Megan looked at the three agents with laser-like intensity. "You will excuse us for a moment. I need a word with Ms. West."

At first, the men didn't move a muscle, weighing which woman carried more clout. Vince Mercado, knowing the serious consequences that would result if this investigation went the wrong way, didn't want the situation to blow up into a media circus. Two federal agencies going at each other would make for a news tsunami and his team would be in the center of the wave. But if he didn't show support for his boss, Agent West could make his life miserable. Comfortable knowing that she needed him more than he needed her, he made his decision. He swiveled his chair towards West and said, "We'll step outside while you talk with Agent Moore. We're done debriefing the raid." He turned to Megan and Peden and smiled. Then he said to Smith and Nichols, "Grab a coffee or something."

The three men stood and exited the office, each giving Megan and Peden their best 'tough guy' glare, but saving the nastiest part for Peden. Megan turned to Peden. "You, too."

Peden turned and left the office, closing the door behind him. As soon as the door closed, Megan Moore shouted that she was reporting West's complete lack of cooperation to Roland Fosco. She accused West of impeding the investigation by coaching members of her team prior to the interviews and by not having the interview rooms ready.

Nila West shot back that the meeting was a debrief of the morning's drug raid, standard procedure, and had nothing to do with the interviews. She said she was highly offended and would lodge her own complaint through her boss, Cliff Metzger.

Megan responded that she welcomed the challenge, that when she was done with her investigation, West would be looking for work in the private sector...if she wasn't in prison.

While the cat fight continued in the office, Vince Mercado walked up to Peden with a smug grin. "If you're in my interview, I'm not saying a word. I'm not giving you the chance to screw me like you did your FBI buds."

Peden, seemingly relaxed, smiled back. "You know, Vince, whether I'm there or not, Megan is going to eat your lunch. She'll get to the truth, so you might want to lawyer up now. Save yourself some time."

"Right." Mercado's tone was laced with sarcasm. His face still wore the grin, but his body was tense. "She's a smart lady. She'll know when to quit wasting her time here and look elsewhere for Deming's killer."

Peden's eyebrows shot up. "And where's that, Vince?"

Mercado inched closer. Peden could smell his breath and aftershave. He'd apparently had time to shower before the meeting in West's office. "She'll figure it out. We bust big time dealers all the time. That would probably be a good place to start. These punks are getting out of prison every week now, so there're a number of low-life scumbags to choose from."

"Yeah, I'm sure. But in this country, we're not supposed to 'choose' who's guilty. There's this pesky thing called 'due process.' Something you should have learned in Law Enforcement 101."

Mercado tried to maintain his façade. The smile was still in place, but his jawbone was tight and a blood vessel in his temple pulsed. He moved in another few inches and said in a low, barely controlled voice, "Shame you're trying to frame the good guys. There's plenty of scum out there that needs our attention."

Peden leaned towards Mercado so that his nose nearly touched Mercado's cheek. "Vince, you back away from me right now or I'll make you cry like a little girl in front of your team."

Mercado backed up slightly, the smile now gone. After a few seconds, he turned and started down the hall. Under his breath, Peden heard him say, "Fuck you. Snitch."

Peden didn't react. He'd heard that and much worse in his career. He figured that Mercado had something to do with Deming's murder. Maybe he wasn't the shooter, but he believed that Mercado knew who the shooter was. From Peden's perspective, the outward attitude was a bit cocky, but he was wound too tight to be completely innocent.

Peden turned towards Nila West's office. The verbal

jousting was still in progress, but the tone was lower. Megan appeared to have the upper hand, which didn't surprise him. Three minutes later, Megan opened the office door and told Peden that Ms. West would be personally guiding them to the interview rooms.

* * *

The five interviews took nearly five hours. They started with Peter Nichols, the most junior of the agents. Initially, he appeared self-confident, even arrogant. When Megan was through with him, the look on his face was one of concern for his future.

At one point, he asked if he could talk with Mercado. Megan berated him for nearly five minutes, starting with his complete lack of law enforcement training. Did he not understand how criminal case interviews were conducted? Her last question to Nichols was if he or any of his peers had ever falsified arrest reports. Even though he denied it, Nichols' near panicked look told them otherwise.

Next was Alex Smith. He was a much harder nut to crack. Throughout the interview he maintained the stone-faced, serious expression of a military infantryman. His body remained upright, like a statue. He showed no emotion and stared directly back at Megan's eyes when answering …except when he was lying. Then his eyes moved to a point just above her head.

Next came Marcus Cook. When Megan asked to question Cook, Nila West seemed surprised. She recovered and called Agent Cook to the interview room.

When Marcus sat at the table, Megan began exactly as she had with Nichols and Smith…no nonsense, just pointed questions. Marcus answered each question in kind. No nonsense, straight faced, serious. There was no outward indication that Marcus knew Megan or Peden. The exchange became confrontational at one point, Cook taking exception to Megan's insinuation that the DEA team was dirty. The interview went on for over forty minutes, at which point, Marcus left the interview room, appearing angry and offended.

Sweat poured from his forehead.

When he passed Vince Mercado in the hall, he quietly remarked, "That is one tough bitch."

Mercado replied, "She's not the one you have to worry about. Savage will smile and shake your hand while he's twisting the knife in your back."

"Yeah, well, they got zilch from me." He took a deep breath for effect. "You're up."

"Good job, Marcus." He patted his fellow agent on the shoulder as he headed towards the interview room.

Marcus maintained his outward appearance, but smiled to himself. He had a pretty good idea that he'd passed the last test to take Deming's position on the team.

* * *

Vince Mercado entered the interview room as if he owned the building and was doing Moore and Savage a favor. He looked from Peden to Megan, then closed the door behind him. He remained silent, standing just inside the door, challenging either one of them to tell him to sit. No one in the room spoke, the only sounds were of each of the agents breathing and the quiet stir of a paper that Megan was reading.

Megan hadn't looked up from the file folder on the table in front of her. She appeared to be nearing the end of a full-page report. She acted as if she didn't care if Mercado sat or stood, or if he was in the room at all.

After nearly five full minutes, Moore, still looking at the papers in front of her, said, "Mr. Savage, turn on the recorder."

Savage did.

"I am Agent Megan Moore of the Federal Bureau of Investigation. Also present in this interview is Peden Savage of Savage Investigative Consultants, and Agent Vincent Mercado, Drug Enforcement Administration. It is Thursday, 6:40 PM, June 18, 2015. Agent Mercado is being interviewed regarding events before, during, and after the murder of Agent Jarrod Deming.

"Agent Mercado, please acknowledge that the previous

statement by me is correct."

Mercado, still standing, shrugged his shoulders, indifference written all over his face and body language. "Sure."

Megan finally looked up at the agent, smiled and said, "Agent Mercado, you know that this is an official record. If you want to come off as being some arrogant jerk when I take this to a judge, that's up to you. Right now, we're looking at a potential murder charge for you and a number of your team members. If you want to blow off this interview, be my guest. It's your prerogative." She paused for several seconds. "Would you like us to start over?"

Mercado knew that he could have Newsome steer the case to Judge Stillwell, so he wasn't particularly concerned. "No, let's just continue, Agent Moore. Yeah, the opening you gave on this recording is correct, but I object to Savage participating in this interview. If he remains, I will not answer any questions."

"Fine." Megan turned to Peden and nodded towards the door.

Peden left the room. When the door closed, he heard Megan say, "For the record, Mr. Savage has left the room. Agent Mercado, are you ready to continue?"

"Sure."

Mercado pulled out his chair and sat, appearing relaxed.

* * *

Peden listened to the interview on a small earpiece with excellent sound quality.

Megan's first question, "Agent Mercado, why did you receive a general discharge from the Army?"

Mercado nearly left his chair and shouted, "What the fuck are you talking about? I was honorably discharge. Where did you get that crap from?"

Megan didn't even flinch. She quietly asked Mercado to sit back down.

Peden wished he had popcorn and a beer. This was going to be fun.

Chapter 18

At 9:20 PM, with the remnants of two submarine sandwiches pushed to the side, Megan and Peden watched the recording of her interview of Agent Vincent Mercado. Peden's vow to eat a healthier diet was going to have to wait for another day.

Agent Mercado's image filled the fifty-five-inch TV screen. Within minutes of entering the room, Mercado wasn't nearly as cocky as when he had first entered. A sheen of sweat glistened on his forehead.

They were looking for information that would help them find Jarrod Deming's killer. Even with Megan's typical, ultra-serious posture, Peden could tell she was enjoying the déjà-vu moment.

Mercado's voice came over the speakers, his hands animated for emphasis as he said, "I was standing with my team about two hundred feet from Deming right before he was shot." He leaned back and moved his right hand, balled into a fist, to his temple. He was looking at Megan, never looking directly at the camera.

"Which members of your team were with you?"

Either Megan's question caught Mercado off guard or he was pretending that it was a stupid question. There was a lengthy silence. While he thought about his answer, his forehead wrinkled and the slightest of smiles crossed his face, his right fist still against his temple.

Megan asked, "Did you want me to repeat the question?"

"No, Ms. Moore. I…"

"You will address me as Agent Moore unless you want to continue this interview at our office in Atlanta, or Washington, D.C. Now, which team members were with you?"

A loud sigh came over the speakers as he leaned

forward, placing both hands in front of him on the table, then he answered, "Smith and Nichols."

"Was Agent Cook with you?"

"No, just Smith and Nichols."

"Was Agent Cook at the press conference?"

"Not that I'm aware."

"Isn't he a member of your team?"

"Yes, he is." Mercado's voice gave away his irritation with the line of questions about Agent Cook.

"Can you account for his whereabouts during the time of the shooting?"

In a loud voice with a large measure of impatience, Mercado explained, "No I can't. Why didn't you ask him while he was in here?"

"I did. I just wanted to see if you knew…being the team lead." She paused then asked, "Were you aware that Agent Cook, like you, also received a less than honorable discharge from the Army?"

At this, Mercado sat up straight and glared at Megan. "First, Agent Moore, I was discharged with honor from the Army. Second, we, the DEA, meticulously screen our recruits. There is no way he left the military with a less than honorable discharge."

Megan paused the video. She looked at Peden. "Marcus is an outsider to this group, but I think he's going to get an invite to take Deming's place real soon. We just have to make sure that the DEA doesn't get their hands on his real file."

Cook's official personnel file from the Army contained multiple commendation letters and glowing FITREPS, or fitness reports. Anyone reading the file would know that Marcus Cook was a stand-up individual who did things by the book. It was the second time Megan had thrown the bait of Mercado's less than honorable discharge in his face. Both times, he responded angrily, but with a hint of concern.

It was obvious that he believed his military records were cleansed of any negative information, but they could see that he wasn't absolutely certain. There was no way to prove otherwise…or so Mercado thought.

Mercado's military file had been purged of negative information, replaced with an honorable discharge and a number of letters of commendation describing acts of bravery and courage, none of which were true. A few, well-placed phone calls provided Megan with the truth about Vince Mercado's military career. During the interview, her eyes drilled into Mercado's as he was thinking back to his personnel file, worrying that something was missed.

Megan said to Peden, "Let's move on."

She clicked the play button. Her voice came over the speakers in Peden's office. "What did you do with Agent Deming's notes, the ones he had in his hands when he was shot?"

Again, Mercado looked at Megan as if she'd grown a third eye. "I got no idea what you're talking about. Never saw any papers."

"You said that you were two hundred feet from Deming at the time of the shooting. Right?"

"I said 'about two hundred feet,' and I wanted to hear his allegations for myself. But I didn't *see* him do anything. We could barely see his head above the crowd."

"Agent Smith said he had a clear view of Agent Deming. Were you and Agent Smith at different locations?"

Mercado answered immediately, his tone angry. "As I've already stated, Smith, Nichols, and I were together. He must have had a break in the crowd from his angle, but I could not see Deming from where I stood."

"I've seen the videos. Deming was standing on the steps in front of the office. Anyone there had an unobstructed view down to at least his waist. If you were looking at him, you would have seen him pull out some notes. Did you see them?"

"I already told you! No I did not!"

Megan hit the pause button again. "I think he was telling the truth at this point. He wasn't all smug and sarcastic."

Peden thought, *Why was Mercado the only one who hadn't seen the notes? Where was he looking if not at Deming, especially since he had such a keen interest in what Deming had to say?*

Savage believed that everyone's attention would be focused on Deming at that moment. He wondered if any of the news footage might have caught Mercado and his team and their exact location.

He suggested, "Lee should review the TV stations' videos and verify Mercado's story."

"It's a long shot. But why?"

"Maybe we'll be able to tell if he has a clear line of sight to Deming. One of them could have taken the shot while the other two covered for them."

Megan countered, "But they said they were to Deming's front-right. That wouldn't be the right position based on the autopsy results. The shooter was definitely to Deming's front-left. Maybe Mercado was looking at the shooter and that's why he didn't see the papers. Maybe they hired a shooter."

"Too many 'maybes' in that equation, but there's got to be a simple explanation. One of which could be that Mercado is lying."

"I think he's lying about any number of things. Anyway, let's move on to Nila West before I get too tired."

Peden looked at the ancient clock. It was nearing 10:00 PM. He asked, "Want any coffee or a soda?"

"Don't you mean 'a pop?' You're from Ohio, if I recall."

"Yeah, but I'm trying to get into the Georgia lingo." He smiled and raised his eyebrows, as if to repeat the question.

"Just water."

When Peden returned to the office with Megan's water and a coffee for himself, Megan said, "Watch her eyes immediately after I ask the first question. You tell me what you think."

She hit the play button and forwarded the recording to the start of the interview with Nila West.

Once Megan was through with the preliminaries, she

asked Agent West, "What did you do with Agent Deming's notes from the press conference?"

She hit the pause button, then looked towards Peden for his reaction.

He stated, "Panic. Just for a second. She recovered quickly."

* * *

The interview with Nila West took nearly an hour. The momentary panic didn't surface again. Her responses were calm, without emotion. She was one cool customer even with Megan's direct, almost hostile manner. Peden could see why she'd been placed in a position of authority. She maintained an outward appearance of control, far from the statuesque facade of Alex Smith or the smug, arrogance of Vince Mercado. She was all business. Considering her earlier jousts with Megan over the rooms, Nila West was the essence of professionalism during her interview.

It was nearing 11:00 PM. Both Peden and Megan were feeling the stress of a very long day. He shut off the playback deck, stood and stretched, tired, but jittery from too much coffee.

He jumped when his cell phone belted out a Ted Nugent song. *Maybe I should change that ringer.*

He looked at the screen. It was Lee Sparks. "Hey, Lee."

"Late night?"

"Yeah. Megan and I just finished reviewing the DEA interviews.

"Good timing then. I just sent you the link to the full videos from the day of the shooting. Was there anything in particular that you were looking for? Maybe I can help you get to it."

Peden asked, "Did you happen to see any of the DEA agents in any of the videos?"

Sparks answered right away. "Yeah. The three guys, Mercado, Smith, and Nichols are behind the crowd. If you look at the clips from Channel 8, there's a spot at the very front of the test portion where you can see all three of them."

Savage's expression was intense. Megan opened her arms with her hands facing up as if asking, "Well?"

Peden held up his pointer finger, telling Megan to wait just a moment. He asked Sparks, "Relative to Deming, where are they?"

"If you're asking what I think you're asking, they're standing by a row of cars about a hundred and fifty to two hundred feet from Deming, to the left of the crowd."

"Do you mean to Deming's left or right?"

"From Deming's standpoint, it would be to his right."

Peden's shoulders sagged realizing that none of the agents could be the shooter. He thought of another question. "How far in advance of the start of the news conference was this video taken?"

"Like less than two minutes."

Peden thought there might have been time for any one of the agents to change positions and take the shots, but that would have been pretty ballsy, knowing that cameras were running.

He asked Lee, "Can you account for those three after Deming was shot?"

"Yeah, Peden. Once one of the cameramen got their shit together, all three were attending to either Deming or Nila West. None of those three took the shots. It doesn't mean they weren't involved, but they couldn't have been the shooter."

The silence went on for several seconds. Sparks said, "I know you're disappointed. Sorry."

Peden sighed, "Yeah, me two."

Megan chimed in, "Me three."

Chapter 19

Vincent Mercado pulled the black Chevy Caprice into the parking lot of the Sam Snead's Tavern near the Savannah-Hilton Head International Airport. The plan was for a quick meeting.

From the front passenger seat, Andrew Newsome's nervous demeanor was as if he expected a SWAT team to pop out of nowhere and surround the vehicle. Mercado glanced at him, hoping that he'd get the message to calm down. Their passenger might notice Newsome's anxiety, potentially giving him an advantage. But they held the trump card: Peter Vega.

From the back seat, their lone passenger, United States Senator Armand Vega, sat quietly. If he was nervous, he didn't show it. Mercado watched the senator from the moment he stepped off the Gulfstream G650ER executive jetliner. He was calm, as if he were ordering dinner, or relaxing after a long day on the golf course. Since his arrival in Savannah, he had shown no weakness – a perfect poker face. The only words spoken since he stepped on the tarmac at Executive Airport were *Let's get on with it*.

Mercado parked the car along the lake that bordered the golf course to the west. He left the engine and the air conditioning running. Judge Stillwell had given Newsome the responsibility to make the deal with the Senator. He feared Newsome would hyperventilate and pass out.

From the back seat of the Caprice, Vega asked, "Was my son physically harmed?"

Mercado waited for Newsome to answer. When Newsome remained silent, Mercado answered, "He's fine. He's been separated from his business partners…"

"Agent Mercado, get to the point. Exactly what is he

charged with?"

Newsome finally spoke. In a confident voice, he said, "Senator, your son is not charged yet. He will be charged later this morning, pending the outcome of this meeting. The charges will be felony-level offenses of trafficking in marijuana, cocaine, methamphetamine, and heroin, with a mandatory prison term of ten years and a fine of $200,000. Even before he is arraigned, the media will have access to his name and the associated charges. They will undoubtedly piece together his family relationship. There will be a firestorm of..."

Vega cut him off in a booming, baritone voice. "Mr. Newsome, I'm well aware of the publicity that will follow. My time is limited. I have only two questions."

Mercado and Newsome both had the same thought. *This guy doesn't waste any time.*

"First, what do ya'll want? Second, when can I see my son?"

Andrew Newsome overcame his bout of anxiety. In a matter-of-fact tone, he laid out the terms of the deal. He added that there was no negotiation and it was good until he exited the car.

First, the Senator was to change his stand on funding for the DEA, including a modest increase. Second, he would pay one and a half million dollars in small, unmarked bills as a show of "good faith." The details of the money transfer would be delivered at a later date in order to give him time to assemble the cash. And third, no one, except the three of them in the car, was to know the details of the deal. If word leaked out, they would know he or someone from his office was the source, and the deal was off. His son would be prosecuted. His political career would be in jeopardy.

Once he agreed to the terms, his son would be released to his custody. No paperwork would be filed. After one year, he would receive all of the original documents of the arrest. It would be up to him what to do with them.

"The others involved in the bust?"

"They will not be charged."

Vega smiled slightly and bent his head down. He had only one other comment. "Ya'll aren't the only ones involved in this. Who else knows?"

Newsome flinched slightly. It was 'the tell' that Vega needed. These two weren't pulling the strings. Someone else was the puppet master.

Mercado said, "Nobody else is involved. You have our word."

Without batting an eye, Senator Armand Vega agreed to the terms.

* * *

The Gulfstream G650ER quickly rose to cruising altitude at forty-one thousand feet. At this altitude, above the clouds and away from any turbulence, the flight was smooth. The pilot announced the flight time to their destination and that the passengers, all three of them, should sit back and enjoy the flight.

That was unlikely for two of the three.

When the Senator's aide, Michael Jess, asked if he or his son wanted anything, the Senator said, "No, Mike, but please give us a moment alone."

"Yes, sir."

With that, Jess moved forward in the jet and closed the door, effectively separating the Senator and his son from the other four people on board.

The Senator turned to Peter Vega, who was dreading this moment. Peter, his face pale with dark, baggy circles under dull eyes, leaned forward with his hands on his knees, the tension evident. Sleep had been elusive since the bust. His crop of dull, red hair was a mess and he needed a shower.

When Peter started to speak, his father raised his hand to stop him. Peter sank back in his seat. He looked aft away from his father's stare.

Peter was not a rebellious young man. He did test his parent's limits of behavior when younger, but he was a decent student. Aside from a bit of alcohol and marijuana use, he was generally a good kid. But being the son of a United States

Senator, the expectations set by his parents were very high.

The compartment was quiet for several minutes, the only sound being the twin jet engines. Armand Vega was gathering his thoughts, keeping his anger in check. He hoped his son would listen. Maybe the arrest and threat of a long prison sentence had scared him enough to humble the young man.

Finally, he said, "First, son, your mother and I love you, unconditionally." He paused, measuring his next words. "I need to know exactly what happened during the bust, and I mean everything."

"Dad, we didn't have all the dope and money that the cops said we had."

"First, it was the DEA. They're a federal agency, not local cops. Second, this is very serious. So please be as specific as you can."

Peter hated it when his dad tried to take everything line by line. Why couldn't they just talk it out? But having been arrested and facing hard time, Peter figured that he should follow his father's lead.

"Alright, Dad. Here's what happened. We did have some pot. It was less that a dime bag, about ten grams. We normally have more than that, sometimes up to an ounce, but it's all for personal use."

"You had no other drugs?"

"None."

"How about your friends, did they have any quantity of drugs?"

Peter looked like he was getting agitated. He emphatically insisted, "No. When I said we've never had more than an ounce, I mean all of us combined. We just don't keep that much around." He paused. Then, as if a light came on, he said, "This was a total set up. They did this to get to you."

The slightest of smiles lit on Armand Vega's face. It appeared that his son was finally getting it. The years of preaching and coaching finally came together in this one moment. From that point on, Peter Vega told his dad everything that happened that early morning, from the moment that the agents knocked the apartment door off its hinges until he was separated from his friends at the jail.

He went on about how they had to do something about the corrupt agents when his father said in a deadly serious tone, "Ya'll must never speak of this to anyone. Ya'll, you and your friends, are free with no charges. But if word of this leaks out, felony trafficking charges will be filed. All ya'll will be hauled back to jail. Do you understand?"

"But we can't just do nothing!" Peter's voice was filled with indignation. In his youthful mind, these men shouldn't get away with this. They should be brought up on charges and tried in the courts. It was the *American Way.*

"Don't worry, son. They won't get away with this, but ya'll have to trust me on this. You, and they, cannot say another word about this." The lines on the Senator's face tightened, his eyes burned into his son's. "Believe me when I tell you this. This is a matter of life and death. Ya'll *must* stay out of this and never speak to anyone else about what happened. Am I making myself clear?"

Peter Vega saw something in his father's eyes that he'd never seen before. It sent a chill up his spine. For the first time in his life, he understood that his father dealt with far more important issues than he had ever imagined. He felt a twinge of guilt for being such a thorn in his side.

"Yeah, Dad, crystal clear."

* * *

Peden Savage parked his dark blue Chevy Tahoe in the parking lot of ReMax Realty on Park of Commerce Way. He had a direct view of the front of the   Drug Enforcement Administration building where Jarrod Deming was gunned down. From this point, a skilled sniper could easily have made the kill shots, but this position was not the correct angle to where Deming stood.

He pulled his Tahoe out of the parking lot, turned right and into the lot of an insurance agency facing the DEA building. A stand of young pines partially obscured the view, but the angle appeared to be correct.

Peden rubbed the scar over his left eye, wondering how someone could determine in advance where Deming's press conference would be held. How could they be assured of a clear shot on Deming when the location wasn't announced until the morning of the conference? The shooter had to know the details of the location. Or they had to be mobile enough to quickly change positions, set up and shoot quickly, then escape the scene without being detected. From where he parked, he believed that he was close to the position from where the shots were fired. In his mind, he drew a line from where Deming was shot to this parking lot. The shooter had to have been set up somewhere along that line…unless the shots were fired from further away.

Wow. That would be one hell of a great shot…no, four shots.

Peden turned away from where Deming stood and looked down his imaginary line. A new office building stood approximately six hundred feet from his Tahoe. The first floor of the building was occupied by a cellular phone business. The second floor of the building had three windows with no blinds or curtains. At first glance, the office space appeared to be empty. From that height on the second floor, there would be nothing obstructing the line of fire.

Peden turned on the DVD player in the console of his Tahoe and played the video from one of the news cameras. He started at about ten seconds before the news conference was to start. He saw Deming get the nod from the man on his left, then from Nila West to his right. He then pulled the notes from his suit. Finally, he looked up and made a slight move to his right, maybe half a foot. Peden stepped the video back a few seconds and watched again. He clicked forward fractions of a second at a time. The nods. The notes. Deming's eyes. The move to the right.

His eyes widened in surprise the instant before he moved.

What did you see, Jarrod? Why did you move?

Chapter 20

Twenty-two cars lined the edge of Flinn Drive on the Isle of Hope on a dark, cloudy Friday morning. Friends, coworkers, dignitaries from law enforcement agencies, and Elizabeth Sanchez had come to pay their respects to the widow of Jarrod Deming just three days after his murder.

Mourners gathered in the living room, kitchen, or back porch, dressed in dark clothing, speaking in hushed tones, uttering their amazement that a fine man was murdered in such a callous manner. A memorial was erected in the library, the centerpiece being a fourteen by eleven, framed studio picture of Jarrod on a tripod, a wreath of flowers below the photo. The tripod was placed in front of the wall containing Jarrod's diplomas, certificates, and licenses.

Sylvia spent most of the morning standing or sitting next to Jarrod's photo with her close friend, Elizabeth, at her side. Those arriving at the home were directed first into the library to pay their respects. From there, they were directed to the dining area to partake in the spread of appetizers and drinks. A few of Jarrod's former team members were in the backyard drinking beer and smoking cigarettes.

Sylvia whispered to Elizabeth, "I really, really hate this."

"I know, Sissy. This has to be tough for you."

"I mean, I don't know ninety percent of them. They're mostly Jarrod's buddies from the DEA or some big-shots from one government agency or another. They're in my house. Most of them could care less that Jarrod was killed." She paused and took a deep breath. "They're just performing some official duty."

Elizabeth didn't have an answer, so she put her arm

around her friend's shoulder. She figured that Sylvia appreciated her just being there. She was glad that she'd made the call, hooking up with her after all these years. She wondered how lonely it must have been for Sylvia not having any close friends nearby. She'd sensed her isolation from the moment she stepped into her home.

Finally, Elizabeth assured, "It'll be over before you know it. Just let me know what I can do to help."

Sylvia put her hand on Elizabeth's and squeezed. She looked up, tears welling in her eyes and mouthed, "Thank you."

Elizabeth pulled her friend closer.

There was a break in the flow of guests to the library and Sylvia took the opportunity to turn to her friend and say, "You know, Liz, Jarrod wasn't the perfect husband. He spent long hours on the job and went out with 'the guys' a lot over the years. I'm pretty sure that he had affairs, too." Her eyes welled up again as she told her friend about her husband's failings. She grabbed a tissue from a nearby box and blew her nose. "But he didn't deserve to die like this."

Elizabeth thought back on the incident in their dorm room when Jarrod had made a clumsy pass at her. There never would be a good time to reveal that episode to her friend. She said, "You're right Sis. Maybe he wasn't perfect, but I know he adored you."

Sylvia's mind seemed to drift far away. Her face twisted into a frown, then she tensed and squeezed Elizabeth's hand. Her eyes refocused on her friend. Tears began to flow anew, but Sylvia's face bore the start of a smile. She pulled Elizabeth into a tight hug. "Thanks, Liz. You're the best."

* * *

Nila West sat in her car inspecting her makeup, hair, eyes, and her black pants and coat. Her plan was to get in, make her official visit, pay her respects, and get out. With the suit she'd chosen, she could head straight for the office.

She hadn't slept well the night before. Dread filled her evening, knowing that she had to face Jarrod Deming's widow for the first time since the agent was killed. Her right hand instinctively went to her left forearm where a flesh-tone bandage covered the bullet wound from the day of the shooting. She took a prescription pain pill before leaving her house, but it had yet to take effect. The combination of the slight throbbing in her arm and the tension from the wake had her wondering whether she should head home.

A knock on her car window startled her. Her boss, Cliff Metzger, stood under a dark umbrella in a light drizzle, looking down at her. He motioned for her to roll down her window.

When she did, he asked, "Are you ready to head inside?"

Through frazzled nerves, she smiled and replied, "Yes. I was just checking…you know."

"Why are you so tense? We're just here to pay our respects for a fallen coworker. Nothing more."

The last thing Nila West wanted to do was walk into the wake with Cliff Metzger. She was concerned that her subordinates might get the wrong impression. She had worked hard over the years to ensure that there was not even a hint that she'd slept her way up the ladder. It wasn't necessarily true, as she had covertly dated men in key positions within the DEA, but she had convinced herself that the handful of trysts had nothing to do with her upward mobility.

She took a deep breath and put on her tough agent persona. "I'm not tense, but if I was, I'd have pretty good reason to be. We have a killer out there preying on DEA agents, an FBI investigation looking at our team, and I know you're getting pressure from your boss to get this wrapped up immediately. So, if you think I'm a bit rattled, I am, but I can handle it." She nodded her head towards the Deming house and said, "I just want to get this over with and get back to work."

She raised her window and stepped out of her car. She moved under Metzger's umbrella and they moved down the line of cars to Sylvia Deming's driveway. They were greeted at the door by a man wearing a black suit. He directed them towards the library.

A number of DEA employees were standing in the living room off the entryway across from the library. When West and Metzger came into view, a noticeable hush filled the room. Heads turned towards the recent arrivals. Nila West's anxiety jumped, but she maintained a stoic outward appearance. Metzger gave the crowd a quick glance, then he and West headed into the library.

* * *

As she and Sylvia hugged, Elizabeth noticed the couple enter the room. She whispered to her friend, "You have guests."

A tall gentleman walked towards them, arm-in-arm with a beautiful, but serious looking woman. Elizabeth noticed Sylvia's expression change in an instant from the sad smile to anger, then to the grieving widow.

The man spoke first. "Mrs. Deming, I'm Cliff Metzger. I was Jarrod's Regional Director. We're all very sorry for your loss. Jarrod was a top notch agent with a promising future. It will be difficult to find a capable replacement with his level of skill. I know you don't care about that. Your loss is so much greater than that. You have my, and the agencies, sincere condolences."

"Thank you Mr...."

"Cliff, please."

"Thank you, Cliff."

Sylvia's eyes immediately shifted to the woman, who was several inches taller than her. Elizabeth noticed that the long, sad face again made a brief, but noticeable shift to a tense, angry expression, then back to the mournful widow.

The woman held out her hand and took Sylvia's in hers. "I'm Nila West, I was Jarrod's direct supervisor. I also share Cliff's feelings that Jarrod was one of the best agents on our team. We're doing everything that we can to help the FBI apprehend his killer."

"Thank you, Nila. Jarrod told me about you." She paused for several seconds, the silence lingering. Nila West's eyes widened slightly as if nearing a panic, then Sylvia continued, "He said you were a great boss, tough but fair.

Thank you."

Nila let her breath out slowly, trying to keep her expression as neutral as possible. She didn't know what to say next, so she simply said, "We're so very sorry for your loss."

When she tried to turn away, Sylvia said, "Wait," and grabbed her arm at the bandaged spot. The pain shot up West's arm to her shoulder causing her whole body to tense. She gritted her teeth as she pulled her arm away and nearly collapsed. Metzger quickly grabbed her around the waist, keeping her from falling to the wood floor.

Sylvia pulled her hands back. She appeared alarmed and in a startled voice apologized, "I am so sorry. I didn't know you were hurt. What happened?"

West was taking deep breaths. "I was shot the day your husband was killed. I was standing behind him at the press conference."

"I'm so sorry." She covered her mouth with both hands. "You could have been killed."

Nila assured, "Mrs. Deming, I'm fine. My wound is healing, no permanent damage. I wish we could say that about your husband."

Nila turned to Cliff Metzger. "We should go." Then to Sylvia, she said, "Again, Jarrod was a good man and a fine agent. We will miss him."

Sylvia just nodded.

* * *

At 11:30 AM, a number of guests began to leave, stopping to convey one last word of comfort to the grieving widow. The crowd had dwindled to ten mourners, including Sylvia's sister and Elizabeth Sanchez. Jarrod's old team came in from the backyard and stopped in the library to pay their final respects. The remaining visitors took the cue and left.

Sylvia's sister offered to stay and help clean up, but Sylvia told her that the caterer was taking care of everything. After a brief moment of uncomfortable silence, she gave Sylvia a kiss on the cheek and headed out the front door.

Elizabeth and Sylvia took a collective deep breath and

headed for the kitchen. Elizabeth asked, "Can I get you anything? You really need to eat something."

"Yeah, Liz. Order us a pizza and let's have a beer, like back at the dorm."

Elizabeth smiled. Then she thought about the weird encounter with Nila West and asked, "What was the deal with Jarrod's boss."

"You noticed, huh?"

"Kind of hard not to."

With a tired, defeated look she stated, "She was fucking Jarrod."

Once Elizabeth picked her jaw up off the floor, she said, "I'll get us a couple beers and order that pizza."

Chapter 21

The interior of The Village Bar and Grille was spacious with a couple dozen tables and booths arranged around a "U"-shaped, raised counter. The air was filled with the aroma of grilled beef. Flat screen TVs seemed to cover every possible viewing angle. Vaulted ceilings with large, exposed beams gave the bar an open feel. Light, natural wood flooring and pale yellow paint above light tongue and groove wainscot added to the bar's pleasant atmosphere.

Seated at a table away from the entrance, Mercado, Smith, and Nichols ordered different craft beers, shrimp skewers for an appetizer, and steaks for their entrées. They took the rest of Friday off after Jarrod Deming's wake, with Nila West's reluctant approval. Anyone coming through the doors would take one look at the three large, muscle-bound men and assume that they were members of law enforcement, maybe off duty military. It was impossible for the three to go unnoticed. They weren't concerned about the attention, but they wanted to be away from the DEA office and West. They also wanted to avoid the downtown courthouse where Judge Stillwell was holding court and Andrew Newsome was reviewing the reports of his Assistant District Attorneys.

Mercado said, "We've got to replace Deming...and fast. Stillwell's keeping the pressure up and Newsome doesn't have the balls to stand up to him. We're out there risking our asses, dealing with all kinds of shit while they sit on their asses behind their desks." He looked from Smith to Nichols. "That's bullshit."

Smith sat like a statue, his face serious and solid as if molded in place. Nichols appeared nervous, picking at his fingernails, his jaw tight, pronounced wrinkles in his forehead.

Smith asked, "Tell me who you have in mind and I'll tell you if I agree."

Mercado turned slightly from side to side, checking to see if anyone was within earshot. "Cook."

His fellow agents didn't have any visible reaction. Mercado continued, "I did some checking. He was Special Forces, did a couple tours in Iraq. Was awarded a handful of commendations, but then he got booted out for shooting up a village. He told his command that the villagers were cooperating with Al Qaeda, but they didn't believe him. Slapped him with a general discharge. He's good with a long gun, won several marksmanship awards. He was considered for sniper school, but the village incident happened first."

Mercado again looked from Smith to Nichols and waited. Smith took a deep breath, though he hardly moved. "Cook's the guy I was thinking of, seems like he'd be a good fit. But what makes you think he'd go along?"

"Several things. He's good at what he does. We know him. That deal in Iraq, he believes his country betrayed him, at least that's how I'd feel. I think we could feel him out, see if he balks at any point. If he does, we stop and find another guy. It would be pretty easy to talk with him about what we do without letting him in too deep." Mercado again looked hard at Smith. "If we bring in a totally new guy, it'll take forever to screen him. Cook has similar military backgrounds to the three of us. With the black mark on his record, it would be easy to convince him that this is one way his country could repay him.

"Another thing. During my interview with that bitch, Moore, she was asking a lot of questions about Cook's whereabouts when Deming got shot. It was like they were trying to pin the shoot on him. I thought that maybe they already knew something about him, that maybe he was high on their short list of inside guys. I don't know why they would suspect Cook, but I let them know that he was nowhere near the office when Deming was killed."

Smith asked, "Since you brought that up, you got any ideas on who the shooter is? I mean, I was ready to do it, and it saved us the trouble, but I think we need to know."

Mercado said, "Hold on." He nodded in the direction of their waitress, who was bringing their beers.

When the glasses were distributed, the waitress said that their appetizer would be out soon. She smiled, turned, and headed back towards the kitchen, her backside followed closely by three sets of eyes.

Mercado waited until she was out of sight. "I don't know who did it, but I do know who we're going to pin it on. We can deal with the real shooter later, in our own way."

Smith asked, "Are you thinking about that Cleaver kid?"

"Yeah. What do you think?"

"It's a stretch," Smith commented. "I'm not sure about the timing of him getting released from Coastal and the time Deming was shot. Might be questions on how it was possible for him to get out, get a gun, set up, shoot and get away …unless he had help."

"We'll build that into the warrant, if we go for it. Plus, I know some folks at Coastal. We can make sure their release logs meet our needs." Mercado looked at Nichols. "You look awful nervous, Pete. What's on your mind?"

Pete Nichols did indeed look nervous. Not wanting to make waves, Nichols replied, "Nothing Vince. I'm okay with bringing in Cook."

"Then what's got you rattled?"

"That FBI Agent…Megan Moore. She rode me pretty good. She makes me nervous, like she knows what I'm thinking."

Mercado smiled, then glanced at Smith who shook his head slightly. Smith turned to Nichols and said in a serious tone, "Don't you worry about her. Their investigation is going to fall flat once we hand them the perp. Plus, we have a backup plan."

Hearing that Smith and Mercado had "a backup plan" to deal with Megan Moore wasn't reassuring.

* * *

The agents were finishing up, leaving their tips when Mercado's phone buzzed in his pocket. He looked at the number and frowned. The only person he knew with a Phoenix, Arizona, area code was Allen Deming. He didn't expect to hear from Jarrod Deming's father ever again. He looked at his partners and said, "I gotta take this."

They nodded and headed for the door.

Mercado hit the answer icon on his cell. "Mercado."

There was silence on the line. Mercado could hear breathing and traffic in the background, but no one said a word.

Finally, Mercado asked, "Deming, is that you?"

"Yeah, Vince, it's me." There was more silence.

"What do you want, Al. I'm busy."

The breathing on Deming's end of the phone got louder and quicker. Mercado was about to tell Allen Deming that he was hanging up when he said, "Why'd ya'll have to kill my kid, Vince? Why'd you do it?"

Mercado wasted no time responding. "Wait a minute, Al. We didn't kill Jarrod. I was at the press conference. So were Smith and Nichols. We were standing together. None of us had a gun. We heard the shots and saw Jarrod hit the pavement. We knew he'd been shot but we didn't have anything to do with it."

"You're a lying son-of-a-bitch. I know you're lying."

Mercado headed for the bar's door. He couldn't take a chance that anyone would hear the conversation.

Once he made it outside, he looked around for any foot traffic. There were a few people strolling along the plaza, but no one close enough to hear.

"Listen to me, Al, I'm telling you the truth. You can check out my story with Smith or Nichols, or even Nila West. We had nothing to do with it. We don't know who it was. We're in the dark as much as you are."

"That's where you're wrong, Vince. I'm not in the dark. I know you did it. You may not have pulled the trigger, but you made it happen. You're as responsible as if you pulled the trigger you...you...lousy..."

"Look man, I don't know what makes you think I did it, but you're wrong. I told you I…"

Deming shouted, "Shut up, Vince! I got proof!" Deming paused while he took a deep breath. In a quieter voice, he said, "I got proof. And I'm going to the FBI with it. Ya hear me? You're toast, Vince! Fuckin' toast!"

"Wait, Al! Wait, don't hang up. I don't know what you think you have, but it can't be proof 'cause I didn't do this." His mind was racing. What could Deming possibly have that would show that he'd shot Jarrod Deming or even ordered him killed? The "proof" had to be manufactured. Sure, he and his team were guilty of planning to do it, but someone beat them to the punch. *Could that be it? Is there something written or recorded that shows we were planning to kill Deming? It's not possible.*

"Al, you'd be a fool to send anything to the FBI because it just isn't true. You can't possibly have anything that would implicate me, or anyone on my team for that matter."

"But I do, smart guy. Don't worry, ya'll'll find out soon enough."

"Al, I'm warning you, you need to talk to me! We can figure this out! Don't go to the FBI! You hear me? You'll regret it!"

"Vince, ya'll can threaten me all ya want. I'm done. Ya killed my sister-in-law, my nephew, and now my son." Deming began to sob. "Ya'll's gonna pay, Vince. All ya'll's gonna pay."

Mercado was about to threaten him, that he wouldn't make it to the FBI alive, but he was listening to silence. He knew that Deming had hung up. He tapped the hang up icon and dropped his phone in his pocket. He was staring out towards the parking lot, but all he could see was Jarrod Deming falling to the ground in front of the DEA office.

He didn't know how long he'd been standing there in a trance, but he shook his head, trying to reset his thoughts. A young woman asked him if he was alright, that he looked pale. He wiped his hand across his forehead realizing that he was sweating. Without saying a word, he turned and started walking slowly towards the parking lot. After a dozen steps, he picked up the pace. He, Smith, and Nichols had a big problem. As usual, they'd have to handle it alone.

Chapter 22

Peden and Megan decided to grab lunch at Debi's Restaurant on West State Street. They walked north along Bull Street from West Liberty to Chippewa Square, passing a handful of tourists snapping pictures of the James Oglethorpe statue. Spanish moss adorned the throng of mature Southern Oaks that provided welcome shade to the square's visitors. Peden asked the woman holding the camera if she would like him to take a group picture. She was delighted and thanked Peden for his thoughtful offer.

After the encounter, they continued their short journey towards the restaurant. The light gray sky continued to darken as the scent of rain filled their senses.

While the stroll was enjoyable, the topic of the conversation was dead serious. Earlier, they'd sat in Peden's car on Flinn Street and watched the guests come and go at Jarrod Deming's wake. There were no surprise guests. Peden had wondered if Allen Deming might make an appearance, but he was true to his word that he would not attend his son's services.

Peden had used a directional microphone from the car, trying to pick up conversations from the mourners as they approached the house and as they returned to their cars. Two comments were of interest to Peden and Megan. First, Vince Mercado and his team planned to take Friday afternoon off after having had a few beers at the wake. At least that's what he told Nila West. He then instructed Smith and Nichols to meet him at the Village Bar and Grille. Peden told Megan that they couldn't risk following the agents. They had to wait for the remaining guests to leave.

The second comment came from Nila West as she and

her boss exited the house. She said to Metzger, "That bitch. She knew why I was wearing that bandage. She grabbed my arm on purpose."

Metzger replied, "Come on Nila. Her husband was just gunned down in cold blood. She's grieving, not thinking straight. Cut her some slack." He paused. "Maybe she suspects that you were sleeping with her husband." A moment of silence passed. When no denial came, he asked, "Were you?"

West replied, "That's ridiculous. It's against the rules. I'm not like you, Cliff. Besides, he wasn't my type."

Megan watched the two as they spoke. She said to Peden, "At first, he rolled his eyes. After that last comment, he frowned. I'm guessing that he's right. She didn't deny it, just made some deflecting comments."

As they walked towards Wright Square past the Juliette Gordon Low House where a Girl Scout troop was about to take a tour, Peden asked about a comment Megan had made about her boss, Roland Fosco, when they saw him approach the Deming house. Fosco was the official representative for the FBI at the wake. When Megan saw him exit his car, she mumbled, "Asshole." Peden wondered what that was about, but opted to wait until they were done with their surveillance to broach the subject.

He asked, "Why'd you call Rollie an asshole?"

Megan stopped next to the William Washington Gordon monument and turned to Peden. She looked both ways. "Yesterday, I asked him if he could set up an interview with Metzger. He said he would. Then, this morning, right after you called about scoping out the wake, he calls and says the Metzger interview isn't going to happen."

Peden's eyebrows shot up in surprise. His face turned to a frown, the question 'why not' written all over it.

Megan explained, "He said that his boss caught wind of his request and told him to stand down, that we were not to interview Metzger or anyone above Nila West. I started to ask him what the hell was going on. He cut me off before I could say two words." She looked up and down Bull Street again, then said, "I thought about going over his head to verify that the order came from higher up, but I thought better of it."

In a sarcastic tone, he asked, "You want me to call my friends at the Bureau?" He smiled because Megan knew he had no connections or friends in the FBI, except her. He said, "Never mind."

As they continued their walk through Wright Square, Peden rubbed the scar over his eye. He went into a trance, thinking about the possible reasons that Fosco would shut Megan down. He nearly ran into a man using palm fronds to make roses and other handmade gifts to pedal to tourists. He apologized and they continued on until they were at West State Street. Megan grabbed his arm before he stepped out into the street in front of a bus.

She scolded him, "Wake up before you get killed!"

He just smiled. They continued crossing the street through the fading cloud of diesel fumes, then angled towards Debi's.

Peden hated to think that his former boss was involved in a cover-up with another federal agency. Roland Fosco was one of the reasons that Peden was able to do business with the FBI despite his being forced out of the Bureau. When no one would work with him, Fosco pulled him aside and gave him the message that the brass at the Bureau planned to trump up charges against him, unless he agreed to keep his mouth shut. Peden had significant evidence that members of the Bureau were railroading suspects with manufactured evidence. He planned to blow the whistle on his fellow agents, but Fosco stepped in and gave him a way out with minimal fanfare. He had assured Peden that the guilty parties would be forced out of the Bureau and he followed through on that promise. The housecleaning was accomplished quietly and efficiently. The press never got wind of the issues. Peden started his own business, which was flourishing.

The only negative was that his former partners talked about his betrayal. Word spread throughout the federal law enforcement family. No one in the rank and file trusted him.

Luckily, he didn't have to do business with them, just their bosses.

As they approached Debi's restaurant, the lunchtime aroma brought Peden out of his trance. He took a deep breath and smiled as he held the door for Megan.

When they were seated, he asked Megan if she believed that Fosco's boss was working with the DEA brass to cover up something bigger. "Maybe this was an inside job. We don't know what Deming was going to say, but it sounded like he was going to blow the whistle on something big."

Megan looked skeptically at Peden as a thin, redheaded, teen waitress with light freckles across her nose approached and set two water glasses on the table.

Peden, in his best Gump accent said, "Hi, Jennay."

With a flirty smile and a sing-song voice, she said, "Hi, Mr. Savage." She turned to Megan. "My name's Jenny, but, like, not the one from the movie."

Megan's expression didn't change. With a deadpan face, she said, "Like, Megan."

Apparently, Jenny didn't catch the dig from Megan and asked about what they'd like to drink.

Peden ordered sweet iced tea. Megan requested lemonade.

The waitress asked, "So, Mr. Savage, are you, like, working on anything, like, top secret or anything?"

He smiled. Again, with a Gump accent he said, "I may have to go to the White House again, and talk with the president again."

Jenny giggled. "Would you like to play a little Forest Gump trivia?"

Peden said, "Uh, not today, Jennay."

"Alright then. Like, I'll get your drinks and be back to get your order."

When Jenny left them alone, they sat quietly, thinking about why Fosco shut down Megan's interview with Metzger. Someone high up was worried. When Jenny was out of earshot, Peden asked, "What do you think Mercado and his buddies are talking about?"

Megan had apparently thought about this already because she immediately answered, "I think they're looking for someone to frame. If they did it, and we're already breathing down their necks, they need a scapegoat right away. I was thinking about how nervous Nichols was during the interview. I think he might break if we keep some pressure on him."

Peden took a sip of water as he thought about Pete Nichols. No doubt he was the weak link. Peden had done some checking. Nichols was relatively new, fresh out of the military, still green for an agent. Maybe he still had ideals about joining the DEA to do the right thing, bust big drug dealers, and clean up the streets of America. Those ideals usually last for a few months before the realities of the job hit you in the face. The daily grind to produce better statistics, bigger busts, and a good sales pitch to increase budgets takes over.

Jenny returned with their drinks, smiling at Peden the entire time. She asked if they were ready to order, but Peden said to give them a few minutes. She smiled. "Sure Mr. Savage." She turned and looked at Megan, then walked off.

Megan looked at Peden, smiled her most plastic smile and in her most sarcastic voice squeaked, "Like, sure, like, Mr. Savage."

He smiled and replied, "You are so cruel. She's just a kid."

"Looking for a sugar daddy."

He smiled back at her and asked, "So, what are you hungry for?"

She smiled and put on her Jenny the waitress voice and asked, "Like, gee, Mr. Savage, like, what would you recommend?"

He shook his head. "I think you'd like chicken salad with the house dressing. I'm getting the club sandwich."

Megan said, "We're reviewing the list of guys who were recently released from prison who were put away by the DEA. We're looking at each one, trying to find anything that points to them as a killer. Most pot dealers aren't killers.

They'd have to be into something heavier. Most of the guys on the list dealt in grass."

Peden began rubbing his eyebrow again. "Here's something that doesn't make sense. Why would a guy looking to get revenge on the dudes who busted him kill the guy on live TV? He had three other agents at the news conference off camera that would have been easy kills, especially for a guy who is obviously a very good shot. He put four slugs in Deming from over a hundred yards. Mercado, Smith, and Nichols were gathered in a tight group. Talking about shootin' fish in a barrel."

"You're right. Doesn't make sense."

"Another thing. In the video clip of Deming right before he was shot, did you see him look up then move to his right. It was a slight move, but it seemed deliberate."

"I noticed, but didn't think too much of it. But if he hadn't moved...wasn't Nila West standing behind him? She was grazed, hit her arm, nothing serious."

"What if Deming wasn't the target?"

Megan frowned. "Meaning Nila West? Why would she be the target? Rumor has it that Deming was going to serve his team up on a platter."

"Yeah, but we still don't know what he planned to say." Peden paused. "I sure wish we could find his notes."

"They're probably in a ditch along Interstate 16 by now."

He shrugged his shoulders. "I hope not."

Chapter 23

The Metallica ring tone from Vince Mercado's cell phone tweaked his already heightened anxiety. *What now? Newsome should be heading home.* After the call from Allen Deming, he needed some down time. Between the FBI's investigation, the pressure from Judge Stillwell to ramp up the bust schedule, and recruiting Deming's replacement, his nerves were shot. He wasn't rattled easily, but he wondered if the money was worth the aggravation.

He had already had three more beers since arriving home. *At least I don't have a wife bugging me.* The persistent grind of the Metallica tune brought him back to the present. He hit the answer icon on his smart phone. "What's up, Andy?"

"Hey, Vince. I hope you're not too relaxed. Stillwell wants to see us at 4:30 at the club."

"Aww man. Shit! What the...I've already had a few beers. I shouldn't be out on the road, much less listening to *His Honor* preach the gospel according to Stillwell. Who else will be there?"

"Just you and me, pal. He's in a foul mood, too. Don't know why."

"Well, just between you and me, we need to talk before we see him. Deming's old man, Al, called me a while ago. It isn't good news."

"Not on the phone. Where do you want to meet?

* * *

The gray clouds had mostly cleared, making way for a hazy, dull blue sky that let in just enough sunlight to jack up the heat. The humidity hammered anyone unable to avoid the outdoors. The Friday afternoon traffic on Skidaway Island was thick with folks heading home, preparing for the weekend. Happy hour was revving up.

Mercado sat in his car, waiting for Newsome to show. He left the car running, taking advantage of the air conditioning. During the short drive, he thought about what the Judge might say. None of it was good. He figured that the pressure would again be ratcheted up. Stillwell had never called a private meeting with anyone other than Newsome, never having direct contact with him or any of his peers. This was a significant change in their communication protocol.

For Stillwell, the change was risky. The meeting, if observed by the wrong people, could implicate the judge if the corrupt nature of the busts came to light. With Stillwell's political ambitions, he could ill afford a tie to any shady dealings.

On the other hand, this opened up a whole new opportunity for Mercado. A certain amount of liability could be deflected. They could now claim that Stillwell and Newsome were the ring leaders. His team was merely following orders.

He shook his head believing that this whole mental exercise was a waste of energy. With luck and planning, it would never become an issue, if he could convince Stillwell that they should slow down a bit.

He knew Stillwell had no intention of backing off. The money was too good and the risk, at least for him, was miniscule. Mercado expected a full court press.

He was rousted from his thoughts by Newsome's tap on the passenger side window. The DA entered and pulled the door shut behind him.

"Sorry to interrupt. You looked like you were in a serious conversation with yourself." He paused, then said, "Man, it feels good in here."

Mercado wasn't in the mood for small talk. He wanted to know if Newsome had any idea why Stillwell called the meeting. Allen Deming's threat was weighing heavily on his mind. He wanted Newsome's thoughts about that situation.

He asked, "So, why does Stillwell want me at this meeting?"

"Us, Vince. He stressed that he wanted us there together."

"I don't take orders from him. What if I blow him off? You can tell him that I'm not meeting with him." He shook his head. "This isn't good, Andy. We, the judge and me, shouldn't be seen together. You know that."

Newsome was already tense. Now Mercado was threatening to back out of a meeting called by one of the most politically powerful men in the county, maybe even the state? He didn't need the stress either, but he wasn't about to snub the judge. He called the meeting, so he must have a damn good reason. It was in both their interests to hear what *His Honor* had to say. As for Mercado saying that Stillwell wasn't his boss...that may be true in a purely legal sense, but Mercado knew all too well that Stillwell called the shots.

"Vince, you're not leaving me hanging here. There's too much at stake for us both. I walk in there without you and Stillwell will go off the deep end." He took a deep breath and continued. "Let's hear him out. You've never heard him in a closed door meeting. I have. He's going to showboat a little. Let him rant. He'll deliver his message and then we," he pointed at the two of them, "can meet again after the dust settles. Then we can plan our next move."

Maybe it was the extra beers, but Mercado wasn't planning on taking any crap from the judge, taking a scolding like he was some junior high school kid. Then he remembered Allen Deming's phone call. The club where they were to meet Stillwell was only minutes away and it was almost 4:25. They had time but Mercado didn't want to keep the judge waiting. According to Newsome, he was already cranky. No sense poking the bear.

"I'll make this quick. Deming's call. He says he has proof that I killed Jarrod."

"What?! He was in Arizona. What could he possibly have?"

"I don't know, but he said he's going to Moore with his evidence. We're going to have to deal with Deming, and soon."

"What's your plan?"

Mercado gave him a look that could burn a hole through steel. "Me?! How quickly we forget. You mean what's our plan?" He looked at his watch. "We have to get going. I'll call you later tonight."

"Not tonight. Call me in the morning, say around 9:00. My wife and I are..."

"I don't give a shit. I'll call you sometime."

Newsome hesitated, then exited Mercado's Acura, heading for his Beamer. Mercado, still angry about Stillwell's meeting, hit the gas, his tires screeching as he headed towards the parking lot exit.

* * *

When the two arrived at the club, a receptionist told them Judge Stillwell was waiting for them in the Gordon Room. Newsome knew the room. It was Stillwell's favorite.

They passed through a coat check room, then continued into the small meeting room. The room was only twenty feet by twenty-four feet. Lighting was subdued at the moment, provided by recessed fixtures with bulbs whose intensity could be adjusted by sliding switches near the room's entry door. The fluorescent lights were off.

Stillwell stood near a wet bar with a small variety of top shelf liquors. The judge, a drink in hand, motioned for the two to help themselves. Newsome headed over right away, Mercado hung back, already feeling a bit rebellious. Finally, he followed suit, dropped ice cubes in a tumbler, then settled on Scotch.

Stillwell took the bottle from Mercado before he could set it down and refilled his own tumbler, adding a handful of ice cubes. He swung his arm out and indicated that they should take a seat.

The room was ripe with tension. Newsome and Mercado were chilled after coming in from the oppressive heat. Not a word had been uttered, the two guests waiting for the judge to start his meeting. Newsome had already downed half his drink by the time he sat at the conference table; Mercado had yet to take his first sip. They had no idea how long Stillwell had been waiting for them or how many drinks he had downed.

Once they were seated, the Judge cleared his throat. In his commanding, baritone, southern voice, he asked, "Have ya'll got a fall guy for Deming's murder?"

Mercado spoke up. "We have a couple possibilities. One in particular is looking pretty good for it."

"Give me a name and I'll issue a warrant for his arrest. Do ya'll know where he is?"

"Not exactly, but he's close. He won't get far. He doesn't have the resources to bolt and we know where his only family lives. If he goes anywhere, that's where he'll head."

"Okay, keep Andy posted. When ya'll give him the word, I'll issue the warrant and get this thing behind us." The judge looked away for a moment. "I don't care which one of you took care of that problem, but we need closure. Let's get this guy."

Mercado's face took on an air of disbelief. The judge actually believed that one of his team took out Deming. He was about to say something, but thought better of it and kept his mouth shut.

Stillwell was ready to move to the next topic. "The bust schedule. We're going to take a break for about two weeks."

He looked at both men, apparently waiting for their reaction. Newsome remained motionless, the anxiety still evident in his body language. Mercado gave a half smile and wrinkled his forehead. It was all he could do to hold his tongue, waiting through the silence.

Finally, the Judge said, "During this time, you need to fill Deming's position and get that person up to speed. They have to be on board with the team."

He again looked at Newsome and Mercado, his face dead serious. Mercado could almost hear the next line before it came out of Stillwell's mouth.

"Once our team is back up to strength, we're going to step up enforcement. We have to…"

"*We?!* Did you say *We?!*"

Stunned by the outburst, Stillwell and Mercado both looked at Newsome. The DA, the consummate *Yes Man,* was standing, eyes wide, mouth open, an incredulous look plastered on his face.

Both men were too surprised to respond. Newsome picked up his drink and downed the remaining finger of Scotch, then slammed his glass down. His eyes returned to the judge's own. Mercado was about to speak when Newsome held up his hand, silencing the agent.

"We've got FBI agents practically crawling up our collective asses because of Deming's murder! We're working our asses off trying to hang someone for it! That bitch, Megan Moore is all over Nila West, thinking that she knows who the shooter is! They don't have a prime suspect, but all of Vince's agents are persons of interest! Add to that, we have a U.S. Senator involved now. Who knows what kind of shit that will stir? We're," he pointed to Mercado, then back to himself, "dealing directly with him! Not you!" He pointed his finger at the judge. "We're on the front lines! And you want to 'take a two-week break?' Are you fuckin' kiddin' me? We need at least a couple months!"

Mercado watched as Stillwell's face colored red from his ears to his cheeks. He was trying to remain calm, but it appeared that all hell was about to break loose.

"Mr. Newsome, ya'll will not talk to me in this manner! I'm the senior judge in Chatham County! Ya'll work for me! Is that clear? Now take your seat!"

Newsome took a step forward, his expression conveying that he had just heard the most ridiculous statement ever uttered. Mercado thought, *This ought to be good.* He sat back and took a sip of Scotch.

Newsome, still standing, looked down at Stillwell. A smile formed on his face. He shook his head slightly. "You may be a very powerful man out there, among all your politically connected buddies, but in here, we're partners...equal partners! We're all in this together! From now on, we make decisions together! A two-week break is not enough! Somebody is going to screw up out there in the field! We can't afford that! Plus, we don't have a replacement for Deming! That takes time!"

Mercado took another sip, mostly to hide his face. When he and Newsome met earlier, Newsome had warned him not to make any comments. *We can meet afterwards and decide how we want to proceed.* But Newsome apparently had his fill of this pompous, arrogant asshole. He wondered how long Stillwell would tolerate this act of rebellion. He could see the Judge measuring his response. His face was still red as he slowly stood, eyeing Newsome.

When he spoke, his voice carried a more conciliatory tone. "Okay, Andy, okay, you're right. Let's refresh our drinks and cool off a bit. Ya'll two can tell me what you think we should do next. Agreed?"

Stillwell looked from Newsome to Mercado, then back. The DA seemed to calm down, the tension dissipating.

Mercado didn't believe a word the judge said. Newsome's little outburst hadn't changed the fact that Stillwell was in charge. In fact, he thought that, from now on, Newsome should watch his back 24/7.

* * *

Following the meeting, Mercado thought about the compromise. As he expected, the judge gave Newsome the appearance that he'd won. In reality, he'd only gotten the judge to delay the stepped up busts by three weeks versus two. Mercado and his team were still under tremendous pressure.

Replacing Deming and locating Cleaver were his top priorities. The sooner they delivered a shooter, the sooner they could get Moore and Savage off their backs.

Chapter 24

By the eighth ring of his third unanswered call to Allen Deming, Peden Savage's tension level ticked up another notch. Deming had a dedicated cell phone strictly for communications with him. It had been only three days since he had hired Peden. He wanted his son's killer caught and brought to justice, or so Peden thought. One would think he'd have the phone close by in case Peden had news. Maybe there was a logical explanation why he wasn't answering.

Peden hit the disconnect icon on his cell and noted the time: 4:05 PM. He changed into a pair of shorts, a tee shirt, and running shoes. He and Megan planned to jog from their separate offices and meet at Forsyth Park. He grabbed his ear buds and hooked them into his cell phone and selected an old Alice Cooper album. He wasn't eighteen anymore, but he loved the songs. He hoped that it would keep his mind off Allen Deming's possible disappearance. *No, it isn't a disappearance. He just didn't answer the call. Maybe he's having a siesta.*

On his way out, he locked up the office and started his jog south on Barnard towards Pulaski Square. He planned to take the three-mile route just to work the kinks out of his system. The run through the historic district with all the mature southern oaks and Spanish moss, the aroma of southern cuisine from various restaurants and freshly clipped grass and hedges always gave his spirits a lift. He hadn't jogged the five-mile route for over a week and decided he had better take the short route today.

He cleared Pulaski Square running south on the sidewalk along Barnard Street when he came to the West Jones Lane crosswalk. He was two steps out into the lane when, over the blare of Alice Cooper, he heard the screech of tires. He turned towards the sound and leapt backwards just in time to avoid being run over. He landed hard on his back and rolled onto his side. Through dust and exhaust fumes, he saw a dark sedan with chrome wheels, dark-tinted windows, and a dark license plate cover. The car sped west towards Montgomery, making a hard left without so much as a pause at the stop sign. His adrenaline spiked as he jumped to his feet. He had his phone out of his pocket hoping to bring up the camera app in time for a quick shot of the fleeing car, but the car was long gone. He took a deep breath, sweat beading on his forehead, dripping down his face. Had he not stopped in his tracks, he most certainly would have been hit. Clearly the driver had no intention of slowing down, much less stopping to see if he had been hit.

His adrenaline continued to race through his body. He stood, doing a quick self-inspection. His right elbow was badly skinned, the strawberry dripping blood. No bones were broken. He thought for a few seconds about what he should do. He could call his computer guy, Lee Sparks, and see if he could track the driver by his description of the car, but without a license plate number, the search would be fruitless. He could skip his run and go back to the office just a few blocks north, but what would he do there except brood. Or he could continue his run and keep an eye out for the offending vehicle.

Settling on continuing, he looked at his phone which had miraculously survived his fall without a scratch. He restarted Alice Cooper's *Love it to Death* and jogged in place for a minute to get his heart under control. Then it was on to Forsyth Park.

As he reached the periphery of the park, his phone vibrated and he heard an electronic ring through his ear buds. It was an incoming call from Megan.

He answered with a winded voice, "Hey, Megan."

In an equally winded voice, Megan said, "Peden, some asshole just tried to run me down."

Peden stopped in his tracks. "What a coincidence. Me

too. Are you okay?"

Megan replied, "Yeah, but I have a hole in the one knee of my good running pants and a pretty decent strawberry on the knee. If I catch that asshole, they're gonna wish they were never born."

Peden said, "Was it a dark colored sedan, chrome wheels, dark-tinted windows, and a dark-colored license plate cover?"

There was silence on the line, then Megan confirmed, "Yeah. That pisses me off. They don't know who they're screwing with, Peedee." After a second she asked, "Are you alright?"

"Yeah. Fine. Just a little jacked up at the moment. Where were you when it happened?"

"I was on Price Street just crossing Hartridge."

"Did you get a look at the driver or anything else useful?"

"No. Damn it!"

"Looks like we're going to have to be more careful."

"We're fine. But when I find the driver…"

* * *

Marcus Cook shut down his computer at 5:30 PM, planning to get out of the office for the weekend. The scent of industrial strength floor cleaner began to fill the air as the weekend cleaning crew started their tasks. He had pager duty for the team, but the call from Vince Mercado assured them that there would be no action for several weeks.

Marcus grabbed his Glock 27 from his desk drawer, checked that the safety was on, holstered it, and was headed for the door when he noticed that Nila West was at the copier station using the paper cutter. She made several cuts, picked up the sheets, tossed the scraps in the trash can, and headed back to her office.

Marcus detoured for the men's room, the path allowing him a brief glance into West's office. He paused just outside her office door.

West, sitting at her desk, facing away from her office

door, was holding two sheets of paper. Two more sheets lay on her desk. The sheets were about half the size of copy paper. He was only ten feet from where she sat, but he couldn't make out the handwritten text. The papers had obviously been folded numerous times.

He continued on, not wanting his boss to see him spying on her. When he got to the men's room, it hit him. *Could those be Jarrod Deming's missing notes? Why would she keep it a secret?*

There was only one way to find out. He had to see them for himself. On his way back through the office, he walked right up to West's office and stood watching for a moment. She was in the same position, but now held three of the four pages. The other page remained on her desk. Marcus took a quiet, deep breath, then knocked loudly on West's door.

Startled, she swung her chair around and quickly placed the pages face down on her desk, covering the page that had remained face up.

Marcus said, "I didn't mean to disturb you, Ms. West. Just wanted to let you know I'm heading out. It's just you and the cleaning crew."

After taking a deep breath, she said, "Sorry, I didn't realize anyone was still here. Thanks for the heads up, Marcus."

"Is there anything I can do for you before I leave?"

"No. Thanks, Marcus. I'll be another twenty minutes or so and I'm calling it a night myself. See you Monday."

"Have a good night then."

He made a deliberate detour again, this time to the copy station. He looked into the waste basket where West had dropped the clippings from the note pages. He noted that the clippings were on top of some other papers in the trash within easy reach, so he snatched the four strips from the trash can and stuffed them into his pocket.

As Marcus turned to leave, his phone rang. He debated blowing off the call, but doing that in front of his boss wouldn't look too good. He crossed the office space to his desk and picked up on the third ring.

"Marcus Cook."

Vince Mercado said, "Marcus, glad I caught you. You have a few minutes? We need to talk."

Marcus smiled to himself. *I'm in.* "Sure, Vince. Where and when?"

"How about…"

* * *

Marcus parked in the lot of the Days Inn, Savannah-Hilton Head International Airport. The sky was clearing, a departure from the morning's gray clouds and light rain. The humidity remained high, so he left his car running with the air conditioning on high.

From his pants pocket, he pulled the four strips of paper that he found in the trash can by the copier. The strips of paper had fold creases and were somewhat wrinkled. The only writing on the strips was 1 of 5, 2 of 5, 3 of 5, and 4 of 5. There was no fifth page. He pondered this, but he needed more information and now was not the time or place to pursue it. He folded the strips and put them in his wallet.

Marcus walked in the door at the Hercule's Bar and Grill on Dean Forest Road just after 6:40 PM. The bar was a small place built over the water of a pond near the hotel. The structure, when viewed from above, was a hexagon. Inside, the lighting was low, craft beer advertisements adorned the walls wherever one looked, outdone only by the dozen or more television screens with continuously running sports programs.

Marcus spotted Mercado at a table and nodded in his direction. He went to the bar, ordered a beer, paid the barmaid and headed towards Mercado with his beer in hand.

Mercado stood and shook his hand. As with the team meeting earlier in the day, the two stood out like sore thumbs in the sports bar catering mostly to a younger clientele.

Mercado got right to the point. "You know, we're kind of shorthanded since Deming's murder. We need someone to step up and take his place. Alex, Pete and I think that you're the man for the job."

Marcus wanted to smile, but kept his face passive, as if Mercado had said nothing at all. "I know the job. I can handle it. When do I start?"

Mercado held eye contact with Marcus, apparently considering his next words carefully. "There's more to this part of the job than meets the eye." He took a sip of his beer, momentarily breaking eye contact. When he set his beer down, he continued, "I know that you had some...difficulties in Iraq. Something about a shooting at a village?"

Marcus expected this line of questioning and was ready. "Man, I can't believe you're bringing that shit up. That was bullshit. Those villagers, they were passing intel to Al Qadea. If we...I hadn't done what I did, a whole lot of my men would have been killed." There was silence as Mercado took another sip of his beer, still watching every move that Marcus made. He continued, "Are you gonna use that against me, keep me on probation or some shit like that?"

Mercado's face gave up the slightest sly grin as he took another drink of beer. The silence between them was punctuated only by the background noise in the bar. "Nope. In fact, we've all had similar experiences. All three of us have a little black mark on our records. Let's just say, we've found a way to serve our country and get paid back, in cash, for the injustice that we endured."

Marcus matched Mercado's grin. "You have my undivided attention."

Chapter 25

Peden was back in his office bathroom showering after his five-mile run. The planned shorter route was put aside after his adrenaline spike from nearly being run over. Jacked up and angry, he and Megan had both decided that running for only three miles wouldn't cut it. They kept running and talking about the case, parting ways at Lafayette Square. She headed home to Tybee Island while he returned to his office.

During their run, Peden told her that Allen Deming failed to answer his repeated calls. He explained that Deming had a cell phone to communicate directly, and only, with Peden. He told her how passionate Deming had been about finding his son's killer. So why hadn't he answered? There were innumerable reasons, of course, but none passed Peden's common sense test, unless there was a serious problem.

Megan agreed that there was a better than fifty-fifty chance that Deming was in trouble. With over two thousand miles between Savannah and Phoenix, they couldn't possibly investigate what might be wrong. Asking for assistance from the regional FBI office in Phoenix was out of the question because Deming wouldn't trust anyone from a federal agency.

Peden lathered up his hair with cheap shampoo, allowing the hot water to massage the muscles in his chest, relaxing in the moment. He swung around, shifting the stream of water to his back. After about a minute, he turned again and ducked his head under the steaming flow. Propping his hands against the shower wall, the hot water flowed over his head, down his face, and dripped from the tip of his nose. He noticed the thin red ribbon of blood flowing down his side. The scab on his right elbow from his near miss with the sedan was still raw. That would require his attention once he dried off. The shower relaxed his muscles, but a number of his bones were bruised.

He let his mind wander, the day's events popping into his brain in random order. In his mind, he could see the cars that lined Flinn Drive in front of Sylvia Deming's house during the wake. Not surprising, there were no black sedans in sight. If someone from the DEA was involved in the drive by, they certainly wouldn't use an agency car or their personal vehicle. He wondered: would Vince Mercado be brazen enough to take a crack at running Megan and him down in such a public place? If the driver had wanted, they could have easily run him down and not just brushed him back. The same was true for Megan. Both attacks were similar and no doubt committed by the same person. The drive by was a warning. Back off the investigation, or next time, they wouldn't be so lucky.

Between them, Peden and Megan couldn't pull together any meaningful data that would identify the vehicle. Neither had seen the driver or any passengers. Identifying the car and its driver was a dead end.

Several other angles bothered Peden. One in particular was Roland Fosco denying Megan permission to interview his counterpart Cliff Metzger at the DEA. It was possible that upper management at both the DEA and the FBI didn't want a messy, public cat fight between the agencies. It was also possible that someone higher up in the DEA was complicit in the assassination. Since Fosco had directly ordered her that she could not interview Metzger, she had no recourse but to comply. For her to pursue that angle was career suicide and another dead end.

But Peden had no such constraints. It might cost his company some business, but would finding the killer be worth the risk? He never was a conformist, which was why he was no longer employed by the FBI.

Peden turned in the shower and leaned against the opposite wall, the hot stream hitting between his shoulder blades, washing away the tension.

He thought about Deming's missing notes from the news conference. *Had the notes just blown away during the mass confusion following the shots or had someone snatched up the papers before they fell into the wrong hands? The 'wrong hands' would belong to whom?*

And why did Deming make that little move to his right just before he was shot? Was there a purpose or was he just expending nervous energy? Nila West sure was lucky that he moved or she might have taken a bullet in the chest, not just her arm. Hmmm. Was it just dumb luck?

Peden dried off, lathered his wounded elbow with anti-bacterial salve, then covered the area with a three-inch square bandage. He dressed in blue jeans, a forest green polo shirt, and sneakers.

He went down to his office and looked at the old schoolhouse clock. It was nearing 6:30 PM. According to the plaque on the wall outside the front door, the office was officially closed. Apparently, someone ignored it because there was a knock on the front door. Peden remained calm, but reached into his desk drawer and withdrew his Glock, tucking the pistol into the holster on his right side. The knock continued. Peden went to a window to the right of the front door and looked out.

A bald, light-skinned black man, about six feet tall and built like a college running back, faced the door with his hands folded in front of him. From his vantage point, Peden was looking at his profile. The man's expression was neutral, even relaxed.

Peden shrugged his shoulders and stood in front of the door. His hair was still slightly wet when he rubbed both hands over his head from front to back. He took a deep breath and opened the door.

In his slight southern accent, he said, "I'm sorry, partner, but we're closed for the day."

The man's expression didn't change. He simply asked, "Peden Savage?"

"That's right."

"I'm Michael Jess, aide to Senator Armand Vega. Do you have a few minutes to discuss some important business?"

Savage did a quick assessment of the man in front of him. If he was a senator's aide, it was clear to Peden that he had other duties, like security. The bulge on the man's right side was due to some kind of holstered pistol. His demeanor was not threatening, but there was a no-nonsense air about him. He definitely had some military training; probably Marines, Navy Seal, or Army Ranger.

"Come in. We can talk in my office."

As they walked the fifteen feet into Peden's interior office, Mr. Jess' head moved only slightly, but Peden could tell he was assessing his surroundings. His stride was smooth and even. Though Jess weighed around two hundred twenty pounds, the normally squeaky floor boards made far less noise than usual.

"Please, take a seat. Can I get you anything, water, soft drink, something stronger?"

"No, Mr. Savage. I'm fine." He sat, unbuttoning his suit coat with one smooth flip of his fingers. He was relaxed, sitting back in one of Peden's guest chairs.

"Call me Peden."

Peden did a quick appraisal of Michael Jess. He wore a comfortable, expensive, light gray suit with a starched white dress shirt, navy blue tie and highly polished black shoes. His relaxed demeanor contrasted with his alert eyes. His hands rested light on the arms of the chair, as if ready to take action.

"I won't take much of your time. As I said, I work for Senator Armand Vega. He would like to hire you."

Peden tried to keep the look of surprise from his face. A dozen thoughts raced through his mind. Since he had no point of reference as to why a United States Senator would want to hire him, he asked, "So, Mr. Jess, what can I do for Senator Vega?"

* * *

The discussion with Michael Jess had taken all of twenty-five minutes. It was a serious conversation, Jess holding true to Peden's first thoughts that the guy would be no fun at a party. He was all business. His facial expression remained passive, not changing from the moment he walked in until he left.

Even while he told the embarrassing story of Peter Vega's arrest by the DEA for dealing drugs, Jess remained calm, as if he were discussing the weather with a close friend.

Essentially, Senator Vega believed that his son was set up because of the Senator's chairmanship of the Senate Appropriations Committee and his goal that the DEA's funding be slashed. The senator had stated on many occasions that the war on drugs was a dismal failure even with the most gracious standard. He had the ear of a number of key members of the committee. It appeared that the committee was ready to yield to the senator's wishes. An unprecedented funding cut was imminent.

That was, until the Senator's son was busted. Pushing the cuts would appear self-serving to his constituents, but more importantly, to his major donors. Senator Vega knew how the game was played. He had received many calls from powerful people both inside and outside the government. Many jobs were on the line should funding be slashed. The standard line that drugs were a danger to the American way of life was used on him countless times. Washington had become so used to passing increased budgets for nearly all federal agencies that anyone proposing a true budget cut was labeled a fool. The mere suggestion of cuts drew harsh criticism from anyone with power and influence. But Senator Vega had never been threatened with a direct attack against his family.

Mr. Jess described how the senator had been contacted by an agent and another man demanding that he change his rhetoric regarding funding for the DEA. If he didn't change his stance, his son's bust would be leaked to the press. The charges could net Peter Vega substantial prison time, not to mention the embarrassment to the Senator and his family.

Jess continued with the personal part of the story. The Senator was expecting a call from a certain agent within the DEA about a personal "good faith" cash donation to the Savannah office. The agent said to be prepared for the donation to be in the low seven-figure range and that it could happen at any time. He said that the Senator should take this seriously. He would not have much time to assemble the cash once he received the call, so he should make plans ahead of time.

Peden had an idea. He told Jess about a program that his tech specialist, Lee Sparks, was working on with the FBI. It was a tracking program for use specifically with cash drops in ransom and extortion cases. He told Jess that he would have Sparks contact him with details.

Jess provided Peden with the names of the men who had made contact; Vincent Mercado and Andrew Newsome.

Peden's eyebrows shot up when he heard Mercado's name, but his jaw dropped when Jess mentioned the DA. And if District Attorney Newsome was involved, who else had their hands in the pot?

Near the end of Michael Jess' visit, Peden asked, "Now that I'm on the clock, what exactly does the Senator want me to do?"

Peden almost detected a smile on Michael Jess' face, but he wasn't sure.

Chapter 26

"I could barely hear you over the music. It's so loud in there."

Elizabeth Sanchez set the pizza on her kitchen counter. She had stopped at the Mellow Mushroom on the way home from work and picked up their large *House Special*. A red sauce-based pizza smothered in mozzarella cheese, pepperoni, sausage, ground beef, ham, smoked bacon, mushrooms, black olives, Roma tomatoes, green peppers, and onions. Elizabeth had them lightly dust the whole pizza with oregano. The aroma filled her condominium.

Wayne Cleaver smiled, but his smile faded. "I can't believe that you're sticking your neck out like this for me. I mean, you're risking everything. I feel…"

"Would you shut up? It's only a pizza. Now grab a plate. Did you put that bottle of wine in the fridge or would you rather have a beer?"

Wayne laughed. "There's beer in there? Heck, if I'd have known that, I'd be passed out by now." He made his way into the kitchen and took a plate from her as she set her own plate on the counter and flipped the pizza box top back. Their sense of smell was overpowered by the mix of ingredients coming from the still hot pizza.

Wayne exclaimed, "Oh man, does that ever smell good."

Elizabeth grabbed one giant slice and headed for the dining room, stopping on the way to get two beers. She said, "Grab a handful of napkins on your way in, please."

While they ate, the only sounds in the condo were of the two of them enjoying dinner. The mood had somehow become starched. Elizabeth had several things on her mind, but she didn't know where to start. He wasn't a fugitive. There were no warrants for his arrest, but she knew that his life was essentially on hold.

She thought she knew who murdered Jarrod Deming. The way those DEA agents pursued Wayne and all but accused him of the crime was more than a little callous. She had known Wayne Cleaver for a long time. They went to high school together. He was a sweet, gentle, young man who wouldn't harm anyone. Maybe prison had hardened him some, but it didn't appear to her that he had changed. She looked across the table and smiled as he took the last bite from his first slice.

Her thoughts shifted to her friend, Sylvia. If what she said was true, she had good reason, *or a good excuse*, to – what – kill her husband? She knew Sylvia well back when they were in college. The old Sylvia from years past was naïve. Back then, she thought that Jarrod, her boyfriend at that time, could do no wrong. Even if she knew that he had cheated on her, she would have forgiven him. Would she feel the same now? Sylvia knew that Jarrod had not been faithful throughout their marriage. Did the affair with his boss really happen? Was it the last straw? Even if she knew and decided to kill Jarrod, there were many opportunities to do the deed in private, away from the cameras and the crowds. For her to kill her husband in such a public forum, what would that gain her? Why take the risk? Besides, everyone was saying that the shooter had to be a professional. She didn't believe that Sylvia had the skills.

Wayne asked, "A penny for your thoughts?"

His smile was genuine as he looked directly into her eyes. He had been watching her as she contemplated his situation. She hoped that he couldn't read what was on her mind.

She leaned back in her chair, but didn't smile back. The moment was at hand to have the serious conversation about what he needed to do next.

"Did you do that write-up?"

Wayne's smile disappeared. Her legal training emerged abruptly. The change was harsh and unintentional.

"Why, yes, counselor, I did. It's on the end table. Let

me grab it for you."

Embarrassed, she looked down at her now empty plate and muttered, "Sorry, that didn't come out right. But, I saw a new case today that is similar to yours."

His eyebrows rose. He leaned forward, pushing his plate back a few inches. "Go on."

"Some college kids were just busted with a large quantity of pot, some other drugs, and cash. The whole thing looked almost identical to your bust. That's why I need your notes."

Wayne frowned. "So, these guys are still at it even though the Deming murder investigation is ongoing. Man, they got some brass ones."

"There's more. Originally, five people were detained. They were held for nearly twenty-four hours, then released. No charges were filed."

Now Wayne frowned. "Any idea why? Sounds like a slam dunk."

"I don't know, but every time I go into my boss' office, if he's on the phone, he keeps his voice down, like a little kid trying to hide something. He's such a jackass. Anyway, I've been sneaking peeks at previous busts. They're too much alike. Similar quantities, perps the same age, just weird. The same DEA team did ninety percent of them."

Wayne frowned. "Listen, you've gotta quit snoopin' into this stuff. These guys may have killed their fellow agent. They wouldn't have a second thought about knocking you off." He paused and shook his head. "See what I mean? As long as I'm here, your life's in danger. I have to get out of here before someone sees me."

"You mean someone else besides my neighbor."

"Damn. Yeah. I've got to stay out of sight. That was careless and foolish."

They were quiet for a stretch, then Elizabeth said, "Your suspicions about members of the team killing their partner may be right, but there are other possibilities. My friend, Sylvia, suspects that Jarrod was having an affair with his boss, that West woman. She's the one who caught a bullet in the arm when Jarrod was killed."

"I saw her on the news. But she's okay, right?"

"Yeah, fine. She was at the wake today with her boss. Sylvia *accidentally* grabbed her arm right on her wound and squeezed. She apologized, but after they left, she told me that she knew Jarrod and her were screwing."

"Did she say how she knew?"

"Nope. Just said it kind of like it was common knowledge. Her whole attitude changed when that woman showed up. She was a grieving widow the whole morning, then when she caught sight of Jarrod's boss, she was, I don't know, devoid of feelings. The change was obvious. They left right after Sylvia did that."

"So, do you seriously think that Sylvia could have killed her husband?"

She grabbed her beer can then looked up at the ceiling, deep in thought for a moment. She took a deep swig of her beer. "I don't think so...I don't know. We were best friends at one time, but that was awhile ago. The way she grabbed that woman's arm...I think she did it on purpose. Maybe it was just a way to send the message that she knew about the affair."

"Hurting a person, even purposely, isn't the same as killing them in cold blood. That takes a special kind of hate or someone without a conscience."

As Wayne picked up his second slice of pizza, Elizabeth thought again about her friend Sylvia and the side of her that she had never before seen. Could she have changed that much in ten years?

"I'm just not sure how well I know her now. When I went to her house the other day, it was just like old times, except for the circumstances, of course. She seemed like the Sylvia that I knew back at school. The thing with Jarrod's boss really threw me. So, honestly, I can't say."

Wayne took a sip of his beer to wash down some pizza, all the time keeping his eyes on Elizabeth as she spoke. He formulated a plan, but wasn't sure how to broach the subject.

He decided that just throwing the raw idea out on the table might be the best approach.

"How about I talk to a couple of my former cellmates from Coastal who told me that they got busted the same way. They could tell us the circumstances of their cases. Maybe there are enough similarities that we could send the information to the FBI."

Elizabeth looked alarmed at the idea. As she pointed her finger at Wayne, she said, "You can't do anything. You can't leave this building and you can't call these ex-cons from my phone. That would lead directly back to me." She stopped as a thought came to her. "But we could get you a throwaway. Then we wouldn't have to worry about it being traced."

Wayne looked at her, not sure what she meant by a throwaway. She explained how you could get a 'throwaway' phone at most any department or drug store. The idea that you could get a cell phone with no name attached was amazing to him.

"When can you get it?"

"It's only 6:10. I'll go now. The only thing is I'd rather go out of town to get it. Less chance I'd run into someone from the office. If I go to Beaufort or even Statesboro, I could be back by about 8:00." She smiled and said, "I don't have to work tomorrow. We can sleep in."

Wayne felt a tingle in his spine. What was that look on her face? He smiled back as she stood and came around the table and stood looking down at him. He swallowed hard, not knowing what he should do.

She remarked, "You have been away for a while."

He pushed his chair back and stood, facing her. She still wore the smile as she moved closer. Her hands rose to either side of his face, her fingers moving to just behind the lower part of his head. She pulled his face to hers, kissing him deeply. His arms went limp at his sides, then slowly made their way around her back. He held her loosely, not sure what to do next. He had never had much experience with women, even before his incarceration. Nervous, he waited for her lead, continuing to kiss her, not knowing if he was doing it right.

She pulled back slowly, looking into his eyes. "I'm going to go get that phone. I want you to remember this moment. When I get back, we can pick up where we left off."

They stood close, looking into each other's eyes for the next minute, not wanting to break the spell. Then Elizabeth took a step back, grabbed her purse from the kitchen counter and headed for the door, detouring to give him a soft, lingering kiss on the lips.

* * *

While Elizabeth was out, Wayne spent the time thinking of the guys who had confided in him about their busts. He wrote down three names on a notepad along with as much information about them as he could remember. Finding their contact information wasn't going to be easy. Not too many ex-cons wanted contact with other ex-cons on the outside. Of the three, Wayne knew that two of them were from eastern Georgia in the vicinity of Savannah. The other was from South Carolina near Newton.

When Elizabeth returned two hours later, she was pleased that he had spent his time wisely. She reviewed the list and smiled.

They sat close to one another on Elizabeth's couch going over Wayne's new cell phone. The size of the screen required that they were shoulder to shoulder. Wayne could smell her shampoo and perfume. He had a hard time concentrating as she went over the cell phone's functions.

"That's about it. Once you use it to contact your friends you can toss it. Then we'll get a new one for you that doesn't have these guys' numbers in memory."

"Isn't this expensive?"

She rolled her eyes. "You've really been out of touch. Didn't they offer computer classes or some kind of technology classes in the joint?"

Wayne smiled, "Yeah. I took the computer class. What they were teaching was already about five years out of date. No classes on cell phones though."

Her sly smile reappeared. Looking into his eyes, she said, "That reminds me, where were we before I left?"

She leaned in and kissed him, soft at first. She put her right hand behind his head and pulled a little, the kiss now more intense. Within a few minutes, they were laid out on the couch, passion building, heat rising.

They made love, learning more about each other than they had planned. Sometime after 10:00 PM, they fell into a deep slumber.

Chapter 27

An elegantly dressed crowd of over two hundred people sat in the DeSoto Hilton's Oglethorpe Ballroom, listening to political speeches and dining on their choice of salmon almondine, chicken marsala, or fillet mignon while drinking a variety of adult beverages. A donation of $30,000 for a table of eight bought this excellent dinner, top shelf wine and liquor, and the privilege of hearing Superior Court Judge Whalen Stillwell announce his candidacy for the senate. A number of party big-wigs from around the state were scheduled for their ten minutes at the podium – most of which stretched to twenty minutes or more – to point out the failures of Senator Armand Vega and to sing the praises of Judge Stillwell. The speeches droned on and on, the message the same. *It was time for someone who was tough on crime and supportive of law enforcement at all levels. Clearly Armand Vega's approach was inappropriate and shortsighted. Funding cuts to one of the nation's primary crime-fighting agencies was clearly the wrong path. Before long, the dealers would control the streets.*

At 9:30 PM, the Master of Ceremonies looked to his right to see if the guest of honor was ready to take to the podium and address the crowd. A young man approached the stage and whispered in his ear that His Honor was not available, but would be momentarily. This somewhat embarrassing moment didn't faze the chairman of the Georgia Democratic Party. He continued to entertain the crowd with stories about past candidates and their successes in the nation's capital, and how he knew that the tide was turning for the party. Good times were on the horizon, pulling us out of the demise caused by policies instituted by the GOP.

The chairman continued his diatribe for more than twenty minutes when a movement from the back of the room caught his attention. A nod let him know that candidate Stillwell was in the building.

"And now, ladies and gentlemen, without further ado, it is my distinct honor and pleasure to introduce a great man with a special message. Please show your southern hospitality with an enthusiastic greeting for our next senator for the great state of Georgia, your friend and mine, His Honor, Judge Whalen Stillwell!"

The guests stood in unison as thunderous applause and whistles welcomed the tall, handsome judge as he bound up the steps of the stage at the head of the ballroom. He turned and waved to the crowd, blew kisses to women of wealth, clasped his fists together and made a gesture of strength as he made his way to the podium. The standing ovation continued for better than a full two minutes when Stillwell motioned with both hands for everyone to take their seats.

Looking out over the ballroom at his supporters, Judge Stillwell smiled as the atmosphere changed from thundering applause to silence. The shift was dramatic. His baritone southern accent boomed, "I am here to announce to ya'll, my dear friends, that I am running for the United States Senate for the great state of Georgia!"

Again, the room erupted into applause, cheers, and whistles. A chant of "Stillwell, Stillwell, Stillwell" arose with loud claps keeping time. Stillwell's smile seemed to send a light beam across the crowd. After nearly another two minutes, he calmed the attendees once more so he could deliver his prepared remarks.

The speech, filled with attacks directed at the standing senator and promises of changes once elected, lasted for twenty minutes. The message remained positive; a change for the better would be delivered and he was their courier.

After the oratory was complete, Judge Stillwell mingled with the crowd, calm, smiling, exuding confidence, and thanking his guests. He might as well have stuck a vacuum hose in their wallets and pocketbooks.

As the crowd thinned, Andrew Newsome and his wife, Meredith, approached the judge. Newsome was in awe of Stillwell's performance. Having had several martinis, his wife was mesmerized by the man. Her eyes locked on the judge's, her smile was like that of a lovesick junior high school cheerleader hoping to gain the attention of the team's all-star quarterback. Newsome felt a twinge of jealousy as his mouth moved from side to side making his nose twist as if he was fighting back a sneeze. He barely kept his composure.

To the judge, he commented, "You sure know how to work a crowd."

Stillwell smiled, taking in the compliment, then turning to the DA's wife. "Meredith, ya'll look lovely this evening."

Newsome thought that his wife was going to have an orgasm right on the spot. She blushed and replied, "Thank you, Whalen. You were wonderful."

Newsome didn't know if she was talking about his speech or some previous covert meeting between the two. His face twitched even more. He felt like an intruder in a private moment between the judge and his wife.

After a few awkward seconds, Stillwell said to Newsome's wife, "Meredith, could I have a brief moment with your husband. I'm afraid that we have some court business to discuss."

She smiled and reacted as if she hadn't heard the judge, then the words sank in and she excused herself after clutching the judge's hand. She turned to her husband, then walked away without another word.

The men watched her leave. Newsome turned back to the judge, only to see him maintaining his eyes squarely on his wife's backside. Again, the jealous tightness worked its way through his body.

Finally, Stillwell turned his attention back to Newsome. "I signed the arrest warrant on Wayne Cleaver. Ya'll need to get moving tonight. Make sure Mercado knows that his team must make the arrest. We don't want the FBI or the local boys involved."

Newsome nodded, his face twitching as he listened. His thoughts were racing, thinking how he was going to contact Mercado this late on a Friday night when the judge nodded his head to Newsome's right. Newsome looked and saw Vince Mercado standing like a soldier at ease near the entrance to the ballroom. Stillwell had apparently already called the DEA agent in anticipation of signing the warrant.

Stillwell instructed, "Alert the press, especially Channel 8, and make sure they get a picture of this Cleaver character. Let's get this done before anyone has a chance to react. Call me with any updates. I'll be at the club for a few hours once I leave here."

"Okay, Judge."

"Oh, and one more thing." The judge reached into his pocket and handed Newsome some papers. They appeared to be notes scribbled on several half-sized sheets of paper. He started to unfold them, but Stillwell's eyes went wide, in a moment of what Newsome thought was panic. Then he recovered just as quickly and his patented smile returned. "Not here. Just stick them in your pocket and get rid of them."

Before Newsome could respond or ask any questions, the judge turned on his heels and headed for one of the few remaining couples in the ballroom. Stillwell immediately turned on the charm, as if nothing of consequence had just happened. Newsome stuck the papers in his suit pocket, trying hard to look nonchalant. Scanning the room looking for his wife, he spotted her with a fresh martini in her hand standing very close to Vince Mercado, smiling with alcohol-induced infatuation. *First order of business is to get her the hell out of here.*

* * *

Elizabeth Sanchez awoke from a deep sleep, the blue digital numbers from the clock appearing slightly blurry. Is that 11:03 or 11:33? She blinked her dry eyes several times to clear her vision. There, that's better, 11:33. The dark room told her that it was still night time and Saturday morning had not yet arrived.

An unfamiliar sound rose from a spot on the bed next to her as Wayne Cleaver's deep breathing filled the room. A mischievous smile covered her face, the thoughts of her and Wayne's lovemaking filling her mind.

Lying on her back under the sheets for a few moments longer, she thought about how Wayne had come into her life. Here she was, working for the District Attorney of Chatham County and she was sleeping with a convicted felon. *This might not be good on my resume.* She smiled again, like a kid who got away with stealing a cookie before supper.

Elizabeth liked to watch the late-night news, but she'd missed it tonight. *Oh well, there's always tomorrow night. I'll catch up then.*

Wayne Cleaver awoke with a start and sat straight up in bed, looking around frantically. He looked frightened and confused. When he looked down and saw Elizabeth next to him staring up at him, he took a deep breath and sighed.

Elizabeth immediately started laughing, amused at his reaction.

She said, "You're gonna have to tell me about that dream. It looked like a doozy."

He smiled at her, then rubbed his eyes. "What time is it?"

"A little after 11:30. Are you okay? You looked pretty scared." She giggled.

He stopped smiling, his face taking on a serious expression. "Yeah, I was. You know that feeling when someone is chasing after you and you're running as fast as you can, but your legs feel like they're in water or molasses? You just can't run fast enough, but the guys chasing you can't quite catch you." He frowned. "It was that bastard, Vince Mercado and his sidekick." He sat brooding.

Elizabeth sat up, pulling the bedsheets up over her chest. She leaned over and put her head against his shoulder. "Let's get up and have a beer. It's almost Saturday. We can relax and think about what we want to do tomorrow."

"How about if we stay here in bed? I can think of something we can do." He put his arms around her and pulled her tight. The blue light from the alarm clock numbers cast a faint glow on the sheets around her body.

They kissed lightly. The first kiss turned into a second. Before long, they were making love for the second time as the late evening turned into early morning. They fell asleep as a late-night news anchor relayed to the public that a warrant had been issued for Wayne Cleaver for the murder of DEA Agent Jarrod Deming.

* * *

Elizabeth Sanchez nosey next door neighbor had just fallen asleep with the television tuned to Channel 8. She vaguely remembered a story about an arrest warrant, but the rest was lost in the fog of near slumber.

* * *

At 12:32 AM, Elizabeth Sanchez's phone vibrated on the night stand next to her head. On the fourth vibration, she reached out and looked at the display. It read Sylvia Deming.

She tapped the screen and put the phone to her ear.

In a sleepy voice, she asked, "Hey, Sissy. You okay?"

Sylvia replied, "Yeah, I'm fine. Did you see the news?"

"No. I fell asleep, I don't know, around midnight I think. Why?"

There was a brief silence on the line, then Sylvia said, "There's a warrant out for Jarrod's killer. Some guy named Wayne Cleaver."

Elizabeth nearly dropped her phone. She was in shock.

"Liz, ya still there?"

"Yeah." Silence. "When did you hear about this?"

"It just came on the TV."

Wayne stirred, making a snorting sound. Elizabeth covered the phone for a moment, hoping that Sylvia wouldn't hear that she had company, but it didn't work.

She said, "Sorry. I didn't mean to intrude."

Elizabeth slid out from under the sheet and walked into the living room, closing the bedroom door behind her. She sat on the couch. "That's okay." She asked, "Did they say anything else? Do they know where this guy is?" Elizabeth was trying to keep the tension out of her voice knowing that Wayne was just feet away.

Her friend replied, "All they said was that the warrant was issued and that the guy was just released from prison the other day. That's it." There was a pause, then she asked, "Are you okay? You sound scared."

"I'm fine, just tired. The big question is are you okay? I mean, this has got to be nerve-wracking for you."

They talked a bit longer, the conversation strained due to the late hour and Elizabeth's growing concern for Wayne. She thought briefly about her own dilemma: harboring a fugitive. She had to get Wayne out of Savannah to a safe location.

The door to her bedroom opened. Wayne took one look at his friend and lover and knew the circumstances had dramatically changed.

Chapter 28

The pounding, though intermittent, wouldn't stop. It was as if someone was near panic, then there was silence. The silence didn't last long and the deep, reverberating drum beat began again.

The source of the pounding confused Peden Savage. *Its Saturday morning. Ignore it.* He normally slept until 7:00 AM on Saturdays but part of his brain shouted *Get up!*

Thump-thump-thump. There it was again. Savage's Marine Corps Drill Sergeant came into his sleepy, foggy mind. *Get up, maggot! Duty calls!*

His eyes popped open. He sat straight up and rubbed his eyes. He was in his own bed. He looked around the room at the single bedside table and shabby lamp, the dresser, the antique mirror on the wall. He stood in his dark blue boxers, donned the flimsy old robe that hung from the hook on the closet door, and wiped a hand across his hair, and flicked away the dried gunk from the corners of his eyes.

Thump-thump-thump. *Damn it!*

He looked at his alarm clock. Red digital numbers burned into his eyes; 6:23 AM. *What the hell?*

Thump-thump-thump. *Who in the hell...?*

Peden hollered towards his open bedroom door. "Just a minute!"

He made his way down the steps of his second-floor apartment to his office, the pinewood floors creaking underfoot. Rotating his head to loosen the neck bones, he felt almost awake by the time he reached the front window next to the office door. Pulling back the curtains, he saw a white man, about five feet-nine inches tall with a solid build, a bit of a gut sticking out over the waist of his blue jeans, and a white golf shirt. Peden put his age at late fifties to mid-sixties. He held a large mailing envelope. *Delivery at this hour?*

Peden let the curtain fall back into place and frowned as he scratched his head with both hands. The man didn't appear to pose much of a threat, so he pulled back the safety chain, flipped back the dead bolt and opened his office door.

"Mr. Savage?"

As soon as Peden heard the voice, he knew. It was Allen Deming.

Adrenaline ripped through Peden's body. "Get in here!" He grabbed Deming's arm, pulled him into his office and slammed the door shut. He locked the deadbolt and put the safety chain back into place.

Peden took several deep breaths. Turning to face Deming, he said, "I thought you were staying away from here. Like, in Arizona?"

Deming's smile was sly, as if to say *If I fooled you, I fooled our enemy.* "I know who killed my son. At least, based on what I've read, I'm pretty sure I know."

* * *

In the kitchen at the back of Peden's office, the two men sat and drank coffee while they talked about Deming's son. He had spread the contents of his envelope across Peden's small kitchen table.

"This is a letter from Jarrod." He handed the sheet of paper over to Savage and continued. "You can read it for yourself, but he is basically confessing that he was involved in a bunch of crimes that ruined a lot of lives. He also implicates others on his team at the DEA."

When Peden finished reading the one-page summary, Deming handed him more papers. These were stapled together, the pages numbered one through twenty-seven.

Deming said, "Jarrod wrote up the details of busts over the last few years. He put together this list because he believed that these busts destroyed the lives of some basically good people." He took a sip of coffee. "You know, there are some guys who deserve to be punished, but the system just can't seem to nail them. Maybe it's wrong to set them up in order to get them off the street, but they are genuinely bad guys." He paused. Peden just stared at him across the table, letting him think about his next lines. He continued, "But the guys Jarrod describes here, they're just kids, mainly, just going to school, trying to get ahead, you know…not hurting anybody." As he spoke, his gravelly voice choked up. It appeared to Peden that his conscience was eating away at him from the inside. Guilt covered his face, though Peden didn't understand why. He remained silent allowing Deming time to get his thoughts together. After wiping the underside of his nose with his finger, Deming said, "They put away dozens of kids. Each got multi-year sentences. They got caged up with murderers and rapists and other really messed up guys. I never followed up on any of their cases…until the last few months. I found out that at least one of these poor kids was murdered during his stint in the joint."

Peden finally asked, "Why are you so broken up about this? Jarrod and his team, they're the ones who put these kids away."

Allen Deming looked at Peden with a half-smile. His face showed the lines of a man filled with self-loathing, the smile, a thin veil trying desperately to hide a soul filled with remorse. "I knew what was happening and I didn't do anything to stop it." He took another drink of his coffee. "I worked as a clerk for the DA's office. I saw the arrest records as they came through the system. It was easy to see the pattern, each bust with almost the same quantities. The pattern was obvious." He looked down at the table covered in papers filled with details of corruption on a grand scale. He looked up again and said, "You know what I did instead? I walked away. I retired and moved to Arizona so I could forget about all this crap, all the while knowing that it was going to continue. Innocent kids were going to prison so that a handful of greedy assholes could get rich off their misfortune…and I let it happen."

Allen Deming looked away, his eyes welling up.

Peden said, "But here you are with all this evidence."

He picked up a handful of the papers, then tossed them back on the table. "You're doing the right thing, but why now? Why did it take you so long to come forward?"

Deming appeared angry, apparently at himself more than anyone else, but Peden wanted Deming to say it out loud. He had to get the truth from him about why he had hesitated, why he had sat on the evidence laid out before them for so long. Finally, Deming said, "I was scared. They threatened to kill me."

"They?"

"Mercado and Smith, and that weasel, Newsome. Even my own son. Jarrod told me I was a dead man if I uttered a word about their operations. They even offered to cut me in on it, just to keep me quiet. I refused the money, but promised I wouldn't tell anyone. That's when they suggested that I retire." A pause. "That's when I put in my papers. I was gone within the week."

Peden sat back, keeping his eyes on the man sitting across from him. He felt no empathy for him. He had been in a nearly identical situation when he worked for the FBI. But he chose to stay and fight, never backing off his principles, even after receiving death threats. He had uncovered corruption where agents were manufacturing evidence to get "the bad guys" off the streets, similar to what Deming described. In those cases, one could have argued that the FBI was targeting some truly nasty people, but Peden knew that his peers were heading down a very dangerous, slippery slope, one that made them no better than the scum that they pursued. Legally, those men had rights regardless of their transgressions. But what Deming described was nothing short of criminal. Like Deming had said, they were just kids, and that really pissed Peden off.

In a tone that came out harsher than he hoped, Peden asked, "So, your kid gets killed and now you want revenge, and you want me to be the executioner, is that it?"

Deming growled, "No, that's not it at all!" He paused. "Jarrod was coming to his senses. His conscience finally caught up with him. I think his wife, Sylvia, may have had something to do with it."

He rubbed his face with a meaty hand and took a deep breath. He pointed to the documents on the table and spoke in a quiet voice. "All this information; Jarrod sent this to me. He must have mailed the package right before he was killed. I think he knew they were going to kill him before he could tell anybody. Before the other day, I had no evidence. It would have been my word against theirs." He looked at Peden, his manner now hopeful. "Maybe this will convince a judge, or the FBI, or someone, to investigate these bastards."

"You told me over the phone that you were scared for your own life."

Deming looked directly at Peden. "I was...but not anymore. I've got no family left. It's just me. I just want to do what's right...what Jarrod wanted to do before he was murdered."

Staring back at Allen Deming across the pile of papers on his kitchen table, Peden was a mix of emotions. On one hand, the man had knowledge of numerous crimes committed by federal agents which were so appalling that he could barely control his temper. If what he read was true, then dozens of young men's and women's lives had been destroyed. Their families and friends were also victims. They watched as their sons and daughters and brothers and sisters and close friends were incarcerated for crimes that they hadn't committed. Even if the pleas and declarations of innocence of the accused were understood and accepted as truth by their loved ones, they had no way to help prove that innocence and help them escape the clutches of a rigged system. Time incarcerated would be time lost. Worse, when they were finally regurgitated back onto the streets, their ordeal wouldn't be over. Reputations were destroyed with no means to rebuild the trust that at one time had never been questioned. They were starting over from scratch with seemingly insurmountable hurdles firmly set in their paths, the black mark of a criminal record ever present.

On the other hand, Allen Deming had just lost a son. Peden thought about his two daughters, now young adults.

Even though they hadn't spoken to him in several years, he knew what a crushing blow it would be if one of them suffered the same kind of injustice.

Peden took a deep breath. Suddenly, he felt hungry. Softening his tone, he asked, "When did you eat last?"

"I got dinner at some fast food place last night about seven."

"Did you drive all the way from Arizona?"

"Yeah. I rented a car. It has Iowa plates."

"Where are you parked?"

"On the street a few blocks over. Why?"

Peden smiled and said, "Just making sure that they can't find you here. They've got some pretty good resources to track people and good reason to want you dead."

"I rented it under a false name. I know what these guys can do. I'm not taking any chances."

"Where did you stay last night?"

"A no-tell motel outside of Statesboro. Joe Smith paid cash."

Peden nodded his head in approval. "Okay. I'm going to whip us up some bacon and eggs. Do you like grits?"

"Love 'em."

"Alright. Bacon, eggs, grits, and toast it is. We'll have breakfast and we can go over these papers in more detail."

Allen Deming took a deep breath, his body slumping into his chair. He started to relax for the first time since his son was killed on a sunny Savannah morning just four days ago.

Chapter 29

Vincent Mercado and Alex Smith sat in Mercado's gray Acura outside the motel room that had been occupied by Wayne Cleaver upon his release from prison. Sitting in the parking lot of the run-down joint near a faded blue, heavily rusted Chevy Impala, the two agents and the Acura were out of place. Now that a warrant had been issued for Cleaver's arrest, they planned to execute that warrant before other law enforcement agencies jumped the gun. The hotel clerk informed them that Cleaver hadn't stuck around after they rousted him four days earlier. Cleaver left without a trace.

Mercado thought out loud, "Where does a guy with no coin, no car, and no connections go? To mommy's."

Smith said, "We got that covered. He hasn't shown up there yet. We'll nail him if he tries. I think he's still in Savannah."

"What makes you say that?"

"I think he's got a few friends left here from school. Or he may try to hit up the guy who snitched on him." He smiled. "Some friend, huh? If I was Cleaver, I'd track that S.O.B. down and kick his ass."

Mercado thought about that. "Let's have Nichols try to track Cleaver's buddy down. He's not doing anything pressing right now. Does Cleaver have any other local friends?"

"Not really, but it's not like we dug deep into the guy. He was a quick, easy target."

"Yeah, he was." His face got serious for a moment. "I felt guilty setting him up like that."

Smith frowned at him, wondering who the soft-hearted guy was sitting next to him. Then he noticed the smile and they both laughed out loud.

Mercado said, "We've heard nothing from our guys watching his mother's place in Anderson. We haven't seen or heard anything about him locally, but we know he couldn't have gone far. Let's have Metro check local homeless shelters, food banks, the usual hangouts. Tell them to contact us if they get a line on him.

"Let's go back to the office. I think you're right; he's still close. Not enough resources to run and too many places to hide. Have Nichols do a search of his past classmates."

"How far back do you want him to search?"

Mercado gave it some thought. "Senior year in high school."

* * *

Mercado dropped Smith at the office with instructions for Nichols. Begin a search for Wayne Cleaver's personal connections.

He hit the call button on his touch screen and called Newsome at his office. After a few seconds, a ringtone sounded from the Acura's speakers. Newsome answered on the second ring.

"Vince, where are you?"

"In my car heading out of the DEA parking lot. We need to chat, but not on the phone."

After a brief pause, Newsome asked, "You eat yet?"

"Just a doughnut."

"Meet me at the Pankake Palace in twenty minutes. My treat."

* * *

The Pankake Palace was a favorite of the locals in the morning, and drunk college kids and tourists in the evening. An attractive black waitress stopped at their table and smiled politely at Newsome. Her nametag said Nashia. She poured coffee and dropped a couple plastic cream containers in front of the DA. When she turned to Mercado, she amped up the charm, her smile brightening. As she poured his coffee, she commented that Mercado looked like he took his coffee black. Mercado returned the vibe with a smile of his own.

Newsome ordered a western omelet with a side of grits. Mercado ordered three eggs over easy with hash browns, sausage, and wheat toast. Nashia flashed her smile again and turned towards the kitchen.

When she was out of earshot, Mercado, still looking at her behind, said, "We haven't found Cleaver yet, but we think he's close. He's got no money and he hasn't contacted his mom in Anderson. He might have help locally so we're tracking down his old friends. We're also checking homeless shelters and hangouts."

Newsome took a sip of his coffee and held the cup in his hands. He was listening to Mercado, but he was thinking about their meeting with Judge Stillwell. He'd lost his composure, but someone needed to stand up to the judge. The current pace of payday busts placed the team in jeopardy, especially with Jarrod Deming's murder and the added scrutiny from the FBI. Without a shooter in custody, that pressure would continue.

Newsome asked, "Nichols looked like a ghost last time I saw him. Is he going to fold on us?"

"Nah." Mercado's response lacked conviction and Newsome's lifted eyebrows showed his doubt. "I had a one-on-one with him. He got the message. Alex is going to talk with him, too, just to make sure the point is driven home. He'll be fine."

Newsome sipped his coffee, then asked, "How sure are you about this Cook guy?"

Mercado started to speak when he saw movement coming their way. Nashia approached the table with a coffee carafe and creamers. As she topped off their coffee cups, she said, "You're order will be out in just a moment." She flashed her pearly whites at Mercado then turned and walked back towards the kitchen, adding a bit of shake to her stride. Mercado smiled while enjoying the show. Newsome watched Mercado and shook his head.

"Where was I? Oh, yeah. Marcus Cook. The scoop on Cook is that he was ousted from the Army on a general discharge. Apparently, he shot up a village then claimed the villagers were harboring Al Qaeda fighters. His command didn't buy it. Said he was a loose cannon and a danger to his team."

"What makes you think he won't be a danger to us?"

Mercado took a sip of his freshly topped-off coffee. "Because it turns out he was right. The Army had a firefight with Al Qaeda in that village. When Cook tried to get reinstated, the Army refused; too much egg on a certain officer's face if they recanted. So, they ruined Cook's career to cover somebody else's ass."

Newsome thought about it. "Sounds like a good reason to get back at your country. Just make sure you vet this guy good. You can't afford to be wrong. *We* can't afford it."

"Relax, Andy. I'll be watching him close."

They sat in silence, drinking coffee, each with their own thoughts. Nashia brought their breakfast plates, asked if they needed anything else, turned and left.

Mercado watched Newsome's face, reading the lines and shifts and nervous twitches. He could tell that the events of the past week were causing his normally high level of anxiety to tick up further. Typically, when they sat and talked through issues that were of mutual concern, by the time they thoroughly discussed each point, Newsome was far less agitated. Not today. Newsome's nerves were like a bomb about to explode. He had let loose some of his angst on Stillwell. Mercado hoped he could get the DA to loosen up.

"You look like you're ready to explode. What gives?"

Newsome glanced towards the server station to ensure no one could hear him. He locked eyes with Mercado and said, "What was that look you gave Stillwell when he said he didn't care which one of you pulled the trigger?"

Mercado felt uncomfortable talking about Deming's murder in public, but the fact was, he and his team had nothing to hide. He leaned forward. In a hushed, baritone voice, he said, "I looked at Stillwell like that because none of us pulled the trigger. Understand? We're clean on this."

Newsome's eyebrows lowered and his nose scrunched up giving him his classic rat-face look. Had Mercado not been so uneasy, he might have laughed, but, under the circumstances, there was little room for levity.

The plan had been for Mercado's team to take care of Deming before he dropped his bombshell revelation. Stillwell, Newsome, and Mercado's team all knew that their world would come crashing down if word got out about the payday busts. The options were few. One way or another, Deming had to go.

Newsome whispered, "But I gave you the order from Stillwell. What happened?"

"Not here, Andy. Not here."

Nashia headed their way, but before she got close, Newsome waived her off. She turned on her heels back towards the server station.

"I need to know, Vince. Who did it?"

"Andy, it can wait until we get out of here."

Newsome didn't say another word while they concentrated on finishing their breakfast. He left over half his omelet untouched though he did finish all his grits. Mercado cleaned his plate as if it was his last meal. When Nashia left their check, Newsome tipped her generously.

They retreated to Newsome's car. Initially, the heat was unbearable. Newsome turned on the car and adjusted the air conditioning to maximum cool. After a few seconds, the vents began pouring out cool air. In less than a minute, the temperature in the car was tolerable. While the car cooled further, they picked up the discussion about Deming's killer.

Newsome asked, "Why didn't you guys take the shot?"

"Alex was getting ready to move. He had the trunk of the car open and was reaching for his rifle when we heard the reports and saw the crowd scrambling. We saw Deming fall back. I looked at Smith, but his gun was still in the trunk. He looked at me like *What should I do now?* He shut the trunk. I motioned to Smith and Nichols to follow me. I wanted to make sure that someone else had actually shot him. Sure enough, he was dead before he hit the concrete steps. We saw that Nila was hit, too, but not real bad. We followed him to the hospital where the ER doc confirmed it."

"So, Vince, who's the shooter?"

Mercado's teeth clenched and he rubbed his jaw. "You know, Andy, I've been wracking my brain, trying to figure that out, and I don't know. I mean, there are a bunch of guys we put away, but of the ones who are out now, none that we know of stuck around here. We're going to go ahead with the plan to pin it on Cleaver, then find the real shooter later."

Newsome's nose scrunched up. Pinning a dope charge on some unsuspecting pot head was one thing, but slapping a guy with a murder charge? That was beyond cold. They were going to completely screw this poor guy's life up. For what? So that they could get the spotlight off themselves? How has it come to this?

Mercado watched Newsome as the gears in his brain spun. He could tell that there was an ethical tug-of-war going on, deciding how much longer he could go along with the status quo. It was the same fight that Jarrod Deming struggled with just before he was killed. He worried that Stillwell might order Mercado to take care of another problem. He wondered, if push came to shove, could he actually pull the trigger and kill his business partner, especially if it meant protecting himself?

That was a decision for another day, one he hoped would never come.

Chapter 30

The aroma of bacon was strong, which conflicted with her view of a mountain stream. She expected pine scent, decaying leaves, burning wood from campfires, and a cool, damp breeze. But warmth engulfed her, as if she was wrapped in a blanket.

A voice called out from the distance. "Elizabeth."

She recognized the voice, but couldn't place it. She kept walking, drawn by the strong smell of bacon, her senses still at odds with each other.

The distant voice again called out. "Elizabeth." A warm hand touched her shoulder. Startled, she spun around to face the intruder. Opening her eyes, she saw a man with short, dark hair. It was Wayne Cleaver.

"Hey, sleepy head, breakfast is almost ready. How do you like your eggs?"

Elizabeth Sanchez blinked her eyes and rolled her head against her pillow. In a low, dry, sleepy voice, she said, "Oh my God, you scared me...but that bacon smells amazing." She sat on the edge of the bed, raised her arms and stretched, looking at Wayne who had already showered and dressed. "Give me a few minutes to wake up. What time is it anyway?"

"Seven-thirty."

"What? It's Saturday. I don't usually get up until at least ten."

"I thought since we hit the hay kind of early last night that you'd want to get up early."

Elizabeth thought back to the night before and smiled. "It's not like we went to sleep right away."

Wayne's smiling face colored a bit. He wasn't comfortable talking about sex, especially with a woman who, up until the night before, was just a good friend. "You can't wait too long. You have to operate that coffee thing-a-ma-gig. Holler when you're ready for me to throw on the eggs. How do you like yours?"

She said in a sly voice, "Over easy."

He leaned closer to her and kissed her on the cheek. Before he knew it, Elizabeth pulled his face close to hers and kissed him lightly on the lips. He stayed still for a few seconds, then smiled. "I think my bacon's burning."

He straightened and headed back to the kitchen. Elizabeth smiled then jumped up and headed to the walk-in closet to throw on a robe.

* * *

After breakfast, Elizabeth showered and dressed in running sweats, a tee shirt and running shoes. She explained to Wayne that she needed to do some grocery shopping, that she'd be gone for a few hours. "Can you stay out of sight while I'm gone? Maybe not strut around in front of my neighbors?"

Wayne looked down at the living room carpet, feigning remorse at Elizabeth's playful scolding. He looked up at her, trying to look serious. "I'll be good, I promise."

He saw her shoes approaching and raised his head in time to see that her face was inches from his. She wrapped her arms around his neck and said, "I'll be back in time for lunch. What are you hungry for?"

Looking at her playful smile, food was the furthest thing from his mind. He opened his mouth to speak and not a sound came out. Before he knew it, Elizabeth kissed him on the lips. It was a soft, playful kiss. He put his arms loosely around her waist. After fifteen seconds, she pulled away. She backed towards the door, keeping her eyes on him as she reached for the door knob.

Wayne stood there, dumbfounded as she left her condo, closing and locking the door behind her. He shook his head, trying to clear the clouds away, but it was no use. He was falling for her like a brick. *You just got out of prison, you dope. You can't fall for the first chick that comes along, especially this chick. You're putting her in jeopardy – her job and her life.*

I know, but she is so beautiful, and smart, and she believes in me. Besides, she started it.

Wayne retreated to the kitchen and started to clean up the breakfast dishes, the internal struggle continuing in his head. By the time he had the pans cleaned, dried, and stashed in the cupboards, a smile was etched across his face. He couldn't stop thinking about Elizabeth Sanchez.

* * *

Elizabeth drove from her condominium across downtown. She parked her car in a lot next to the Colonial Park Cemetery, her nerves causing involuntary pulses along her spine, as she thought about the task at hand. Her thoughts jumped to her friend, Sylvia, and what she must be going through, knowing that her husband had cheated on her just before he was murdered. Elizabeth had to know if it was true, that Jarrod's boss, Nila West, had been sleeping with her best friend's husband. She walked south on Habersham towards Liberty Avenue.

At 9:40 AM, the sun was already making its way into the sky, heating the air, the humidity already brutal. The day promised to be a scorcher.

Elizabeth passed from a stretch of sidewalk exposed to direct sunlight to East Liberty Avenue where the ample canopy of the Southern Oaks provided some relief from the hot sun. She feared that her deodorant was already failing. As she made the turn onto Liberty, her destination came into view.

Nila West lived in a two bedroom, two bath condominium, part of an historic, three-story building. The exterior sported pale gold stucco, beautifully maintained with entrances to individual units from Liberty Street, Perry Lane, and either side of the building down narrow alleys. The entrance to Nila West's first-floor unit was on the west side of the building accessed by a wrought-iron gate which was set back from the front edge of the building by about eight to ten feet. A five-foot-wide alley separated Nila West's building and another building to her left. Like many charming alleyways in Savannah, the gate was partially hidden from the street by a number of trees and bushes planted in front of the structures.

Elizabeth walked up to the gate and looked around. There were several people walking on the sidewalk on either side of Liberty Street. They looked like students out for their morning walk. All wore running suits and had ear buds planted in their ears. She turned to the gate, lifted the latch, and pulled the gate towards her. The loud squeal made Elizabeth cringe. There was no turning back now. She walked another fifteen feet down the alley and came to Unit H, Nila West's condo.

Elizabeth stood facing the ornate, solid wood door, rehearsing what she would ask Nila West. *Why were you sleeping with my friend's husband, a co-worker and subordinate of yours? Are you that arrogant that you think you can take anything you want? Does this have anything to do with his murder?*

A cold shiver ran down her spine. The combination of her thoughts and the fear of what Nila West might say back to her, plus the cool, damp feel of the concrete walls of the buildings on either side of her whittled away at her confidence. She looked left towards Perry Lane, then right towards Liberty Street. No one was in sight. *Show time.*

Elizabeth rapped on the door hard with her fist two times and was in mid swing for the third knock when the door eased open slightly from the force of her blows. The hinges squeaked under the weight of the ancient, heavy wood. She drew in a deep, sharp breath as her nerves went into overdrive. The door was open just a few inches, but Elizabeth felt uneasy about pushing the door open further.

What started as the desire for an angry face-to-face confrontation now turned into self-doubt. Elizabeth nervously looked both ways down the alley. She didn't know what to expect or how she should proceed, but she had come this far. Maybe West had forgotten to close her door tight or maybe the door latch didn't work right.

She took another deep breath, cleared her throat and called out, "Ms. West?"

The only sound was rustling leaves on the trees on

Liberty Street.

Again, louder this time. "Ms. West? Are you home?"

Again, nothing. Elizabeth was now chilled to the bone, her body shivering from the adrenaline rush. She pushed on the door with her closed fist. The door was heavy. It resisted her attempts to open it and she had to apply more pressure to get it to swing further inward. When the opening was large enough for her to move inside, she took one hesitant step in and called out again, "Ms. West? Are you home? I'm a friend of Sylvia Deming."

Elizabeth looked around the condominium. Little natural light made its way into the first-floor unit. She let her eyes adjust to the dark interior. It was hard to tell what color the walls were painted. No lights were on and curtains were pulled shut on the few windows that she could see.

It was eerily quiet as she moved a step deeper into Nila West's home. A loud click made her jump. Then she heard a quiet buzz coming from the kitchen and realized that the refrigerator had cycled on. She exhaled, relieving some of her tension. That relief didn't last long as she picked up a scent that she recognized from other crime scenes that she had visited. The foul odor of human waste emanated from inside the condo. Elizabeth's first instinct was to turn and leave, but she had to find the odor's origin to confirm what she suspected.

She stepped into the unit, looking left to right, then straight ahead. Just inside the door, the living room was neat and clean, nothing out of place. To the left, a hallway led to the bedrooms and bathrooms. Straight across, a large archway opened into the kitchen. Elizabeth followed the foul scent.

She was still six feet from the archway when she saw Nila West on the kitchen floor, face up, her body twisted in an odd position. A pool of blood seeped from under her back. She wore a tank top, shorts and running shoes. She was either preparing for a run or had just returned from one. The front of the tank top was soaked in blood from an apparent gunshot or knife wound.

Elizabeth covered her mouth to keep from screaming

aloud. She took repeated deep breaths through her mouth, trying to keep her composure. Her first instinct was to turn and run, but she stood still, continuing her deep breaths. There was no need to take Nila West's pulse. The blood on either side of her body was dry, her skin was pale, her open eyes clouded over. Elizabeth knew that she had to get out of Nila West's condominium immediately, but she had to remain calm until she was far away from what she knew was a crime scene.

Elizabeth took one last look around, trying to find anything out of the ordinary. She didn't see a single object out of place. The unit looked pristine – save for the dead body on the kitchen floor.

* * *

Peden Savage and Allen Deming reviewed the information that Allen had received from his son, Jarrod. The information confirmed what Peden, Megan Moore, Marcus Cook, and Lee Sparks believed to be true. The local DEA office was framing low-level pot dealers so that they could enrich themselves with taxpayer seed money and confiscated drug money. They now had convincing evidence that major crimes had been committed by the agents. The evidence had to be presented to the FBI, another federal agency that Allen Deming didn't trust. Peden tried to convince him that Megan Moore was on his side. He conceded that she was, but what about her boss and her peers? His big question was, to whom was *she* going to present the evidence?

Chapter 31

Elizabeth Sanchez sat in her car taking deep breaths. She had walked away from Nila West's condominium as fast as she could, while trying to not draw undue attention. Sweat poured down her face, back and chest, soaking her gray tee shirt. The combination of the heat and humidity, and the adrenaline rush after finding Nila West's body, pushed her sweat glands into overdrive.

She calmed down long enough to put the situation into perspective. Her first thought - *Did anyone see me at the condo?* Regardless, getting far away from Nila West's condominium was her first priority. Second, find a pay phone and call Savannah-Chatham County Metro Police and report – what – a murder? A possible break-in?

She couldn't say that she found a body. If someone had seen her at West's home, and she was identified as the person making the call, she could at least say that she never entered the condominium. She just saw the door ajar and thought that something was wrong. Chances were slim that anyone saw her in the alley…she hoped.

She found her way to the Harry S. Truman Parkway and headed south. Staying under the speed limit was a challenge as was keeping her composure. She still had no idea where to stop and make the 911 call.

She exited the parkway at East Derenne Avenue and pulled into the Twelve Oaks Plaza. She had no idea how long she'd been driving. It felt like hours. Finding a pay phone was difficult; cell phones rendering them obsolete. But there, at the edge of the lot and away from foot traffic was a pay phone.

Elizabeth's next concern? Cameras catching her car and license plate. She parked in the middle of the lot between a van and a large SUV, then walked towards the Publix Supermarket. Once near the store, she detoured to the phone. The short walk helped calm her rattled nerves.

After a series of deep breaths, she lifted the receiver and held it away from her head. She hung up the phone again when she couldn't decide what to say. Should she use her real voice or try to disguise it? Can they trace this call right away? Will they send the police here? *Stop! Just calm down and make the call. Don't make it obvious that you're freaked out.*

Elizabeth rehearsed what she would say then picked up the phone and dialed 911. The dispatcher picked up immediately.

A calm, female voice asked, "Nine-one-one, what is your emergency?"

Elizabeth's nerves were still off the charts but her voice came out as if she were reciting a script. "I think there's been a break in at 312 Liberty Street."

"Is that East or West Liberty Street."

The question threw her off for a second. She answered, "East."

"Are you the resident?"

"No."

"Did you witness the break in?"

"No."

"Do you know the number of perpetrators?"

Frustrated by the questions and getting angry with being drilled about the 'break in,' Elizabeth said, "No. Listen. The door to my friend's condo was ajar. The woman who lives there never leaves her door open like that. Can you have the police check it out please?"

After a pause and the sound of the dispatcher pounding on a keyboard, she said, "A car is on the way. Did you say that this is your friend's condo?"

Elizabeth hung up the phone and turned towards the store. A loud horn blared, startling her. She had walked into the path of a car. Luckily, the car was moving slowly and the driver was paying attention. The middle-aged black man shouted out his open window that she should watch where she's walking. Elizabeth mouthed *Sorry* to the man then made tracks for the store entrance.

She entered the store and went to the produce department where she grabbed a couple bags from the roll at the end of the fruit aisle. She put four apples in one of the bags and three oranges in the other bag. She walked back to the dairy section and picked up a dozen eggs and a half-gallon of milk. With her groceries in hand, she headed for a self-serve checkout then detoured to a line with a cashier.

The young man at the register noticed her sweat-soaked tee shirt and asked, "Been out jogging?"

Her face momentarily looked alarmed. "What?"

"You've been sweating. I just thought that you'd been out for a jog."

She relaxed, realizing that his comment was a great alibi. She said, "Yeah. I just did a couple miles. I'm still kind of beat."

He smiled. "I jog, too. Be sure to drink some water. Your cheeks look a little flushed."

She flashed a weak smile. "I will. Thanks."

He finished ringing up her few groceries. She paid cash and headed for the exit. As she approached the exit, she noticed a Savannah-Chatham Metro police car moving slowly through the parking lot. *Damn.* She took a deep breath and walked as normally as possible through the exit towards her car. Tossing her bags in the passenger seat, she started her car and backed out at what she hoped was a normal speed. The patrol car continued its transit of the lot, paying Elizabeth no mind.

The trip back to her condominium was tense but uneventful. When she unlocked the door, Wayne greeted her with a concerned look and an appraising stare.

He asked, "Did you run a marathon or something?"

She started to cry as she ran into his arms. Through deep sobs, Elizabeth wailed, "She's dead."

Wayne's eyes grew wide. It took a moment for her statement to sink in. As he tightened his arms around her, he asked, "Who?"

"Nila West."

"You mean, Jarrod Deming's boss?"

"And mistress. Yeah."

Wayne's thoughts were crashing into each other like high voltage bumper cars. He felt like running, but held on to Elizabeth even tighter.

* * *

"We get cash to make 'buys' from dealers. We use undercover guys to make the buys over a period of time to gain the dealer's trust. The buys are recorded and kept for evidence. Then we set up a major buy, record it, and bring the hammer down. It seems simple, but over the years we've found that we get convictions on only a handful of cases."

Marcus looked surprised. "You mean, after all that work, these cases aren't a slam dunk?"

"Some are and some aren't. That's why we got smarter than the system."

Mercado's sly smile displayed a touch of evil. "We still get the seed money, and we do use it for buys once in a while, but not often."

Marcus watched the monitor in his home office. He couldn't see his own face, but was able to see Mercado's face on the recording of their meeting at the Hercule's Bar and Grill. Mercado had no idea that Marcus wore a micro camera and microphone combination during their meeting. He was reviewing the recording for the third time. The evidence was damning for Mercado, Smith, and Nichols, as well as the late Jarrod Deming.

Mercado explained why he and his team got frustrated. Hardcore dealers were either escaping conviction or were getting out of prison early after shortened sentences. The public thought that they were cleaning up the streets. In reality, it was a revolving door at the penitentiary. The dealers were back in business before the books were even closed on their cases.

Mercado leaned forward and said, "That's when our team was approached by a guy who's pretty high up in the judicial system with a plan. At first, I was skeptical, that maybe they were trying to set us up for some corruption sting or something. Then I thought, *Why would they do that?* They got nothing to gain from it. I dug a little deeper and the plan sounded solid."

On the monitor, Marcus remained silent. At that time, he was trying to move Mercado along without appearing too anxious. He remembered taking a sip of his beer just to do something with his hands to hide his emotions. On the monitor, Mercado also took a swig from his beer. Then he continued.

"So, these guys, the Judge and the DA, approach me about their plan. They had noticed I was complaining about dealers being back on the streets and they say to me, *Vince, would a cash bonus from time to time get you to stop bitchin'?* And I said, *Maybe. Depends on the amount.* They say, *You'll be happy.*"

Marcus remembers smiling at Mercado at this point. He was smiling because Mercado just gave him evidence that the team was extorting money and that there were more people involved than just the DEA team members.

Marcus heard himself say, "Tell me more."

He listened as Vince Mercado explained how the Judge, the DA and the DEA team split the buy money and busted low-level punks. He explained that they used the same fifty to sixty pounds of grass as evidence against the dealers. The Judge and the DA made sure that all the cases pleaded out. The perpetrators really were dealers, but most were small-time. They wouldn't have received jail time, much less time in the big house. They were so scared of doing hard time that most begged their defense attorneys to accept a plea.

After Mercado finished, Marcus heard himself ask, "What would my take be?"

Mercado answered, "About twenty grand a pop. And we usually do fifteen or more busts each year. We are taking a break because of Deming's murder, but we'll be back at it with a vengeance once this is behind us."

Marcus knew it was time to contact Megan Moore and

Peden Savage. He had already made several copies on jump drives for his friends and one for safekeeping. He reached for his desk phone. When he did, the phone rang. Damn poor timing.

He picked up and said, "Cook."

Vince Mercado was on the other end. "We got a big problem, my man."

Marcus got nervous thinking that Mercado had found out about his recording of their meeting. "What's the problem?"

"Nile West was murdered."

It took a second for Marcus to comprehend what he had just heard. "Say what?"

"You heard me right. They found her body just minutes ago in her condo. Shot in the chest. Needless to say, things are on hold for a bit, maybe longer than we discussed."

The news was delivered with cold calm. Their boss was murdered and Mercado said it like he was reading the baseball scores from the sports page. Marcus rubbed his face with his free hand. "Any suspects?"

"Yeah, the whole team and about half a dozen dope dealers." There was a pause. "We have a guy that we want to pin it on, but we have to find him first."

He asked, "What do you need me to do?"

Mercado told Marcus to meet him and the rest of the team later that afternoon so that they could come up with a game plan. Marcus agreed and they ended the conversation.

Once off the phone, he knew one thing that he had to do immediately; search Nila West's office for the notes that he saw her reviewing. He would call Peden and Megan while on the way to the DEA office. He shut down his computer and snatched the four jump drives of his meeting with Mercado. He stuffed them in his pocket, holstered his Glock, and headed for the door.

Chapter 32

The blond anchorwoman for *Channel 8 News* recited the Breaking News to the television crowd.

> *Less than one week ago Drug Enforcement Administration Special Agent Jarrod Deming was assassinated on the front steps of the Savannah DEA office. Now, a second DEA agent has been murdered. The body of Special Agent Nila West, Deming's immediate supervisor, was found in her Liberty Street Condominium earlier today, the victim of an apparent murder.*

> *Savannah-Chatham Metropolitan Police need your assistance in locating this man, Wayne Willis Cleaver, in connection with the murder of Deming. A police spokesman would not say whether Cleaver is a suspect in the West murder, but a warrant for his arrest was issued last evening. Drug Enforcement Administration's Clifford Metzger, Nila West's supervisor, stated that it was far too early in the investigation to make any comments. He asked only that anyone knowing the whereabouts of Cleaver contact the Savannah-Chatham Metropolitan Police immediately.*

Wayne Cleaver's less-than-complimentary mug shot, taken immediately after his drug arrest, was displayed on the television screen behind the anchorwoman. She continued.

> *Cleaver was released from the Coastal State Prison in Garden City on Tuesday, the same morning that Deming was gunned down*

during a news conference. West, who was standing behind Deming at the news conference, was injured by a bullet fired from the murder weapon.

Channel 8 News contacted Roland Fosco, Special Agent in Charge of the Savannah office of the FBI and asked what part Cleaver may have played in Deming's murder and whether the murders of Deming and West are linked. He had this to say.

The television screen switched to an old file photograph of Roland Fosco. The audio of a phone conversation played for less than thirty seconds. During the call, Fosco stated that a number of law enforcement agencies were working together on the case. When asked if the FBI believed Cleaver to be the gunman in the murders, he said that he could not comment on an ongoing investigation.

The caller then pressed Fosco on why the Savannah-Chatham Metropolitan Police called the station about Cleaver and not the FBI. He again stated that law enforcement agencies were working together and that he had no further comment. He abruptly disconnected the call.

The television picture switched back to the anchorwoman. The picture of Wayne Cleaver was again posted on the screen behind her, this time with a telephone number prominently displayed. She said,

The Savannah-Chatham Metropolitan Police Department will only say that Cleaver is possibly armed and dangerous. You are advised that, if you see him, do not approach him and call the number on your screen.

In other news this evening...

Elizabeth Sanchez and Wayne Cleaver sat in dumbfounded silence, staring at the television screen as the Channel 8 anchorwoman moved on to a story about a lost dog. Elizabeth's mind raced. *What should we do? Did the police know Wayne was staying with her? Did her nosey neighbor get a good enough look at Wayne to recognize him from the mug shot on the television? Did she even see the news broadcast?*

She turned to Wayne. He was already looking at her, fear and doubt plastered on his face. His eyes screamed *I'm so sorry*. His posture sagged, an outward sign of defeat, as if he was saying to her, *They got me...nowhere to run.*

"Snap out of it," she said with some force in her voice. "They're trying to pin this on you because you're an easy target."

He looked at her, the hopelessness still evident. "I'm not worried about me, Liz. You're in danger of losing your job, maybe worse, because of me. I can't let that happen. I've got to leave, right now."

She sat up straight, her face flushed with anger. "Bullshit! You're not going anywhere! You didn't have to convince me to help! I did it willingly! We're in this together!"

The forcefulness of her voice hit him like a two-by-four. Even knowing that her career could be in jeopardy, she still believed in his innocence, in his integrity. It broke him out of his malaise.

"Liz, these guys could come in here with guns drawn, fully intending to kill me. They want me dead so they can pin the whole mess on me. I can't put you in that kind of danger. Chances are that they're planning their move as we speak. How can..."

"Stop! Just stop!" She squared around on the sofa to face him. She grabbed his hands in hers. "If they knew you were here, they'd have already been here and busted you. They're asking for help. That means they don't know where you are and they're hoping someone has seen you. The only person we know of who has seen you is my neighbor."

He put on his best fake frown and said, "Guess we'll have to kill her."

She smiled wanly. "Not funny. She's nosey but she's sweet. Besides, she's got dementia...a little bit anyway. She probably doesn't even remember what you look like."

"She is nice. She complimented you on your green

thumb."

Elizabeth looked alarmed. "What, did you go over and have tea with her?"

He smiled, then his face turned serious. "No, but I think that we shouldn't take any chances. It might be a good idea if I didn't stay here. Someone's bound to figure out that I'm here."

Elizabeth had to admit that he was right. Her condominium was less than a quarter-mile from the courthouse. Many city and county employees lived nearby.

The bottom line: either he stayed put in her condominium or she moved him to another location. If he stayed, they took the chance that her neighbor didn't recognize him on the news or didn't see the broadcast. That was a big risk. If he moved to a new location, they had to ensure that he stayed out of sight and that it was a location where the Feds wouldn't think to look.

* * *

Gertrude Francis chopped celery and carrots at her kitchen counter while a large pot of chicken broth heated on her stovetop. Five large chicken breasts cooled in a casserole dish on a metal rack next to the sink. She loved homemade chicken soup. When she whipped up her mother's recipe, she made enough to fill a dozen single serving containers for freezing.

The *Channel 8 News* aired as she cut the chicken breasts into one inch cubes. A picture of Wayne Cleaver popped up on her TV screen. She frowned. Recognition ran through her mind. *Where have I seen that face before?*

She hit the button on her remote control to un-mute the sound just as the anchorwoman advised the viewing audience that the man pictured was wanted for the murder of Drug Enforcement Administration Special Agent Jarrod Deming. The number to call was plastered on the screen below Wayne's picture. Gertrude reached for a pencil and wrote down the number.

She muted the TV sound again and reached for a towel to wipe the chicken residue from her hands, all the while asking herself, *Where have I seen this man before?*

She reached for the phone and dialed the number. After just one ring, a woman with a strong Georgia accent answered, "Savannah-Chatham Metro Police hot line. How may I help ya'll?"

Gertrude hesitated a moment. "That man on the news...I've seen him before."

The woman asked, "Ma'am, are you referring to Wayne Willis Cleaver?"

Gertrude again hesitated, thinking, *What was the name on the screen?* Then she asked, "Was that the name of the man on the TV during the news?"

"Ma'am, what is ya'll's name?"

"My name? Why do you need my name?"

"Ma'am, it's just so we know who made the report."

"It's Gertrude...Gertrude Francis."

"Now, Ms. Francis, when did you see the person on TV?"

"It was on the *Channel 8 News*, just a few minutes ago."

The operator paused before she spoke again. "No, ma'am. I mean when did you actually see this person? Where was he?"

Gertrude was confused, her mind working overtime but mired in a fog that was thickening with every thought. "I can't remember. I recognized the face when I saw it on the television, but I can't remember where I saw him."

The woman on the phone replied, "That's okay, ma'am. You have our number. If you remember just call us back. We'll be here."

Gertrude hung up the phone and noticed steam rising from the pot on the stove. She remembered that she had to get the chicken cut up into cubes and add it to her soup. Her full attention shifted to finishing her mother's recipe.

* * *

A young waitress at Sandra's Seafood Restaurant in Ellabell, Georgia, saw Wayne Cleaver's picture on the television that hung in one corner of the dining area. She stopped and looked closer. She immediately recognized the guy who came in with a well-dressed young woman just a few days earlier. She couldn't believe that he was wanted for murder. He looked harmless. They looked like a nice couple. When the hotline number appeared on the screen, she jotted it down on her pad, deciding that she would call after the dinner crowd thinned down.

As time passed, she forgot about the broadcast. In her haste, she tore off the ticket with the hotline number and turned it in with a dinner order. The number was lost in a stack of orders for the evening.

When she finished closing out her evening tickets and cleaning up the restaurant, she remembered the picture of Wayne Cleaver and that she had planned to call the hotline. Thinking about the couple, she decided that there was no way it was the same person. Besides, she was tired after a fast-paced shift and needed to get home. She still had homework to do before her classes the next day.

* * *

Sylvia Deming sat on her living room couch reading a romance novel, her eyes fluttering shut as sleep took over. She had been packing boxes of Jarrod's belongings, as well as her own, all day in preparation for putting the house on the market. Jarrod had been dead less than a week, but Sylvia decided it was best that she get a fresh start in a new city and state. Even her renewed friendship with her best friend from college, Elizabeth Sanchez, couldn't keep her in Savannah.

She looked up from her book at the muted television and saw the face of Wayne Cleaver on *Channel 8 News* at 11:07 PM. Reaching for the remote control, she un-muted the sound and listened to the anchorwoman talk about the warrant that had been issued for the ex-con. She was shocked to hear that Jarrod's boss, Nila West was also murdered. She jumped from the couch and went around the house, locking doors and windows as she went. Finally, she went to the gun cabinet, pulled out her 9mm Sig Sauer, checked that the clip was full and cycled the slide, driving a bullet into the chamber. Only then did she check that the safety was engaged.

I wonder if Elizabeth has heard about Nila West? Is it too late to call?

Sylvia moved to the kitchen, leaving the television in the living room on. She grabbed the cordless phone from the table and hit speed dial number for Elizabeth's cell. Her friend picked up on the third ring.

* * *

Elizabeth saw Sylvia's number on the screen and answered with a pleasant but tired, "Hey, Sissy."

"Hi, Liz. I'm so sorry bothering you at this late hour, but I just saw on the news that Jarrod's boss was killed. Did you hear about it?"

Elizabeth's heart raced. She had to say something quick and she had to calm down.

"Yes. I heard about it on the six o'clock news." She looked over at Wayne and mouthed *Sylvia*. He frowned, but didn't seem too concerned. "They're looking for this guy, Wayne Cleaver. He just got out of prison the day Jarrod was killed."

"This is getting to be too much, Liz. I was packing up some of Jarrod's things today." She paused. "I'm going to move. I can't stay in this house anymore. But first, I'm taking a week and going to Florida, maybe the Keys. I've got to get away."

Elizabeth asked, "Do you need me to watch the house while you're gone?"

This seemed to brighten Sylvia's mood just a bit. "I was thinking that you might go with me, but I'm leaving tomorrow morning. I don't suppose you could call off work for a week on such short notice?"

"Sorry, Sissy. I can't. I'll come by in the morning and get a set of keys."

"Liz, you're the best."

Elizabeth felt guilty hearing her friend praise her for her kindness, especially since she was going to take advantage of Sylvia's absence.

Chapter 33

"One-point-five million dollars, non-sequential bills divided equally into two duffle bags. Tomorrow afternoon, fly into the Savannah-Hilton Head Airport. See Jarvis Davidson at the National rental desk. He will give you the keys to your rental car."

Vince Mercado barked the orders into a throwaway cell phone. The Senator listened to Mercado on a throwaway that he had been given on his last visit. Mercado continued, "When you are in the rental car, call me and I will give you further instructions. Be alone. Dress casually. No law enforcement. No tricks." He added, "We'll be monitoring your votes and actions in the Senate. Don't screw with us, Senator. Your son's freedom is at stake."

"Mr. Mercado, I know exactly what is at stake. I will do exactly what ya'll say."

Mercado smiled and disconnected the call, surprised that Vega didn't put up a fuss about the short notice to gather the cash. He apparently had the cash on hand and was ready to go.

If all went according to plan, Mercado would meet the Senator and make the pickup at a shopping center in Statesboro, tomorrow around dinnertime. Vega would be given instructions to drive to a hotel near the interchange of Interstates 95 and 16. Once there, he would receive new instructions to head north to Hardeeville, South Carolina, and pull into the Burger King restaurant. Mercado would let him sit there for a while then give him the final instructions to go to Statesboro, Georgia, on back roads, avoiding the freeways. Smith and Nichols, in separate cars, were to tail Vega making sure he wasn't followed. His rental would be equipped with a tracking device and a voice recorder. If he had any conversations with law enforcement while in route, they would hear at least his side of the conversation.

Once Mercado had the money, he planned to drop the bags and the cash at a house that he had rented outside of Swainsboro, Georgia, in an anonymous name. Smith, Nichols, and Cook would then pick up the cash, transferring the bills to six separate bags, one each for the six partners. Marcus Cook would get a small cut to lock in his loyalty to the team.

Mercado smiled. Another year and he could retire to a tropical island or a mountain retreat, if he could stand another year of Stillwell and Newsome. Mercado sighed as he thought about a white, sandy beach, aqua blue water, and a Bacardi and Coke. His thoughts were interrupted by his cell phone blasting out a Metallica song. Newsome again.

Crap. Now what?

* * *

Peden Savage looked around at his nineteenth-century office, listening to a recording of Senator Vega and Special Agent Vincent Mercado. It was crystal clear that Mercado was calling the shots for the money drop. What wasn't clear was where the money would flow once it was delivered. Peden hoped to capture more details, but Mercado was too smart to spill his guts during a phone conversation.

Peden yawned as the clock in his office hit 10:15 PM. *Thank God all I have to do is walk upstairs to get to bed.* He still had to chat with Lee Sparks about the recording. As Peden listened in his office, Sparks also listened from his own condominium. The plan was for them to compare notes after the Senator's call to Mercado, but Sparks always reviewed his work before commenting. Savage figured that he would be hearing from Sparks by 10:20 PM.

The conference with his technical man was put on hold by a blinking light on Savage's computer screen, indicating that a call was coming into Mercado's personal cell phone. The caller was identified in a text field on Peden's monitor. *Newsome, Andrew.* Savage smiled and clicked the

Monitor/Record button.

He listened as Newsome spoke with Mercado. Their voices were crystal clear, as if Savage was on a three-way connection with the other two. He was almost afraid to breathe for fear that they could hear him, but Lee Sparks had assured him that no one on the lines that they were tapping could hear anything other than their own conversation. Peden was still skeptical and remained as quiet as possible.

He knew that Sparks was making a digital recording of the new conversation, backing it up at the same time. The recordings were evidence of wrongdoing, but would never be used in any court proceedings. Once the recordings were turned over to the party paying the bills, Senator Armand Vega's security team, Peden had little interest in the recordings.

"Any problems with our man?" Newsome was trying to keep from using the Senator's name on the phone, his paranoia off the charts. He proposed that he and Mercado meet later to discuss the call, but Mercado declined, stating the late hour and the long day ahead, driving around in two different states.

"Andy, try and relax. It's not like we're on the terrorist watch list." He yawned, but the gesture was more for show, trying to calm Newsome. "I gave him the instructions and he said he'd follow them. No questions asked. He knows what's at stake."

"What if he's got…you know…a backup plan? He's got a lot of power, even if we're holding a trump card. I mean, things are getting crazier, especially with the West thing. What the hell. We don't know who did Deming. Now West. Who's next?"

Mercado believed more and more that Newsome was going to crack. He had been concerned about the pace of payday busts before Nila West was murdered and before they decided to extort money from a U.S. Senator. He agreed that things were tense, but it was now time for the team to pull together, not fall to pieces. He was comfortable with his partner, Alex Smith. The guy had nerves of steel. From time to time, Nichols needed to be reassured, but he was coming around. Newsome was the obvious weak link in the chain. He appeared to be in command when they spoke with Senator Vega at the first meeting, piping up when Mercado least expected it. Now, he sounded like a scared little kid in the face of bullies trying to take his lunch money. Mercado's anger spiked. He needed to nip this in the bud, and fast.

In a forceful voice, he said, "Andy, get your shit together! He can't touch us as long as we got his kid on a short leash! Now man up!" He paused then said, "Remember how you took the ball and ran with it the first time we met with Vega? You need to take that attitude all the time from now on out. We're fine. We're golden. With Vega's money and the increase in funding in next year's budget, we're set to make a killing. We'll all retire at a young age and enjoy life for a change. If Stillwell wants to go into politics, that's up to him."

There was silence on the line as Newsome processed everything Mercado had said. He took a deep breath to calm his nerves. When he spoke, it was tentative, still laced with doubt. "Okay, okay, I got it, but we gotta figure out who killed Deming and West. It's great that we want to pin this on Cleaver, but that just means there's a real killer out there. And we're still talking about starting up operations again in less than three weeks. Man." He, again, let out a deep, anxious sigh. "I don't know, Vince."

"Andy, you've got to switch to decaf. You're freaking yourself out. Tomorrow night, we're gonna add a nice chunk of change to our pockets. Another step towards a well-deserved retirement. Believe it, man."

"I'm trying, Vince. I really am."

Mercado heard Newsome's wife asking who was on the phone. Newsome answered that it was one of his Assistant DA's. Apparently, that satisfied her curiosity because she didn't saying anything else. Newsome said, "I gotta go. Meredith is getting too curious. We'll talk in the morning."

"Okay, Andy. Listen, just relax. It's gonna be fine. You've got to trust me on this. Okay?"

"Sure, Vince. Whatever you say."

* * *

Almost immediately after Newsome and Mercado disconnected, Peden Savage's phone rang. It was Lee Sparks.

"Who is Cleaver?"

"You caught that, too. I'm pretty sure it's the guy from the six o'clock news today. There's a warrant for his arrest in Deming's murder. They're gonna try and pin both murders on him. He was released from prison the morning of Deming's murder and hasn't been seen since. Megan was going to look into that. She hasn't called yet. But if what they're saying is true, they don't think he's the trigger man. Mercado says nobody on his team did it." Savage paused. "So, who did?"

There was silence on the line. Peden could almost hear the gears in Spark's head grinding. After several seconds, he asked, "How does a guy just released from prison know where a DEA agent is going to be giving a news conference and how does he get a high-powered rifle and the ammo to carry out the murder? Not to mention arrange the transportation to the shooting location and get away unseen. Plus, the shots were marksman skill level. That whole scenario doesn't work for me."

Peden replied, "Yeah, you're right. Sounds like somebody's blowing smoke up a lot of people's asses. We'll see what Megan finds."

"And he said 'Stillwell.' Is he talking about Judge Stillwell? Judge Whalen Stillwell, the guy who just announced that he's running for Senator? If it's the same guy...man, this is big shit."

Peden said, "Oh, yeah."

"Call me when you hear from her." Lee paused to shift gears again. "So, this recording, we got them on the extortion. But we can't turn this over to Megan. We know they're guilty of extortion and Vega knows they're guilty, too. Where does this go from here?"

Peden didn't want to think about it. His client asked for some surveillance on Mercado's phones and Peden obliged. Michael Jess, the Senator's aide said he would keep the information 'under the radar.' That could mean only one of a very few things. Before he turned the recordings over to his client, he had to make sure that his close friend, Marcus Cook, was out of harm's way. With Cook supporting the cash pickup tomorrow, that was going to be challenging.

Peden thought that with Newsome so close to losing control, maybe it was time to apply a little pressure. Not too much, just enough to push him over the edge. Peden was sure of one thing: Neither Newsome nor Mercado were the ring leaders. Could it be Judge Stillwell? Was he calling the shots? Or maybe Mercado's boss, Cliff Metzger? Was Roland Fosco investigating his counterpart at the DEA? *Could be why he won't let Megan near Metzger.* He was certain that finding the puppet master would lead them to Deming's and West's killer.

Peden's phone rang, jolting him out of his deep thoughts. It was Megan Moore.

"There's no way Wayne Cleaver is the shooter, at least for the Deming murder. He was still being processed out. The logs were tampered with, but the guard who did the processing swore that Cleaver wasn't checked out until several minutes after 10:00 AM. Deming was shot right at 10:00."

Peden rubbed his face and asked, "Does the guard know who altered the log?"

"If he does, he's not saying."

Peden wanted to tell Megan that he and Lee heard Mercado say they planned to implicate Cleaver, but she didn't know about the illegal tap. "This whole thing stinks. We're no closer to finding the shooter than we were a few days ago."

"You're right." She paused. "I have to corner Roland. He's holding something back. I think Metzger knows more than he's letting on."

"You call me as soon as you hear anything." He paused, debating whether to tell her about his new client, Senator Vega, but he thought it could wait until morning. "I'll talk with you tomorrow. I'm headed for bed."

"Me, too. Night, Pedee."

Damn it, Megan. "Night, Megan."

Chapter 34

Megan Moore was troubled and frustrated. Every lead that she followed in the Jarrod Deming murder investigation hit a dead end. The interviews that she conducted pointed her in one direction, then evidence led her in another. The murder had the feel of an inside job, but Jarrod's wife believed that her husband was having an affair with her boss – definitely a motive for murder. Now both parties to the alleged affair were dead. Would Sylvia Deming murder her husband and his lover knowing full well that she would be a potential suspect? Murder investigation 101 – the spouse is a suspect until proven otherwise.

Originally, Sylvia Deming was on the short list of potential suspects. When Megan questioned her at her home, Deming kept talking about a change in her husband's personality. Megan hoped to find out why. Was it related to the busts? Maybe his conscience began to bother him. Maybe he wanted out and he realized that there was no way out. Or maybe that's when the affair with Nila West started. Could it have been that all these issues were piling up on him and he felt trapped? The news conference was his only way out. Who would have lost the most had he been successful in blowing the whistle on his team?

Megan thought about the conversation that she had just finished with Peden Savage. She and Peden had always had a great working relationship; sharing information, working as a team, pooling resources, usually culminating in a successful investigation. Putting bad actors away was their passion, regardless of whether they were common street criminals or whether they hid behind a badge. They knew each other well enough, professionally, that they could read each other's signals.

That was why, when she clicked off from talking with Peden, she was angry. Why was Peden hiding something from her? *We're supposed to be a team, like Mutt and Jeff, Cagney and Lacey, Batman and Robin. Well, that last one was stupid. I should read him the riot act. But, maybe there's a good reason for his holding back.*

And Rollie, keeping me from interviewing Metzger. He's been a real roadblock.

The clock on the living room wall read 10:48 PM. Late, but it was Saturday night. She picked up her cell phone and hit the speed dial number for her boss, Roland Fosco. He answered after five rings.

"Damn it, Megan, it's nearly eleven. My wife's going to think I'm having an affair." He yawned. "Okay, she really won't, but this better be important."

"We're not making any headway on the Deming murder. Now we've added the West murder. We've processed West's condo. All the evidence is at the local lab and I have our forensics team coming in tomorrow to oversee and assist in the processing. That will take time, even with a rush order on the lab. Rollie, I need to interview Metzger."

Roland Fosco didn't reply, almost so long that Megan thought he might have hung up on her. Finally, he said, "I had to move to my office. You can't interview Metzger and I'm not authorized to tell you why."

Megan had had enough of people telling her who she could and could not question. The murders of two federal agents should be at the top of the FBI's priority list. She was the Special Agent in Charge of the investigations. Fosco was her boss, but she knew him well enough that she could speak freely to him, even to the point of shouting.

She angrily barked, "Rollie, this is bullshit! Deming and West are both dead! Who's next?! You?! Me?! Mercado?! You know something and I have a need to know! I've never threatened to go over your head. Don't tempt me now!"

She was afraid that her boss would jump back at her

with a tirade of his own. Instead, he said, "Okay. Calm down, calm down. We can't talk about this on a non-secure line. Let's meet in the morning. Breakfast is on me."

"When and where?"

"Just be ready by 7:00. I'll call you with the location. In the meantime, call Savage and tell him that we're going to need some special gadgets."

"Anything specific?"

"Yes, but we'll discuss that in the morning. His guy Sparks helped create what we need, so it shouldn't be a big challenge for him."

This seemed to take the edge off her frustration, but now her interest piqued. There was obviously more to the story.

* * *

"Damn, Megan. It's after 11:00. I was just about to head up to bed."

Megan smiled as she glanced at the clock. It was 11:02 PM. She knew Peden liked to be in bed by now, but that was too bad. It was the price he paid for keeping secrets.

"So, Pedee, Rollie wanted me to let you know that you and Lee are on the payroll first thing tomorrow morning. He said we need a special gadget. Something that Lee helped create? Do you know what he's talking about?"

Peden suspected that Roland Fosco was going to want surveillance on the DEA team. This was going to get complicated real quick since he already had a tap on Vince Mercado, by way of Senator Armand Vega. If there was a willing judge out there in the Federal Court System, he might be able to make his tap legit. But that also opened the door to having any legal tap thrown out of court due to it starting out as an illegal tap. That was a twist he would leave up to the lawyers and judges.

He stammered, "Well, yeah, um, I think I know what he means. I don't think we should be talking about this right now…I mean, on the phone. Can we meet for breakfast?"

"Sorry, I already have a breakfast date. I'll stop by your

office after. Oh, and by the way, we've processed West's condo. Nothing obvious, but all the evidence is at the lab."

Peden scratched his head, rubbed his eyes and said, "Yeah. Okay. See you then. And, Megan…"

"Yes, Pedee?"

"Never mind. We'll talk in the morning."

* * *

After Megan's call, Peden couldn't sleep. He wanted to tell her about the illegal tap and about his visit from Allen Deming, but he knew all too well that phone lines had ears.

Usually when an investigation progressed, pieces started falling into place. The puzzle picture became clearer, people realized that they were cornered and filled in even more pieces. In the case of Jarrod Deming's murder, the pieces of the puzzle were coming in, but the puzzle was expanding. Originally, it appeared to be murder to keep a whistleblower quiet. Hearing conversations between prime suspects, that might not be true.

Several things were bothering him. The video of Deming as he was shot. He had notes in his hands that were never recovered. What did those notes say? Who would suffer if that information got out? Then he moved slightly as the shots were fired. Was that just a coincidence or did he intentionally move to shield Nila West? Now West was murdered. Maybe she was the original target and Deming was collateral damage.

Something else poked Peden's brain, something off about Sylvia Deming's library. He couldn't put his finger on it, but it was there, taunting him. *Maybe it's worth another trip to the Deming residence?*

And why was Roland Fosco so protective of Cliff Metzger? He didn't even like the guy. Was the DEA brass involved in Deming's death? Was there an active investigation into the Savannah office and they wanted the FBI to back off until their investigation was complete?

Now a local judge and his DA were implicated by Deming's team. What was their part in this whole mess?

Finally, Senator Vega entered the picture due to his son

being in the wrong place at the wrong time. Did Mercado's team set up Peter Vega so they could put the squeeze on his father? If so, they were playing a very dangerous game, and Peden's friend, Marcus Cook, was caught right in the middle of it all.

Damn.

* * *

Elizabeth Sanchez smiled. "Sylvia is headed out of town. She said she needs to get away. It'll be perfect."

Wayne Cleaver listened as she explained her plan to keep him out of sight in a place where no one would look for him. He wasn't convinced that it was such a great idea, but the more she talked, the less apprehensive he became.

"So, you're sure she's leaving the area? She won't just pop in on me while I'm lying around on her couch?"

Elizabeth replied, "Yes, I'm sure. She's planning on going to Florida, maybe the Keys. I can't imagine what she's going through right now, especially with Jarrod's boss murdered. The police questioned her, but she had an alibi. She was at home packing up her husband's belongings. Her sister was with her the entire time."

Wayne was still skeptical. "Won't her sister have a key?"

"She does, but she's going to Maine for a week with friends. I'm picking up a set of keys tomorrow morning. She's leaving around eight. If we play our cards right, we can have you over there by ten."

Wayne took a deep breath. He knew staying here with Elizabeth was a bad idea. The longer he stayed, the more potential danger she faced. At the very least, her job was in jeopardy, at worst, maybe her life.

The move to Sylvia's house seemed like a good, short-term solution. While there, they could work on a long-range plan. With any luck, the killer would be apprehended soon and he could get his life back.

He turned to Elizabeth. She asked, "Penny for your thoughts?"

His face remained somber. "If you think that moving to Sylvia's place is the right move for now, then I'm with you. Does she have a garage so that I can sneak in?"

"Yes. I'll see if I can get her opener along with the keys. I'll go shopping in the morning so you have food while you're there. You have to be careful to not move anything around. She can never know that you were there."

"Didn't you say she was packing up Jarrod's stuff? Maybe the house will be in such disarray that she won't notice a thing or two out of place."

She smiled at him. It was a look that said *You don't know Sylvia Deming.* "Let's just say that she'd notice. She's kind of a neat freak. So, when she says she's packing up Jarrod's stuff, she means that she's packing it in boxes and doing a mental inventory of everything. She will notice if anything is out of place, trust me."

This last bit of information worried Wayne. How was he going to live in the house and make sure nothing was moved? Then he realized he wasn't going to be there when she got back.

He looked up into Elizabeth's eyes. "I think it'll work."

Wayne stood and stretched. He looked at Elizabeth. "We need to get some rest tonight if we're going on an adventure tomorrow."

Elizabeth stood and put her arms around his waist. She studied his face and smiled. "Mr. Cleaver, we're going to get these guys and clear your name. Do you trust me?"

He smiled down at her as he put his arms around her shoulders. "Yeah. Yeah, I really do."

Chapter 35

Vincent Mercado had a rare third Scotch on the rocks. He normally quit at two, typically confining his hard liquor drinking around dinner. Having a drink after 11:00 PM was highly irregular.

But these were highly irregular times at the DEA. When Deming was murdered, Mercado and his team were surprised, but relieved. That job was taken out of their hands by some, as yet, unknown gunman, which was good and bad.

It was good because they could honestly say that they had nothing to do with the murder. And they had an alibi. They were at the scene at the time of the murder, on film, unarmed. Their guns had not been fired.

It was bad because they had no clue who the real shooter was. And it appeared the killer wasn't finished. He and his teammates wondered *Who's next?*

He was also concerned that Andrew Newsome was going to fall apart and spill his guts to the FBI. Maybe Stillwell could calm him down. It was time to make the call.

Mercado looked at the time on the screen of his cell phone. 11:34 PM. Not too late to call a guy who gets to the office at 8:30 AM. He dialed Stillwell's private cell.

After three rings, the judge answered in a clear and powerful drawl. "Vince. This can't be a social call at this hour."

"No, sir. It isn't. Do you have a moment? I have some concerns about a mutual friend."

"You mean Andy, right?"

Mercado was surprised. Stillwell must have picked up the same vibes from Newsome. "Yes, Judge. Andy's having a problem keeping his shit together. Pardon my language."

Stillwell laughed. "No problem, Vince. Andy's never had nerves of steel, not like you and Smith." He paused for a moment then asked, "How serious do ya'll think this case of frazzled nerves is? I mean, when he blew up at me at the club, I thought that he was growing a pair, which would have been a good thing, in my opinion, but maybe it was his nerves busting out instead. What do ya'll think?"

Mercado thought for just a second. "He did the same thing when we met with Sen…"

Stillwell cut him off, probably not wanting Mercado to mention Senator Vega's name over the phone. "Hey, Vince, I think I get the picture. I'll talk with Andy late tomorrow. I understand that ya'll're busy so won't have that luxury, but I think we can get him calmed down. He knows the stakes."

Mercado wanted to press one other issue with Stillwell before he finished the call. "The other thing, Judge, is that we've had two DEA agents murdered within the last week and we don't know who the shooter is for either murder. I know we have a guy in mind, but…" He stopped before finishing his thought. He wanted Stillwell to know he was concerned that, even though they had a patsy for the killings, his guys didn't do either of the murders. There was still a real killer on the loose and they didn't have anyone high on the suspect list, or even a person of interest.

There was a period of silence as the Judge was apparently thinking about what Mercado said. Then, in a measured manner, he said, "Vince, ya'll keep pursuing the path that we laid out. We'll handle ya'll's concerns, but right now we need to get this officially behind us. Understand?"

"Yes. Yes, I do. And you're probably right. Good to get the heat off us first. Once everyone's off our backs, we can handle this little problem on our own time."

"That's right." There was another moment of silence on the line, then Stillwell asked, "Anything else, Vince?"

"No, Judge. I think that answers my questions. Good luck with your campaign. You've got my vote."

"Thanks, Vince. I may need ya'll for some extra

security work during the campaign. Think ya'll and that Smith character could handle a little extra cash on the side?"

"Yes, sir. I think we could work something out."

"Good man. I'll let ya'll know how my chat with our friend goes."

Mercado hit *End*. He thought about the work he might do for the judge's campaign. It would probably be some scheme to raise money or plant evidence of wrong doing on his opponent, Senator Armand Vega. Either way, it would be lucrative.

Mercado finished his Scotch in one deep gulp. He had to get some sleep. Tomorrow was going to be a long but profitable day.

* * *

Peden was tired, but his mind was in overdrive trying to put the pieces of a very complex puzzle together. His computer chirped indicating that another call was outgoing from Vince Mercado's cell phone.

Within seconds he received a text message from Lee Sparks asking if he was monitoring the call. He hit the *Monitor/Record* button on his computer screen and put on a set of headphones. Mercado was talking with Judge Stillwell about Andrew Newsome. Mercado expressed his concerns and Stillwell said he'd handle it.

Then Mercado spoke about the Deming and West murders, that they had a guy who would take the fall for the murders, even though they knew he wasn't the shooter. They were saying that they'd worry about the real shooter later. Peden frowned. *Why would they pin a murder on an innocent man?* He could feel his blood begin to boil as he thought about some poor, unsuspecting bastard being slammed with a murder rap. It bolstered his resolve to expose these guys, one way or another.

One thing became obvious; Judge Stillwell was the puppet master. Could he have orchestrated the murders? The motive for Deming's murder was to silence him. But why kill Nila West? Peden thought about West's time of death. Stillwell was attending his own fundraiser, kicking off his candidacy for the U.S. Senate. That's a pretty tight alibi, being in front of hundreds of people most of the evening.

He thought about the distance from the DeSoto Hilton to Nila West's condominium, a mere three blocks east on East Liberty Street, and thought *Would it be possible for him to slip out and kill West then slip back in without anyone noticing?* He shook his head. Where would he keep the murder weapon? What if West's blood got on his tuxedo? Would he chance walking down the street in a tuxedo? People would notice that. How could he keep his cool in front of a crowd of potential donors after committing a murder? There were so many things that could go wrong.

But was it possible?

Savage heard Stillwell's and Mercado's phones click. He hit the button on his computer to end recording. His cell phone vibrated. Sparks sent a text message that he successfully recorded the conversation. He would call Peden in the morning.

It had been a long day. With Senator Vega's impending visit, Sunday looked even longer. He needed to get Megan up to speed regardless of the consequences.

* * *

Marcus Cook had as much information about Mercado's plan as he was going to get. It was time to pass the details on to Peden. It was late, but he figured it was now or never. Sunday he'd be teamed up with Pete Nichols and might not have a chance to call anyone.

At 11:50 PM, Marcus tapped in Peden's number. A tired sounding Peden answered, "Hello."

"I didn't wake you, did I?"

Peden yawned. "No. I was just heading upstairs. It's been a long night. What's up, my man?"

"Wanted to tell you about tomorrow. The Senator's coming in to Savannah International, but he'll be all over before he finally makes the money drop. Vince has a rental car reserved for him. He'll be driving to a bunch of different parking lots and restaurants before they connect in Statesboro. Vince will take the money to a place near Swainsboro and drop it. I don't know the address, but it's a rental home, supposedly away from any neighborhoods – maybe a farm house, something like that."

Peden yawned again. "I think we'll be able to follow him wherever he goes. You said he's going to drop the cash. What happens to it from there?"

"Me, Smith, and Nichols are supposed to pick it up and take it with us. It'll get passed out to the team sometime in the next couple days, probably Monday or Tuesday."

"It'll be interesting to see how well these new bill trackers work."

The 'bill trackers' were a brain storm that he came up with about a year ago. He mentioned the idea to Lee Sparks and Lee went to work designing the devices, which were basically the guts of an electronic tracking device superimposed on a strip of fabric of the type used internally on U.S. currency. The FBI liked the idea and helped test the strips. Testing went so well that they decided to prepare hundreds of thousands of dollars – twenties, fifties, and hundreds – in "ransom money" for use in kidnapping cases. This was to be the first time the strips were used in the field.

Marcus said, "If it works, Lee's neck will snap from the weight of his head. We won't be able to stand him."

Peden laughed. "I'll put up with him if this helps us get these guys."

"Amen to that, brother."

Peden was quiet for a moment. When he spoke, his tone was serious. "Marcus, you be careful out there. Watch your six, okay?"

Marcus almost said, *Sure, Dad,* but instead said, "I will."

* * *

Sleep eluded Andrew Newsome. He lay awake, tossing and turning, trying to chase the demons from his mind. There was no escape from his own mental torment.

There was at least one killer on the loose. Instead of looking for the real killer, they were concentrating on finding a guy they knew couldn't be the killer. *What the hell sense does that make? I could walk out my front door in the morning and get plugged.*

Newsome thought about the insanity of extorting money from a U.S. Senator. Even if all went as planned, what happens afterwards? Was the Senator just going to forget about one-point-five million dollars? Maybe it wasn't directly out of his pocket, maybe it was campaign funds, but it was still his money. He wouldn't just chalk it up to a bad experience. There would be hell to pay.

Mercado had told him to chill. Everything would be fine. They had his kid as insurance. No way would he expose his son to a prison term.

Newsome's wife awoke from a deep sleep, sensing her husband's restlessness. In a sleepy, still half drunken voice she asked, "Hey, Sweetheart, can't sleep?"

"I'm okay, honey. Go back to sleep."

"It's Saturday night, you should leave that stuff at the office."

"I know."

Newsome leaned over and kissed his wife on the cheek. He rolled back, facing away from his wife, who immediately started to quietly snore.

Newsome stared at the wall beyond his bedside table. He tried to clear his mind and think of nothing but sleep. The face of Judge Whalen Stillwell appeared like the head of the Wizard of Oz. Fire and smoke rose on either side of his head. In a booming voice Stillwell said, *Andy, get me the head of Wayne Cleaver.*

Newsome awoke with a start. His wife had rolled over and pulled the covers with her. He was trembling like the Cowardly Lion.

He looked at the digital clock on his night stand. It read 5:30 AM. He gave up and went downstairs to fix coffee and a big breakfast. Sleep would have to wait for another night.

Chapter 36

Megan sat next to Peden on Sunday morning as he approached the Harry S. Truman Parkway. Peden noticed that her scowl was more pronounced than normal, meaning that she might actually be angry. The tension was evident. Peden decided it was time to clear the air.

"So, how'd breakfast with the boss go?"

"Fine."

Peden knew the mood, but didn't like having to play games, so he came right out and asked, "What's got your panties all twisted up?"

Without looking at him, she said, "Well, Pedee, it could be that you're not being completely honest with me. I could tell by the way you talked to me on the phone last night. You're holding back. How long have we been partners, business associates, and friends? Hell, I helped you get away from that witch, Susan. You know, your ex-wife. You'd be dead right now if it wasn't for me. She was going to kill you eventually."

Peden knew that it was an exaggeration, but they had been colleagues for a long time now, and close friends for almost as long. Megan may have been the reason his wife had left him, but she had suspected a workplace affair that didn't exist. She even tried to catch her husband in the act and ended up busting in on a sensitive surveillance operation. Peden was angry and embarrassed. Megan was furious.

"Well, just because my wife left me because she thought we were having an affair, I don't think that allows you to take credit for getting rid of her. And I don't think she'd have killed me…maybe just cut a little."

"Yeah, well, you're lucky she's gone. She was a real bitch." Her perpetually angry face tightened. "Seriously, what are you not telling me?"

Peden's anxiety level jumped a notch. He could either tell her about the illegal wire tap and force her to make the choice of not reporting it, or he could keep it to himself and suffer her never-ending death stare. *Maybe I should just shoot myself now.*

He took a deep breath and plowed ahead. "I got a new client Friday. He has a problem related to our current case."

She looked at him and said, "Go on."

"He's a guy in a powerful position in the Federal Government. His kid's a student at SCAD. The kid got arrested for dealing dope here in Savannah. The bust was carried out by Mercado and his team. They pulled their signature move by loading up the kid's apartment with way more drugs than he had."

"Are you going to keep dragging this out? Who is your client?"

"Senator Armand Vega." He waited for her reaction, but she continued to stare. "Here's the twist. He wasn't charged. Neither were any of his friends. They were held overnight and released."

"How did that happen? Anyone else gets busted by Mercado's goons and they get prison time."

"Yeah." Peden remained quiet for a few seconds. "Do you know anything about Senator Vega? Politically, I mean?"

"Just that he's more for civil liberties than most in his party, but a financial conservative."

"Exactly. He wants to cut funding for agencies involved in the War on Drugs, including the DEA. He believes that it's a waste of taxpayers' money, doing more harm than good. I think they arrested Vega's kid so that they could twist his arm, maybe get him to change his vote and keep their funding."

Megan's face turned more angry than usual. "So, why did he hire you? You don't have any pull with the DEA. Quite the opposite, in fact."

Peden was quiet for a few seconds. He wondered just how much he should tell Megan.

"Okay, here's where it gets...dicey."

Peden told Megan about Senator Vega's security man visiting his office and hiring him to do some covert surveillance. He came clean and told her the entire story about the phone taps and monitoring Mercado's cell phone. He also told her about the extortion money and the threat to reopen the charges against his son if he didn't follow through with his votes in the Senate.

Peden was sure that Megan was going to call him a hypocrite. He was, after all, mister "by the book." It was why he was forced out of the FBI.

So, he was surprised when Megan said, "Let me get this straight. Senator Vega contracted with you to listen to DEA agents' private conversations? He can't use it in court."

Peden turned towards her and said, "I know."

Megan became reflective. The silence stretched for several minutes as they approached the Montgomery Cross Road interchange. Peden took the exit and turned left heading towards Isle of Hope.

Finally, she asked, "In monitoring these conversations, have you found out who killed Deming and West?"

"No, in fact we're pretty sure that no one on Mercado's team is the killer. They're still trying to pin Deming's murder on Wayne Cleaver. You already know that he couldn't have done it. He was still at Coastal being checked out."

"Yeah. He's not the type anyway; passive, quiet, like a lot of pot heads."

"I wish we could find Deming's notes. They might give us a clue."

They approached the Deming residence, hoping to find Sylvia Deming at home. No cars were in the driveway. Compared to the scene the day of the wake, with cars parked on both sides of the road, the neighborhood looked abandoned. As they pulled up in front of the house, the garage door began opening. A gray Chevrolet Malibu backed out. Peden thought it might be Sylvia Deming leaving so he pulled up to the end of the driveway, cutting the driver off. As he did, he loudly honked his horn to get the driver's attention. The car stopped.

Megan caught movement from the corner of her eyes as a curtain from one of the front windows moved. Someone glanced out then quickly let the curtain fall back into place.

Peden and Megan exited his car, Peden heading for the driver's side of the car, Megan for the passenger side. He recognized the woman, but couldn't remember where. He motioned for her to lower her window. When she did, he said that she should also lower the passenger window so Megan could hear the conversation.

The young woman asked, "Why are you blocking me in?"

Peden smiled. "We thought you were someone else. Is Sylvia Deming home?"

The young woman seemed nervous, her eyes bouncing from side to side. "No. She left town for a few days. She's been through a lot. Her husband was killed earlier…"

Peden cut her off. "We know. I'm Peden Savage." He motioned to the other side of her car. "This is FBI Special Agent Megan Moore. She's in charge of the investigation."

He let that sink in for a moment. "So, if Mrs. Deming is out of town, what are you doing in her house?"

"I'm her best friend, Liz Sanchez. I'm watching her house while she's away."

Megan spoke for the first time. "Liz, who's helping you watch the house?"

"No one. Just me." Her panic-stricken face said otherwise.

Megan asked, "Well who looked out at us from the front room?"

She was caught red-handed. She never was good at lying, so she tried to think of a way to avoid going into the house. She was a lawyer and knew all the tricks to keep law enforcement from exercising an illegal search, but she also knew that it was a stretch saying that they didn't have probable cause. She also knew that Wayne was cornered with no way out. The last thing she wanted was for him to get shot by an

FBI agent.

"Liz? You seem awfully nervous for someone who hasn't done anything wrong. Do we have reason to enter Sylvia's home with our weapons drawn?"

"No. No, you don't. Look. I'll let you in, but the person in there hasn't done anything wrong. He's being set up. I swear."

Peden and Megan shot each other concerned looks. Peden asked, "Who are you hiding in there?"

"My friend...Wayne Cleaver."

Their eyebrows shot up. *What were the odds?*

* * *

Elizabeth and Megan entered the house through the front door while Peden covered the service door to the garage. When the women stepped into the foyer, Elizabeth called out to her friend.

"Wayne. Come out here, please." Wayne slowly stepped into the hallway from the kitchen, his hands held open at shoulder height, not sure what to do with them, but instinctively knowing that they should be in plain sight. He looked like he was surrendering.

Megan said, "Mr. Cleaver, you can relax as long as you don't make any sudden movements. Okay?"

Wayne slowly lowered his hands to his side. "Okay. But call me Wayne. Mr. Cleaver makes me sound like a TV show dad from the 1960s."

This made Elizabeth smile. *Wayne and his corny sense of humor.* She said, "I'll let your partner in."

Megan offered, "How about we all sit down and talk for a bit." She looked at Wayne. "First, we know you couldn't have killed Jarrod Deming. You were still at Coastal. Second, you have no motive to kill Nila West."

They moved into the living room where all of the pictures were taken down off the walls and boxed. None of the boxes were sealed. They were pushed against one wall, the folding tops of the boxes sticking up.

Elizabeth and Wayne sat next to each other on the

couch while Megan took a seat in an overstuffed chair across from them. Peden remained standing and roamed the room, looking in the boxes without actually moving anything.

Megan continued, "The big question is why are they trying to set you up?"

Wayne raised his eyebrows, shrugged his shoulders, turned his palms upward and said, "Hell if I know. When I got out of Coastal, I checked into this flea-bit motel. I wasn't there too long when Mercado and some other goon showed up and told me to stay put and not leave town. Asked me a couple questions, like where I'd been since getting out. Hell, I went straight to the motel, grabbed a sub sandwich from the sub shop across the street and went back to the motel. When they left, I turned on the TV and saw the news about Deming's murder. I knew right then that they were gonna try and pin that on me. So I moved to a different place."

From across the room, Peden looked from Wayne to Elizabeth. "What's your connection to Liz?"

Wayne turned to Elizabeth and smiled briefly, then his face turned serious. "We went to high school together, many moons ago. When I got out of Coastal, I planned to head home. My mom lives in Anderson, South Carolina. I have a few bucks stashed there, unless Mom needed it for bills. I told her to keep it for me, but if things got tight, to go ahead and use it. When they rousted me, I figured I'd better stay away from Mom. That'd be the first place they'd look. I knew I needed legal help and Liz was the only lawyer that I knew. I was afraid that, since she works for the District Attorney's office, she might not want to talk with me. She took a big risk even taking my call. Now she's in deep."

Peden and Megan looked at each other, both thinking the same thing. Peden asked, "Liz, do you work for Andrew Newsome?"

"Yeah. He's my boss. Why?"

There was silence as Peden and Megan thought about how to answer. Megan said, "Let's come back to that. Wayne, how did you end up at Coastal?"

Wayne told his story about the bust, the amount of pot and money that he had in his possession, and what the DEA claims he had. He told them about others at Coastal who had the same experience as him. He knew then that this whole DEA thing was much bigger than just him.

That brought the discussion back to why they wanted to set Wayne up for the Deming murder. Megan said, "Listen, Wayne, they want to pin this on you because they figure that you're an easy target. Maybe we can use that against them. Liz, your boss is one of *them*."

Chapter 37

By 2:00 PM, the sweltering morning threatened to deteriorate into a stormy afternoon. As Senator Vega's jet approached the Savannah-Hilton Head International Airport, Lee Sparks reported to Peden that the tracking program picked up weak signals from the extortion money. As soon as Senator Vega exited the private jet, the tracking program locked in on the cash. The signals from all twenty "tagged" bills were strong, the location clearly displayed on Lee's computer monitor.

Peden noticed the indicators on his own monitor using the repeater program Sparks installed on Peden's office computer.

"Got it, Lee. Perfect. This is a really cool program."

Peden had been monitoring Vince Mercado's cell phones all morning. He made only one call. That was from his personal cell to Alex Smith. He told Smith to contact Nichols and Cook and get them moving. Peden figured that they had choreographed their moves in advance and were heading out to begin their assignments. Peden hoped to hear from Marcus Cook by now, but he wasn't concerned. He would get a call when Marcus felt it was necessary.

Megan Moore and Michael Jess, Senator Vega's personal assistant, were monitoring the calls and the computer program at Lee Spark's home office. There was no plan for anyone to intervene with the money exchange. They decided that they shouldn't be anywhere near Mercado and his team so that they wouldn't be accused of attempting a sting operation. Megan didn't like the plan and she let Peden know it.

* * *

At 2:20 PM, Vince Mercado waited in the parking lot of a Lowe's Home Improvement store southeast of Statesboro, Georgia. His stomach was growling, the grease from the double cheeseburger working on his stomach. The impending money drop rattled his nerves.

He scrutinized every car that passed and watched the sky for aerial surveillance. He listened to the police monitor for any sign of a sting operation. So far, he noticed nothing suspicious.

He remained on edge. Both his personal cell phone and the throwaway were on the front seat within easy reach. He was tempted to call Alex Smith to make sure that he was at his post, but he knew Smith was where he needed to be. He trusted that Marcus Cook, as the new guy looking to impress his team lead, would also be on post carrying out his part of the plan or awaiting other instructions.

Off to the west, Mercado noticed the gathering dark clouds. A whale of a storm was closing in. *The weather. Just one more thing to worry about.*

When Mercado's throwaway cell phone buzzed, his muscles flinched. He took a deep breath and tapped the answer icon. "Senator."

"I'm in the rental. Where to?"

"Do you have the package?"

"Yes, Agent Mercado. Let's get on with it."

"I just want to remind you. No tricks. You know the consequences."

"Let's stop with the games. Now where am I going?"

Mercado smiled and gave the Senator directions that would take him south on Interstate 95 to exit ninety-four.

* * *

"The money's on the move."

Lee Sparks let Peden, Megan, and Michael Jess know that the Senator was heading out of the parking lot of the car rental agency. The triangle on Peden's screen glided smoothly along the map, the signals from the tracking devices maintaining a strong output. Peden had told the Senator that he was not to make contact with the team in any way, figuring that Mercado was monitoring any calls made from the car. If Vega made a call, even on his personal cell, Mercado would know that they were on to his plans and abort the money drop.

Vega turned onto the southbound entry ramp for Interstate 95. The team watched as the triangle picked up speed. After a few minutes, Vega's car passed exit one hundred two, then passed exit ninety-nine. After another five minutes, the triangle on their screens took the ramp for exit ninety-four. The triangle turned right off the exit ramp then took another right turn. The triangle came to a stop at the EconoLodge hotel parking lot. Peden, Lee Sparks, Megan Moore, and Michael Jess wondered, *Was this it?*

* * *

Mercado's throwaway buzzed as the first big raindrops hit his windshield. They made a loud *splat* on impact. He answered the call. "Senator, tell me what you see around you."

Vega was confused. "What do ya mean?"

"Tell me what you see from where you're parked. It's not a trick question."

"I'm in the parking lot of an EconoLodge Hotel just off the highway."

"What else is around you?"

"You mean other businesses? There's a Shell gas station, a Hooters, a Shells Restaurant and a new hotel being built just up the road. And there's a business by the Hooters but I don't know what it is."

"Okay, Senator, you've passed the test." The rain began to fall harder in Statesboro. "Now, get back on I-95 and head north to exit five in South Carolina. Take Highway 17 north and park in the back of the Burger King."

In a loud, clear voice, Vega said, "Mercado, this is bullshit. You better..."

"Senator, do as you're told. We'll be finished soon enough. You better get moving."

The line went dead. Mercado smiled then noticed that the rainfall was getting heavier. The dark clouds swirled for as far as he could see to the west. It was going to be one hell of a storm.

* * *

Peden watched his screen as Vega's car headed north on the interstate. He wondered if the money had been transferred. His cell phone buzzed. It was Marcus Cook.

"Hey, Peden. Just lettin' you know that Vega still has the money. You monitoring the throwaway?"

"Yeah. I kind of figured that Mercado wasn't anywhere near that exit." He asked, "Aren't you with Nichols?"

"Not exactly, we're in separate cars. I'm not in his sights right now so I thought I'd call. I'm heading out to Swainsboro now. Have to be at the house when Mercado drops the money. Nichols is going to get ahead of Vega and make sure he goes to Hardeeville. Then he's taking backroads and meeting me in Swainsboro."

"Okay, Marcus. Call when you can if anything happens."

"Will do, my man."

Peden wondered about the noise on Mercado's throwaway phone. It sounded like rain. He clicked on the weather program on his computer. Sure enough, a storm lay west of Savannah. It stretched from the Florida Panhandle to the south up through Winston-Salem, North Carolina. The front edge of the storm was passing through Statesboro. Mercado was sitting in his car up that way. No matter, they would follow the money from a distance and move in only when they were sure they had all the players cornered.

He saw that Vega was making good time on the interstate. After twenty minutes, he was crossing into South Carolina. Another five minutes and he parked behind the Burger King Restaurant. Peden imagined the aroma of flame broiled hamburgers. His stomach growled.

* * *

Rainwater rushed to drains in the Lowe's parking lot. Puddles formed everywhere. A flash of lightning lit up the area followed by a thunderous boom. It was so loud that Mercado missed the first vibration from the throwaway cell phone.

He hit the answer icon and, without waiting for Vega to say anything, he said, "Okay Senator, head back on Interstate

95 south, to Interstate 16. Head west on sixteen to exit one twenty-seven. Go north towards Statesboro. I will call you in one hour with your final instructions."

Vega hung up without saying a word. Mercado didn't like that. Everything was going as planned...except for the weather...and that last call where Vega said nothing. *That was strange. Maybe I'm just spooking myself.* Another flash of lightning lit up the plaza followed immediately by a loud boom that shook his car.

Somebody trying to tell me something?
* * *

Twenty minutes later, Peden watched his screen as Senator Vega headed west on Interstate 16. The triangle that he had been following suddenly froze in place. He frowned. Maybe the Senator slowed down because of the heavy rain. Then again, maybe he needed to zoom in to see any movement. After three clicks making his screen show two thousand feet per inch, the triangle still hadn't moved. The triangle then jumped across the page further up the interstate. He zoomed back out as the triangle continued its trek west, as smooth as before. After another minute, the triangle froze again.

He waited for a full minute. Nothing happened. He waited another minute, but the triangle remained in place. Suddenly, the triangle disappeared from the map completely. *Damn.*

Peden's cell phone buzzed. It was Lee Sparks.

"Peden, we lost the tracking signals...all of them. Vega's driving through a bad storm right now, so once he gets through, we should get the signal back."

"Should? You're not positive?"

Lee hesitated before he answered. "This is new technology. I'm pretty sure we'll be good, but you never know. Hell, the lightning from this storm is intense. You'll see in about ten minutes when this hits Savannah. But like I said, we should be okay. We'll just have to ride it out."

Peden was frustrated, but he knew Lee was right and it certainly wasn't his fault. They had taken a chance using the tracking strips because the technology hadn't been thoroughly tested. Up to this point, they had worked flawlessly. Hopefully, they would weather the storm and come back strong.

Just as he ended the call with Lee, his screen made an electronic sound indicating that there was another call from Mercado's throwaway phone. He hit the *Monitor/Record* button and quickly put his head phones on.

He listened as Mercado spoke to Senator Vega.

"The drop's off. You guys are playing games."

Vega responded angrily, "What the hell are ya'll talking about?"

"You got the FBI involved, didn't you? You bastard. You know what happens next. Your kid's going to jail and your career is going up in flames. Turn around and take your money back to Washington, but don't get too comfortable. You won't be there much longer."

"Agent Mercado, I don't know why ya'll's doing this, but I've been straight with ya'll. There's no one else involved. I'm alone out here with the money. Nobody knows I'm here. Nobody knows about the money. Just you and me."

There was silence on the line until a loud boom sounded over the phone. Peden knew it was thunder from the storm. He was hoping that Mercado was just bluffing, that he had no real proof that Vega was being monitored. *How could he know?*

Mercado said, "Alright, Senator. You get a room for the night. Sit on the money. I'll call you in the morning. If I find out your screwing with me, I will follow through on what I told you from the start. You got that? Am I making myself clear?"

"Crystal clear."

The line disconnected. Peden hit the *Monitor/Record* button and thought, *So, what's our next move?* He sat back in his chair and rubbed the scar on his eyebrow. He was in deep thought when his cell phone buzzed. It was Megan.

Damn.

He answered with a touch of irritation in his voice. "Yes, Megan?"

"So, Pedee, where do we go from here?"
Double Damn.
"We sit tight."

Chapter 38

Senator Armand Vega's assistant, Michael Jess, cancelled all of Vega's Monday commitments. There were questions, but Jess downplayed the inquiries, stating that the Senator just needed a day or two off from his grueling schedule. That satisfied most everyone, but word got back to the Stillwell camp that Vega was cancelling some important meetings. They sent out a press release that Vega was missing important meetings and not properly representing the good people of Georgia.

Jess called Savage's office at 9:00 AM, Monday morning. Megan sat next to Peden in one of his hideous green chairs. The conversation, on speaker phone, was business-like, to the point, with no levity. Peden knew that Jess was concerned that the money drop was in jeopardy, that the Senator had no idea how long he'd be tied up in this mess. If Jess was in a bad mood, Peden couldn't tell.

"Mr. Jess, the Senator hasn't received any word from Mercado since yesterday at 4:10 PM. That's when he called and cancelled the drop. You've heard the recording. He gave no valid reason."

"Well, he did say that he suspected that the Senator wasn't being honest. You said Mercado was just bluffing. He's dragging this out."

Peden thought for a moment. Megan jumped in. "Mr. Jess, we think this is all a head game that Mercado is playing, trying to get the Senator to make a mistake. It's a good ploy, but we should sit tight and wait until Mercado makes his next move."

There was silence on the line as Michael Jess thought about Megan's comment. Jess was a smart, calculating guy.

Peden believed that he would go along with Megan's recommendation. There really wasn't another reasonable option. Nothing had changed except that the timeline was slipping with each passing moment, but that couldn't be avoided. Mercado was in control...for now.

"Alright, I agree. We have all of our assets in place. There's no reason to panic. I actually briefed the Senator on this possibility, so it isn't totally unexpected."

Peden was impressed with Michael Jess. He wondered if the man might be interested in joining Savage Consultants after this fiasco was over.

Megan brought him out of his trance with an elbow to his arm. She asked, "Anything further for Mr. Jess?"

"Just that we'll contact you as soon as Mercado calls your boss. We're all frustrated, but we need to stick to the plan. Remember, we're not taking any action until the money is distributed. So, we're still pretty early in this whole scenario."

Jess didn't hesitate when he responded, "Agreed."

With the call disconnected, Peden sat back in his chair and Megan relaxed. They both took deep breaths and sat for a moment.

Peden asked, "Need your coffee freshened?"

"No. I'm okay for now." She sat deep in thought for more than a minute, staring off at some image that only she could see. When she spoke, it seemed labored, like she was dragging the words from her mind. "How does all this tie together? I mean, we've got two murders, extortion, and a federal agency that is systematically destroying lives...for what...personal gain? Is it all about money and power?"

"If you assume that, you leave out the one other big motivator...love."

Megan thought about that for a few seconds. "Do you really mean love or does that include sex...and jealousy?"

Peden didn't have to think about that. In his opinion, most people confused all three for just love. "Love, sex, and jealousy, it's all part of the same package. How does that apply to our case?"

"Good question."

Megan was about to continue when Peden's cell phone buzzed. He looked at the screen and recognized the number. "Allen Deming."

Megan's eyebrows rose slightly.

"Allen. How you holding up?"

"Just okay. I found some of Jarrod's notes that ya'll should see."

"Okay. I can't really leave my office right now. Can you drop them off?"

"Be there in ten minutes."

"Use the back door. Less chance you'll be seen."

* * *

At 9:25 AM, Allen Deming knocked on the back door to Savage's office. Peden let him in. He introduced Megan and the three sat at Peden's desk. Deming appeared nervous with Megan listening in, but Peden assured him that she was on their side. He laid a business-sized envelope on Peden's desk. It had been opened.

Deming explained, "I found this along the passenger seat in the rental car. It must have fallen off the stack of papers that we looked at the other day. It was unopened because it was in my mailbox at home. I grabbed what was there as I headed out on the road to drive here. I didn't even know what was in it."

Peden and Megan sat silent, allowing Deming to continue.

"There are six pages. One is a personal letter to me. He believed he was going to be killed before he got to the press conference, said he deserved to die for ruining people's lives. He apologized for killing his cousin. That happened in one of the early busts. The other five pages are basically a summary of what his DEA team did."

Deming took a deep breath and motioned for Peden to pick up the envelope. He nodded for Megan to join Peden.

Megan walked around his desk and read the letter over Peden's shoulder. They moved along to the first page of Jarrod Deming's notes. They could tell Jarrod had been nervous as he wrote out the summary of illegal busts that his team had executed. On the next to last page, Deming implicated a local District Attorney, Andrew Newsome, and a local Judge, Whalen Stillwell, in the illegal embezzlement of funds from the federal government. The details of how the scheme worked could be found in a safe at his home on Flinn Drive in Savannah.

As they got to the final page, both of their eyes widened as he apologized to his wife for the affair between him and Nila West. He sincerely regretted the pain that he had caused her. He hoped that, over time, she could forgive him.

He closed the notes by offering his sincere apologies to all of the victims of the busts. He hoped that their cases would be reviewed and that they would be released from prison.

His final remarks were that he intended to surrender to the FBI at their office in Savannah and provide whatever information that they needed to prosecute the guilty individuals, including himself. He believed his team committed a number of egregious violations of the law and severely damaged the public's trust in all law enforcement agencies.

When they finished, they both looked at Allen Deming. The man was visibly shaken. All of the ingredients of what Megan and Peden had been discussing before Deming showed up were in Jarrod Deming's notes. Murder, extortion, greed, power, love, and sex.

Allen Deming had aged several years in the few days since Peden had seen him last. The weight of the evidence that he presented had crushed his spirit.

"I told ya'll a lot about why Jarrod had a change of heart, but I didn't tell ya'll what triggered the change. My sister, Paula, married this great guy, Richard Ross. He treated my sister like a queen. They had a son, Weston. Wes grew up and started hanging out with the wrong crowd, ya know, heavy drinkers and dope heads. He started dealing and getting into trouble before he could even drive. I remember Rich telling me what a shit he was. Paula used to try and defend him, but ya could tell, he was trouble. They kept throwing Jarrod up in his face, asking him why he couldn't be more like his cousin. That only made it worse."

Peden and Megan listened in silence as Allen told his version of events surrounding his son.

"Rich threw Wes out when he turned about sixteen. Paula tried everything she could to convince him that their son was just going through a phase. Rich gave the kid chance after chance. He told Paula they needed their lives back and Wes was taking that from them.

"Shortly after he tossed Wes out, Richard was killed in a car accident. Paula was devastated. She let Wes move back in, mainly for companionship, but it quickly turned bad. Wes started dealing drugs and having parties at the house. At first, Paula tried to stop it, but then she started drinking and doing drugs to forget her troubles. It wasn't long before her life completely fell apart.

"When Jarrod heard about it, he figured that Wes would be a good target for one of his team's busts. He set it up with Mercado and they hit the house. What Jarrod didn't plan on was Wes and Paula getting killed during the bust. It took a while for it to sink in, but Jarrod finally realized that he'd helped kill his aunt and his cousin.

"That was the first attack on his conscience. As the busts accumulated, the guilt mounted. Finally, it became more than he could bear. I think he may have told his wife, Sylvia, about it and she piled on, telling him what a monster he was. They were already having problems in their marriage, mainly because of Jarrod's infidelity."

The three sat in silence for a moment while Peden and Megan tried to process all that they had just heard. Peden's face lit up as if he'd just realized something.

"Do you know if and when Jarrod ended the affair with Nila West?"

"No. To my knowledge, it wasn't over. He admitted it was wrong, but I think they kept it going."

Peden said, "I want you to watch something with me."

He clicked a few keys on his computer and pulled up a

video of the news conference. He forwarded it to the point just before the press conference was to begin and clicked play.

Jarrod had just pulled his notes from his coat pocket and raised his eyes. His expression appeared tense as he scanned over the crowd. A change occurred in his facial expression, and he shifted his body slightly. Then his body jerked and fell backwards as he was struck with the high-powered bullets.

"Did you see him shift right after his face registered, what, maybe recognition?"

Megan agreed, "Yeah. So?"

"I think he saw the shooter right before he was killed. I think he shifted his position to protect Nila West. If that's true, then your daughter-in-law might be the shooter."

Deming stared at Peden for a moment. "I guess I couldn't blame her if she did it, but my money's still on Mercado."

Both Megan and Peden's eyebrows shot up in surprise. They knew that Mercado, Smith, or Nichols couldn't have shot his son. Could they have hired a professional? Maybe, but hiring a private assassin had additional risks for a federal agent.

"What makes you so certain that Mercado had your son killed?"

"Because he told me Mercado threatened to kill him. I believed him because Mercado threatened to kill me, too."

Chapter 39

Elizabeth Sanchez left her office at noon on Monday planning to head home and eat a microwave dinner for lunch. The previous day's storm raised the humidity to near unbearable levels. The short walk to her car left her wishing that she had opted for a cold cut sandwich and a glass of tea from the cafeteria.

Once in her car with the air conditioning on max cool, she dialed the number for the throwaway phone that she had bought for Wayne Cleaver. She wanted to make sure he was comfortable and had everything he needed for the next few days. He answered after the first ring.

"Hey, Liz. Checkin' up on me?"

She smiled and replied, "Yes, as a matter of fact I am. I'm just starting my lunch break. Do you need anything."

In his mind, he thought of kissing her passionately, but said, "Yeah, I'm good. Just lying low, staying out of sight."

"I hope you're doing a better job of it than you did at my place. You haven't gone over to Sylvia's neighbors and introduced yourself, have you?"

They both laughed. Elizabeth's phone beeped in her ear indicating an incoming call. She looked at her display and saw that Sylvia Deming was calling her. To Wayne she said, "Oh crap. Sylvia's calling me. Let me call you back."

"Okay."

She hit the icon to connect to the incoming call. "Hey, Sis. Enjoying the Key West beaches and bars?"

Sylvia laughed lightly, almost politely, like the joke wasn't really funny. "Neither, Liz. I'm not doing anything. I got down here, got a hotel room, and took a long shower. I've been sitting in the hotel room ever since with the TV on, but I'm not into it. I can't even tell you what's on. I'm really bummed."

"Sissy, what you need is to go get something to eat...and drink. Go to one of the local bars, eat a Cheeseburger in Paradise, have a margarita and some chips and salsa. Forget about this place. That's why you went down there, isn't it?"

"Yeah. I guess."

Elizabeth noticed the complete lack of energy in Sylvia's voice. She was worried about her friend. Could the trip to Florida, without any company, have been a mistake? She thought quickly, trying to come up with something that would boost her friend's spirits.

She said, "Listen, you took this trip with good intentions. Maybe if you just give it a few more days, see what happens. Stop at a bar. Talk to the first good looking guy you see."

Elizabeth heard Sylvia sigh loudly. Her advice wasn't helping.

"Thanks for the pep talk, Liz. I know you're trying, but I'm staying tonight, then I'm heading home. Or what was home. I'll get the place cleaned out and get it on the market by Wednesday. I might even call a realtor today and have them get a contract ready."

Elizabeth was in a slight panic, but she managed to maintain control. "Whatever you want, Sissy. If you need a place to stay while you house hunt, I've got a couple extra bedrooms. You let me know."

"Liz, I already told you, you're the best." There was a pause, then she said, "I should be back in town late afternoon tomorrow. I'll call when I get to the house."

"Okay. You drive careful. Call me tonight if you need to talk." A moment passed and Elizabeth said, "You're gonna be alright, Sis."

"Thanks, Liz."

A few moments after the phone went silent, she said, "Bye, Sis."

Elizabeth was still sitting in the parking garage with her car running. Her feelings were all over the board. She felt a terrible sadness for her friend, who lost her husband to a violent death. She may have lost him even before the murder, her marriage already in shambles.

Then she felt guilty for using Sylvia's house without getting her permission. It had appeared to be a gift from heaven, but now that gift was being pulled away. Was it Karma or just bad luck? Or had circumstances deemed this change inevitable? She rubbed her eyes, hoping that when she opened them, things might look differently. But the sun was still shining, the heat and humidity were still unbearable, and she still had to get lunch.

She took a moment to reflect on the recent changes that had occurred in her life. Two old friends from different eras in her life were now back. Both had experienced tragedies and both leaned on her for support. At this time last week, she had few friends outside the office because she was so tied up in her work that she had little time for a social life. She vowed to herself that had to change.

Elizabeth hadn't had time to head home between calls and she really didn't want to drive with her head spinning from Sylvia's news and talk to Wayne at the same time. She dialed Wayne's throwaway again.

"Hey, Sweetie, that was quick."

"Don't panic, but we've got trouble."

"What now?"

"Sylvia's coming home. She won't be here until tomorrow afternoon, but it looks like you're heading back to my place. Maybe late tonight."

Wayne's mood immediately went into the dumper. He had hoped that this would be over before he had to move again, but that didn't appear to be in the cards.

"Are you sure that she won't just walk in on me later today?"

"Yeah, I'm sure. She's still in Key West, staying over tonight. But we're getting you out of there tonight so we won't have to worry about running into her tomorrow. She might not appreciate that."

"At least I don't have much to move."

"See, it's looking up already."

They both laughed nervously. The entire ordeal was weighing on them both. Elizabeth's phone beeped in her ear again. She thought it might be Sylvia calling again, but it said Private Caller on her display. She said, "I have another call coming in. I'll call you back in a little bit."

"Busy woman. Go."

She answered the new call, "Hello."

"Elizabeth, this is Special Agent Megan Moore. We have something that we want to discuss with you, but it needs to be in private. Can we meet for lunch?"

Elizabeth didn't know how to respond. She asked, "Can you tell me what this is about?"

"Not over the phone. Can we meet at your condo? We'll bring lunch if you haven't eaten. You name it. We'll get it and meet you there."

After a nervous pause, she said, "Okay. How about..."

* * *

The cold cut combo sub from the local deli, the glass of cold, sweet iced tea, and the seventy-two-degree air conditioned kitchen were just what Elizabeth needed. Megan Moore and Peden Savage sat at her kitchen table going over the details of the quickly assembled plan. They knew that she didn't have much time left for her lunch and they needed time that afternoon to get their plan set up.

Between bites, Elizabeth told her two visitors that their timing was perfect, that Wayne had to get out of Sylvia Deming's house tonight. Sylvia would be back in Savannah tomorrow afternoon, unless she had a change of heart. So having Wayne back at her condominium by dinner time would work out perfectly.

"You want him to make contact with Mrs. Francis, my nosey neighbor?"

Megan replied, "Yes, the more visible, the better. We want your neighbor to see him and call the police hot line. If she doesn't, we can have someone make the call, but it would sound more authentic coming from your neighbor."

"And you think that word will get to the guys who are trying to frame him that he's here?"

Megan replied, "We're pretty sure that it will, yes. We'll be monitoring her telephone, so we'll know if she makes the call."

Elizabeth listened to the explanation again and gained confidence that their plan would work. She looked at the digital time on her microwave and said, "I need to get back to work. What do you need from me?"

Peden replied, "We need you to pick up Wayne after you get off work and bring him here. That's all. I think we have everything else we need."

Elizabeth headed back to work. Special Agent Megan Moore and Peden Savage stayed at her condominium. Now all she had to do was keep her cool in front of Andrew Newsome for the afternoon. She hoped that she could do it. Wayne's freedom, maybe even his life, depended on it.

* * *

Andrew Newsome's Administrative Assistant buzzed his phone at 1:02 PM. "Mr. Newsome, Judge Stillwell is on the line."

"Put him through."

Judge Stillwell, in his normally booming drawl, said, "Andy, how are you?"

"Busy, Judge. How can I help you?"

"Well, Andy, I've been thinking. Things have smoothed out a bit in the last couple of days. Sounds like the team's back at full strength. Marcus Cook, ex-Army Special Ops tough guy. Vince called me and said he appears to be a perfect fit. What do you think?"

Newsome's eyebrows sank down in the middle; his nose started to twitch upward as he sensed that this call might ruin the rest of his day. He wondered what was coming next.

"Well, Judge, he seems okay, but we haven't even had a chance to test him in the field. Why do you ask?"

"I'm asking because I think we should get back in the

business of busting bad guys. Since we have a full team again, we should start back up later this week."

Newsome's face turned bright red. His nose twitched faster, his stomach started to churn, and he could feel sweat form on his forehead. He needed to release some pressure or he would have a stroke. He yelled, "Are you fucking kidding me? I thought we agreed that we'd take three weeks off. It hasn't been three days." He paused to take a deep breath. "Does Vince know about this?"

"No, he doesn't. I wanted to run it past ya'll first. I think it would be good to get back into the habit and…"

Newsome cut him off, shouting, "We're not fucking doing it, Judge! No way!"

Newsome's assistant opened the door a crack and asked, "Are you…"

She stopped as Newsome angrily waved her away.

"Andy?" The Judge's voice was calm and quiet, much more than normal. "Ya'll aren't stroking out on me because I'm just pulling ya'll's chain. Vince called and said he was worried about ya. He said ya'll's a bit tense. I just wanted you to blow off some steam."

"That didn't help, Whalen! Not one fucking bit!"

"I think it will after ya'll get home tonight and relax. You need a break."

Newsome thought, *You got that right. I need to get away from you lunatics.* He said, "Let's just get past the murder investigations and your election campaign, then we can relax. There's just too damn much going on right now."

"Andy, it's going to be fine. Relax. Forget about this stuff for now. Do your job. Love your wife. Take a vacation. Just unwind a bit."

"Maybe I will take a vacation. And a cruise sounds like a good idea."

"Good man."

Chapter 40

Senator Vega sat in his room at the Marriott Springhill Suites Hotel on the southeast side of Statesboro, Georgia. From his north facing third-story window on a beautiful Monday afternoon, he could see the rooftops of the Georgia Southern University campus buildings poking above the trees.

Since the previous afternoon, he had worn a path from the window to the bathroom door, back around the bed and back to the window again. The temptation to call Peden Savage for an update was nearly unbearable. The only calls he made were for room service and about the availability of the room for another night should Mercado drag this out for another day.

He turned for the hundredth time and looked at the throwaway phone sitting on the dresser, willing it to ring with news that the money drop was on. It was 2:20 PM. He had checked in nearly twenty-two hours ago. Sleep had eluded him into the early morning hours, thinking that Mercado would call while everyone was tired and slow to react. The call never came.

He turned to head for the bathroom to splash water on his face when the phone vibrated and let out an electronic ringtone. He took three quick steps, snatched up the phone and hit the answer icon.

"Vega."

"Good afternoon, Senator. Sorry to keep you waiting."

"Agent Mercado. Are we going to do this?"

"Yes, Senator, we are. When I complete my instructions to you, I expect that you will quickly carry them out. When you are finished, you will go directly to the airport, board your plane and fly back to Washington. You will not contact anyone. Is that clear?"

"Yes," Vega replied.

"Good. Take the two bags and turn left onto Highway 67, then an immediate right onto the 301 bypass. Take the second right, Route 80, and pull through the Applebee's parking lot to the Lowe's parking lot. There is a white van sitting four spaces into that lot. Pull next to the van on the passenger side. Put the bags in the cargo area using the side door. Open the passenger door and lock the van. Check and make sure the doors are locked. Then leave." Mercado paused. "Any questions?"

"None."

"Go. Don't waste any time, Senator."

The line went dead.

Vega quickly grabbed one of the duffle bags of money and threw it over his shoulder. He grabbed the other bag in his left hand, headed for the door, and closed it behind him. The money felt heavier than it had the day before. He went to the front desk and tossed the keycards to the clerk. "Room 312, checking out."

He was out the front door before the stunned clerk could ask anything about how he enjoyed his stay.

* * *

"The money's on the move."

Michael Jess looked over Lee Sparks' shoulder at his computer while Lee called Peden and Megan.

Peden and Megan were set up at Elizabeth Sanchez's kitchen table. Peden tapped the touchpad and the screen lit up. He saw the triangle on the map. It had indeed moved. It was displayed on Highway 67 angling for the Highway 301 Bypass. This was great news. The tracking devices' electronics hadn't been damaged during yesterday's thunderstorm. Everything was working fine.

The triangle picked up speed, tracking along the Highway 301 Bypass, achieving a smooth motion after about eight seconds. After two minutes, the triangle slowed and eased off the bypass onto Route 80. It turned off the road and pulled into a large parking lot. It stopped and remained that way for five, ten, then twenty minutes. By 3:30 the team was beginning to wonder if Mercado and his team had been scared off.

Peden rubbed his face, hoping they hadn't spooked Mercado. They literally didn't have anyone in the field, except Marcus Cook, and he was playing as if he was on their team. Peden worried about Marcus, hoping that his cover hadn't been blown.

At 3:42, the money moved again. The triangle pulled out of the parking lot and headed west on State Route 80. The triangle moved at a choppy pace as it moved through Statesboro. Once the triangle hit the open space west of the city the pace smoothed out. The tracking software showed the vehicle maintaining a steady sixty miles per hour, a safe speed on a two-lane state highway.

After thirty-five minutes, the triangle turned south on South Old Reidsville Road. Another ten minutes and a few turns in the country, the triangle stopped on a road that looked to be farmland. Peden zoomed in, switched to a satellite view, and saw that the triangle stopped at a farmhouse. The only other structure close by was a large barn. The closest house to this one was nearly three thousand feet away on the opposite side of the road.

Peden texted Lee and Michael Jess, *They chose the location wisely.*

Sparks texted back, *You got that right.*

It was now 4:20 PM. There was nothing more to do for the next hour except wait. They needed to get confirmation from Michael Jess that Senator Vega had gone back to Washington, D.C. They hoped that he knew enough to just stay out of the way.

* * *

Senator Vega locked the door to the nondescript white Ford van and jumped back into his car. He didn't waste any time heading out of the parking lot, turning left onto Highway 80, then south on Highway 301 Bypass. From there, he picked up State Route 67 South to Eastbound Interstate 16. It took all his willpower to keep driving and not turn around to confront

Mercado, or whoever was to pick up the money. It wasn't the money that bugged him. It was the loss of pride, losing the war of wits and nerves to these guys. He hated to give in. *I'm a United States Senator, for God's sake. How...why did I let this happen?* He felt the rumble of the grooves on the side of the road as his rental car veered too far off course. *Damn. Concentrate.*

* * *

Wayne Cleaver paced through Sylvia Deming's house all day. He ate a ham and cheese sandwich for lunch and chased it with a glass of sweet tea. The caffeine gave him a burst of energy and heightened anxiety as he thought about his role in the FBI's plan. He was waiting for Elizabeth to pick him up so he could ride in her car, laying down in the back seat all the way to her condominium. He was already nervous about the trip. Passing the time with nothing to do didn't help.

As he paced through Sylvia's house, he couldn't help but wonder about their lives, most of which was now packed in boxes. How much of these household goods would Sylvia keep, how much would go to charity, and how much would end up in a landfill. Elizabeth had told him that she wasn't the type to accumulate a lot of trinkets. She liked things in their place with no clutter. If it wasn't used, it was gone.

Jarrod, on the other hand, was the one to display trophies. Sylvia had told Elizabeth, and she repeated it to Wayne, that one wall in their library was devoted to Jarrod's certificates for various achievements, such as college diplomas, qualifications on small arms, completion of specialized courses for DEA Agent certification as well as plaques for competitive shooting. Jarrod had called it his "I love me" wall. As Wayne strolled into the library, he looked at the boxes along the wall, all of them open, containing dozens of framed certificates, along with a few pictures. He stooped down on his haunches and pulled a framed certificate up so he could read it. It was Jarrod's 2011 recertification for small arms. He pulled several more frames from the box and noted that they were all for similar achievements: recertification on long rifle, recertification on shotgun, recertification for Basic First Aid.

He moved to the next box. There were two more certificates in front, followed by a picture of Jarrod in his DEA raid uniform, holding what Wayne believed to be an M-16 military assault rifle. For all he knew, it could have been a plastic toy, but it looked real enough.

Wayne was about to get up and look for something else to keep him occupied when he lifted the next frame from the box. It was another qualification certificate, but this one was for initial certification as an expert marksman on long rifles. It looked much the same as the previous framed certificates, but with two, glaring differences. The glass in front of the frame was cracked with a chip of glass missing. The second difference was that the certificate was issued on Tuesday, May 20, 2014…to Sylvia Deming.

Wayne sat down in place, his mind racing. Not only was he sitting in the house of a murdered DEA agent. He might be sitting in the house of that agent's murderer.

Wayne looked at the clock on the wall; 4:58. *Come on, Elizabeth. I have to get out of here.*

* * *

When Elizabeth unlocked the kitchen door to her friend's house, she heard Wayne walking in her direction. He was moving quickly. When she saw him round the hall corner, she could see that he was anxious about something.

She said, "What's wrong?"

"Let me show you."

Wayne led Elizabeth into the library to the boxes containing the framed certificates. He pulled Sylvia's Marksmanship certificate out and handed it to her. She frowned as she read it. After a moment, her jaw slowly dropped, her eyes widened, and her hands began to quiver. She gawked at Wayne. She said nothing, but her expression exclaimed, *Oh my God.*

"Where did you get this?"

In a voice filled with tension, he said, "Right there. It was in that box. I was bored so I looked at all these certificates.

I thought that they were all Jarrod's."

She said nothing, but looked back at the framed certificate in her hand, trying to will it to say something other than what it did.

Wayne apologized, "I'm sorry, Liz. I know you two are close."

Again, she didn't respond as her mind flooded with the possibility that her close friend may have murdered her husband. She finally said, "I think we'd better put this back right where you found it and get out of here. She said she wasn't coming back until tomorrow afternoon, but she may have changed her mind. We'll take a quick look around. We need to leave everything exactly as it was when we got here yesterday."

Wayne said, "All I have to do is get the kitchen cleaned up and clear the few things out of the fridge and we're set to go."

Elizabeth took one last look at the certificate with her friend's name in bold script across the center. Tears welled up in her eyes as she set the frame back in the box. Wayne came back to the library and stood at a distance until Elizabeth turned and faced him. She moved close to him, putting her arms around his waist as he embraced her.

She cried on his shoulder until he coaxed her, "We should really go. I have to go expose myself to your neighbor."

She looked up at him and laughed as tears streamed down her cheeks.

He said, "I guess that didn't come out right."

They embraced again then headed for her car.

Chapter 41

At 6:20 PM, Wayne Cleaver took a deep breath to calm his nerves. On the drive to Elizabeth's condominium, he had been quiet, fretting about the task at hand. Now, standing in her living room, he held a cold bottle of water in his left hand. He flipped the lock on Elizabeth's sliding patio door, turned towards Peden, Megan, and Elizabeth, and took another deep breath. All three gave him a thumbs-up. It didn't instill much confidence but he was determined to do it no matter what. He slid the door to the side and stepped onto the concrete patio. The heat was still oppressive, even into the early evening. He heard Elizabeth's neighbor, Gertrude Francis, humming to herself. She was watering the plants that surrounded her patio.

He walked further out on Elizabeth's patio, making sure that he was in view of her neighbor, then turned in her direction. A bumble bee took flight from one of Mrs. Francis' flowers, narrowly missing Wayne's face. It landed on another flower a few feet away.

He said, "Hi. What's that tune?"

The elderly woman looked back at Wayne with a confused stare. She asked, "Pardon?"

"That song; you were humming a song that I recognize, but I can't remember the name."

Mrs. Francis continued to look at Wayne as if she hadn't understood. Then the light seemed to come through. "Oh, that old song. I heard it on Lawrence Welk last night on television. I don't remember the name either. It is so relaxing to sit and listen to those wonderful old tunes."

"That's nice. Your flowers look beautiful."

"Why, thank you. You're Elizabeth's friend."

"Yes. I'm Wayne. We went to school together a long

time ago."

Wayne wasn't sure if she recognized him from the other day or if she had seen the news broadcast where his picture was prominently displayed. He now doubted whether this part of the plan would work. He ran his hand through his short hair and roughed it up as much as he could, then he turned back towards Mrs. Francis again. "Have you seen the news lately? Sounds like we're stuck with this heat for a while."

"Well, it is summer in Georgia." She looked at Wayne closer without saying anything then suddenly excused herself. "I've got a pie in the oven."

Mrs. Francis forced a nervous smile then headed into her condominium. She finally recognized Wayne Cleaver, the murder suspect from the news. He was pretty sure that she would be calling the police hotline within the next few minutes, if she could find the number and concentrate long enough to make the call.

Four minutes later, Lee Sparks reported that Gertrude Francis was making the call.

* * *

The man who answered Gertrude Francis' call wasn't sure about the call's validity, but he was instructed to forward all information to the on-duty detective. He dialed the Detective Bureau.

"Hey, Detective, we've got a potential sighting on Wayne Cleaver, the guy who the DEA is trying to find. I've got the recording of the call. Bring up file R0622151825. We're supposed to call the DEA Special Agent in Charge. Name's Vince Mercado.

Detective Rick Jenkins was annoyed. He had hoped to have the evening off, but couldn't line up a replacement in time. Reading the notes on the hotline procedure, he saw that he was supposed to call the Chief about any plausible tips. He dialed the chief's direct line.

Chief Robert Chastine answered on the second ring. It was now 7:18 PM.

"Hey, Chief, this is Jenkins."

"Hey, Rick. What's up?"

"I've got duty this evening. We got a call on that Wayne Cleaver guy, the one from the hotline. We've got a location on him. Do you want me to assemble a team and grab this guy? I think we might need a warrant."

Chief Chastine thought about the consequences of taking Detective Jenkins advice. They could get a few at-a-boys from it, but the instructions were to contact the DEA first and they would decide how to handle it. Chastine was a by-the-book kind of law enforcement officer, so he opted to make the call to the DEA agent...what was his name...Mercado?

"Hey, Rick, send me the file number on the call. Then pass it on to the DEA agent. Let them handle it. No sense spending manpower on something that isn't our problem."

"Okay, Chief. Will do."

Immediately after the call disconnected, Rick Jenkins dialed the number for Vincent Mercado.

He answered, "Mercado."

"Agent Mercado, this is Detective Rick Jenkins with Savannah Metro. We have a tip call that places Wayne Cleaver at a local address in Savannah. Let me know when you are ready to write down this information, sir."

Mercado almost couldn't contain his excitement, but he kept his composure. "Yeah, Detective, I'm ready."

"A caller identified as Mrs. Gertrude Francis called the hotline shortly after 7:00 PM this evening. She said she saw Wayne Cleaver on the patio of her neighbor's condominium. She was certain that the man was Wayne Cleaver. The condominium where Cleaver is located is 620 Berrien Street, Unit D.

Mercado smiled. He repeated the address information back to the detective to ensure that he had the right address. "Thanks Jenkins. We'll take it from here."

Mercado hit the disconnect icon on his phone. He looked over at the bags of cash from Senator Vega. He rubbed his face with both hands. He was tired from the long, busy day.

Now they had to take care of Cleaver.

Mercado dialed Alex Smith's cell phone. As he waited for his partner to pick up, he took the throwaway phone from the table, placed it on the floor of the farmhouse and smashed it with the heel of his shoe. He stomped on it several times until the phone shattered into pieces. He hadn't heard Smith pick up.

"Vince, you there?"

"Yeah, I'm here. Just got rid of a loose end."

"I hope you didn't draw any blood."

Mercado smiled. "It was just the throwaway phone. No big loss. Anyway, we've got a line on Cleaver. You guys get over here so we can get these packages split up. When we're done, we're gonna tie up one more big loose end."

Mercado smiled as he thought about Cleaver and how much fun it was going to be shutting him up permanently.

* * *

Mercado looked at Nichols and Cook and instructed, "When we get to the condominium, you two take the back doors. Alex and I will take the front door and the main garage door. I don't think he'll be expecting us. If Sanchez tries to play hero, well, tough luck for her."

Mercado was looking at his laptop computer's screen. He did a search of owners for the condominium complex where Cleaver was reportedly staying. He saw that the neighbor was indeed named Gertrude Francis, so that much was consistent with the report.

Alex Smith asked, "You calling Newsome to let him know?"

Mercado was in deep thought for a moment. "Yeah. I've got to take his cut to him anyway. So let me call him and get that out of the way. In the mean time, you guys head back to Savannah. It's 7:50. You should be back to town by 9:20. We meet in the parking lot of the Civic Center at 11:00. The Sanchez place is just a minute from there." He looked at Smith, Nichols, and Cook. "Be in full gear. Bring your silencers. Let's go."

All three stood, nodded, grabbed their duffle bags of

cash, and headed for the door. It had been a long, but prosperous day. They all felt excited about the move on Cleaver, all except Marcus Cook.

Marcus hoped that Peden and Megan were following his moves throughout the day. He also hoped that they were ready for Mercado's next move. If he had to, he could handle Nichols, no problem. But taking out Mercado and Smith? That would be a tall order.

As the three men made their way to the door, Mercado said, "Hey, Marcus, hang back. Give me a hand."

Marcus stopped in his tracks. A thousand thoughts raced through his mind, but all he said was, "Sure, Vince."

When Smith and Nichols were out of earshot, Mercado said, "I thought I noticed you tense up when I said that we found Cleaver."

"Not me. I'm okay with this."

He said, "This is your first op. Just keep your cool and follow Nichols' lead. It'll be fine. We'll be in and out before Cleaver knows what hit him."

"What about Sanchez?"

"We'll cross that bridge…you know. Hopefully, she won't be home, but if she is…it's sad, but she shouldn't cavort with murderers."

Marcus forced a smile. Inside, his gut twisted into knots, wishing he could take out the three agents right now. That wasn't to be. He knew he had to play along.

"Well, let's get this show on the road." Marcus held out his fist for a bump.

Mercado obliged and the two men headed for the side door with four bags of cash in tow. Marcus dropped the extra duffle bag in Mercado's trunk. Mercado threw in the other two and shut the trunk lid. Marcus took his own bag of cash to his car. Nichols and Smith were already on the road.

This is going to be a long drive. I sure hope the good guys are ready at the other end.

* * *

At 8:05 PM, Mercado was driving east on Interstate 16 as the sun neared the horizon in his rearview mirror. He was deep in thought about the ensuing confrontation with Wayne Cleaver. The scent of three duffle bags of money drew his attention and he grinned. He had no idea that cash in an enclosed space, like a car, had a distinct aroma, like dirty tee shirts, or Converse tennis shoes...no, like old leather. He settled on his belief that there was no other scent like it in the world...and he loved it.

He thought about Elizabeth Sanchez. Smith was right. The name sounded familiar. Where had he heard that name before? The realization hit him like a two-by-four to the head. He met Sanchez at Deming's wake. *What the hell?*

He decided he'd better call Newsome to arrange to drop off his and the Judge's cut. This little wrinkle might be significant, but maybe not. He hit the speed dial for Newsome's cell.

"Hey, Vince."

"Andy, are you going to have a few minutes free around 9:20? I've got something for you."

"Sure, Vince. Where do you want to meet?"

"Can you meet me in the parking lot of Planet Fitness on Ogeechee?"

"Yeah, Vince. See you there."

"Wait. You still there?"

"Yeah."

"Do you remember seeing Sylvia Deming's friend, Elizabeth Sanchez, at Deming's wake?"

Newsome was quiet for a moment. Why would Mercado be asking about Sanchez? "Yeah, I remember. Why?"

"We got a tip that Cleaver is hiding out at her place. Do you know anything about her?"

Mercado thought he heard the DA having a stroke, the intake of air was so loud.

"Andy, you there?"

"Yeah. Is your source reliable?"

"Well, it was a hotline tip and we checked out the lady's location. She lives next to Sanchez. She said she saw Cleaver there about an hour ago. I wanted to let you know that we're going in tonight. Just wanted to know if you knew who she was."

"I ought to know. She's an Assistant DA in my office."
Shit.

Chapter 42

11:12 PM. The night was dark, aided by a thin veil of clouds partially obscuring a crescent moon. Still driving the dark blue Ford Fusion that he had rented early that morning, Mercado parked one full block past Elizabeth Sanchez's condominium on Berrien Street. The canopies of several ancient Southern Oaks with thick patches of Spanish moss left large stretches of near complete darkness on the block.

Sanchez's condominium was also dark. No exterior lights were on and the curtains were drawn over dark windows. It appeared that Sanchez was in bed, resting up for tomorrow's workday. Cleaver was probably in bed as well. His plans for tomorrow were of no consequence.

Alex Smith sat in the passenger seat looking at the neighborhood, allowing his eyes to adjust to the darkness. What he saw confirmed what they had observed on the satellite image they looked at moments ago in the Savannah Civic Center Parking lot. The plan would work just fine.

Pete Nichols and Marcus Cook moved in from West Jones Street to cover the rear of Sanchez's condominium. Once Mercado and Smith heard the signal that they were in place, they would wait thirty seconds and move to the front door, ring the doorbell once and give Sanchez five seconds to open the door. If she did, they would quickly move in and take out Cleaver first, then Sanchez. If she didn't, they would break the door down and finish the job. Mercado had a plant weapon for Cleaver, a Glock 9mm. Smith had one for Sanchez, a short barrel Smith and Wesson .380.

The team had their standard issue LAR-15 assault rifles and Smith and Wesson MP40 side arms. Their rifles had silencers. No sense waking up the entire neighborhood. If they had to crash their way in, they could always remove the silencers before local law enforcement arrived.

Smith continued to survey the area, looking for movement of any kind. So far, it appeared that the neighbors had rolled up the sidewalks and locked their doors, planning on a quiet evening.

Smith said, "Roll your window down. Let's listen for a few seconds."

They both lowered their windows. The heat and humidity rushed in, overtaking the car's cool air. Smith reached over and turned the air conditioning fan to low so that he could hear his surroundings. The only sounds he and Mercado heard were truck and car traffic on the entry ramp to nearby Interstate 16 and the quiet engine of their rental car.

Smith whispered, "Quiet night, just how we like 'em."

Mercado only nodded. He picked up his LAR-15 from between him and Smith and looked over the weapon in the dark. He had already prepared it with a fully loaded, thirty-clip magazine locked in place and two more inside the pocket on his left pant leg. He was ready to go, getting antsy, waiting for the signal. He was about to say something to Smith when the double-click signal came through over both their radios. They donned their helmets, opened their car doors and headed for Sanchez's condominium.

* * *

Behind Elizabeth Sanchez's condominium, Nichols and Cook made their way along a row of mature arborvitae that separated the condominium complex from property once used for light industry. The trees provided cover for their approach from West Jones Street. In full, black gear, they looked like shadows moving through the night. Nichols led the way, Cook following close behind, both keeping silent, listening for any instructions from Mercado. If all went as planned, no voice communications were necessary.

At 11:15, Nichols and Cook were in place on either side of Sanchez's patio door. Cook nodded to his partner who clicked the talk button on his communications head set twice.

He received a single click in reply. They were to wait until they heard Mercado and Smith enter the front door before entering the back. Nichols was looking at the locking mechanism as best as he could in the darkness. It was difficult to see what type of lock it was but most doors of this type had cheap, easy to break locks.

Marcus' nerves were going wild. Seconds ticked by, but it seemed like an eternity. He stared at Nichols, waiting and wondering what would come next. *If Savage and Moore are out here, they're doing a hell of a job hiding. I haven't seen any support vans or cars.* He looked at his watch. He thought that it might have been a full minute since Nichols sent the signal, but his watch said it had been only twenty-five seconds. He wasn't sure how long it would take Mercado and Smith to reach the front door. He looked around the yard, making sure that no one could see them. As he did, he heard the doorbell from inside the condo. He counted one thousand, two thousand, three thousand, four thousand, five...

Marcus heard the sound of Sanchez's front door smashing open and felt a tremor as the building shook. He heard Mercado yelling, "Cleaver, get on the ground now!"

Pete Nichols grabbed the handle of the patio door and forcibly slammed the door open. The cheap, aluminum lock shattered into pieces. Nichols went through the door first, raising his gun to eye level as he went. He veered off to the left and flipped on the flashlight attached to his gun. Marcus followed a step behind, moved to his right, raised his weapon, and flipped on his light. As he did, he heard several staccato rushes of air and saw flashes of light. He knew that Mercado or Smith, or both, had fired multiple shots. *Awe shit. That can't be good.*

* * *

Mercado waited the full five seconds before stepping back from the front door. He nodded to Smith and both men flipped on the flashlights attached to the undersides of their assault rifles. Mercado took a deep breath and charged the door like a linebacker charging an opposing lineman. The door stood no chance against the solid mass weighing more than two hundred thirty pounds. The door frame splintered leaving sharp shards of wood sticking out into the entry. The deadbolt lock stuck out of the edge of the door at an odd angle. The door flew open and smacked against the wall. One of the door sidelights broke out, sending glass flying.

Mercado rushed to the end of the foyer, darting to the right, facing the hallway leading to the guest bedroom. Smith followed a step behind to the left, looking at a closed door that led to the master bedroom.

The condominium was dark except for the beam from their flashlights. Clouds of dust rose into the light stream giving the room an eerie feel. Mercado motioned for Smith to go into the master bedroom while he shown his light around the living room. He heard Wayne Cleaver's voice from down the hall. As he swung his gun in that direction, he heard the patio door open with a loud metallic crunch. Nichols and Cook came in from the back. His light caught a face standing in the open doorway to the guest bedroom. The voice was yelling, "What the hell is going on here? Who…"

Mercado smiled to himself. The problem with who was to blame for Jarrod Deming's murder was about to go away. He aimed his weapon and fired three quick shots. They hit Cleaver's body in the chest, but he didn't go down. Mercado fired again, another burst of three shots.

Then he heard Cleaver's voice continue with, "…are you? What are you doing in here?

Mercado's mind raced. Cleaver was hit with six well-placed shots to his chest. His heart should have been destroyed. He should be dead! Behind him, he heard the screaming of a woman, he presumed it was Elizabeth Sanchez. Then he heard a three-burst shot from Smith's weapon. The screaming continued. Smith didn't take a second shot. Mercado turned around and saw Smith walk out of the bedroom with his weapon lowered even as Sanchez's screaming continued.

Pete Nichols and Marcus Cook stood inside the patio door their weapons slowly lowering. Suddenly, a series of flashes from different points in the room caused the team to shield their eyes.

Mercado walked to the hallway and flipped a light switch. He could now clearly see the face of Wayne Cleaver. It was a life-sized photograph of his face attached to a mannequin dressed in pajamas. It was propped up inside the bedroom aligned perfectly with the doorway. The pattern of bullet holes in the prop's chest was tight, but that didn't matter.

Alex Smith looked over Mercado's shoulder, the setup becoming crystal clear. He stepped back to the bedroom and flipped on the light switch. He pulled back the covers. Another mannequin lay in the bed with three bullet holes in the torso. He exclaimed, "We're fucked!"

Smith moved back into the living room with Mercado. The four men stood trying to think about their next move when Megan Moore's voice could be heard as if she was in the room with them. "Gentlemen, put your weapons on the floor...all of them. Remove your gear and sit on the floor. Don't move a muscle."

Less than one minute later at 11:19 PM, Elizabeth Sanchez's condominium unit was swarming with FBI agents. They cuffed the four DEA agents who would be transported in separate vehicles to the FBI office in downtown Savannah.

* * *

Peden Savage removed Marcus Cook's handcuffs as they sat in the backseat of a black Chevrolet Suburban, still sitting on Berrien Street in front of Elizabeth Sanchez's condominium. Marcus rubbed his wrists, trying to get more blood to flow in his hands. The two men were still pumped from adrenaline flooding their bodies from the evening's events. It was 11:23 PM, but their night was just beginning.

Marcus asked, "Did you get everything on tape?"

"Well, yeah, except we don't use 'tape' these days, but Lee got it all, clear as a bell. Mercado and Smith pretty much sealed the deal with their shoot first, talk second move. They had no plans to take Cleaver alive."

"I kind of figured that when I heard the shots inside the

condo. Where are Cleaver and Sanchez now?"

"They're at FBI headquarters, locked away from everyone else, for their own safety. We got their statements recorded earlier along with Elizabeth's permission to use her property for the sting."

The Suburban pulled into the parking garage next to three other identical vehicles. Marcus was the last of the four DEA Agents delivered to FBI headquarters. Peden put the cuffs loosely back on his friend then stayed behind while two FBI agents escorted him into the office building. He waited in the parking garage until Lee Sparks pulled up with his video recording equipment. He helped Lee carry the gear into the building. Peden wasn't sure how chatty the three agents would be. It was likely that they had already requested lawyers. *I would if I was in their shoes.*

Peden was surprised when Megan told him that Pete Nichols requested that she contact Cliff Metzger, that he wouldn't need a lawyer. Megan called Roland Fosco and asked if she should follow through on Nichols' request. Fosco had instructed her to keep Nichols away from the rest of the team and not interview him. This had Peden scratching his head.

* * *

By 1:20 AM, Tuesday morning, everyone at Savannah's FBI satellite office was exhausted. Mercado and Smith requested their lawyers and weren't talking. All four of the DEA agents involved, including Marcus Cook, were placed in holding cells, isolated from each other. Pete Nichols quietly repeated his demand that Megan speak with Cliff Metzger. He would not tell Megan the purpose of his request.

Just after midnight, Lee Sparks called Peden. Vince Mercado's cell phone had multiple calls from Andrew Newsome. Starting at 11:30 PM, Newsome called roughly every ten minutes and hung up after four rings. He left no messages. At 12:45, he called and left a message wanting an "update on the situation." He closed the message ordering Mercado to call him first thing Tuesday morning.

Peden smiled. He told Sparks to get some rest. The next

few days were going to be busy.

Peden and Megan made a visit to Vince Mercado while he was in the interview room. Peden was tempted to smile but maintained a serious expression. He just had one question for the agent.

"Was that you driving the sedan that almost ran Megan and me over the other day?"

Mercado didn't answer directly. He simply said, "Just business, nothing personal."

Megan quipped, "Spoken like a true thug."

They turned and left Mercado alone to think about his future.

Chapter 43

Mitchel Abernathy, Vince Mercado's lawyer, entered the FBI offices at 8:00 AM sharp and demanded to speak with his client. Noting his sculpted white hair, perfect white teeth, and an expensive Armani suit, Megan Moore greeted him and led him back to Mercado's holding cell. When he demanded that his client be allowed to sit in an interview room, Megan informed him that his client was being held on murder and attempted murder charges. He would not be allowed out of his cell, but she offered to have a table and chair brought in.

After conferring with Mercado for only half an hour, he requested a meeting with the Special Agent in Charge. Megan said, "Let's talk."

Abernathy sat across from Megan Moore and Roland Fosco in a conference room. In a loud, confident voice, he declared, "Ya'll have nothing on my client. I want him released immediately!"

Megan, with her usual angry stare, said, "Before you go on boasting about your angelic client, you should watch this."

Megan picked up a remote control, pointed it at a flat panel screen at the end of the conference room and hit a button. The screen came to life.

When the video began to play, Cliff Metzger looked back at them. It was a recording made late last evening. Metzger described an ongoing internal investigation of DEA Agents Vincent Mercado and Alex Smith. Metzger stated, "Specifically, we are investigating the loss of over $1,000,000 seed money, the loss of accountability of confiscated drugs, the relationship between our agents and Chatham County District Attorney Andrew Newsome and Superior Court Judge Whalen Stillwell. The investigation has been active for eight months. We were preparing to bring charges against all four individuals but were sidetracked by the FBI's recent murder investigation and sting action. Our internal investigation did include DEA Agent Jarrod Deming, but he is the murder victim in the FBI investigation."

When the interview with Metzger was complete, Abernathy said, "Nothing's changed. There was no evidence presented in that statement."

Megan and Fosco again said nothing. Another video started. This time, Special Agent Peter Nichols looked at the camera and spoke. "I'm Peter Nichols, DEA Special Agent with the Savannah satellite office. I was assigned to this office specifically to investigate Special Agent Vincent Mercado, Special Agent Alex Smith, and deceased Special Agent Jarrod Deming. The investigation expanded to include Chatham County District Attorney Andrew Newsome and Superior Court Judge Whalen Stillwell when it became apparent that Newsome and Stillwell had direct ties to the aforementioned agents."

Nichols went on for the next twenty minutes detailing the illegal deeds of the DEA team, including extortion, falsifying drug confiscation reports, wrongfully targeting, arresting, and framing low-level drug dealers, and conspiracy to commit murder. That charge was in regards to the plan to murder Jarrod Deming, which never materialized, and the murder of Jarrod Deming's cousin Wesley Ross during a drug raid.

Abernathy had seen enough. "I have to confer with my client."

Megan replied, "While you're 'conferring,' let your client know that he has no bargaining power. We have everything we need to convict all four of the living conspirators." She looked Abernathy straight in the eye. "And tell him I didn't appreciate him trying to run me down the other day."

* * *

By 9:30 AM, Lee Sparks set up a camera so that DEA Special Agents Vincent Mercado and Alex Smith could make their statements. Both statements, made independently, corroborated the fact that Judge Whalen Stillwell had initiated the whole plan and used Mercado's team to extort money from the federal government for personal gain.

* * *

Peden Savage called Michael Jess with the news that they were paying a visit to Judge Whalen Stillwell at 1:00 PM. Peden wanted to know if he and Senator Armand Vega wanted to watch a live video and audio feed of the visit.

Jess said that it would make the Senator's day.

* * *

After Nila West's murder, the FBI searched her condominium and office. The crime scene technicians forwarded their preliminary report to Megan Moore.

In West's home, agents found half a dozen cryptic notes referencing clandestine meetings for dinner and late-evening trysts. The notes, found in a locked desk drawer, always closed with the letters *WS* in a fancy script. The crime scene technicians put a rush on all evidence related to her murder. To their surprise, late Monday afternoon, the fingerprints of Judge Whalen Stillwell were all over the notes. The judge's fingerprints were also found on the headboard of West's bed.

In the desk drawer of her office, they found a file folder with personal notes about each of her agents, District Attorney Andrew Newsome, Judge Stillwell, and her boss, Cliff Metzger. The notes spanned nearly thirty pages, each man getting his own "chapter." Marcus Cook and Pete Nichols were the smallest chapters. They had been on the team the shortest period of time.

Vince Mercado rated eight pages. She described him as an arrogant bastard with aspirations of running the DEA, making his own rules, and eliminating anyone who stood in his path. He cared for no one but himself. Women, at first, are drawn to him because of his cocky attitude, but soon are repelled by his cruel treatment of them. She made a follow-on note that she knew from personal experience.

Alex Smith she described as all business, but not a good

leader. He followed orders and carried them out, regardless of the consequences. His stance was that the brass knew what they were doing. He was as loyal as a lapdog and as fierce as a bulldog. West noted that she planned to stay away from Smith as his loyalty was obviously to Mercado.

The weak link, according to West's notes, was Andrew Newsome. He was a nervous, whiny, wimp of a man. He was also a sexist pig. His wife was going to bankrupt him if he didn't put a stop to it, but he was too *pussy-whipped* to do anything about it. She noted that the cash he was making on the side might keep him ahead of her perpetual shopping spree.

Whalen Stillwell, she noted, was indeed a powerful man, but he wanted more of everything: more money, more power, more women, faster cars, and more prestige. She noted that he planned to run for the Senate, then for the presidency. She wrote, *I told him I wanted in on the payday busts. He told me that he didn't know what I was talking about. I laughed at him. I confided that Jarrod had told me everything. I know the team is making a fortune and I want in. He laughed at me. That was two days before Jarrod was killed. The day after Jarrod's murder, I told Whalen that I wanted in or I was going to the FBI with what I knew. He said to calm down, that he and the others would talk about it first, but that it wasn't going to be a problem. He's coming over tomorrow night to tell me what I need to do.*

Megan said to herself, "There it is, the smoking gun." *Tomorrow night. The night West was murdered.*

Megan moved on to the next person in West's notes. The longest chapter was about Jarrod Deming. The last few pages were the most revealing. She wrote, *He was a good man, though a bit misguided. He was a good lover. His wife was a cold fish, so it was easy to get him in bed. Just before he was killed, he told me that he expected to be sacrificed for the good of the team. I told him that I'd protect him, that he needn't worry. He laughed at me. He said he was going to tell the FBI about the payday busts in a news conference. "I need to clear my conscience," he'd said. He wanted me to set it up. When I said I would, but that I wanted to know what he planned to say, he said he would let me know. He let me read his notes before he walked to the microphones.*

She went on to describe how she had grabbed the notes that flew from his hands. They had practically landed on her when Jarrod fell backwards onto the concrete steps. She had not realized that she had also been shot until she saw the blood on her clothing. With the notes secured, she moved towards Jarrod, but she was quickly moved away by some person that she didn't know, tending to her wounded arm.

West also had a few notes about how Sylvia Deming had squeezed her wounded arm at Jarrod's wake. *It was no accident. That bitch.*

Megan took a deep breath. It was nearly 12:30 PM on Tuesday. The plan was to be at the courthouse in front of Andrew Newsome's office at 1:00 PM. They would arrest him then immediately go to the fourth floor to Judge Stillwell's chambers. They would show him the video clips of Mercado and Smith stating that the Judge was the mastermind of the payday busts from the beginning. The Judge would then be placed under arrest. If all went well, they would wrap up the arrests no later than 1:30 in the afternoon.

Megan laughed to herself. *These things never go as planned.*

* * *

Megan Moore and four agents from the Statesboro and Brunswick satellite offices exited the elevator on the third floor of the Chatham County Courthouse. Megan held up her FBI badge to the surprised receptionist and asked which office was District Attorney Andrew Newsome's. She pointed to her left and said in a deep southern voice, "Down the hall to the end, then to your right. His office is the second door on the right. May I…"

Megan said with some force, "Do not alert Mr. Newsome. Stay at your desk and do not notify anyone of our presence. Understood?"

"Yes, ma'am."

Megan led the four agents down the hall, their heels clicking on the tile floor. The sound echoed off the narrow walls of the grand hallway as they made their way to Andrew Newsome's office. They entered the office and were surprised to see a beautiful, young black woman sitting at a desk in front of a closed door. Megan asked, "Is this Mr. Newsome's office?"

The woman replied, again with a slight southern accent, "Yes, it is." Her response slowed as she noticed the five people standing in front of her desk. "He's in conference with…"

"His conference is over." She put her hand over the telephone and ordered, "Do not alert him."

She turned and pointed to two of the agents and gave them instructions to stand guard at the doorway. "Do not let anyone in. Jim, Stan, come with me."

Megan opened the door to Andrew Newsome's office. He was sitting on the front edge of his desk talking with a young woman who sat in one of the guest chairs. He looked up in surprise and barked, "I'm in a meeting. You're going to have to wait for a few minutes. Miss Chambers can get you…"

Megan cut him off. "Mr. Newsome, your meeting is over." She flashed her FBI credentials and said to the young woman, "You are excused. We need to have a word with the DA."

The woman looked up at Newsome. He nodded then stood up from his desk. As she left the room, Newsome made his way around to his chair. Megan could tell he was nervous and trying to hide it, but his nose twitched continuously.

"Mr. Newsome, I'd like to show you a video then get your response."

She opened the *Microtel* tablet, tapped the screen several times then set the tablet on Newsome's desk so he could see the screen. Vince Mercado's face came up on the screen and his voice filled the room.

"Andrew Newsome was our go between. He got orders from Judge Stillwell and sent those orders through me to be carried out. It was Stillwell's plan from the start. Newsome was just the messenger. He was also involved in the prosecution of the perpetrators, knowing full well that the evidence against them was planted."

Megan reached down and hit the screen to stop the video. "Mr. Newsome, do you have anything you'd like to tell us?"

Andrew Newsome stared straight ahead. He knew that life, as he knew it, was over. His thoughts flashed to his wife, Meredith. What would she do now? She would be ostracized from her social life. He thought briefly about Judge Stillwell, that it was his idea from the start. His insistence that Newsome be involved as the go between put the DA in a no-win situation.

"Am I under arrest?"

Megan asked, "Are you serious? Of course you are. Please come out from behind the desk, turn and face the wall."

Megan cuffed the District Attorney, read him his rights, and motioned to the two agents to take him away. As the group made their way into the hall, stunned faces stared out of offices. As they passed Elizabeth Sanchez's office, Newsome looked in at her. They briefly made eye contact. When Megan passed her office, Elizabeth Sanchez smiled.

Chapter 44

Megan and the remaining two agents rode the elevator to the fourth floor of the Chatham County Courthouse. She turned right off the elevator and approached the receptionist's desk. A woman asked, "May I help you?"

Megan held up her FBI credentials and said, "Judge Whalen Stillwell's office."

The woman pointed to her left. "Second door on the right. The judge is finishing his lunch, so you..."

The receptionist stopped talking when Megan turned and gave her a death stare. "Do not alert the Judge."

The team marched the twenty steps down the hall and came to a closed door with a gold plaque that read *The Honorable Whalen Stillwell, Chief Judge.* Megan's lips crooked up on one side. She motioned for the two agents to follow her in. Grabbing the door handle, she forcefully opened the door and marched in.

Judge Stillwell demanded. "What do ya'll think you're doing, barging into my chambers like this?"

One of the agents closed the door behind them.

She turned back to the judge, holding up her credentials. "Judge Stillwell, I am going to show you a short video. The reason for our visit will be quite clear."

She tapped the screen on a tablet that she had brought with her. On the small screen, Vince Mercado faced the judge and began, "My name is Vincent Mercado. I am an Agent with the Drug Enforcement Administration at the Savannah, Georgia, satellite office. For the last three years, my team and I have been carrying out raids on low-level drug users and dealers and planting evidence to make it look like they were much higher-level dealers. We have been doing this to make our office look like we've been performing above the level of other offices. We also did this for personal gain. I will provide specific details of this scheme, but I first want to go on record stating that the person who came up with this entire scheme is Judge Whalen Stillwell. He planted the idea in our heads, planned how we could profit from the drug buys, and steal money from these dealers. I will provide details..."

"Stop. This is nonsense. I don't have any contact with this man. How is it possible for..."

Megan held up her hand and picked up the tablet from his desk. She tapped the screen a few times and set the tablet back on his desk. This time, Alex Smith stated his name for the record and described his job with the DEA. He began to describe a similar scenario as Mercado. After thirty seconds, Stillwell waved his hand and brought it across his throat. He was either asking that the video be stopped, or he knew his goose was cooked.

Megan savored the next few minutes. "Judge Stillwell, please stand and come around your desk. Keep your hands where we can see them."

Stillwell looked from Megan to the other two agents then back to Megan. He stood, staying behind his desk, looking around at his office at all the pictures of himself with any number of powerful men. He smiled sadly and shook his head, then slowly made his way around the front of his desk, his hands at his side, shoulders drooping down in defeat.

Megan said, "Please turn and face the back wall and place your hands behind your back."

He asked, "Is this really necessary, Agent Moore?"

As Megan put the cuffs on his wrists a little tighter than necessary, she exclaimed, "You're damn right it is!"

Megan Moore read Judge Stillwell his rights and asked that the two agents escort him to the waiting car in front of the courthouse. She took a deep breath and pulled out her cell phone. She dialed Roland Fosco and said, "It's done."

When she disconnected from her boss, she called Peden Savage and asked, "Did you get all the video?"

Peden replied, "Oh yeah."

* * *

Armand Vega and Michael Jess watched the image of Judge Whalen Stillwell as Megan Moore played the videos of Vince Mercado and Alex Smith naming him as the instigator and ringleader of payday drug busts. The once cocky, arrogant man was speechless. He was smart enough to not make any statements. He would fight the charges. He knew the best lawyers in the south, but for now, he was silent. His bid for the U.S. Senate was over.

Michael Jess said, "This will give you a load of new ammunition for taking away some of DEAs funding. If this is what they're doing with the taxpayers' money, imagine what's going on at other agencies."

Senator Vega shook his head. "This is a start, but where do we go from here?"

Jess raised his eyebrows and turned his hands up in the universal *You got me* sign.

Vega said, "One place we're going to start is finding out all the kids that these jokers have put in prison and make sure their sentences are overturned. Then we're going to make sure that they and their families are compensated. I'd like for you to work with the Chatham County DA on that...the new Chatham County DA."

Jess smiled and said, "Yes, sir."

* * *

Elizabeth Sanchez dialed the number for Wayne Cleaver's throwaway phone. He answered after just one ring. "Hey, Liz. What's the good word?"

"It's almost over. The FBI just arrested Newsome. I think they were on their way up to get the Judge. I think you're in the clear."

Elizabeth heard Wayne sigh loudly into the phone. She could almost feel his tension wither away. She wished she could be with him now. He was at a hotel room, paid for by the FBI, while they continued to process Elizabeth's condominium in the wake of the DEA's failed assassination attempt. It would be several days before her home was restored to livable condition.

Elizabeth said, "What do you think about a few days away? I'm sure whoever my new boss is will approve some time off. We're going to need it in case I have to be deposed. What do you think?"

"I'm all for it. How would you like to take a trip to lovely Anderson, South Carolina? It's not the beach, but I know Mom would love to meet you."

Elizabeth smiled. "That would be perfect."

Elizabeth heard four quick reports outside her window. There was a pause, then three more reports followed. Elizabeth said to Wayne, "I've got to go. I'll call you back in a few minutes."

"What's going…"

Elizabeth hung up and looked out her window. Two people were lying on the sidewalk at the entrance to the Chatham County Courthouse. Two men and a woman in blue blazers were standing over them both. Elizabeth covered her mouth with her hands as she looked down at the horrific scene.

* * *

Megan Moore walked behind Judge Stillwell and his two FBI escorts. Everyone that they passed in the hall of the courthouse stopped and stared, or pointed at the judge with their mouths agape. The agents, each holding an arm and guiding Stillwell through the lobby, kept looking around, anticipating where to move next. The courthouse wasn't particularly busy, but the agents remained vigilant. They wanted to get Stillwell to the FBI office downtown before any of the news stations caught wind of the arrest.

The Suburban was parked in a tow away zone. As they passed through the front doors of the courthouse, a second Suburban carrying Andrew Newsome pulled away. Megan and the other agents saw Stillwell and Newsome make eye contact. A stocky man in a light gray hooded sweatshirt angled towards them as the agents looked towards the departing vehicle.

Four loud pops in quick succession caught their

attention. Stillwell collapsed, the weight of his bulk causing them to strain to keep him upright. They looked towards the source of the reports and saw an older man aiming a pistol at them. He had pulled back the hood. Megan recognized Allen Deming immediately. He jerked the gun towards one of the agents, but hesitated. Megan Moore drew her service weapon, aimed, and pulled the trigger three times. Deming's arms flew back wildly as he fell backwards onto the pavement.

Megan kept her weapon pointed at Deming while she grabbed her phone and punched in 911 with her thumb. "We have shots fired at the main entrance to the Chatham County Courthouse! I repeat, shots fired! Two men are down! We need medical assistance immediately! Shooter has been neutralized!"

The dispatcher asked for Megan to identify herself. The ensuing discussion seemed to take forever, but was in reality only twenty-two seconds. In less than two minutes, two ambulances and eight Savannah-Chatham County Metro Police cars pulled up to the front of the courthouse. Paramedics told Megan that both men were dead.

* * *

Elizabeth called Wayne back after she got word that Judge Stillwell and Jarrod Deming's father, the shooter, were both dead. She told him what had transpired right under her office window. He asked if he could do anything and she said no. As she spoke with Wayne, her phone beeped in her ear, telling her that she had an incoming call. She looked. It was her friend Sylvia. How was she going to tell her friend that Jarrod's father, her father-in-law, had been killed after he killed a judge?

"Wayne, I'm sorry but Sylvia is calling. I'll call you back again."

She answered Sylvia, "Hey, Sis. You decide to stay in Florida?"

"No. I just got home. I wanted to call and thank you for watching the place. I know I wasn't gone that long, but I just felt that I needed to get home and get the house ready to sell."

That reminded Elizabeth of the marksmanship certificate that she and Wayne had seen in one of the boxes. She said, "How about if I come over and help you. I have to tell you a couple things anyway."

"Okay. I'll see you in a bit."

* * *

Sylvia greeted her friend at the front door of her home. They hugged in the entryway. The dread of the events of the day hung heavy in the room.

Elizabeth said, "Sis, your father-in-law was shot and killed this afternoon."

"Oh my..." Sylvia covered her mouth with her hands, her face displaying the shock. "What happened?"

"The FBI arrested Judge Stillwell at the courthouse."

"Judge Stillwell? Why? What does that have to do with Allen?"

"That announcement that Jarrod was planning, it was about some illegal things that his DEA team was doing. Did Jarrod tell you anything about that?"

Elizabeth watched her friend closely for any indication that she knew what her husband had been doing. Sylvia didn't miss a beat.

Her facial expression tightened into shock. "No, he didn't." Her expression changed to deep thought. "Judge Stillwell was involved with Jarrod's team? What were they doing?"

Elizabeth spent the next twenty minutes detailing Jarrod's and his peers' sins. She told her about how her own boss was involved and the number of people that they had put in prison unjustly. Sylvia appeared genuinely astonished.

Finally, Elizabeth said, "I have to apologize to you. I'll pay to have it replaced."

Sylvia looked puzzled. She asked, "What do you mean?"

"Well, when I was over here yesterday, I accidentally bumped into one of the boxes and a framed certificate fell out. The frame broke."

Elizabeth walked over to a box and pulled out the frame with cracked glass and a certificate. She handed it to Sylvia to make sure that she could see the words on the certificate.

This Certificate is Presented to Sylvia Deming Acknowledging that She has been Designated as an Expert Marksman by the National Firearms Association of America.

Elizabeth said, "I know this is important to you. Let me know the cost."

Sylvia's expression changed for the briefest moment. "You don't have to worry about it, Liz. I probably won't keep it anyway."

At that moment, Elizabeth knew. Sylvia murdered her husband.

Chapter 45

We interrupt your regularly scheduled program to bring you breaking news from the Chatham County Courthouse in Savannah. I'm Stephanie Willard, Channel 8 News. Superior Court Judge and recently announced candidate for the U.S. Senate, Whalen Stillwell, has been shot dead at the entrance to the Chatham County Courthouse. Stillwell was in the custody of three FBI agents and was being escorted to a transport vehicle when the shooting occurred. A man, identified as Allen Deming, a former employee of the courts and the father of murdered DEA Agent Jarrod Deming, allegedly approached Stillwell and the agents as they exited the courthouse. He withdrew a handgun from under a hooded sweatshirt and fired multiple shots, killing Judge Stillwell. FBI Agent Megan Moore returned fire as Deming was allegedly turning to fire on the agents. Deming was also pronounced dead at the scene.

In related news, Chatham County District Attorney, Andrew Newsome was arrested on a number of charges and was transported to the FBI office in Downtown Savannah. Sources claim that Newsome, Stillwell and three Drug Enforcement Administration Agents were involved in an extortion scheme, the extent of which is currently unknown. We will bring you updates as we continue our investigation on this developing story. We now return you to your regularly scheduled program.

Wayne Cleaver just shook his head as the television switched back to some ridiculous talk show involving two cheating spouses and a host who was antagonizing the ex-wife into berating the ex-husband. He was amazed at the number of lives destroyed by the actions of a handful of men in positions of trust. They were already successful in their careers, but apparently not satisfied with their success. They wanted more. The cost to others was of no concern to them.

Wayne shook his head, hoping to clear the dark thoughts. He smiled as the face of his friend – no – his love, Elizabeth Sanchez, came to mind. A week ago, his future was no more than a blur, a cloud, an unknown. With Mercado and Smith making their presence known at his motel room, his future looked bleak. Now, he had purpose and someone with which to share that purpose. He planned to make the most of his second chance.

* * *

Thursday, September 10, 2015.

The slim, platinum blonde sat alone at a table on the deck of the 1748 Restaurant. She was dressed in a bathing suit top and a pair of shorts. A beautiful necklace dangled against her tanned chest. Her hair blew back with the sea breeze.

The open-air restaurant was on the grounds of the Long Bay Beach Club on the north coast of Tortola in the western section of the British Virgin Islands. The aqua blue waters of the Eastern Caribbean Sea, the waving palm trees, and the year-round moderate tropical temperatures made Tortola Island the perfect place to get away from it all. It was not an American territory which made it all the more attractive to the young woman.

The restaurant was empty at 3:30 PM, except a bartender, one server, a handsome couple, apparently on their honeymoon, and the blonde who sat alone with a view of Long Bay. The woman glanced up from her drink, not expecting the man who approached her.

"You look like you could use a friend. Mind if I join you?"

The woman looked at the man's face. Recognition immediately registered, followed by fear. She had hoped that her disguise, changing her hair color and getting a perpetual tan, would allow her to grow old without any contact from her previous life. Since Peden Savage had now found her, it appeared that her plan was either ill-conceived or her disguise was too weak. She looked back out at the aqua waters of Long Bay. "Sure, why not? It's a beautiful day, like most are here."

"They certainly are."

Savage waved to the server. "Blue Moon, please."

The server nodded and slowly walked to the bartender. The pace was slow, which Peden didn't mind. These were billable hours.

He turned his attention back to Long Bay. The view was as fantastic as any that he had seen in his life. It brought a smile to his face. He looked over at the woman and said, "With such beautiful surroundings, you should be happy, but I think that something is keeping you from enjoying your stay here." He fell silent, hoping that Sylvia Deming would talk openly about her husband, even though he hadn't asked a question. When she remained silent, he said, "You know, there isn't any place on earth, no matter how beautiful, how peaceful or calming, that you can run and escape from yourself."

"How do you know I'm running from anything?"

"I'm pretty good at reading people. You're running, but maybe you don't need to."

She looked back out over the aqua water. A warm breeze blew her hair back as the server brought Peden's beer. He took a deep pull on the ice-cold brew. After the server retreated, she said, "You're right. I'm running. My husband was a real bastard. But he wasn't a bastard to me directly." She paused to think for a moment. When she spoke again, she smiled a wistful smile and said, "He cheated on me almost from the beginning of our marriage. He would act as if he deserved to be unfaithful, like it was his right, because other than his skirt chasing, he was a good husband. He gave me everything that a wife could want."

Peden took another drink from his glass. "Except fidelity."

She smiled again. "Yes, except fidelity. But he was a real bastard when it came to others." Her face darkened as she thought of some of his horrific deeds. "He screwed over so many innocent people. A lot of them are sitting in prison because of him. They have to deal with the damage that he caused. Families are broken because they don't trust their loved ones, the guys that my husband put away. Parents, wives, families have gone bankrupt paying for attorney fees. I found out about it when I overheard him and that asshole, Vince Mercado, joking about it over a beer on our back porch. I confronted him about it, explained to him the people whose lives he was destroying. At first he laughed it off, like it was some joke. The whole thing was like a big game to him. I finally told him that I wanted him out of the house. I put up with his cheating and lying, but I wouldn't tolerate him destroying people's entire lives. I think in the end, he tried to make amends, but the destruction was so great, he hardly knew where to start. I couldn't be a part of it any longer."

Peden remained silent as she continued with the confession of her husband's sins. He was in no hurry.

"You know, he didn't even do it for the money. I had enough money that neither of us had to work. My mother was murdered several years ago. She left me a fortune. The money wasn't important to my husband. It was the thrill of his job, or the thrill of a conquest, or the thrill of a fast car. It was always the next thrill. I'm so straight-laced, so conservative in my ways that I couldn't provide the next best thrill. I just wanted to live a quiet, comfortable life. I asked him if he'd like to retire and move to a tropical island." She paused for a moment, allowing the breeze to blow her hair back. "He said *Maybe someday*. Maybe someday? I told him that someday may never come.

"You want to know the worst part?" She looked at him to make sure he was paying close attention to her. "The worst part is I lost my best friend, Liz Sanchez. We had finally reconnected after ten years. We met in college. We did everything together – went on double dates, helped each other with homework, shared an apartment in our last couple years at Athens. When I…When Jarrod was killed, she called me to see if I needed a shoulder to cry on. It was like we were never apart." She was silent for a time as she looked longingly out over the water. "I should have called her years ago when Jarrod started to cheat on me, but I thought I could handle it on my own. I lost touch with her and, by the time we'd reconnected, it was too late. Jarrod had, pretty much, destroyed our marriage. And I let him do it."

She took a drink then swirled the ice in her glass and looked out over the bay once again. She seemed to drift into a sad state, bemoaning her losses.

Peden wanted to comment that she had profited from her husband's misdeeds, but he had no idea what became of all the money that Jarrod had essentially stolen from innocent people and from the government. He didn't plan to press her on the issue because he knew that she came from old money, but she must have read his mind.

"You're probably wondering about the money."

Peden took another sip of his beer and remained silent.

"I donated every penny to the Civil Liberties Union. I sent an anonymous note along that they should use the money for the defense of inmates incarcerated for marijuana possession and sale. Maybe the money will be put to good use."

Peden eyed her closely as she again looked out over the water. He didn't plan to have her arrested and extradited back to Georgia. She was already serving a life sentence. She had financial freedom, freedom from the law, and freedom to travel anywhere in the world. But she was imprisoned by the most cruel form of confinement...her own tormented mind.

Peden stuck out his hand as he said, "Mrs. Deming, it's been nice talking with you. I hope you can stop running from yourself. I'm pretty sure that no one else is chasing you."

Peden finished his beer, stood, and looked out over the beautiful waters. He wondered how one could live in paradise while being stuck in hell.

He left Sylvia Deming to battle her personal demons.

Epilogue

November 1, 2015
Peden Savage
Final Case Notes and Report
To: The Honorable Armand Vega, United States Senator, Georgia
Cc: FBI Special Agent in Charge Roland Fosco

It has been approximately six months since the murder of Agent Jarrod Deming, Agent Nila West, and Superior Court Judge Whalen Stillwell and the arrests of former Chatham County District Attorney Andrew Newsome, Agents Vincent Mercado, and Alex Smith. The subjects were charged with extortion, falsifying arrest records, falsifying drug logs, conspiracy to commit murder, attempted murder of Wayne Cleaver and Elizabeth Sanchez, and a number of other financial crimes under the RICO statute. Details of all charges are found in the indictments for the individuals listed. The date for the first trial in this case is not yet scheduled, but is projected to be at least six months from now.

FBI Agent Megan Moore has been exonerated in the shooting death of Allen Deming. It was determined to be self-defense where Moore clearly feared for her own life as well as the lives of her fellow agents and Judge Whalen Stillwell, who was in custody at the time of the shooting. Mr. Deming had already successfully discharged his weapon, mortally wounding Stillwell. The agents were in clear and immediate danger as were members of the public in the vicinity.

Judge Whalen Stillwell, had he survived, would have faced charges similar to those now being faced by Newsome, Mercado, and Smith. During independent depositions, the three men implicated Stillwell in the plot to extort money from the

U.S. Treasury, as well as aid in the improper conviction of twenty-seven innocent men and women. Planted evidence, coerced testimony, and improper interview techniques were all part of the plan allegedly introduced by Stillwell. Seed money and other goods wrongfully confiscated during bogus drug raids were pooled and distributed to the co-conspirators after the arrests of their victims. At this writing, one hundred percent of the victims have been identified and their convictions overturned. Eighty-five percent of the victims have been compensated for their unlawful incarceration, but litigation is still pending regarding any further compensation. Two of the victims died during incarceration. Their families have legal action pending.

Allen Deming's death was ruled "suicide by law enforcement." Based on his actions, his intent was to kill the man that he believed to be responsible for his son, Jarrod Deming's death. In his initial discussion with me, he said that he believed Vince Mercado or one of his team was the actual shooter. After learning of the involvement of Judge Stillwell, he then believed that Stillwell was responsible, regardless of who actually shot Jarrod Deming.

It has not been determined who murdered Jarrod Deming. After thorough questioning and review of the news footage of the actual event, Agents Mercado and Smith could not have been the shooters. They were visible on the video immediately before and after the shooting. They were far away from the direction from which the shots came. Andrew Newsome was at the Chatham County Courthouse at the time of the shooting. Therefore, the actual shooter may still be at large.

It is highly likely that Nila West was shot and killed by Whalen Stillwell. There are several factors that point to this likelihood. Nila West recorded details of an affair with Stillwell in a journal in which she also detailed her intention to become part of the extortion plan. She revealed in her journal that she approached Stillwell regarding her intentions. She stated that if Stillwell did not include her in the extortion plan that she would report him and his partners to the FBI. This threat of exposure occurred two days prior to her murder.

Nila West also recorded details of an ongoing affair with Agent Jarrod Deming. Deming was going to admit to the affair at the press conference on Tuesday, June 13, but was murdered before he was able to make those details public.

Special Agent Peter Nichols (not his real name) has returned to his original unit. For the purposes of this report, I will continue to call him Peter Nichols. He posed as a junior agent, placed on Mercado's team specifically to infiltrate the team and determine the extent of their illegal activities. He is actually relatively senior, though his physical appearance is that of a much younger and less experienced agent.

Nichols was placed in the unit at the request of Clifford Metzger. The DEA was performing an internal investigation into the illegal activities of Mercado's team. They were close to making arrests when the FBI became involved due to Jarrod Deming's murder. Pete Nichols had to stand down and allow the FBI's investigation to move forward. That was a good strategic move since he was not aware that Marcus Cook was working with the FBI. A confrontation between the two may have exposed the agents and jeopardized both investigations.

Marcus Cook is a personal friend of mine. He was a junior DEA Agent after spending eight years in the Army Rangers. He was honorably discharged after a distinguished career. We had his official Army Service Record removed and an altered record placed into the Army Human Resources Command database. There was a write up about an altercation in Afghanistan with local tribesmen that got him the reputation as a loner, not a team player, and not trustworthy. We had Marcus' record indicate that he was less than honorably discharged in order for him to appear like a good candidate for Mercado's team. Mercado and Smith asked Nichols his opinion. He went along with their opinion so that he wouldn't have his own cover blown.

Cook and Nichols working side by side as the junior guys worked well. They were able to avoid being ordered to carry out any illegal activities, including the attempted murder of Wayne Cleaver and Elizabeth Sanchez.

Marcus Cook has resigned his position with the DEA. Since being portrayed as a whistleblower, fellow DEA agents are reluctant to work with him. Senior agents have requested that he be transferred to other teams or job duties. He found working conditions to be unacceptable. He has formed a limited liability company for the purpose of providing investigative services to law enforcement agencies nationwide. I expect that Savage Investigative Consultants will be using his expertise. I have trusted him with my life. He is brilliant, physically fit, and loyal to his friends. I expect that his business will do extremely well. We could not have succeeded with this investigation without him.

Elizabeth Sanchez and Wayne Cleaver have been cleared of any wrong-doing: Wayne for dealing drugs, Elizabeth for harboring a fugitive. They have become engaged and still live in Elizabeth's condominium. The condominium has been repaired, paid for by insurance. What wasn't covered by insurance was paid for by the DEA. They are not pursuing legal action against the DEA despite being contacted by a number of law firms offering their services.

Elizabeth has been promoted to Senior Associate District Attorney position, working for another woman, Yvette Wilson. Ms. Wilson has been in the District Attorney's office for seventeen years and is a tough prosecuting attorney. Elizabeth told the newly appointed Superior Court Judge of her intent to resign until he told her that Yvette was going to be the new DA.

Wayne Cleaver has reenrolled at Savannah College of Art and Design. He's trying to catch up on the advances in technology that he missed while incarcerated at Coastal. When I spoke with him last week, he was making great strides, enjoying his freedom. He expressed appreciation to all of the people at the FBI and at my firm who helped him break free of this travesty of justice. He and Lee Sparks have become friends. Lee has contracted him on a couple tests of new spy equipment; we call them 'gadgets.' It seems to be a good match and helps Wayne pay for his college courses, not that he needs it after his settlement with the Federal Government.

Sylvia Deming has disappeared. We have tried, without success, to locate her. She sold her house within two weeks of the murder of her husband. The sale was an all cash deal and therefore an expedited closing was possible. She left the title agency after receiving the check from the sale and stopped down the street at her bank. She cashed the check and took the cash with her in a large handbag. We tried to track her travels but after her stop at the bank, no one has seen or heard from her. Her friend, Elizabeth Sanchez, remains tight-lipped about her friend, saying only that we should leave her alone because she just lost her husband. She has no idea where she went and has not heard from her since the day Judge Stillwell was killed. She expects that Sylvia will contact her when she is ready.

You will receive a final invoice for this case in the mail sometime next week. If you have questions regarding the charges, please do not hesitate to contact me. It has been a pleasure working for you both. I am pleased that we were able to bring these cases to a successful conclusion.

Very Truly Yours,

Peden Savage

Savage Investigative Consultants, LLC

* * *

Peden sat back in his office on West Liberty Street and wondered if Sylvia Deming would ever return to the United States. In his mind, he saw her image in her tropical get up and thought, *What a waste to be in such a beautiful, tropical setting and not be able to enjoy it.* Maybe over time, the wounds would heal, the mental scars would fade, and a new love, a true love would find her.

He was jarred from his thoughts as his phone rang. It was Megan Moore.

"Hey, Peedee, want to go for a run?"

"Megan, I wish...ah hell, forget it. Sure, let's go. Where should we meet?"

"Forsyth Park, at the fountain. See you in twenty minutes."

"And, Megan, watch out for black sedans with crazy drivers."

"You got it, Peedee."

Damn.

The End

Other PJ Grondin Suspense Novels

All titles are available in trade paperback and various eBook formats.

A Lifetime of Vengeance
McKinney Brothers Book 1

A Lifetime of Deception
McKinney Brothers Book 2

A Lifetime of Exposure
McKinney Brothers Book 3

A Lifetime of Terror
McKinney Brothers Book 4

A Lifetime of Betrayal
McKinney Brothers Book 5

Visit www.pjgrondin.com
pjgron@pjgrondin.com

Author Information

Pete 'P.J.' Grondin, born the seventh of twelve children, moved around a number of times when he was young; from Sandusky, Ohio to Bay City, Michigan, then to Maitland and Zellwood, Florida before returning to Sandusky, OH. That is where he married the love of his life, Debbie Fleming.

After his service in the US Navy, in the Nuclear Power Program, serving on the ballistic missile submarine U.S.S. *John Adams*, Pete returned to his hometown of Sandusky, OH where he was elected to the Sandusky City Commission, serving a single term. He retired from a major, regional, electric utility after twenty-six years of service.

Drug Wars is his sixth novel, the first in the Peden Savage series. His previous works, all in the McKinney Brothers series are *A Lifetime of Vengeance, A Lifetime of Deception, A Lifetime of Exposure, A Lifetime of Terror, and A Lifetime of Betrayal.*

Made in the USA
Charleston, SC
29 December 2016